To: Steven —

For a pers
enjoys read;)
may you enjoy
this book very much!

Axel Hansen
Linda Hansen

THE VENGEANCE TRAP

THE VENGEANCE TRAP

their only escape was love

AXEL & LINDA HANSEN

Ophir Publishing

OPHIR PUBLISHING

Publisher's Cataloging-in-Publication Data
provided in part by Cassidy Cataloguing Services, Inc.

   Hansen, Axel & Linda
     The vengeance trap: their only escape was love /
   A. L. Hansen.—1st ed. – Winter Haven, FL : Ophir Publishing, 2007
   (Vengeance series)
     ISBN 978-0-9787658-1-1
     ISBN 0-9787658-1-8
     1. Family—fiction.   2. Revenge—fiction.   3. Love–fiction.   4. Love
   stories.   5. Adventure stories.   6. Picaresque literature.   7. Didactic fiction.
   8. Erotic stories.   9. Bildungsromans

   PS3608.A574 V46   2007
   813.6–dc22   2006933873

Interior book design by Susan Mark
Coghill Composition Company, Inc.
Richmond, VA 23237
john1@coghillcomposition.com
www.coghillcomposition.com

*This book is dedicated to those brave souls
who choose the path of love and understanding.
Thanks for giving us all hope in a world of chaos.*

Some Special People Deserve a Big Thank You for Making *The Vengeance Trap* a Reality

A lot of wonderful people worked hard and tirelessly—quite selflessly—to bring this first book of *The Vengeance Trilogy* to the printer. Among them, two generous and multi-talented souls stand out: John Coghill and Susan Mark of Coghill Composition Company. They chose the way the type looks in this book, they set the type, arranged the pages to look their best, and then accepted *countless* changes and corrections of errors, most of them made by the author and the publisher. Without John and Susan this book would still be on a dark desk somewhere, unfit for printing. Not only did Coghill Composition do a fantastic job, *they did it for free!* They wanted to be part of the team that helped launch this book program for wounded veterans, and they largely made it possible that the program's launch be a success. Thanks, Coghill Composition!

Another generous couple of guys are Steve Talacka and Bob Kernag, co-owners of Green Button Press. Steve and Bob donated the first printing of the Advance Review Copies (ARC) of this book. These ARCs went to the newspapers and magazines and other important media people who gave this book its good reviews. Steve and Bob helped us reach the media with this first book of *The Vengeance Trilogy*, and they did a great job of it. They, too, donated their time and talent (and printing!) and they gave the first printing of ARCs for free. Thanks, guys!

Acknowledgment and kudos go to Giselle Fernandez, *artiste extraordinaire*, for her great cover art for this book. We love your work, Giselle, and we look forward to your art for the next two covers of *The Vengeance Trilogy*.

There's another group that deserves thanks. They include our "amateur" reviewers who turned in our first reviews and helped us get the attention of the professionals. (In case someone reading this doesn't know it, the word "amateur," which comes from the Latin for "love," has *nothing to do* with skill level, Webster notwithstanding. At its root, the term refers to someone who does something *mainly out of love*.) These loving amateurs include (in no particular order) Colleen Martin, Nurse; Sharon W. Storm, Nurse; Scott McGrath, Building Contractor; Lou Ann Plasse, Medical Transcriptionist; Denise Richardson, Business Co-owner; Rhonda Tackett, Accounts Manager; and last of the "amateurs," Dr. Jean Reynolds, College Professor of Literature. Dr. Jean wrote the book's first review and also served as the book's first vigilant mentor in grammar and punctuation. And where would *The Vengeance Trap* be today without the loving care and uber-professional skills of Terri Snyder, a woman of wisdom and sensitivity who edited this book up to a higher level for story development and depth of character. From the heart you are thanked, Terri, for going *far* above and beyond in giving of yourself. You *absolutely must* be a permanent member of the team!

Many thanks to you all!

1

The Beach

NORTHERN IRELAND, 1983

here is that damned Arab with my guns? She searched the horizon. *My soldiers are freezing. How much more of this can they take?*

She was worried about her adoptive father, too. Tom's boat was somewhere out there in the cold darkness again, looking for the Arab's ship. This was the third night in a row. She'd already lost her birth father; she didn't want to lose this one to the sea.

Her eight soldiers—all young women—were watching the shoreline for any sign of trouble. She had them divided into two squads, under team leaders Hawk and Mongoose. Kathleen's heart, too, was divided. Part of her could sympathize with her commandos. Another part was steeled to the mission.

"Me diddies is ice, Mother," said a voice on the military radio. Kathleen, code named Mother, recognized Bridie's Dublin twang.

"Mine, too!" another voice said with a giggle.

"Whist!" Mother admonished. "No guff on the radio!" Order must be maintained, no matter how she felt.

Bridie smirked at Kathleen's reprimand. The fighters revered their young leader, but after three days and nights of bivouac, they were tired. And damned cold. Discipline threatened to break down just a bit as frustration set in. A little snap from Mother and her soldiers were back in the moment. Mother knew this was all it would take; she trained them to be tough.

A November gale screamed in from the Irish Sea. The fierce wind blew the sky clean of clouds. The surf was thrown high in the air, and it slammed against the black stone beach. The roar was deafening.

Braced against the icy wind, Kathleen stared out across the water toward the black horizon. Usually she liked the sharp smell of salt air, but tonight it seemed acrid.

Where the hell is he?

She searched the water for a signal. It was ebony ink out there. The only hint of where the sky ended and the sea began was the dim twinkle of a few stars.

Kathleen was twenty years old, petite, with a body kept solid by a strict regimen of martial arts and proper diet. Her gray-blue eyes could be gentle and tender, they could be hard and unforgiving; but, always, they held a glint of sadness, and rage.

Kathleen O'Toole's real name wasn't known to many beyond the seaside town of Glenarm. In a cemetery on the outskirts there were three O'Toole headstones. Many O'Toole gravestones dotted Northern Ireland cemeteries, but her own mom, dad, and big brother Tim were in the Glenarm graves.

As a young child Kathleen was anything but sad and knew nothing of rage or revenge. In those days, she preferred to climb trees than play with dolls, and her big brother Tim was her best friend.

A photo of herself and her brother, taken on Kathleen's seventh birthday, was her favorite and she carried it always. The picture showed her wearing Tim's birthday gift: an American cowboy outfit complete with chaps, red boots, jeans, and two pearl-handled six-shooters slung low and forward for a quick draw. A ten-gallon hat of white showed she was a good guy; the fancy braid all around the edge and the dangling tassels said this good guy was still a girl.

In the picture, she is standing next to her brother, her feet wide-spread in a defiant pose. Her fists are on her hips, elbows out, and on her face she is wearing the best imitation of a tough-guy scowl a seven-year old angel can make. Later, she learned Tim saved a long time to buy her that outfit.

One night, when she was fifteen and her brother nineteen, Kathleen heard Tim and his friends in the back yard. Their voices were low, so Kathleen knew this must be important.

Ever the snoop, she slipped out the front door, went around the side of the house, and crept under a bush just in time to hear Tim say, "All right, then. It's time for us to show *why* we're in the Irish Republican Army. We'll get together in the cellar at yer house, Barry, to work out the hit. Two o'clock okay? Yer people asleep by then?"

"Most nights by ten."

"All right. Two o'clock it is. See ye're not followed."

Kathleen hurried back inside and waited for Tim in the kitchen. "You're IRA!"

Tim froze, shock on his face. "Yer ears are too big, little sister!"

"I'll never tell. I swear it!"

"Some things ye're just better off not knowin'."

"Can I go with? I promise I'll not say a word."

"Go with?"

"I heard. Whatever it is, I want to be in on it."

Tim laughed. "Ye'll do no such thing."

"I want to go!"

"And I said ye'll not be after goin'." He put his arm around his sister's shoulders and added in a gentle voice, "Ye'll stay at home, where a kid belongs, and all."

"All right, then, Mr. IRA! See if I care!" She stuck her tongue out at him and ran to her room.

Later that night, it turned out Tim wasn't as good at not being followed as he expected his friends to be. All the way to Barry's house, Kathleen tagged along stealthily. She could have waited ahead, as she knew very well where Barry O'Sullivan lived, but it was more fun to play "I Follow." Long practice through the years had made her good at it.

Peeking through the cellar window, she saw the group huddled around a table. Tim was saying something. He looked so bold, so much a grownup. Kathleen wanted to be part of it. The door was right there beside the window. *If he catches me, he'll be really mad! Maybe I should go home*, she thought.

Kathleen tried the door. It wasn't locked. Without making a sound, she eased it open a crack.

It was Tim's voice, and he sounded angry: "They grab at every girl who walks by, for Chrissakes! Now they've raped two girls from Dublin. It's got to stop. They have to be taught a lesson. What the fek are we, then, if we let those bastards take our women? Are we in the IRA or not?"

Tim pounded his fist on the table as he added, "It's time for killin' some British soldiers, I say! We'll hit their Dublin outpost. Anybody wants out, it'll be okay. No one's gonna hold it against ya, then."

"I'm in."

"Me, too."

A chorus of like replies came from around the table.

"Ye understand, maybe not all of us is comin' out of this alive, then," Tim said. "We could all of us be in deep shit, as of right now."

Startled at hearing that maybe her brother might be killed, Kathleen stumbled. Her foot slipped and the door hit the wall with a bang.

There was a mad scramble at the table. In seconds, guns were pointing at Kathleen.

"Wait! Don't shoot!" Tim screamed as he recognized his little sister beneath her getup of big dark glasses, black pullover, black jeans, black (though shiny) shoes, red socks because she didn't have black ones, and an oversized baseball cap—black, of course—with her thick auburn hair tucked all up inside.

One of the young men at the table screamed, "Damn!" and lunged toward Kathleen. She jumped in alarm. The glasses slipped, the big cap fell off, and her long hair spilled.

Tim grabbed the man by the arm and swung him hard against a wall. "Ye don't touch her!"

Tim pointed his finger at Kathleen. Fire in his eyes, he yelled, "Get-yerself-*home!*"

Kathleen turned and ran hard, headed anywhere but home, trying to keep back the tears. *I've mucked up real bad this time.*

In a few minutes, she found herself in front of Glenarm's Catholic rectory.

I'll tell a priest what I did. The good priest would calm her, she thought, maybe quote soothing words from the Bible and tell her Tim would forget all about it by daybreak.

A priest will calm me? All I ever got from any priest was an angry look.

Her brother said priests didn't like her face because it was too pretty. She wondered what the priests really saw in her that made them scowl; she didn't believe her face was all *that* pretty, so they must have been scowling at something else they saw in her, something unforgivable. She didn't believe Tim would ever get over what she'd done this night, either, and he was her life.

Kathleen sat down on the rectory steps, laid her face on her knees, and wept.

She wished she could do like other girls and talk to her mom about this. *Ma and Da would never understand. They don't even know Tim is IRA. What'll I do, then?*

AFTER HE'D SENT KATHLEEN away, Tim restored order. The one he pushed against the wall squawked a lot and needed his feathers smoothed. Tim reassured everyone that his little sister would keep quiet, and the meeting concluded with a renewed pledge that the British soldiers who'd raped the two Dublin girls would die. The cell would attack the Dublin army post at dawn in five days.

THE PHONE RANG at the Real Order of Orange Protestant headquarters in Dublin. The man on duty recorded the call. "This is Ros Doyle from the Tim O'Toole cell. He plans to kill some British soldiers."

"Oh, *does* he now?" the man said.

"Aye. Will ye call the Brits?"

"Hm. Maybe. Or maybe we'll take out this trash ourselves."

TIM WALKED HOME with a big problem on his mind. It wasn't about his plan to attack a British army post. He was worried about his sister. Her snooping could get her hurt.

As soon as he entered the house Tim went to Kathleen's bedroom door. "Katie?" he called softly. No answer.

"Katie, I just want to say—" He pushed the door open and saw her bed hadn't been slept in. He flew out of the house.

Which way? He remembered once when Kathleen was a little girl she'd run away from home and gone to the rectory. His heart went out to her when he found her sitting there, crying. Tim shook his head and, with a smile, he extended a hand to her. "Katie, me girl, what *am* I goin' to *do* with ye, then? *Hmm?*"

"I'm sorry, Timmy."

"Come on, then, Katie. Let's go home, now, and we'll just talk it all out."

And as they walked home in the gathering daylight, Tim's arm around his kid sister's shoulders, he gave her his best big-brother talk. Even before he started his little lecture, Kathleen knew she wasn't going to like it.

"Ye've got to stop bein' such a bleedin' tomboy, then. Ye must stop wastin' yer time followin' me around, and all."

This wasn't what Kathleen wanted to hear, but her brother's arm made her feel safe.

"Ye must start behavin' more like a girl, then, and less like a guy, ye know. Yer growin' up now, I'm after sayin'. Almost a woman, or I'm damned."

Kathleen looked up into her brother's stern but gentle eyes. She loved those eyes, but she didn't like where this conversation was headed.

"Ye must start thinkin', girl, about havin' a good Catholic boyfriend. God willin', someday you'll get married and have kids of yer own, then."

"But I don't *want* a boyfriend, Timmy. I don't *want* to grow up and get married. I . . ." She turned her head away, embarrassed, and added in a low voice, "I just want to be like you."

Tim stopped. He laughed and asked, "And what would God think of ye, lass, if ye don't marry and have kids, hmm? Come on, then, let's go home now." He started walking again.

Kathleen hung back. "Wait, Tim!"

He turned to face her.

"What was that I heard, then? About killin' British soldiers? And what about you being IRA, and all?"

"The less ye know about that, child, the better off ye'll be. I'm sorry ye heard any of it at all. Killin's a dirty business and whoever must do it has a dirty soul. Now come on, then."

That morning, Kathleen sat in her bed, worried about what she'd overheard. *Who can I tell?* A voice deep within her answered: *Absolutely no one!* She knew that to tell could put her brother in prison.

But Tim might get killed. Next she thought: *Maybe the deal won't happen. Yes! The whole thing will get called off. I just know it!*

Her thoughts drifted. She was angry with Tim; in fact, she was furious.

Stop being a tomboy so's I can get a boyfriend? Hah! I can get any damn boyfriend I want! Right now! Just as I am! In fact, I'll do it first thing Monday! I'm almost sixteen years old. It's high time! And doin' it is no big deal, anyway. I know scads of girls that have done it. Yes, I'll do it! So there, Mr. Tim IRA Smartass!

WHEN KATHLEEN SET OUT for school the following Monday, she walked with an angry, determined stride. She would prove Tim wrong. She was sure she could. She decided her boyfriend would be Danny Quinn, the good looking captain of the school's soccer team, The Glenarm Raiders. He had always been interested in her, but Kathleen had constantly snubbed him.

She approached Danny at his locker as school was letting out.

"Hello, Danny." She gave him her best smile.

"Well, hello back at ya, then." He was surprised she was talking to him.

"Will you come for a walk with me? I think we should get to know each other better. Much better. Interested?"

"Am I *interested?* Is the Pope interested in *heaven?*" Danny thanked the good Lord. This was his lucky day.

Kathleen led Danny to a supposedly secret place she'd heard about. It was under the bleachers, and Danny knew it well.

"Sit down here with me on the grass, then," she said. Danny was so eager, he nearly tripped over his own feet.

"Do you think anyone might come along?" she asked as she leaned near him to look down the way. She leaned a little more, and her breast pressed firmly against Danny's arm. She didn't move away but turned her face up to his as she closed her eyes and parted her lips. She knew exactly how; from movies and from the tattered paperback she kept under her mattress. Danny thanked the Lord again as he leaned toward her. Her hair gave a light scent, a little like roses Danny thought. Their lips met. Danny reached for her breast. She didn't resist.

Kathleen lay back on the grass and drew Danny down to her. Nervous someone might come along, they didn't fully undress. She took Danny's hand and placed it inside her panties.

"Like that, Danny," she whispered, moving his hand for him. The paperback helped her practice, alone in her bed, in the dead of night way under the covers where she dared to think that maybe—just maybe—God couldn't see.

"Like this?"

"That's fine, Danny! Fine! Mmm! Yes! Right there! Yes, yes! Gently, slowly!"

Kathleen was eager. The lad was amazed things progressed so far so fast. He was a little nervous as he unzipped his pants and freed himself.

"I'm ready! Do it! Do it now!" Kathleen whispered as she wrapped her legs around Danny.

Danny pushed. He pushed a bit harder. She gasped.

"Did I hurt ye, darlin'?" Danny asked as he pulled back.

"It's my first time, and all."

"Oh, Jayzus!" Danny complained. "I'm after wishin' somebody else done it to ye before me, then."

"It's all right, Danny! Go ahead!" Kathleen whispered in his ear.

She wrapped her legs tighter around his hips and pushed up against him, hard. Surprised by the pain that shot through her, she stiffened and bit her lip.

"I'm stoppin'!" Danny gasped. "I heard about a guy who done it with a virgin, and she lost so much blood, they had to call an ambulance."

"And were you *there,* then? Did you actually *see* that, then?"

"Well, no, but Joe Martin told me—"

"And Joe Martin's a big fat liar! Now come *on,* then, Danny. I want you *so* much!"

He pushed again, a little deeper this time. He felt a hot trickle.

"I'm gonna pull out."

"No!" Kathleen replied and pulled herself tighter to him. "*Do it!*"

He pushed all the way in, then stopped. "Is it all *right,* darlin'?"

"Yes, for the love o' *Jayzus!* Will you just *do* it, for God's sake!"

"Okay, okay!"

Kathleen could see Danny's passion was racing. She'd heard he was too fast. *Is he gettin' finished already, then?*

She heard him whisper, "Hail Mary, full of grace, the Lord is with—"

"What the hell are you praying for?"

He gasped, "If I say prayers, it helps me, you know, to go longer. Okay?"

Kathleen shrugged.

"Okay, Danny. Fine." she whispered. She was feeling no more

pain. "You go ahead and pray, then." She pulled him tighter. "Say the whole rosary."

Danny closed his eyes, his brow furrowed. ". . . and give us this day our daily bread . . ."

Kathleen noticed Danny had his prayers mixed up.

Soon he was thrusting faster. Kathleen sensed his praying wouldn't help much longer. She heard, ". . . our trespasses as we forgive . . . we forgive . . . forgive. . . ."

His torso and legs went rigid. He threw his head back, his eyes squeezed shut, and a grimace on his face. Danny shuddered once, once more, and a third time.

It was over.

As she rearranged her clothes Kathleen thought, *That was nice, but it wasn't the rocket ride to the moon some girls brag about. I wonder if there really is such a thing.*

FROM WAY OUT ON THE WATER, Kathleen caught the dim flashlight signal she'd waited three days to see.

She wanted to believe it wasn't her mind playing tricks on her. Her body ached from lack of sleep. *I'm wild tired. Was it the blink of a star, then? Low, near the water?*

Again she saw it. *That's no bloody star!*

Her heart leapt! Her fingers were stiff with cold, clumsy, and the flashlight almost fell as she rushed to return the signal. A second time she returned it. From the water came confirmation.

Finally, after three bloody days, the damned guns are here!

"The bread is in the oven," she said into her radio.

Her commandos tensed.

There could be a fight if this gun buy went sour. Behind the tension, though, there was a sense of relief. If the deal went down as it should, they would soon go home. Some to a worried mother and father, some to a husband and kids, some to the arms of a lover—always kept a careful secret in Northern Ireland so the Catholic Church won't come knocking at the door. Literally.

In a few minutes, the waves rolled the flat-bottomed motorboat over the shoal line, out some hundred meters from where Kathleen stood at the water's edge. She spoke into the radio, "Brew the coffee."

The muscular woman in the delivery van parked thirty meters behind her answered, "Yes, Mother." A good soldier, she'd already made sure her M60 machine gun was ready. The oversized satchel beside it contained one hundred thousand dollars, American.

The waves rolled high, their tops whipped away as foam. No moon shone this night, but by dim starlight Kathleen could see the vague outline of two men gripping the gunwales of a small heavy boat as it lurched on the sea. The smaller man and owner of the boat was Tom Mulcahy, her dear adoptive dad ever since her own father's death. She knew Tom better than she had known her first father. Her real parents had been reserved in manner, polite to one another but a bit distant. Tom was older than her father but younger at heart. He was stern as senior in command of the local IRA chapter, but always gentle and fun-loving with Kathleen, his protégée—and the beloved daughter he and Peg had never had.

Kathleen smiled as she remembered how pleased and proud Tom was when she presented him with his birthday present last month, a Beretta with underarm holster. A few days later, Peg complained, laughing, that he wore the damn thing to bed.

Kathleen wore the same sidearm and holster. But, because it showed authority, she also liked to carry on her shoulder the classic Kalashnikov automatic rifle, also known as the AK47.

The Arab was bringing her the IRA's purchase of three hundred new 74s, much improved over the magnificent 47 prototype, and Kathleen was eager to try out this wonder gun.

She had pointed her rifle in anger only once. An IRA operative became determined, with no encouragement from her, that she would be his sex toy. Kathleen pushed his hands away and screamed at him. When he wouldn't stop, she sprayed the floor in front of him with a burst of gunfire. He vanished through the window behind him without bothering to open it.

The only time Kathleen had ever had sex was that one time with Danny. She got hit hard with guilt over it the same day, and she vowed sex before marriage would never happen again. God's punishment was too great. Far greater than the sin.

During the next four years, she found little incentive to end her celibacy, but she decided if she ever did have another man before marriage—as unlikely as that was—she wouldn't be at it with some bloke who backed her into a corner, like the spalpeen she'd scared off that day with a blast from her AK47. She would choose who, where, when and why. When it came to men, Kathleen would always be in charge. She was clear about that.

The stranger in the boat she knew only by reputation as "the Arab."

She wondered if he was armed. Mulcahy had decided he wouldn't pat him down, in deference to political courtesy. Kathleen thought that a bad decision and had said so at the time.

"Bring out the jam now. The bread will soon be on the table," Kathleen radioed the woman in the van.

"Yes, Mother. Coming."

The machine gun and the large bag of money were a load too heavy for many men. The big woman carried both easily to the edge of the wooded area near the beach. There, she set up the M60 on its tripod and lay the money bag beside it. Carrying them brought a warmth to her well-muscled arms and legs, and she smiled with satisfaction at her body's great strength, congratulating herself once more for years of routine weight lifting. She connected the gun's cartridge belt and lay down behind it in the snow to make a final adjustment to the sights. Last, she pulled back on the loading shuttle and let it snap the first round into the chamber. If that gun merchant wanted a fight, she was ready. She almost hoped he would.

The boat made a loud scrape on the rocky bottom. Mulcahy jumped out with a splash and pulled on the frayed old bow line to haul up the heavy boat. The man in the rear of the boat stood up and stepped out onto the shiny stones. He wore a backpack over rough seaman's clothes.

Hmph. Doesn't impress me much, Kathleen thought.

He walked up to her and swept off his cap with a flourish, flashed a large toothy grin and made a shallow bow.

Saints preserve us! The bastard thinks he's pretty! She never moved. Her face showed nothing.

And he doesn't look exactly Arab. He reminded her of an old-time movie actor whose name she couldn't recall, and whom she'd always disdained as overblown and thinly talented.

"Hello!" he shouted over the wind. He smiled again, and extended his hand. "I'm . . ." She ignored the proffered handshake. Her arms remained folded, her eyes locked on his in an angry glare. His smile turned to a frown. He felt insulted. All he could see of her face were gun-metal eyes. The extended hand balled up into a stiff fist as he returned it to his side.

"Something wrong, little girl?" he shouted over the crash of the surf in his best attempt at an Irish accent.

Oh, sweet Jayzus! Little girl, is it? And insulting the Irish way of speaking! If he puts that hand out again, I'll show him what's bloody wrong! And he'll not be after using it for a long time!

Mulcahy understood what was going on, for he knew the lass well. He placed a hand under Kathleen's elbow. "Will ye have a word with me, then, Mother?" he shouted over the surf's roar. "And will ye, sir, just wait here for a moment, then? There's a good lad."

Kathleen and Mulcahy walked away from the thundering shore-line and back to the trees, near where the machine gunner lay concealed. Kathleen's mind was in turmoil.

"He's late!" Kathleen said with a stamp of her foot. "Damn it, he's three bloody days late!" She felt the heat of anger deep in her stomach—a sensation so familiar it almost felt good. In front of her soldiers she would never display this undisciplined side of her, but with her adoptive dad she knew she was safe.

"Aye, I know, Katie, I know. But he's not the devil, after all, now then is he? And he's got the guns on his ship. I went aboard. I saw them."

"Did you check the shipment? Are they the new seventy-fours?"

"Aye, of course, lass. I dug down and unwrapped two. They're genuine. Let's pay him and take delivery. Sun'll be up in a few hours, and he's got to be far off by then. So do we, for all of that."

Kathleen said nothing as she looked into Mulcahy's face for a long silent moment. She trusted his judgment. Her own, she knew, could get clouded by anger.

"Come on, lass. Let's bring him the money," Mulcahy said.

"You're right, Tom," Kathleen smiled. "As always." She walked to the machine gunner's lair, picked up the bag of money and carried it to the stranger.

Kathleen scowled at him. "One hundred thousand, American.

As agreed. Now bring me my damn guns!" she shouted against the wind.

The Arab looked from Mulcahy to Kathleen. He fixed her with a stare and said not a word. After a silence that seemed to go on forever, he chose three bundles of the money at random and riffled them to check for stuffing. Finding the payment genuine, he made two clicks of the transmit button on his belt radio. The signal told his ship, the *Thea*, to send in the motor launch with the guns.

A reply of three clicks would affirm; but his radio was silent.

He turned the volume all the way up and repeated the two clicks. Again silence.

The Arab's radio barked, "Thea to Hyperion." Voice communication meant trouble.

"Go ahead, Thea."

"British task force, three ships. On site in about thirty minutes."

The Arab calculated the ride back to the *Thea* would eat up the half hour window. *If there is some delay?* The plan for today did not include an engagement with a British task force.

He decided to take the contingency. The *Thea* would pick him up in Belfast. No time to deliver the weapons.

"Hyperion to Thea."

"Go ahead, Hyperion."

"Go to flank speed at once. *Get the hell out of there!*"

"Wilco," the OD confirmed. He knew how much the skipper regretted it when, on rare occasions, he was stuck on land and missed a game of cat and mouse, especially when, as in this case, the cat didn't stand a chance.

"I'm afraid I have to return this to you, Miss," the Arab shouted over the wind as he handed Kathleen the satchel of money.

"*What?*" She let the bag fall before her feet and turned her Kalashnikov on him.

"Whoa!" He threw his hands up over his head.

"Easy, lass," Mulcahy said and tilted the barrel of her gun toward the ground.

The Arab said, "My ship is being hunted by a British task force. Which means delivery of the merchandise is impossible. I've returned your money. May I put my hands down now?"

Kathleen glanced at Mulcahy. His expression said, *Let it go!*

"Put 'em down," she said in a voice full of mistrust.

"Hawk to Mother, come in!"

"Mother here, Hawk."

"Movement!"

"Where?"

"Merlyn Rock!"

The ancient rock, bigger than a two-story house, was north at water's edge and even in the best of weather the surf pounded it with the force of madness.

"In the water?"

"Yes. I thought I saw a raft. Something got flipped by a breaker. It was big, and flat."

"Can you get a closer look?"

"I'll try."

"Mongoose, did you copy?"

"Roger."

Kathleen thought, *What the hell could this be? Probably not a wild animal. Most are hibernating. And animals have better sense. At Merlyn Rock the breakers kill.*

"Tom, go cover the van," Kathleen said. "We can't afford to lose it." Her real concern, though, was the possibility that in a gunfight she might lose him. "Right," Mulcahy replied. He suspected her real motive, but she was mission commander.

EARLIER THAT DAY in London there was much interest in the guns and the ship. "Sir, we have a photo of the, uh, *freighter,* sir. And a dossier from upstairs." The communications technician was in the basement of MI6's War Office, Britain's center for military strategy. "Upstairs" was a reference to MI6's team of crack analysts—rarely wrong.

In peacetime, MI6 monitored national threats to Great Britain and linked Scotland Yard to the CIA, France's *Sureté*, Israel's Mossad, and other intelligence services throughout the free world.

Rear Admiral George Binkstrom, Her Majesty's Royal Navy, was Officer on Deck.

"Some problem about the identification?" Binkstrom asked.

"Well, sir, it's bloody well not like any freighter *I've* ever seen before. Our surveillance plane got a quick snapshot before the fog rolled in. Here, sir, take a look."

"Hmm."

Binkstrom read the dossier. According to the MI6 analysts, this was the famous, or infamous, mystery ship he'd heard about. With a quick response, the ship and her captain might just be Binkstrom's plums for the plucking. Any contraband on board would be an extra treat.

Binkstrom knew where he could get the quick response that could turn the trick. He radioed an old school chum, captain of a small flotilla in that area.

"Captain Maddox here."

"Good morning, Maddox! This is Binkstrom over at the War Office." He sounded chummy.

"Binky! You old sea dog! How are you?" A flotilla captain does not call an admiral an old sea dog on military radio. But Maddox and Binkstrom graduated in the same class at war college, and they had quaffed a few pints together in their younger years.

"I'm fine, Peter! Fine! Yes, it's been a long time, hasn't it? Listen, I have a bit of news. We just got a photo on the wire from Corsewall Point."

"Oh?"

"Yes. A snapshot we took about an hour ago of a renegade ship."

"What is she? Freighter?"

"Well, yes, I do believe she *is* a freighter, Peter, *of sorts*. But she's not *built* like a freighter at all. More like one of those speed boats the drug runners use in the Carib."

"All right, then, she's a small fast craft, probably carrying a bit of exotic cargo. Not a problem, I'd say, unless she's *so* fast that—

"Fast she is, I'm sure, Peter. But small she isn't."

"How's that, Binky?"

"As best as our analysts can judge, she's far too bloody big for a sports craft. Our people have measured the size of the whitecaps, factored in wind conditions, altitude, the pilot's visuals, and well, Peter, this craft, this *warship*, I'm afraid it's the size of one of your destroyers! And probably more than twice as fast!"

"A hundred meters long, and . . . *moving at more than a hundred knots?*"

"'Fraid so" Binkstrom said. "Can't *see* any guns. But there are some boxy shapes on deck. I'm sure that's where she hides them."

"*Hides* them?" In his experience, a ship of war displays her guns. Proudly. She doesn't hide them.

"Right. Hides them. She's designed for stealth as well as speed. Probably covered with a material like mylar or Teflon. Won't return radar. Any surface that *could* return a signal, like a steel gun barrel, is shielded.

"Our analysts think the big compartment on her poop deck is a helicopter hangar. That makes her a threat by air and by sea. She's lovely, though. Got a long bow that comes almost to a needle point like an old pirate sloop. She's sleek and she's slick, Peter. In this photo she looks like a big plastic toy."

"Hmm. A stealth warship. What's she called? Do we know whose she is?"

"Yes, I just received all that from upstairs. Ship's name is Thea. Says here the owner is a modern pirate, munitions trader, smuggler, and sometimes-legit merchant. I've seen reports of this fellow and his Thea. He's been spotted in the Indian Ocean, the Black Sea, and the Aegean.

"Until today, though, I don't think MI6 knew he's in *our* waters. Half the navies of the world have chased the Thea at one time or another. I've heard she likes to move under cover of darkness or heavy fog. I don't think anyone's ever gotten close."

"Do we know what this fellow is up to in *our* pond?"

"Gun delivery to the IRA, is what upstairs thinks. I'd bet the coordinates have already gone to Royal Air Command. RAC will try a capture, Peter. But I want you to find that ship before they do. I want the whole package."

"I gather I'm to take the ship . . . *or sink her*, of course."

"Well, before I got these orders I'd have said yes, if she won't surrender, blow her out of the water. But now I'm afraid a fight is out."

"How so?" Militarily, this made no sense.

"Apparently, our people want this vessel in one piece, and everyone on it very much alive. You are to search for her, and try to give chase. My hunch is, she'll see you and be off like a shot. Nevertheless, your orders are to try a capture. If you get close enough, you are to fire across her bow, but do not, I repeat, do *not*, engage the vessel in combat. If she fires back, you are to break off."

"*Break off*, Binky?" This was insufferable.

"I know it's galling, Peter. It would bloody well gall me, too. But our navy and MI6 want to find out exactly how this craft is built and who built it. The Thea is to be captured if possible, but *not* damaged! Is that *clear?*

Binkstrom's voice was ice, the warmth of camaraderie frozen.

How the bloody hell do we catch a ship that does a hundred knots when our best speed is less than forty? was what Maddox wanted to say. Instead he replied icily, but with proper military bearing, "Aye, aye, *sir.*"

The orders were clear. He was to look for a giant invisible speed boat that flew like the wind and might be armed like a destroyer. *If* he found her, his orders were to ask this ship, politely, to come along with him to the pokey. And he felt like a damn fool doing it.

Captain Hosseini Wessam, the Officer of the Deck, the man in charge on the *Thea,* grinned as he turned down the volume on his scanner. There were no radio frequencies this jewel could not pick up. Captain Wessam glanced at his radar screen. Being invisible to another ship's radar didn't mean he couldn't see them with his. The *Thea,* he reflected with considerable pride, possessed what were probably the world's sharpest eyes *and* ears on any sea.

Like Maddox, Wessam, too, was told to avoid a fight. A warrior at heart, he didn't like the order any more than Maddox did. But, like Maddox, Wessam would obey.

Britain's highly secretive Special Air Services, or SAS, was widely regarded as one of the finest and best-trained special forces in the world. It was a model and teacher for many other nations' special forces, and justly commanded the respect of all other military arms of the British government.

The SAS paratrooper unit at Stranraer in Scotland was on alert. These might be the weapons reported stolen not long ago in

Czechoslovakia. To snag them on delivery to the IRA was an exciting possibility.

SAS's intel was conclusive, but before any mission could be launched, regulations required that final approval come from the War Office because that was the source of the enabling data.

When the call came in, Binkstrom told his technician, "Let it ring. It's not for us."

"But—"

"I said it's not for us. Got it?"

"Aye, aye, *sir.*"

Binkstrom unplugged the phone. "In two hours, you can plug it back in."

And this was why SAS Brigadier Allan Rogers had to wait two hours to get authorization for his parachutists to take action—which was well after Maddox's flotilla of ships was on its way to the target.

Finally, as the War Room phone was plugged back in, Rogers did get through. Binkstrom gave him the clearance required by regulations, and then Rogers phoned the air strip and the ready room.

Within the hour, the SAS DC3 throttled down to a whisper as it approached the drop zone. The likelihood anyone on the ground could hear this incursion team was next to zero.

Binkstrom's delay of the SAS clearance failed to give Maddox the edge in this mission. Maddox lost the target and, in disgust, was headed back to port.

In the DC3, the ready light went from yellow to green. The Royal Marine Commandos stood. Each man checked the man next to him to make sure he was properly strapped into his parachute pack, black for this night jump.

Rogers went to the door. The green light began to blink. Time to go. Rogers pulled open the jump hatch and locked it to the plane's bulkhead. The icy blast of wind that filled the plane was staggering.

He threw out a small parachute attached to the team's big rubber raft which would inflate automatically when it hit the water. He shouted to his men, "At two-second intervals, *jump!*" and he dove out the door. One after another, into the subzero slipstream his faithful team followed like lemmings.

The five men plunged through the blackness and soon were falling at 120 miles per hour. The ultra-short-range radio and tiny red light built into each man's helmet allowed the team to keep track of one another, and well-rehearsed body movements helped them stay in tight formation.

"A-way, a-way, *ho!*" Rogers called softly into his radio. Like a night flower eager to open its dark petals, the team peeled out six or seven meters from tight formation.

"We-pull-*now!*" he said, and the team yanked their rip cords in unison. The chutes blossomed into a five-sided black dahlia.

The men splashed as one into the icy Irish Sea. Unprotected in this water, a man would freeze to death in minutes. But these SAS paratroopers were insulated in their chemically heated wetsuits. Even head cover and face mask were caloric.

The men were unanimous that this thermal suit would never replace the warmth of a woman's thighs, but they were glad to have it keep them alive.

Moments after splashdown, the five soldiers were in their rubber boat, paddling over the waves and toward the shore line.

Rogers's waterproof map showed Merlyn Rock and, next to it to the north, an open stretch of rocky beach where MI6 said delivery of the guns would be made.

The SAS team would capture buyer, seller, money and merchandise. According to plan.

Automatic rifle fire came from Hawk's team to the south. A burst answered from the water.

Kathleen's radio blared, "Abort! Abort! Enemy in the water!"

More gunfire.

"Your people?" Kathleen yelled. She was ready to shoot the Arab.

"I swear not!" He clicked on his radio. "Hyperion to Thea."

"Go ahead, Hyperion."

"Belay seven! Belay seven, Hosseini! We're under attack! Small arms fire from the water. Flank speed to shore! Mind your keel! Unless you see a ship, your target is the big rock on the shore line. Signal when you're in range. I'll give you a flare. Fire for effect! Fire for effect!"

"Aye, aye, Skipper. Will you come aboard?"

"If I can. Now, *move it!*"

Squad One came off the high ground to the north and set up an intensive fire pattern south at water's edge. Squad Two fell back to the west, away from the water. Both groups fired nonstop, and IRA bullets whined off Merlyn Rock.

Kathleen grabbed the money bag. The Arab pulled out a handgun, a long-barreled semiautomatic. He snapped off a few shots toward the water but couldn't see any targets.

"Come on! Come on! Follow me!" Kathleen yelled at him.

She ran toward the van, the Arab close behind.

"Mongoose to Hawk."

"Yeah! What?" She was taking heavy fire and giving it back.

"I think we can keep their heads down. *Run for it!*"

Mongoose's team continued its protective fire pattern. Hawk's team dodged backward through a cover of darkness and foliage, and popped off random shots as they ran.

ROGERS HEARD ONLY FEMALE voices on his radio. *Who the hell are these people? Mission brief said fewer than ten. Got to be more.*

His troopers were taking fire from two directions, straight ahead to the west, and from their right, or north, along the water's edge.

Damn good shooting, too, Rogers observed. They seemed to be everywhere, moving all the time.

His men couldn't see well enough through the brush, even with their night vision gear, to pick out targets. They were pinned down behind the big rock and chest deep in icy water because their raft got flipped and pushed out of reach by the breakers.

Rogers wanted to go ashore to the south, but in that direction a cliff rose straight up, six or seven meters, and seemed to run as far as the eye could see.

Nobody told him he might need climbing gear.

Icy breakers kept knocking the men down. The cold sapped their strength. Rogers worried that the chemical heaters in their wetsuits wouldn't last much longer.

Kathleen moved back toward the van. To her right she saw one of the Hawk team grab at her thigh and go down with a scream. Another commando helped the wounded soldier back to her feet.

As soon as the Hawk team got safely behind the machine gun, the weapon began its clatter. The Mongoose team started a half-circle back away from the beach to also come in behind the machine gun.

Kathleen realized the big rock was protecting the enemy. She knew her people would start taking a lot of hits. The gun buy was already scrubbed. Now she had to get her people out. She fired constantly as she signaled her two teams into the van. Return fire from the water grew heavier.

From the corner of her eye, Kathleen saw the Arab run in a

crouch back toward the shore. About halfway there, he pulled a flare gun from his backpack and aimed it high beyond the rock.

Moments later a brilliant white light showered the water. Through the trees Kathleen saw a silver ball of flame hanging in the sky. Less than ten seconds later came the cannonade of five-inch ship's guns. Two rounds hit Merlyn Rock where the SAS troops were pinned, and the small arms fire from the water dropped to almost nothing.

The Arab ran back to the van, radio in hand.

"Thea to Hyperion."

"Go ahead, Thea."

"Sonar! We're painted!"

"Take seven!" the Arab yelled into his radio. *"Go, go, go, go!"*

As he turned his ship, Wessam took one more shot at Merlyn Rock and missed. The round buried itself in a large tree about six feet from the van.

The Arab made a mental note to ask the supplier—a Turkish broker who bought all his goods from China—why one of his five-inch projectiles didn't explode on impact. That it would have killed them all if it had gone off was beside the point.

From the water came a deep whine as the *Thea*'s turbines revved for speed away from the coast, her goal the misty Irish Sea.

Kathleen's troops were all in the van. The Arab stood a few meters away, looking at Kathleen as she stood at the van door. *Can't very well leave him, what with his ship gone and all*, she thought. "Well, don't just stand there! Come on!" she yelled. The Arab grinned and jumped aboard.

Mulcahy kept the gas pedal to the floor as the old van rocketed down the bumpy dirt road out of the woods and back toward Glenarm.

Kathleen turned to check on her wounded soldier.

"How're you doing, Bridie?"

"Hurts like hell," Bridie said. She looked scared and was trying hard not to cry. One soldier supported Bridie's head in her lap while another held her hand. Hawk cut away the left leg of Bridie's trousers to expose a hole in her thigh. A tourniquet had stopped most of the bleeding.

Hawk smiled at Kathleen and said, "She'll be fine. It went clean through, missed the bone and main artery. The morphine should take effect soon."

With her free hand, Bridie made a gesture of despair. She smiled through her tears as she said to Kathleen, "I'm sorry to be such a baby. Can't seem to help myself."

"Now don't you worry about *that*," Kathleen said. "You go ahead and cry, lass. It'll do you good. And you're still gonna look great in a mini skirt."

Bridie wasn't so sure about that.

THREE FIVE-INCH ROUNDS hit Merlyn Rock. Rogers and two of his men were dead. The two survivors were dazed and battered by surf. One bled from a head wound where a slice of rock peeled a wide trough in his scalp.

He shook his head to clear it, and with his sleeve he kept wiping the watery blood from his eyes.

The one who wasn't injured spoke into the small radio pinned to his shoulder.

"SAS to HMS Oak."

"This is Oak," came the response from the submarine. "That you, Rogers? What the bloody hell's going on?"

"Sergeant Peterson here. Brigadier Rogers is dead. Two survivors. Me and Sergeant Thomas. Our life raft is lost. No prisoners. Send a pickup."

In the debriefing, the conflict in orders and the escape of the mystery ship were questioned. The submarine captain was told not to fire on the mystery vessel, but when the SAS people came under fire he was supposed to support them. When asked why he didn't shoot, he said the target raced in on a zigzag course, fired, and raced out again. He managed to ping her twice, but she was gone too fast for a shot.

"What the hell *was* it, big as she was and moving so fast?" the sub's captain wanted to know.

A FEW HOURS REMAINED until daybreak when the van pulled into Glenarm. The wounded soldier was first to be dropped at a medical safehouse called Doctor Delaney's where she would receive advanced care. The other soldiers were driven to their homes and, last, Kathleen and Tom brought the Arab home with them.

Peg answered the door.

"Ah, ye're home!" she said with a breath of relief.

Mulcahy bussed his wife on the cheek, muttered "Mornin' Peg," and walked in. In the doorway, Kathleen said, "Mornin', Peg. This is—"

"I'm known as the Arab, ma'am," he said with a slight bow.

"Ye must all be froze, right enough. I've kept the fire up, and there's hot tea. We won't be havin' any. Keeps us awake," Peg said with nonchalance as she adjusted the hair at the back of her head. "Is there anythin' else the two of ye'd be after needin', then, before I'm back in the scratcher with old Tom here?"

Kathleen laughed as she pulled off her heavy coat and cap, and shook out her thick hair. "I'm sure not, Peg. You're too kind. Thank you." She took the Arab's coat and hung it with her own in a closet.

"Good night, then," Peg said. "And to ye, too, sir." She shot a sly glance at Kathleen and curtsied to the tall good-looking stranger, who made another shallow bow in return. "Now ye don't be long, Tom," she said to her husband as she went up the stairs with a smile.

Mulcahy took Kathleen in his arms for a hug. "Silly woman, that Peg. Are ye all right then, child?"

"I'm fine, Tom. A bit tired is all."

"And ye," he said with warmth to the Arab. "If ye wasn't with us on that beach tonight, I'm hatin' to think what—"

"We're alive. All of us," The Arab said as he put a friendly hand on Mulcahy's shoulder. He glanced at Kathleen. "It's all that matters tonight."

"Aye," Mulcahy said. "And right proud I am to have ye in me home. 'Tis right welcome ye are, and all."

"Thank you, sir. You are a gentleman."

Mulcahy shook hands with the Arab and turned to Kathleen, "Ye'll show the gent his room, then? Peg's makin' up the bed. Be ready in a minute."

"Right," Kathleen said. "We'll just sit here by the lovely fire and have our tea. Good night."

The parlor was dominated by a huge fireplace of fieldstone slabs, its hearth almost high enough to stand in. A fire of dried oak gave the room a pleasant warmth and aroma. In front of the fireplace was a love seat, and a long low table. On it was a dish of chocolates. Kathleen noticed the Arab studying them. A strong interest in a dish of fancy chocolates didn't fit her idea of this rough man. She would more have expected to see him sink his teeth into a leg of wild boar roasted over an open fire, or maybe he'd rip into it raw.

"Chocolates fascinate you, do they?" she asked, trying hard not to smile.

"Yes, as a matter of fact they do. Good ones, that is. If I'm not mistaken, these are Butlers from right here in Ireland."

"I believe they are." She paused. "You seem an afficionado."

"I'm hardly an expert," he replied, looking up at Kathleen with a modest smile. "But I think this one is a walnut ganache," he said, pointing, "and this a butter praline, and this is a hazelnut slice."

"Have one?"

"Don't mind if I do," the Arab replied. "Now let's see . . ." he bent over the dish and pondered his choice. He took one and smiled up at his hostess. She seemed amused.

"What?" he asked.

"I'm sorry. It's not what I expected of a gun runner."

"You think you can know a man inside out in just one evening? The truth is, when it comes to chocolate, I simply melt," he said with a careless air, and with that he popped the chocolate into his mouth.

The Arab smiled again and licked his finger tips.

"Another?" Kathleen offered.

He shook his head. "Thanks, but no. Good things are best taken slowly. That way, the pleasure lasts."

Kathleen blushed. She felt the heat in her cheeks and mentally kicked herself for letting it show.

At either side of the table were two small upholstered chairs. Here Kathleen and the Arab chose to sit, some distance apart.

For a long time they were silent. They sipped their tea and watched the fire, with a glance at one another from time to time.

Kathleen had to admit he was good looking, dark, mysterious. She saw his gracious manner with Tom and Peg, a certain Old-World charm. And his fondness for chocolates spoke of a gentleness to the man's nature. Apparently, she thought, he wasn't afraid to show that side of himself—at least a little. Kathleen recognized she'd never known any man quite like this one. Nevertheless, she was determined to remain angry with him for making her wait three days in the cold. *And,* she reminded herself, *strangers are not to be trusted. Especially men.*

The only sounds were the fireplace's friendly crackle and the wind at the shutters. The silence seemed to fill the room with something uncomfortable.

Kathleen spoke first. "And what do I call you, then?"

"Omar."

Kathleen laughed. *He could have come up with a better name than that.*

"Omar the tent maker?"

"Sure," he said with a chuckle. "Tent maker. Gun runner. Chocolateer. Whatever you like." A brief pause. "And what do I call you?" he asked in a gentle voice. His earlier harsh manner seemed gone. Kathleen wanted to hold onto her anger, keep it handy. She turned the cup of tea in her hands, pressing its warmth into her fingers.

"I'm . . . Kathleen." She intended to throw her name at his face like a stone. But to her surprise, she spoke in a soft voice, almost a whisper.

Conversation wavered, like the fireplace flames that smoldered down and sparked up again.

"I'd like to finish up our . . . transaction," Kathleen said.

"Oh, yes," Omar replied, as though being reminded of something that had grown unimportant.

Kathleen thought his tone strange. "When can you arrange delivery? Again." she said, her manner suggesting clearly that he had fouled up the transaction by permitting the British to find him.

"How about three days from now, say three in the morning, just a bit southwest of Bushmills? Good beach there."

"You know that country?" Kathleen asked in surprise.

"I once visited the Bushmills distillery. Best whiskey in the world."

"Our whiskey and our chocolates. Anything else you like about Ireland?" Kathleen asked with a laugh.

Omar looked at Kathleen a long time before he answered in a low but warm tone, "In time, possibly."

Kathleen felt herself blush. She looked away from him as she answered just above a whisper, "Sunup. I'll be there. With the cash."

There followed a long silence. A log shifted softly as it burned. Kathleen looked over at Omar. He seemed to be dozing off.

She had sat before a crackling fire in this fireplace many times, and always with pleasure, but tonight for some reason the fire brought painful memories.

Five years before, when she was only a few days shy of sixteen, she'd known another kind of fire. That fire had charred her soul. Much later, probing her soul's ashes, she never could find the strong faith she once had enjoyed as an innocent Catholic girl. That was dead cinders. God was a cruel murderer, and she would have nothing more to do with Him.

She began to drift off to sleep herself, her thoughts drawn back to that afternoon, on her way home from school, after sex with Danny under the bleachers.

One last corner to turn and she would be on her street.

What would she tell her parents about why she was late? Would her brother Tim read her face? He thought he was so smart, and him only four years older. Some day she would—

A loud radio voice came from around the corner.

A short burst of static, and: "Signal ten. Strength four. Upper Waterford Road, niner-five-three."

Nine fifty-three? That's my house! She ran around the corner. The police radio barked again: "Residence of Aidan and Cliona O'Toole." Kathleen almost fainted at hearing her parents' names.

On the roof of a black car, blue lights flashed on and off. They illuminated the next car's door and made the painted words seem to blink: *POLICE. POLICE.*

A big fire truck stood in front of her house, a smaller bomb squad truck nearby.

Kathleen's chest turned to pain as she looked at her house. Much of the front was exploded out, pieces of it blown everywhere.

She saw a great black hole four times bigger than the front door. Deep inside the house, flames roiled.

The blackness of the hole invaded her like a phantom. It settled between her shoulders, made its own black hole in her back. The phantom began to push her to the blazing house.

Oh, Dear God! she prayed.

Toward the horror, Kathleen ran, at first with wooden legs, then faster and faster, her arms outstretched for her family. She tried to scream, but her throat choked with pain. In the distance a siren wailed.

Three firemen stood in the street near their truck, hosing down the house's roof. They didn't see Kathleen coming. As she flew past, one of them shouted, "Hey! *Ye,* there! *Stop!*" Kathleen leaped easily over the broad piece of lumpy brown canvas someone had laid in front of the house.

She sprinted for the hole of black smoke and fire. She would get in there. She would find them. Her mother, father, Tim. She would—

Two firemen were smashing out the house's last window to hose the inside; they heard their comrade's shout and turned just in time to catch the girl who almost shot past them into the flames.

"*Whoa*, now!" one of them said as he grabbed Kathleen around the waist. "Whoa, now, lass! Ye can't be after goin' *in* there!" The two men held the girl as best they could, but she kicked and flayed at them. Twice, she almost broke free.

Her voice came back. The screams that poured out of her throat were pure hysteria. Her heart was breaking. A savage will drove her. She would get into the blackness of the hole, there where the fire was, there where she knew her family waited for her to come get them. She screamed. And screamed.

The ambulance pulled up and a medic jumped out, bag in hand. He injected a sedative into Kathleen's arm.

Her whole body, her mind and her will, fought the drug for a few seconds.

She went limp. The firemen carried her away from the house.

They were careful to walk around the broad piece of brown canvas, the one Kathleen jumped over, without a thought, moments before. A thin curl of smoke drifted out from under the stiff and kinked material.

Under it lay the blasted and charred bodies of her mother, her father and her big brother Tim.

PEOPLE CAME to the funeral from everywhere. Kathleen saw a tall elderly gentleman at the back of the room. A stranger. He looked wealthy, foreign somehow, yet in some strange manner she felt she knew him. She wanted to ask him who he was, but she turned her head away for just a moment and he disappeared. She asked about the visitor, but it seemed no one had noticed the man. She never saw him again.

At the wake there was music, dancing, good food and ale, and lots of noisy celebration about the lives of the deceased. Tim's friends were there, including some who'd been in that cellar meeting just nights before.

Tom Mulcahy held his hand up for silence. His face was serious. "This is not the time or the place for words of anger and vengeance. Later for that. Our goodbyes will last forever. In our hearts, we hold the O'Toole family as though they were alive. Always here among us. And the last one who is alive, Kathleen, is now me own dear daughter. From this day forward, for as long as she likes, this girl lives with me and the missus. Let word go out from this place. Kathleen O'Toole now lives free under my protection. Beware to any and all who might do her harm, or even think it, for they are surely dead."

After the funeral, Mulcahy held Kathleen in his arms to console her. She cried until the tears wouldn't come any more. "If only I'd told," she whispered, holding her head in her hands. "They'd still be alive."

"Told?" Mulcahy asked.

"Told somebody that Tim was IRA. They might have stopped him. He'd be alive today. And Ma and Da, too. It's my fault they're all dead! It's my fault! I killed them!"

"No, child! No!" Mulcahy wrapped his arms around her again. "Never think that for a moment. Never! It's not yer fault at all! Ye did the right thing, tellin' no one. Ye were right, child. Ye were right!"

Kathleen heard the words but her heart doubted them.

Her heart was sure, though, that God had used the bomb to punish her for having sex with Danny. And she *hated* God for it.

Two days later, on her sixteenth birthday, Tom Mulcahy swore Kathleen O'Toole into the IRA. She took her oath in a rage, swearing not on a faith in God but on faith in her own power to hate. She was determined to wreak vengeance on those Protestant bastards. And she would be part of the fight to drive the British out of her homeland.

OMAR HAD COME out of a light sleep and was thinking of adjusting the logs in the fireplace. He also was watching Kathleen's head and shoulders shift back and forth in her sleep. She apparently was having an unpleasant dream.

In her dream, Kathleen saw her mother and father, and with them Tim—always Tim, and all three wrapped in flames, coming toward her with their fiery arms outstretched as though to embrace her in their eternal suffering. Her head thrashed, horror and pain on her face, as she struggled to break free of the familiar nightmare.

What do they want of me? What do they want?

The answer screamed from the deepest part of her, as it always did: *Vengeance! Vengeance!*

Still asleep, Kathleen moaned. Omar jumped from his chair. He touched her arm and said softly. "Kathleen, wake up!"

She opened her eyes and looked up into Omar's face, so close to hers. His touch was warm; his deep brown eyes were filled with concern.

Coming out of the dream she had a sense of being alone, vulnerable. It seemed her anger was in hiding, like a monster that rips at its victim and then slinks back into its den. Without that familiar beast controlling her, Kathleen was bewildered. Without the anger to lean on, she was like a lost child, or like a one-legged woman who can't find her crutch. She searched, tried to bring back the phantom, but Omar's eyes threw her out of focus. She couldn't hold on. She was slipping.

On impulse, hardly aware of what she was doing, she reached up from her chair and slipped her arms around Omar's neck. Her heart was filled with pain. She didn't want to come apart, let this stranger in. But she had to let go. It couldn't be stopped. Her soul's anguish poured freely. It reminded her of the night on the rectory steps, but this was different. She felt like she might actually be washed clean of something old and stale. It would take many years and many tears, but her heart somehow knew tonight could be the beginning, and she sobbed.

"There, there, now," Omar whispered as he lifted her to her feet. He took her in his arms and gently rubbed her back. He held her close. She felt the warmth of his body flowing into her, and it made her feel secure. Her sobs softened.

I think I could trust this man. The thought surprised her.

Kathleen whispered through her tears, "In my back, between my shoulders, there's a great black hole. Sometimes it feels like I'll fall in it and disappear."

"Here?" he asked, placing his hand on her back at the level of her heart.

"Yes," Kathleen murmured softly. She turned her face to his neck while he continued the gentle massage. His body scent reminded her of fine new leather.

"Better?" His voice vibrated deep and soft against Kathleen's breast.

She felt his lips brush her cheek.

A delicious shiver flooded her body. A desire she hardly knew could exist coursed through her. In his eyes, she saw passion and knew he saw the same in hers. Their first kiss was tentative. Their lips touched again, a bit more surely. Kathleen hungered. The instinct of ages inspired her as she searched his open mouth with her kiss. She drew him in. Their tongues danced in spirals.

Kathleen's past nagged at her. She pushed it away, denied it, but it rose up again, strong from deep inside, a familiar phantom. She was forced to stop. Kathleen's heart belonged to rage, and rage was a jealous lover.

She gasped, "We'd better stop. They might come in."

Omar looked deep into Kathleen's eyes. What he saw puzzled him. It didn't seem to be fear the Mulcahys might walk in on them.

"What is it, Kathleen? What's wrong?"

Kathleen felt an urge to open up, share her terrible secret. She decided to take the risk. She sat on the loveseat and he sat beside her. Kathleen took one of Omar's big hands in hers.

"My family . . . my parents and brother . . . were burned to death. A bomb was thrown through our window because my brother was IRA."

Kathleen's words struck Omar in the heart. His eyes went wide. His breath all but gone, he muttered, "Good God!"

He thought: *Both our families were murdered!* The shock of that kismet showed on his face.

Kathleen saw in Omar's response something more intense, more personal than she expected.

"What?" she asked.

Omar shook his head. He didn't want to turn the conversation away from whatever Kathleen needed to say; about his own hell, he would tell her another time.

"When did it happen?" he asked when he got his breath.

"Four years ago." She explained about Tim and his plan to attack a British outpost, and about how the firebomb was thrown through their window and her entire family killed.

"Ever since then, I've sworn to fight the bloody bastards and they know it. I've taken an oath of vengeance. It fills me." She turned her face away and whispered, "That's why I can't. . . ."

Omar took her face between his hands and searched her troubled eyes.

Kathleen felt his tenderness, his concern, and she turned her head from him as tears started slipping down her cheeks. With strong but gentle hands he brought her eyes back to his. "Please. Stay."

Kathleen's demon was still in control, but she felt a new excitement, too.

"Omar," she whispered. Her heart pounded. She felt dizzy, overwhelmed, flying too fast. "Not now, Omar. Not yet. I'm sorry."

Omar smiled and put his hands on her shoulders. In her eyes he saw a conflicted woman of great depth, a woman of passion.

"Let's sit together and talk. Okay?" he said.

Kathleen smiled as she nodded, sniffling once.

"Here. Blow," Omar said gently as he pulled a handkerchief from his pocket. He got up to stoke the fire.

Kathleen watched his muscular arms work the fire tongs as he rearranged the logs in the hearth. *Your arms felt safe. Do I dare get to know you?*

As Omar put the tongs back in place, a log spit a large spark at him. It landed on the front of his pullover and the garment began to smolder and smoke. Suddenly a patch of flame licked up toward Omar's face. He grabbed at the bottom corners to yank it off over his head. As he spun away from the fireplace, his hands pulling the flaming sweater off, Kathleen said, *"Jayzus, Mary and Joseph!"* Reacting on reflex, she flung her cup of tea at the flame.

Her aim was poor. The tea, now only lukewarm, hit Omar square in the face.

The pullover was off but still in flames, and Omar flung it into the fireplace.

"You okay, then?" she asked as she jumped to her feet.

"Yes. I didn't get burned."

Kathleen pointed at his face. She laughed, yielding to fatigue and the stress of the moment.

"What?" he asked with a grin, as she continued to laugh and point.

He felt around his face and finally found it. A tea bag hung from his right ear. He pulled it off, grinned, tossed it into the fireplace, and the two turned to the loveseat. Kathleen's laughter had awakened a thirst in him that he had denied most of his adult life.

"I'd like very much to be your cup of tea," he joked softly, "but this wasn't exactly what I had in mind."

Kathleen was still giggling. She said, "I'm sorry. I shouldn't have laughed. I suppose it's because I'm so tired."

Omar grinned. "I guess I did look pretty funny. I usually wear my tea bag over my *left* ear." He reached for a napkin to wipe his face.

Kathleen giggled again and said. "In Tahiti, you know, a flower on the right ear means a girl is available."

"Well, if that applies to men wearing tea bags, we must be in Tahiti."

"No," Kathleen said. "If this is *Tuesday* we must be in Tahiti."

Omar's face grew serious as he heard his mind whisper, *And if my heart is telling the truth, I must be falling for you.* The thought surprised him. Could he be falling for this woman? Falling was not in his experience. Taking, yes, but not falling.

"Are you really okay? Did you get burned? Do you need some ointment?"

"No. I'm fine. It was good to hear you laugh." They looked into each other's eyes for a long silent moment. The attraction was strong. "Feeling better?" he asked.

Kathleen nodded and smiled. She was feeling better than she had in a long time. They sat on the love seat and settled into one another's arms. The flames dwindled to embers and conversation ebbed.

As dawn approached she fell asleep, her head on Omar's shoulder and a childlike smile on her face. Omar saw the child, but in her smile he also saw the woman.

2

Bushmills, Northern Ireland

THREE NIGHTS LATER

Tom was behind the wheel and Kathleen sat next to him, the satchel with the money on the floor between her legs.

The big truck lumbered down the main highway from Ballycastle, and entered Bushmills at around two in the morning. Tom had been careful to hold his speed down. The old diesel was rapping hard, and a failed engine was the last thing he wanted this night—even less: some pleasant cop stopping to help two stranded travelers, and then getting nosy.

"Are ye certain ye know the place, child?" Tom said. It was the tenth time he'd asked since they'd left Glenarm.

"I have the map, Tom," Kathleen answered, for the tenth time, her teeth on edge. She clutched the slip of paper Omar had given her showing his drawing of the protected inlet just a bit southwest of Bushmills, and the beach where the boat from the *Thea* would land.

"But does Omar know the place? I hardly know it meself. And you neither, I'm after saying."

"Omar knows the place, Tom," Kathleen said, shoving down her impatience. She loved her adoptive dad with all her heart, but he did sometimes get on her nerves. This was one of those times.

She was looking forward to. . . . *What?* she asked herself. *Completing the munitions buy?* That wasn't it, and she wasn't going to try to deny what it really was. It was him. He'd been on her mind constantly since that night, three nights ago, when they fell asleep in each other's arms in front of the fireplace. *Are you daft, then?* she'd asked herself dozens of times. *A damn good thing you didn't let it happen, too!* she said to herself crossly. *You'll take delivery of the bloody guns, pay the damn man, and be off. Forget about anything else.*

They had put the sleeping town of Bushmills just behind them when Tom eased the truck around a sharp bend in the road, and there ahead were the flashing blue lights of a police car.

"Oh, Jayzus, Mary and Joseph!" Kathleen said quietly.

"Easy, now. Easy," Tom said gently. "We don't know what they want. Might be nothin' at all."

"Oh, aye," Kathleen said derisively. "Maybe they're selling tickets to the policeman's ball."

"Well, if they are sellin' tickets, I dare say we've enough money to buy a lot of 'em, then." Tom eased the truck to a stop in front of the policeman with his hand up, and lowered his window. It was a cold wind that blew in from outside and the young officer looked frozen.

"Where ye headed?" the policeman wanted to know.

"Me son's house in Coleraine," Tom replied. "It there a problem, officer?"

"Truck's turned over in the road ahead. Driver killed," the officer replied while shining his flashlight around inside the cab. He let it rest on Kathleen's legs, then her face, then the bag between her legs.

"What's in the big bag?" he wanted to know.

"Sheets, a rubber cover, some sterile things. Me daughter here is a midwife. Me daughter-in-law is about to have her first baby, unexpected like. We got a phone call."

"And why would ye be needin' the likes o' this truck to go deliver a baby? Is it a buffalo that your daughter-in-law's expectin', then?" the officer wanted to know.

Tom laughed. "No, but this is the only thing I got what's runnin' right now. Me car is down."

The police officer turned his light on Tom's face and held it there while he seemed to be studying to learn whether this was the truth.

Apparently he was satisfied. "All right, then. Take this red flag. Give it to the officer at the other end of the crash scene. Drive careful."

"Oh, aye," Tom said. "Thank ye, sir. And a good night to ye," he added as he rolled the window back up to where it caught against the flag and propped it out to be seen. "Good night, then," Tom called loudly to the police officer as he pulled back onto the road.

"Jayzus, Tom," Kathleen said, "but you're a damn fine liar. Where the hell did that all come from, out of nowhere like that?"

Tom laughed. "Not out of nowhere. Out of a romance novel I read a couple days ago. I Lost My Baby To The Night."

Kathleen laughed hard. "I Lost My . . . Oh, Tom, I didn't know you like to read romance novels!"

"Only if they're clean. No hanky panky," he said, with a wink. Up ahead a red flashlight was slowly waving side to side, a signal that meant pass carefully. "There's the wreck," Tom said. They passed a truck on its side, a front wheel missing. No other vehicle involved. "And there's likely what made that truck crash," Tom said. "Damn thing lost a wheel." He wondered how good were the wheels of the borrowed truck he was depending on.

A bit farther down the road, another flashlight was signaling them to stop again. "Ah, and here's our friendly policeman number two," he said, rolling down the window.

"Here you are, sir. Good night," Tom said as he handed the officer the flag and rolled his window back up. The officer smiled, touched the tip of his cap in salute, and said, "Drive carefully, then."

"Oh, aye," Tom called loudly to the man through the closed window as he pulled away.

"Whew," Kathleen said. "Glad that's over. What if that first one had wanted to see what's inside this bag?"

"Don't even think about that, me darlin'," Tom said. "Don't even think about it. It's too ugly."

A few moments of driving passed and Tom said, "Ye'd better be after checkin' that famous map. We're passin' a cove right now," he gestured to his right with a nod of his head. "This could be the place."

"Aye. Look! There's the tree with the broken branch hanging. And there's where Omar said you could pull off."

"Aye," Tom replied, bringing the big truck to a stop on the gravel shoulder of the road. Tom and Kathleen climbed down and looked around. Other than the whistle of the cold wind, there was nothing and no one.

"What's your name?" a voice called out of the darkness surprisingly close. Kathleen saw low bushes. She thought the voice was familiar.

"Pudding and tain. Ask me again, and I'll tell you the same," she called out with a glee she had totally not expected to feel.

The bushes gave up a laugh and a man stood. He came forward, and in the light of a partial moon Kathleen saw the grin.

Her heart began to pound. *Careful!* her head warned. *Nothing's changed here!* Her heart wasn't listening. They walked slowly toward each other, each reaching out for a handshake. The hands came together, and the two bodies continued to close the remaining inches that separated them.

For Kathleen, the universe had gone into ultra-slow motion. The two faces came closer, slower than eternity, and they met cheek to cheek, first on one side, then on the other.

The slow motion snapped. "Omar! Nice to see you again!" Kathleen said. The two stood there, motionless, their four hands joined, and looking intently at one another for a long moment.

"Ahem," Tom said quietly. "If we're holdin' hands to keep warm, then, I want to hold hands, too. You've got the bigger hands, Omar, so I choose you."

"All right, funny man," Kathleen said to Tom, laughing. "Now go get the money."

Omar made two clicks of the transmit button on his belt radio, his standard signal ordering the *Thea* to send in the motor launch with the guns. Three answering clicks said the motor launch was on its way, and soon its muffled engine could be heard approaching.

"I think it's about time for the British ships and paratroopers to arrive," Omar said with a wry smile.

"Not likely, me lad," Tom said. "We rewrote the script. This time it's just you gettin' paid, and us gettin' the guns. No Brits at all!"

"I think I like your new movie best," Omar said. Kathleen said nothing. Her mind had wandered back to the evening in front of the fireplace, and the man she had discovered there. She looked closely at the man in front of her now, and found them to be one and the same. The idea made her pulse quicken.

The *Thea*'s motor launch scraped the rocky bottom. The three men in the boat jumped out and pulled the heavily loaded craft onto the shore. A tarp covered the boat's cargo, and the men pulled it off. Nothing was said. Two of them gripped one of the heavy boxes, lugged it to Kathleen, and placed it gently on the sand before her.

Omar pulled at one end of the box's wooden lid. It came loose with a loud noise as the nails were pulled free, revealing its content, each gun individually wrapped in a heavy brown waxed paper. Omar smiled at Kathleen, and made a gesture that said, "Have a look!"

Kathleen felt a little strange—as though she were guilty of an unwarranted mistrust—as she reached down into the box, moving the top guns aside, and pulled one out. She handed it to Tom, burrowed deeper into the box, and pulled out another gun for herself. The paper was stripped to reveal the dark gleam of the new AK74 automatic rifle. Tom pulled back on the loading shuttle and let it snap forward. It made the satisfying click of well oiled newness. Kathleen did the same, just for protocol. Tom replaced his gun in the box and walked back to the truck. Omar signaled his men and they picked up the box of rifles and followed. Tom returned with the satchel of money and placed it on the sand in front of Kathleen's feet. She opened it, pulled its mouth wide, and made the same gesture Omar had used to say, "Have a look!"

For a long moment Omar waited, as though trying to decide, then he smiled and closed the bag without looking inside it.

It took more than an hour for Omar and his men to transfer the crates from the boat to the truck. Twice during that time, a car was heard coming. The truck's rear doors were quickly pulled shut, and both times the car passed without incident.

Halfway through the transit, Kathleen said, "I've a large thermos of tea in the truck. More than enough for us all. I'll just go get it."

Omar watched her walk away and said softly to Tom, "I may be a bit old fashioned, but I would like . . . that is, I wonder if I could . . . if you might permit . . . ." He was amazed to find himself tongue-tied.

Tom smiled. "I get the sense this isn't something ye ask every day, lad."

Omar shook his head and sighed. "I've known a few ladies in my time, but not in the way I want to know Kathleen."

"Are ye askin' me permission to court me daughter, young man?" Tom asked, drawing himself up.

Omar grinned, "Well, yes. In a manner of speaking, I guess I am."

"Ah," Tom replied. "I see. Well then, in a manner of speaking, I guess me answer is. . . ."

Omar folded his arms and stared hard at Tom, a grin at the corners of his mouth, as he knew he was being played with.

"I guess me answer would have to be. . . ."

"I'm about to shoot you, old man," Omar said with a broad smile.

"Are we doing some shooting, then?" Kathleen asked brightly. Tom and Omar hadn't heard her coming.

"Just me shootin' off me mouth is all," Tom replied. "And me answer is yes," he said to Omar.

"Your answer to what?" Kathleen wanted to know.

"Mind yer own business and pour the tea, girl," Tom growled, but winked at her at the same time.

With a sense that most women find handy when they need it, Kathleen knew she should let the subject drop. She served tea.

After the last crate was in the truck, and the load cinched for safe travel, Omar signaled one of his men to put the bag of money in the boat. He turned to Kathleen and said, "Well, I guess that's it." Something in his voice said he wished the evening wasn't finished.

"Yes," Kathleen responded. "I guess that's it." She felt an ache in her throat.

"Oh, well now, that's it!" Tom mimicked in a high-pitched voice. "You know, I just can't believe that's it. Is that really it, then?"

"Tom!" Kathleen growled through clenched teeth, fists rigid at her sides, and a grin trying hard to break through her façade.

"I think I'll just wait in the truck then," Tom said as he scampered off like a boy who's been teasing. "Don't be too long, now," he called from the truck. "It'll be days before that moon is full!"

"That Tom!" Kathleen said to Omar with a shake of her head. "Sometimes he acts more like my little boy than my father." Omar took her hand in his, without saying a word, and led her toward the beach for a walk in the moonlight. Kathleen realized she'd never been for a walk in the moonlight, and as cold as it was, she didn't want it to end.

Omar stopped and turned her to face him. "I asked your father for permission to court his daughter."

Kathleen felt her pulse rush. "Oh!" she said. She looked away. "And what did he say?"

"He said no. That's why I said I was going to shoot him."

"What?" Kathleen said loudly.

"I'm lying. He said yes."

"Oh," Kathleen said softly and moved a few inches closer to Omar. He took her in his arms and kissed her.

She broke away, laughing. Omar looked confused by her laughter, unsure whether he should be hurt, angry, or something else.

"I'm sorry. I just got a picture of you and me walking side by side down some lane, not daring to touch, with some ladies walking a dozen paces behind as chaperones. Like Maureen O'Hara and John Wayne."

Omar laughed. "The Quiet Man. I saw the film." He paused. "Am I too old fashioned? Asking permission to see you?"

"Well," Kathleen said. "Certain things do seem a bit old fashioned. And we might live without them. Like air. And the sun. She reached her arms around Omar's neck and pulled him close. They kissed again, and this time neither pulled away.

The truck horn sounded, four beeps that were short but insistent.

"Our chaperone," Kathleen said with a smile.

"Good lord!" Omar added, "I've got three men sitting in that boat freezing! I forgot all about them!" He started to move off.

"Wait!" Kathleen said, holding Omar's arm. "When will I see you again?"

"One week from tomorrow. I have business in Belfast. May I phone you?"

"Of course," Kathleen said, and kissed him quickly on the lips. "You have my father's permission," she said with a mischievous grin, and ran off toward the truck.

"CAR'S PULLIN' UP THE DRIVEWAY," Tom called out from his post at the parlor window. "I'll just step out—"

"Don't bother," said Kathleen as she flew out of the kitchen past Tom. She scooped up her sweater and was out the door.

"Hello, Omar," said Kathleen as she ran across the yard. It was already dark but she could see Omar's face clearly in the light from the open car door. "We've been holding supper for you."

"Hello, yourself," said Omar. "Sorry I'm late. Business took longer than expected."

Kathleen watched as Omar seemed to unfold his large frame out of the small rental car. He wore a business suit and seemed to Kathleen to be the image of an elegant gentleman.

"I . . . uh . . . well," Kathleen spluttered.

"Come here," Omar beckoned with arms open wide.

Oh lord, there's that lovely smile, she thought, and ran to his embrace.

Their kiss was long and sweet. *If he lets go, I'll slide right to the ground*, she thought. *My knees have gone watery.*

After a minute, Omar said, "Will you help me with these?" as he reached into the back seat and brought out some packages.

"Oh my, what's this?" said Kathleen with the excitement of a little girl on Christmas morning.

As they walked toward the house Omar explained that he brought small gifts for them. "For your many kindnesses to me."

Inside, after warm welcomes and quick hugs, Omar said to Peg, "I hope I haven't spoiled dinner."

"Not at all," said Peg. "Let's sit for a while. It's Irish Stew. The longer it sets, the better it gets."

"I think that's true of many traditional dishes all around the world," Omar replied. "And I'm really looking forward to trying your authentic Irish Stew!" He stood to take off his suit coat and put it over a chair.

"Do we have time for these?" said Omar as he patted the wrapped packages.

"What's this?" said Tom as he accepted the box Omar handed

him. In his typical manner, Tom tore off the wrapper like an eager child, and that made everyone laugh.

"Bushmills 21 Year Old Single Malt! Where did you find this lad? It's rare even in Northern Ireland."

"You had to have it," said Omar, "In honor of our successful venture last week."

"Well thank you, lad, and we'll toast to that success right now!" Tom said as he got four glasses down from the cupboard and opened the Bushmills.

Meanwhile Omar brought Peg a large box and said, "For the keeper of the hearth. Here, let me help you open it."

Peg looked under the tissue paper and gasped, "Ohhhh, now lad, ye shouldn't have done . . ." She put her hands in the box and turned them this way and that. Finally she said, "Please, lad, ye take it out. Me hands are shaking."

Omar lifted the Waterford Crystal lamp for everyone to see. The base was clear, and the shade was amber. Omar put the lamp on the side table by the window. He found a socket and turned the lamp on.

Peg burst into tears. Tom hopped to his feet and said, "Let's lift our glasses to Peg, the keeper of our hearth. No more fittin' tribute can be given to a one such as she." After the toast, Kathleen, with tears in her eyes, gave Peg a big hug.

"Ye've got a good eye for seein' into the heart of people, lad," said Tom. "I appreciate what ye've done. Peg's not told often enough how important she is to us all."

Peg jumped up and wiped her red face with her apron. "Me stew! I forgot about it! I'll be right back."

Omar took Kathleen's hands and led her to sit beside him. "And this is for you," he said handing her a small slim box.

Kathleen looked down at the package, then up into Omar's eyes. Tom leaned forward in his chair for a better look.

Kathleen smiled and tore into the packaging.

"That a girl!" laughed Tom.

"Omar! It's beautiful!" said Kathleen lifting the necklace up to admire. At the end of a thick white-gold chain was a pendant. The center of the pendant contained a pearl embedded in a stylized flower of white-gold. The flower was framed by a few emerald leaves.

"Here," said Omar, as he helped her put it on. "That's a Tahitian pearl, and the flower is a gardenia—the flower of Tahiti."

Kathleen turned to Omar. She could hardly hold on to her emotions, and with great self control gave Omar a proper hug and said, "It's a beautiful gift and a beautiful sentiment. Thank you."

Peg came to announce dinner. "What have I missed, then?" she asked. Kathleen stood to show Peg. "Omar gave me this necklace. Here's a pearl from Tahiti, and a gardenia from Tahiti—"

"And bright green leaves from Ireland!" Peg said with a merry laugh. "It's lovely, child." Peg looked around the room and asked, "Now who's for some Irish stew?"

During dinner Tom said, half joking, "I was thinkin' we might all go down to the pub after dinner for a few pints and some entertainment. But I don't think the locals will let you in all dressed up so fancy, Omar."

"I'd love to join you. I've got my luggage in the car, with a change of clothes. It'll be good to get out of this suit." Omar continued, "I've got a flight out to London tomorrow at 10:30 in the morning. Got a room right by the airport."

"A room!" said Peg. "Why ye'll stay here with us. Then we can have a proper night out and ye'll be off to Belfast in the morning."

IT WAS AN UNUSUALLY mild evening, and the two couples decided to walk to the pub. Tanner's Pub was full and the Friday night songfest competition was getting underway, a weekly event known in Glenarm more for its nonsense and tomfoolery than for any singing skills. The bar itself was below street level and the walls of chiseled rock constantly seeped cold water, to be carried off by the floor's system of small gutters that fed the runoff to a sump pump.

The main excuse for opening a bar in this cold, damp hole was that the place was purported to be the site of an ancient Druid prison, with iron shackles still attached to the walls. The little club's genesis was invented by Tanner, and the shackles were as faux as all the other artifacts along the walls, and the tourists generally knew that as well as the locals but they all loved the place just the same.

"All right, now," the master of ceremonies said. "It's open night at the mic comin' up. So wet yer whistles and don't be shy—all are welcome to join in. First prize in tonight's competition is a pint for everybody at yer table."

A loud cheer rolled across the room, and the servers were kept busy delivering new rounds of Guinness. The local band was introduced, and soon their fiddle, flute, guitar and tambourine filled the pub with sad songs about making love and merry songs about making war. The master of ceremonies joined in with his accordion, which he played badly. It was no use to complain; the accordion player was Mr. Tanner.

"Ye know a lot of old ballads, Tom," Peg said. "Why don't ye go up there and sing us one? Ye might win first prize."

"Aye, I might just do that. But let me build up some courage first," Tom replied, waving his empty mug at a passing waiter. "Besides, I always like to go last."

"I'll join you in that, Tom," said Omar, as he held his empty glass high.

"Well, while you boys are taking on more courage, I need to spend a penny," Kathleen said as she got up from the table. "Care to join me, Peg?" Peg smiled and got up to follow Kathleen.

At the line of sinks in the ladies' room, Kathleen asked Peg, "So what do you think of him?"

"What do *I* think of him?" Peg replied hesitantly. "Well, he's a good man, generous too. The question is what do *ye* think of him."

Kathleen tried to be rational. "Well I have to admit, I'm smitten. I mean he's charming and handsome . . . but . . . ."

Peg giggled, "Well he's sure got the attention of all the girls in the pub tonight. Why there's been a regular parade goin' by our table."

"Don't you see?" Kathleen continued. "He's different from us. That's part of his attraction. But could he really fit in here when the novelty's worn off? And more important. Why would he ever even want to fit in here?"

"So what are ye saying, Katie?"

"I guess I'm trying to say, I'd like to see him, date him, whatever you want to call it. But that's it. I mustn't let myself think that we could have a real relationship. Could ever fall in love. *Oh God, I think I already have.*

A few moments later as they walked down the short hallway from the ladies' room, they heard a male voice singing.

"Is that Tom?" Peg asked.

"Sounds like," Kathleen replied.

The two women just barely got seated when Tom wrapped up a rousing version of an old rebel classic. The audience rose and applauded their appreciation. Over the din, Tanner yelled into the mic, "It looks like Mulcahy's stolen the show. Last chance, now! Anyone else want to give it a try?"

Omar stood, walked forward and jumped easily onto the stage.

He looked a bit menacing with his black turtle neck and black pants and dark features. Then he smiled broadly and said, "My name is Omar Jabri. I'm from Persia. I would like to sing you a song."

"Well, I'll be!" Kathleen said as she and Peg nudged each other.

Omar began to sing with one hand holding the mic to his mouth and the other gesturing. The song was in a language other than English. It had a lively pace and the customers were toe tapping. The musicians didn't know the tune but were adding a note or two, here and there, and everyone seemed to be enjoying the performance.

Omar had a deep rich voice, and was quite expressive. Kathleen couldn't know what the song was about, but Omar's facial expressions, gestures, tempo and intonation suggested to her that this might be a powerful patriotic song—probably about victory at war.

Omar's song ended abruptly, fortissimo, with a stamp of the foot and then a bow. The room jumped to its feet and applauded as he made his way back to the table, grinning at Kathleen and wearing a light sweat on his brow.

"Well, now," Tanner said on mic. "Do we have a first place winner here?" The audience shouted, whistled, and clapped their approval.

"Care to tell us what that song was about, sir?" Tanner asked.

Omar stood and spoke loud enough to be heard across the noisy room, "Thank you. I enjoyed that very much. The song tells the story about a warrior who lives only for battle," Omar said, looking intently at Kathleen as he added, "until he meets the woman of his dreams." In a softer voice he said, "And then he has a new reason to live." The message was obvious to everyone in the pub and a roll of "Ahhh!" reached across the room.

"Thank you, sir!" Tanner said, and signaled the waiter to bring a round of drinks to the table.

"Somehow I knew that song had something to do with war," Kathleen said proudly.

"It doesn't," Omar said, laughing. "I just made that up. It's actually an old folk song about plucking chickens."

Tom roared. "Oh, that's perfect! Plucking chickens instead of war, is it? Perfect!" He slapped his thigh and laughed until the tears rolled. Everyone else at the table laughed along with him.

After finishing her pint, Peg said, "I think we should be leavin' these two children on their own now, Tom."

"Eh?" Tom said.

"We should be gettin' on home," Peg said insistently.

"What fer?" Tom wanted to know. "Shank of the evenin'."

"You know . . ." Peg said, as she nodded toward Kathleen and Omar across the table.

"Oh!" Tom replied, understanding finally what Peg was saying. "Yes, of course! Come on, woman. We're off." He turned to the waiter. "The bill," he called out.

"Nonsense," Omar replied. "My treat."

"Eh?" Tom said. "Oh." The beer had gone to his head. "All right, then. Yer treat."

"Is he going to be all right?" Kathleen asked, some concern showing on her face.

"Nothin' a little fresh air won't take care of," Peg replied. "Come on, then, Tom. Let's be goin', now."

"Aye," Tom said. "Let's be goin'. You two be good, now, ye hear?"

"Yes," Kathleen replied. "We'll be good. And you mind your step."

"Oh, aye," Tom said glumly, with a wave of his arm, as though disgusted with the suggestion that he needed to be careful. Peg winked at Kathleen and gestured that she'd be in charge. The two left, Tom walking just a bit unsteadily.

"Good people," Omar said.

"Yes. I'm lucky to have them," Kathleen said with a sigh.

Some time later, after another round and some small talk, Kathleen said, "It's getting late. I hate to be the one to say it, but we ought to be getting home ourselves."

"Are you sure I won't be in the way at your house? I could get a room in town."

"Of course not," Kathleen said. "No trouble at all. Come on."

Omar paid the bill and the two walked out the door and headed home. Kathleen had her arm wrapped around Omar's and nothing was said for a long while.

"It's been a long time," Omar said.

Kathleen looked up at him, a question in her eyes. "A long time?"

"Since I just relaxed and had a good time. With no agenda."

"Agenda?"

"Sometimes it's business. Sometimes . . . pleasure."

"No . . . business . . . on your mind tonight?" Kathleen asked, with a mischievous grin.

A car roared around the corner from behind. It screeched to a stop at the curb. Kathleen saw three men inside, their faces covered by improvised masks.

"Kathleen O'Toole! The Arab fucker!" one of the voices called out.

"Hey, Arab! Get the feck out o' this place! Keep yer filthy hands off our women!"

Kathleen flew to the side of the car, Omar not far behind her. She reached through the driver's open window, grabbed the man by his throat and pushed him hard. Then she reached in and ripped the keys out of the ignition. The stunned driver squawked, "No, no! Let us go! We were just havin' a bit of fun!"

A rear door flew open and another of the car's occupants jumped out, also masked and with a gun in his hand. "All right, then!" he screamed, his voice high-pitched with hysteria. "Who wants it first?" He was waving his gun back and forth.

Omar took a quick step toward the assailant and kicked. The tip of his boot caught the man's wrist and the gun flew high in the air and down the street behind him. The young man grabbed his wrist with his free hand and howled in pain. The last of the three jumped out of the car and charged at Kathleen, a police night stick high above his head. He never saw Omar coming.

Omar jumped behind the youth and threw a choke hold on him. The night stick fell. "You want this one, or can I have him?"

Kathleen walked up to the immobilized attacker and ripped off his mask. "Arnie McCloud!" she said in amazement. To Omar she said, "Father's a policeman."

"What the hell are you up to?" she asked the boy and slapped him across the face. "Does your father know you've got his nightstick?"

"Behind you!" Omar yelled, just as the one with the injured wrist was about to jump on Kathleen.

She spun on one heel, grabbed this one by his good wrist, and swung him in midair like a wheel. He landed hard and screamed in pain.

"You're gonna have to do without that hand for a while, now aren't you, boyo?" she said.

She ripped off his mask. "Tommy Frazier! Another policeman's son! Was that your father's gun you had, then?"

Kathleen turned back to the car. The driver, now cowering in the front seat begged, "Please, don't hurt me!"

Kathleen dangled the keys outside the window just out of his reach. "Mask off, if you please," she demanded. With hands shaking, the driver complied.

"And I could of guessed. Another policeman's boy. Fatty Glaird."

Omar was still holding Arnie around the neck. "Let the little boy go, Omar, before he pees his pants." Kathleen threw the keys at Fatty's face and turned away. She walked to where the gun landed, picked it up and put it in her pocket. "Home, then?" she said to Omar. They continued on their way as if nothing had happened.

The car sped off, its three occupants shocked at the fight they'd been in.

"That was fun!" said Kathleen. "Those boys have been needing their comeuppance for a long time."

"Whew, remind me to never get you mad at me," said Omar.

Kathleen laughed, "I wasn't really angry you know, that was just show biz. You sure kept yourself cool though. Very impressive."

"That type of stupid behavior doesn't bother me," said Omar. "It's happened before. I was concerned about you getting hurt."

Then he chuckled, "I can see I was worried for nothing." Omar pulled her close to his side, and they continued to walk, their laughter and chatter echoed off the silent, darkened homes along the way.

3

From Glenarm to London

Glenarm. It's on the east coast of Northern Ireland, not far north of Belfast. Just a typical Irish village.

A child plays with a spotted dog as they run along a narrow sidewalk. An old woman walks with her head down as she carries her bundles home. The buildings that border the street are all joined in an unbroken row. Some are tall, some not so tall. Most have red or gray roofs, stuccoed walls of green, white or yellow with the trim painted a different color. On nearly all the buildings the trim paint is weathered and chipped, revealing other trim colors from many a yesteryear. There are the typical small town shops: bakery, tavern, greengrocer, shoemaker, butcher. It's a pretty town. Peaceful.

On Fridays, the women come to church to confess their sins—a rosary said too fast or daydreaming during mass, mostly. Five "Hail Marys" and a good "Act of Contrition" is nearly always enough to wash the soul clean again.

Sometimes, though, a girl gets in bad trouble and then the Church's penance goes far, far, beyond prayers.

Somewhere in the hodgepodge of short streets and crowded

buildings there is a police station. The officers are sincere and dedicated. Their job isn't terribly sophisticated. They haul in the occasional drunk who becomes too rowdy; they respond now and again to a domestic complaint—here, too, alcohol is often behind it.

A few years ago there was a murder in the village. Not *in* the village, actually, but on the northern edge. A young man from Belfast held up a gas station and killed the proprietor. He was caught. Once during the War a wounded German paratrooper was captured in Glenarm by a woman at home alone. She wrestled the German's gun away from him, and he fainted from loss of blood. She got him to hospital in time to save his life.

Hers was a brave and well-mannered Irish village, Kathleen reflected with a smile. But she traveled far from bucolic Glenarm. As the main buyer of munitions for the Irish Republican Army, she was trusted to travel the world with a great deal of money to purchase guns, rockets, and components for the bomb makers in Belfast. She was levelheaded and mature far beyond her years, intelligent, could memorize long lists of facts and figures, was a convincing actress, and she could think on her feet.

When she joined the IRA to become a commando, she was severely tested as part of her training. On three occasions her handlers set up some elaborate theater. They wanted to know if Kathleen would kill to protect the IRA.

In one of these fake killings Kathleen "shot" a twelve-year-old Protestant boy. She was told he stole critical information and was running to give it to the British. She thought of what her brother said about killing. *A dirty business and whoever does it has a dirty soul.* Then she muttered, *The damned ugly deed needed doing, right enough.*

In another exercise, a woman was made to look pregnant. Kathleen's handlers wanted to find out whether their trainee would shoot an enemy who was an expectant mother. She did. It wasn't until much later, after she finished her training, that she was allowed to know that the boy and the woman were both actors, and had not actually been shot. Her handlers had loaded her gun with blanks.

Before she knew her training included fakery, she was given her third and final test in killing, and that one almost did her in. She was told the Kearney family in Dungiven, over near the west coast, were traitors. All three members of the family, the father, mother and teenage son, were guilty. They had provided names of IRA fighters to the British.

The family's punishment was bitter for Kathleen, and she almost refused it. She was to throw a bomb through their window. Mission code name: *broken shamrock.*

On the appointed night, two of her handlers drove Kathleen from Glenarm to Dungiven and arrived at the Kearneys' street shortly after ten. Kathleen got out of the car, walked up to the house and was ready to throw the bomb through their front window. Her whole body shook, and she felt she might throw up. The grass on her own family's graves was new, and here she was about to put another family into the ground—and in the same horrible way.

Before she could pull the bomb out from under her coat, a man ran around the corner. He screamed, "Broken shamrock! Stop! Broken shamrock!" Kathleen froze. Her mind went blank.

The man snatched the fake bomb from her hands, stage-whispered, "Get back in the car!" and ran off.

As the car sped away and the driver was hanging up the car phone, Kathleen demanded, "What the bloody hell was *that?*"

"We just got a call to cancel the mission! We got some bad feckin' information on the Kearneys! They're *loyal!*"

"You mean I almost killed an innocent family?" Kathleen shrilled hysterically. She shook and sobbed all the way back to Glenarm. When she got home, she locked herself in her room for two days. She ate nothing, took only water, and slipped in and out of a tormented sleep. When she awakened, her first thought was of the person, the bomber, who killed her own family with a fire bomb.

Was that bomber anything like me? she asked herself.

No amount of consoling was of any help, and Tom said to Peg, "Let it be. She'll come 'round."

When Kathleen learned the Broken Shamrock mission was staged to test her determination, at first she was angry; then she was relieved. She completed the training because her mission was to avenge her murdered family by helping to throw the British out of Ireland. When deadly mistakes were made along the way, she would have to find a place within her heart to contain the anguish.

Kathleen had read Karl Von Clausewitz and she accepted the maxim, *"War is politics by other means."* She couldn't tolerate the mealy-mouthed phrase "collateral damage," but the wrongful death of innocents, in error, was the warrior's dilemma, and she would have to live with it. Kathleen understood.

"Katie, it's for ye," Peg said.

"Hello?"

"Hello, Kathleen. This is Omar."

It had been three weeks since the night at Tanner's Pub. They had talked on the phone several times, each time more and more like two persons eager to become lovers, and Omar filled Kathleen's thoughts every day. Now the sound of his voice gave her a weak sensation in her knees. Her hand began to tremble.

"Yes." One word, uttered breathlessly, was all she could manage.

"I hope that will be your answer."

"My answer?" She struggled to breathe.

"I want . . . I want to invite you. To London. Invite you to London for a long weekend."

"Oh!" Kathleen kicked herself for her replies. *You sound like a kid out of school!* She forced her mind to focus and her throat to unclamp.

"I know how you feel about the Brits. How do you feel about coming to London?"

"I'm fine with being in London. I have no quarrel with the English people. My enemy is the British government, and only in Ireland."

"Then you'll come?"

This is too fast. This is what I want. I don't even know him. I want him.

"Yes! Yes, I'd love to, Omar!" Her heart raced. "When?"

"Today."

"Today?"

"Can you?"

"Well, let's see. I don't know. I don't have a ticket."

"Don't need one. I'll come get you."

"You mean you'll fly here yourself, then?"

"Not with my arms, no. I think I'll use a small airplane."

Kathleen laughed. "No. People will talk if you land an airplane here to pick me up."

"All right, then. I'll fly in *without* any airplane! That should give them plenty to talk about."

"Be serious," Kathleen said, laughing.

"How about I wire you an Air France ticket to the Belfast City Airport? You'll have it before nightfall."

"Have the ticket made out to Margaret Bigsby. That's the name on the passport I'm using these days." She stopped a moment. "Oh, about that plane ticket."

"Yes?"

"Round trip?" she asked, a tease in her voice.

Omar said softly, "Certainly, but I understand a round trip ticket can be used only one way, if that's what the lady decides."

Kathleen's heart pounded, her voice dropped an octave and she said, almost in a whisper, "Sounds good. But give the lady time to pack, will you?" *What is going on with me?* She didn't know the answer; only that she felt good. *Too fast!* She didn't care.

"First thing tomorrow morning, then? There's a direct hop at ten."

"Okay," she said. "Omar, you know . . . if we do . . . *get involved,* a price could be put on your head by the Brits."

"Iran already has a price on my head. The Brits will have to stand in line."

"All right, then, if you're sure." She was feeling sure herself. But the *'why'* of it was a great mystery. "See you tomorrow."

"Right. 'Bye."

"'Bye."

Kathleen hung up the phone and turned to Peg.

"Katie, dear, yer cheeks are bright pink," Peg said.

Kathleen laughed and grabbed Peg around her ample waist and began to waltz with her as she hummed a ditty about forever and love. In her heart, love's opposite was being squelched. For now.

Mulcahy walked in and said, "Well, what's this, then? Can a fella cut in?"

Kathleen let go of Peg and spun around the room with old Tom's arm around her until she collapsed, laughing, on the sofa.

"She got a call," Peg said in a stage-whisper. "From *him!*"

"Ye *don't* say! *Did* she now?"

"Oh, Tom! I'm so excited! So *happy!*" Kathleen said.

"Well, lass, I'd o' never guessed it! Come on now, tell me all about it, then."

"Omar's invited me to London. I leave tomorrow morning. Isn't it *grand?*"

Mulcahy saw his Katie look like a schoolgirl invited to the autumn dance. He sat back against the sofa. Peg straightened up in her chair.

"London, is it? And ye leave tomorrow. Hmm," Mulcahy said as he rubbed his chin.

"What?" Kathleen asked. "What's wrong?"

"Ah, me lass," Mulcahy said. His voice cracked, his eyes turned sad and he looked like he might cry.

"Oh, Tom," Peg said. Her hand reached out to her husband, for she understood his pain. What his Kathleen was about to do brought back bitter memories. He knew how violent the Catholic Church can be when it thinks a girl is immoral.

"What is it, Tom?" Kathleen said.

"What's wrong, ye ask?" He pulled out a handkerchief and blew his nose. "In a sane world, there'd be *nothin'* wrong, child. Oh, listen to me, then, still callin' ye child. And ye a grown woman, and all."

"But what is it, Tom?"

Mulcahy said nothing.

"You don't want me to go to London? Is that it? Because I'm with you in the IRA?"

Mulcahy pulled out his Meerschaum, pain on his face. He pressed the tobacco into place with great care and lit it.

"Fifty-five years ago—no, wait—it was fifty-seven, a Glenarm girl of eighteen, unmarried she was, got pregnant. I was five years old at the time. She was me big sister, Colleen. Da called her Princess. All I knew was, one day Colleen was here to play with me, and the next day she was gone. Da never called her Princess again."

Mulcahy stopped to take a few puffs on his pipe. There were tears in his eyes.

"I didn't know you had a sister," Kathleen whispered. "What happened to her, then?"

"The bleedin' Catholic Church is what *happened* to her, that's what!"

Peg gasped, "Tom! Ye mustn't talk that way!"

Mulcahy cast a long, level look over his pipe at his wife. "That's the one subject Peg and I ever fight about: The bloody Catholic Church." Mulcahy's voice cracked again.

Peg sat next to Tom and slipped her hand into his. She was crying, too.

Kathleen cleared her throat. "Let's talk about something else, then, shall we?"

"No!" Mulcahy said firmly. "We'll talk about this. It's about us *all*. And it's mainly about ye, then, now as ye're about to become a woman."

"About to become a woman? If by that you mean lose my virginity, Tom, I did that when I was sixteen."

"Right ye are, lass. Losing her virginity never made a girl a woman, I'm bound to say. And I've long known all about what ye did when ye were sixteen."

"*What?* You've *known?* But how *could* you? I told no one!"

"Right enough. Ye never told. But Danny Quinn did."

"The *bastard!*" Kathleen gasped.

"Well, he didn't get to talk to many, and the priests never did hear of it."

"I haven't seen him since the funeral," Kathleen said. "Some say he went off to the French Foreign Legion."

"Yes, well the Legion's as good a place as any to tighten up a loose tongue. The point is not where he went, or how. What's important is, he was gone before he could blab much."

Peg's eyes dropped and she looked ashamed. Kathleen saw that, and a question formed in her eyes. Mulcahy became defensive. "What was done, had to be! I didn't want *ye* to end up where the Princess went, damn it!"

Peg wanted to move the conversation away from what was done with Danny Quinn. She lifted her eyes and whispered as a fearful conspirator, "Tom's sister was put away."

"Put away?" Kathleen asked, astonished. "You don't mean—

"Aye. The Magdalene Laundries!" Peg said just above a whisper, first glancing left and right, as though a terrible enemy might be eavesdropping.

"Oh, dear!" Kathleen said. She knew the Magdalene Laundries were a string of Catholic convents throughout Ireland that deviated from the meaning of Christianity and the rule of Rome. "Wayward" girls were locked away in these hell holes, some for life, to endure slavery and abuse of all kinds. This might include girls who's only crime was to have had sex, maybe just once, girls who'd gotten pregnant, and even girls who'd been raped. The Laundries were a blemish on Ireland's soul.

"Did Colleen ever come out?" Kathleen asked in a hushed voice.

Mulcahy puffed hard and fast on his pipe. It glowed bright red. Big tears ran down his cheeks.

"No, she didn't." His voice was cracked and shaking. "When I got older, I tried to see her many times, but the sister superior would never let me in. I did speak one day with a young nun in the convent garden who was a friend of my sister's. She told me what happened, who got Colleen pregnant. Me sister died in that damned convent. So did her child. Ma and Da were never even let in to see the graves. Nor was I."

"I'm sorry, Tom." Kathleen reached out and placed her hand on his. "Who got her pregnant, then?"

"Now there's a tale, lass. There's a tale no one wants to hear. Not anyone. Not ever."

"Best not to ask," Peg whispered, tears in her eyes. "Tom's told me, and I can't believe it."

"Ye mean ye don't *want* to believe it, woman," Mulcahy said gently as he stroked his wife's hair, which he always did to calm her.

He turned and looked at Kathleen in silence for a long moment before he sighed and said, "I suppose it's wrong of me to burden ye with my past. What's with ye and this Omar fellow, then, hmm?

"He did ask my permission to court ye, which I thought had died out with the last century, and I was so surprised that I told him he could." He paused and added, "But what does this mean for *ye*, then?"

Kathleen made a naive smile and raised her shoulders in a gesture that said, *I don't know.*

"Then why are ye goin', and all?" Mulcahy demanded.

"Because I *want* to, Tom! I know it's too fast, and all. Believe me, I've told myself I'm a fool. But it makes no difference. More than I've ever wanted anything, I want this man!"

"More than . . . even more than . . . to avenge yer family?"

Kathleen hung her head. "I don't know," she whispered. "I'm so confused."

Mulcahy felt a rush of tenderness toward his adopted daughter. He put his arm around her and whispered, "I've heard it said that confusion is the doorway to knowin'." In a louder voice he added with a laugh, "Makes me wonder why I'm not the most *knowin'* bastard in the whole damn world!"

Peg said, "Ye've known to love me all these years, right enough. And I'm right proud of it, too!"

Mulcahy patted his wife's hand and smiled at her, "And always will. Lovin' ye is easy, me Peg. I win no award for it, then."

To Kathleen he said, "Ye say ye *want* him. *How* do ye want him?"

"Oh, Tom! *Please!*" Peg said, and gave him a bit of a shove.

"No," Kathleen said to Peg. "Fair question." To Mulcahy she replied, "I think . . . what I feel . . . must be like . . . the early days when a woman believes she might have her first child inside her. She doesn't want to get her hopes up, but she's too excited to get it out of her mind."

Mulcahy's eyes grew large. "Are ye tellin' me that ye're—"

"No! My heavens, no!" Kathleen said laughing. "I told ye, I haven't been with anyone since Danny. Not even the elephant stays pregnant for four years! What I'm trying to say, dear Tom, is that I think . . . I think I could *love* him." *What am I saying? How could this be?*

Mulcahy scratched his head. "Has this fellow declared his intentions, then?"

Kathleen laughed. "Oh, faith, Tom! We've only just met!"

"But ye're goin' off to London to be with him, and all!"

"Should he be a calling on me here in Glenarm, then? How would that be? I'm sure people are already talking."

"Hmm. Good point. Good point. And it's not as though ye're sixteen any more." He finally chuckled and relented. "Go on, now. Off with ye, then! Ye'll be wantin' to pack yer Sunday best, if I remember what a young woman is like," he said with a gentle slap on Peg's rump as she rose from her chair to go help her daughter.

"Oh, the likes of 'im!" Peg said with a laugh.

Mulcahy's show of good humor was just that. A show. Inside he felt conflicted, and that night he lay awake.

Kathleen, too, found it hard to sleep. *What of my vow I'd never have sex again before marriage?* It was a vow made in fear of God's punishment, she admitted. *God's already taken everything. What more could He do to me?* She knew this was blasphemy, and she didn't care. What she cared most about was the next thought she had: *My main vow isn't about sex. It's about getting those Brit bastards out of Ireland.*

Another thought kept knocking: *That time with Danny can't be all there is. Why would anyone bother?* Her family's murders were on her mind. She still felt the old lust for revenge. Now she felt a new kind of lust. The two feelings were at war.

On the way to the airport next morning Kathleen noticed Mulcahy was quiet, withdrawn. "Tom," she said gently, "I need to know how you and Peg feel about me getting involved with this fella. You've both been so good to me. I'd never do anything to hurt you."

Mulcahy looked over at her and smiled sadly. "And look at what I've got ye into, then. What's yer life been like? Ye've given yerself entirely to the IRA. Ye've had no life of yer own. No parties, no boyfriends. My doin', that."

Kathleen put her hand on Mulcahy's shoulder. "No, Tom. It's nothing you did. I wanted it this way. For my parents. For Tim." She allowed herself, for the first time, to see how much she had closed out of her life. She felt her throat hurt and tears sting her eyes.

Mulcahy looked straight ahead. "Aye. Well, what's so is so. What's done is done. And now there's a new day a comin'. I've given it a lot of thought, lass. Didn't sleep much last night. Peg and

I talked about it before breakfast. We both think ye should start to live yer own life."

Kathleen felt the tears come down her cheeks.

Mulcahy looked at her. "What's wrong? This is a happy time."

"Yes, a happy time." She said it again, trying to learn it. "A happy time." She smiled, sadly, and added, "I'll get the hang of it."

"And know this, lass. What e'er ye do, I'm behind ye. I'll always be there to cover yer back. None shall harm ye, or even criticize. And that includes the bloody Catholic Church."

"Thank you, dear Tom. You're the best father a girl could have."

Mulcahy looked at her, and saw her for the first time as the woman she might become. "It's high time ye be joinin' the dance."

KATHLEEN FORCED her feet to walk, not run, when she saw Omar's smiling face at the Air France off-ramp. When she was but a few yards from him, Omar reached out.

Kathleen felt a thrill go up her spine as she flew into his arms.

For a long wordless moment, they held each other and Kathleen's heart raced as, once again, she felt herself melt in the safety of this man's embrace.

"Kiss me," she whispered. She looked in Omar's eyes. In her own eyes was the plea *Take me!* Their parted lips touched lightly, touched again. Omar found her mouth and captured it. Kathleen got those weak knees again and held tight. She wanted this kiss to go on forever.

"Come on," Omar whispered. "This will be even better when we're alone."

Kathleen smiled and Omar reached for her bag, then stopped abruptly.

"Whoa!" he said. "The first time I handled your bag, you almost shot me."

Kathleen laughed. "What's in this bag isn't worth shooting you for. Besides," she whispered, "I forgot my gun, so you're safe."

"Oh, that's a relief!" He picked up the bag. "Shall we go to London?" he said with a bow.

"Let's do!" She took his arm and together they walked outside into England's best December weather: a sky of cold gray but no rain.

Kathleen had never given a thought to what Omar might be driving, but when she saw his convertible it surprised her. The little sports coupe reminded her of everything she'd read about art deco. The car featured three hood ornaments, three headlamps, and exaggerated curves. It was bright red.

"I love your car!" Kathleen said. "How darling! What is it?"

"It's called the Austin Atlantic. Made in the early fifties. Not many left. A wild design."

As they started out of the airport garage, Kathleen asked, "Does it take a wild man to own this wild car?"

Omar grinned like a carnival barker who sells Kewpie dolls. "Ah, my dear. Both me and the car are wild beasts, ma'am. Why, we're the genuine article!"

"Why don't I believe that?"

"That I'm genuine?"

"No. That you're wild."

"Smart girl. The truth about both of us, me and this car, is it's only the *design* that's wild. Under the bonnet we're both completely tame, actually."

"Hmm. I'm not so sure *that's* true, either."

"About me or the car?"

Kathleen laughed. "Let's find out about the car right now. Later for you."

Omar didn't push his Austin but the drive was fun for Kathleen anyway. As they passed through London's districts, she found Omar to be the perfect tour guide, with a broad knowledge of English history, architecture, and customs.

Omar lived at the end of a tree-lined pedestrian lane in one of London's most prestigious neighborhoods off High and Church Streets in Kensington. A small row of Victorian houses with delightful front gardens and trees faced each other along the short street. Omar's was the last, a charming two-story home with entry through its own little garden of lilac and roses. Kathleen could hear the sounds of children playing at the small primary school nearby. The quiet street, the dignity of the architecture, plus the well-kept garden looked transported from another century when the sun never set over the British Empire.

The overall impression was that the person who lived here treasured a life of serenity.

Kathleen was astonished at this counterpoint to the man she first new as a pirate and gunrunner who sailed the seas in his own warship.

"Well?" Omar said as he saw the surprise on her face.

"I thought maybe you'd live in Soho. Or some other place like that, where the action is."

Omar laughed, "Plenty of action in my life already. Peace and quiet is what I want." He took her face in his hands and said. "And you? What do you want?"

"When I find *that* out, you'll be the first to know," she said with a warm smile.

Omar chuckled and opened the door.

As she stepped into his home, Kathleen was stunned by its beauty. She found herself first in a sitting room where two decorative balconies overlooked the front garden. Fawn was the color of the heavy drapes at the floor-to-ceiling windows and of the elegant portico that framed the great Victorian fireplace. This contrasted with the room's L-shaped leather sofa in deep burgundy and, nearby, a large table in sycamore and maple. A bit deeper shade of tan in the lush carpeting together with a lighter tint at the ceiling wrapped the room, and everything or everyone in it, with a sense of well-ordered calm. Throughout the house, well placed for maximum exotic impact, were the Persian rugs and artifacts Omar had collected from some of the world's most trusted purveyors.

"This is beautiful, Omar! And so peaceful!"

"Thank you." Omar made a sweep with his arm. "Welcome to my home. I gave the help the day off. Take the half-penny tour?"

"Mmm. Love to."

As Omar showed Kathleen through his home, she felt herself relax into its ambience.

The tour reached an upstairs sitting room when Omar said, "Can I interest you in a glass of wine?"

"I'd like that." Kathleen was relieved. Her excitement needed a breather.

On a table near the window, she saw a bottle of wine in a bucket of ice, some glasses, and a dish of chocolates.

"Butlers?" Kathleen asked with a grin.

"What else?" Omar replied with a shrug of his shoulders. "Please, take one. Those in the middle are Cerice au Kirsch and surrounding them are Double Chocolate."

"Double?" Kathleen asked.

"Dark chocolate outside, white inside," Omar replied, holding the dish out to Kathleen.

"You really are an afficionado, aren't you. Or do you work for Butlers' publicity department?"

Omar laughed. "Do you think they could afford me?"

"Come to think of it, no," Kathleen replied. "This is good. May I have another?"

"Please," Omar replied. "Do try the pralines."

They sat together before the window and looked out onto Omar's winter gardens.

"Spring is my favorite season," Omar said. "The heliotrope and the jonquils fill my garden with perfume. Later, in summer, it's the roses. I grow a few that still have a great scent."

"You are a man of many parts, sir," Kathleen laughed. "No end of surprises."

Omar grinned and shrugged in a self-deprecating manner but offered no reply.

Conversation was light. There were comments about the chocolates, the wine, the house.

But eventually the banter ran out. Kathleen glanced at Omar, then away, and he did the same.

"Penny for your thoughts," he whispered.

Kathleen's smile was inviting. Omar went to her side. He bent and kissed her lightly on the mouth.

She got up and moved into in his arms, looking into his eyes.

"Just a penny?" she said softly. "I'd have offered more for yours."

"You couldn't possibly afford mine," Omar replied with a smile. "I was just thinking that if heaven isn't like this, I'm not going."

Her lips were parted slightly for Omar's kiss, a light touch of his mouth against hers. She felt him press more firmly. His tongue invaded her mouth, searching, finding, entwining itself with hers. She felt unsure of what to do. She pressed against him, feeling herself grow moist.

"You were right," she said softly when they stopped for a breath.

"About?"

"This is better now that we're alone."

Omar laughed, swept her off her feet and carried her to the master bedroom. They sank together to the bed. Their hands fumbled with each other's buttons.

Panic surfaced in Kathleen. "Omar, wait."

He stopped.

"I don't know . . . how."

"How what?"

"To please a man."

He smiled. "Let's make it easy then. I'll please you."

Naked. Kisses everywhere. Little ones, lingering ones. Kathleen was passionate now, and she wanted him with a fire she'd never known before. She ran her fingers up his back and squeezed the muscles in his shoulders. Omar's lips hovered over her breast and she could feel his hot breath on her nipple. She let her instinct guide her. She thrust her breast up to his mouth and gave it to him. His fingers brushed her thigh and sent an electric tingle through her. He came nearer and nearer but never touched her silken pubic curls. Kathleen was wild with wanting him. She didn't know what should happen next, but once again she let her instinct take charge. With a delicious kind of embarrassment, she reached for him and felt how hard he was, how ready.

He entered her with no hesitation, and soon he was lodged so deep she thought she could feel him throughout her entire being. When he moved, it was with a gentle force. He made her feel taken, possessed, and glad to be. Rhythms changed and positions did, too, with many deliberate stops and starts. Mouths explored every possibility, found each other's musk, loved its taste. They raised in each other storms of passion, which they enhanced, prolonged, and gave every possible nuance.

They couldn't delay it any longer. They climbed together to a place where their passions fused, exploded, rushed upward, and exploded a second time, a third, and yet again. Finally, they drifted down through several lovely plateaus into a blessed surcease.

Now Kathleen knew that, yes, there is such a thing as a rocket ride to the moon.

The next morning, Omar woke Kathleen with a kiss and said, "Good morning, my lady. Sleep well?"

"Like a baby," Kathleen answered in a sleepy voice. She reached for Omar, but he jumped aside. "Later for that. How about a typical English breakfast, served to the lady in bed?"

Kathleen laughed. "I'm wild hungry. But all I want for breakfast is you."

"Good plan. Hold the thought. But I'm hungry. For food."

Kathleen sat up. "Shall I make us something, then?"

"No. I want to show off," Omar said as he slipped on a robe.

Kathleen smiled and shrugged. "Breakfast in bed. I've never been so catered to."

In a short time, Omar returned and knocked on the bedroom door.

"Are you decent?"

"Must I be?"

"I have someone with me."

Kathleen flushed. "Oh!" She quickly slid down and snatched the cover up to her chin.

Omar came in followed by a short thin man with dark brown skin and shiny black hair.

"This is my man, Hakim Jamal. Hakim, meet Kathleen."

"Madam," Hakim said with a polite bow. He set a large tray down on the table by the bed and again bowed, more deeply this time. "At your service, Madam." He bowed again slightly as he closed the door behind him, and was gone.

"What charming manners!" Kathleen said. "Who is he?"

"Hakim is many things. He's my best intelligence agent, with global connections. He's also my cook, my manservant. Manages this place and also my hacienda in Spain."

"You have a home in Spain?"

"Yes. On the Mediterranean coast. Place called Florenza," Omar said with a grin and added, "If you're a good girl, maybe I'll take you there some time." Omar slipped off his robe and approached the bed.

"Why, sir, I am *always* a good girl," Kathleen said with a sexy smile.

Omar sat on the edge of the bed. Kathleen glanced down and saw he was half-way ready for more lovemaking.

"Mmm. You were quite a good girl last night."

"You weren't so bad yourself," Kathleen said, stroking his arm gently. Then she pulled her hand away. "But tell me about your home in Florenza. You said Hakim manages it?"

Omar busied himself with the breakfast things. "Sometimes. Actually, I have a full time staff in residence there. Hakim is more than a manager. He's also my hawaladar and my most loyal servant. I trust him with my life."

"What's a hawa . . . what was the word?"

"Hawaladar. One who practices hawala, or paperless banking. I'll tell you about it sometime. If Hakim wanted to, he could send me to the poorhouse with one word. But right now, let's see what he's fixed us to eat."

"I thought you were going to cook."

"Would have, if Hakim wasn't home yet. But he had everything nearly ready. Makes the best English breakfast in the world."

On the tray by the bed was a large pot of coffee and two platters piled high with eggs, bacon, sausages, ham, scones with clotted cream, fried bread, mushrooms, and baked beans.

"Oh, my!" she said. "This all looks delicious. But there's so much! How many are we expecting?"

"Eat. You're too skinny."

"You sure know how to flatter a girl! I didn't hear you complain last night," she said as she pinched Omar's naked rump hard enough to make him jump.

"Hey!" he yelled. "Don't bruise it! I've got to sit on that!"

Kathleen laughed. "I'm *not skinny!*"

"All right, then. You're fat. See if I care."

Kathleen swung a pillow at his head but missed. On purpose.

Breakfast was a slow affair, with lots of laughter. As they finished eating Omar glanced at the bedside clock and said, "I've got a big day on the town planned for us. Care to take a shower with me?"

"Oh!" Kathleen said, lowering her eyes. She didn't understand why this should make her feel shy, but it did.

"Try it," Omar said as he took her hand and led her into the shower.

Slippery soap bubbles soon were everywhere. Though she was noticeably sore from all the delights of the prior afternoon, Kathleen couldn't resist the mounting passion in her breasts and deep inside, between her legs. This was all so new. For one fleeting moment, she had a vision of herself a thousand years ago as a Celtic woman loving her man. The thought streaked through her mind that race memories were guiding her, instructing her now. With Omar standing behind and pressed against her, she began slipping her back up and down, ever so slightly, against Omar's chest and abdomen, and slipping his hardness in and out between her thighs.

Omar gasped, "I can't last much longer."

"Me neither," she whispered as she leaned forward and reached between her legs to guide Omar and tickle him with her fingertips as he slid into her until he was pressed tight against her rump.

Kathleen found she could control her thrills, direct Omar's movements inside her, by slightly changing her position; raising her back a little to feel his thrusts high against her womb, then curving her back downward to accept his deepest thrusts. Yesterday, she thought sex couldn't be more thrilling. But this was. Her sensations were spreading. Her entire being was responding. She felt she must faint unless she let go. She screamed her joy. Omar's pace quickened, became animal. He slammed into her, hard, again and again, not even aware that he was screaming, too.

Kathleen turned and looked Omar full in the face. Her smile was grand. Exotic. It was lustful; it was tremulous. It was strong; it was helpless.

Never before had Omar found an entire woman, the entire soul of a woman, in her smile.

A little actual washing up did get done, and while she was drying her hair and Omar was still in the shower she heard him sing an old pop tune.

I like a man who sings in the shower, she thought. She blushed. *I talk like a woman who's had countless men. And I've had only one before today—and we were both kids.*

Kathleen noticed the singing had stopped, the water was turned off, but Omar wasn't coming out of the shower. She waited. Listened. Nothing; no sound, no movement. She became startled. "Omar? You okay in there?"

Still nothing. Now genuinely afraid, Kathleen whipped the glass shower door open. As she did so, Omar turned his back to her. He said nothing.

"What's wrong?" she said, a chill racing up her spine.

Still no answer. She reached for him, touched his shoulder with her fingertips. He pulled away, still with his back to her.

"Who taught you?" he asked in a low voice, his head tilted up, the words aimed at the ceiling.

"Taught me what?" she asked, and pulled at his shoulder, trying to turn him toward her. Suddenly she understood. She felt her blood boil. "Taught me *what?*"

Omar's head dropped forward. He leaned his forehead against the shower wall, his back still to Kathleen.

Her first impulse was to hit him. Her next was to run; get back to Ireland as fast as she could. *This is crazy!* she thought. She saw a tremor go through him, and when he turned to look at her she saw pain and sadness in his eyes.

"Omar?" she whispered, her anger gone. "Talk to me." She stepped into the shower and took him in her arms.

He wrapped his arms around her and whispered, "I'm sorry! I'm so sorry!"

Kathleen held him away a little so she could look into his face.

"Talk to me," she said.

Omar shook his head, as though trying to clear it. "I don't understand it. It's always there, ready to jump out. Like a wild animal. I hate it."

This sounded familiar. "What is it, Omar?"

"I'm jealous. I'm crazy with it. I make things up. Stupid, crazy things. I'm jealous of every man you've ever known. Jealous of who taught you to be such a wonderful lover. Jealous of a man you might meet tomorrow." He regained his composure and added, "I'm sorry. I'll get dressed and take you to the airport."

"Is that what you want? To take me to the airport?"

"No," he said. "That's the last thing. But you must—"

"I must . . . what? What must I, Omar?"

"But after what I just—"

"Yes. There was a moment, there, I wanted to go. But now, I'm not so sure anymore."

"But I don't understand. How could you—"

"You talked. You opened up to me. That means a lot, because it's something I find hard to do myself."

"But my jealousy. I—"

"Your jealousy is just what you said it is. Crazy. But if you're willing to deal with it, so am I." After a moment she added, "I think." She stepped back out of the shower, as though to give Omar space.

He took a deep breath. When he let it out, he felt a weight slip—just a little—from his mind. The look on his face was hopeful, but uncertain.

Kathleen smiled and tossed him a towel. "You're all wet, sir. Meet me in the sitting room and tell me your plan for our day. Remember that? For now, this subject's closed. Okay?"

Omar nodded, stunned. His eyes followed Kathleen as she walked out of the bathroom.

Who is this woman? he asked himself. He felt as though for the first time in his life, someone else was in control. And he liked it. It scared the daylights out of him, but he did like it. *Could I, finally, conquer this demon? With her help?*

As he was toweling, a rogue thought slid into his brain: *She got away with not telling me who taught her how to make love.* The thought had barely registered when he pounced: *Stop it! That's crazy!* His next thought made him weary: *This isn't going to be easy.*

Waiting for him in the sitting room, Kathleen was having similar thoughts. She doubted she could help him much. Both concealed their fears and doubts behind lighthearted smiles, and planned their day.

OMAR TOOK KATHLEEN to some of the stores in the upmarket shopping district of Kensington Church Street. The mood in the street was gay. Christmas strollers greeted one another with smiles, a breach of reserve English passers-by permit themselves once a year. Shoppers were loaded with ribboned bundles.

The aroma of baking from the confectioners and the perfume from flower shops scented the air as one carol followed another along the street.

The two lovers visited Genel's, where Omar insisted Kathleen try on a black evening dress they saw in the window. It was deep off the shoulder, a one-piece that wrapped tight around waist and hips, went to the floor, and left the entire back bare.

"It's a smash. You've got to have it." Omar said. His demon reared. *And who will slip it off her some day?* Omar mentally replied, *Go to hell!* He felt brave for dueling with his demon, but he was unsure—like a knight whose shield has a big hole in it.

"Where on earth would I wear something like this?" Kathleen asked.

"To the theater. With me tonight."

There was a whirlwind of fashion shops, perfumeries, shoe stores, and jewelry stores.

Omar insisted, and Kathleen bought it all, with faithful Hakim at a discreet distance to write the checks and carry the packages. Before the morning was out, Hakim looked not like a short person carrying things, not like a person at all, but like a tall pile of boxes equipped with legs.

There were places that sold lingerie that made Kathleen blush. The thought of wearing the sexy garments for Omar caused a delicious stirring between her thighs and she blushed deeper as she felt herself grow warm and moist.

These lovely things will stay in London. Only for us, Omar thought.

FOR LUNCH, THEY WENT TO CLARKE'S.

The maitre d' greeted Omar and Kathleen at the door. "Reservations?"

"Jabri," Omar replied.

"But of course, sir." He made a large overhead wave of his arm to summon their waiter.

"Jacques will attend you," the maitre d' said with a plastic smile, common issue to all arriving guests.

"Good afternoon," Jacques said with a heavy French accent. He bowed slightly from the waist, his hands held at the chest and cupped together at the fingers. A gleaming white napkin, folded perfectly, was draped over his arm. This was one of the last of the Old-World continental garçons, waiters whose main objective is to charm.

"Permit me to show you to your table." He turned, his head high, and strode out onto the dining floor in the imperious manner of a general on parade.

At their table, Jacques gave a chair a ceremonial swipe with the end of his napkin and, directing a glance at Kathleen, said, "If you please."

"Thank you," Kathleen murmured. Jacques' bow was very nearly imperceptible, and, as Kathleen sat, he made a symbolic little push at her chair.

The same napkin swipe was made at Omar's chair, the cloth barely touching it, and Omar was seated with the same subtle bow.

As Jacques handed his two guests their menus, Kathleen noted his attire. He wore black trousers with a strip of shiny black silk up the outside of each leg and a white linen jacket heavily starched. Perched above his large Adam's apple was an impossibly small bow tie, also black and showing its elastic where the little shirt collar tips turned up and then down again.

Over one arm, he wore his badge of honor, the large white napkin, now perfectly refolded by a neat flick of the wrist.

"May I offer a recommendation?" His manner said he intended to.

"By all means," Omar replied, closing his menu.

"Today the chargrilled Dover sole is *délicieux!*" Jacques said with a noisy kiss that exploded in air on his finger tips. "*Mervellieux!*" he added and rolled his eyes as though in unbearable ecstasy. "She is stuffed with clams in white sauce and served with a baby spinach *salad*."—he isolated the last word in exaggerated French. "I suggest with that a 1949 white Jean Lafitte. Properly chilled, of course. Jean Lafitte is quite correct for a light midday *repas*."—he puffed out the word with a roll of the 'r' back in his throat. "Would that please M'sieur *et* Madam?" he intoned, as he half-shut his sharp black eyes and aimed an aristocratic gaze down his Gallic nose.

Omar gave Kathleen an inquiring smile as he tried to hide his amusement. "Lovely," she said, her eyes sparkling with fun. Omar nodded to the waiter who murmured, "Merci, m'sieur, madame," promptly turned toward the kitchen, his head high again, and strode imperiously away.

Kathleen placed a hand before her mouth to hide a giggle. "He's too funny!"

Omar also laughed. "Funny, and damn near *unbearably* correct!"

Several times throughout the meal Kathleen felt that the glow of love burning her body must be apparent to everyone in the restaurant, and she glanced nervously around her, half fearing the other patrons would see how sexual she had become, half hoping they would.

That night, they attended the grand London National Theater in a private evening for invited guests produced by and starring Hume Cronyn and Jessica Tandy. The evening was a potpourri of the couple's favorite scenes from myriad plays, and to close the soiree, Mr. Cronyn read Ms. Tandy's favorite poem, a bucolic elegy about the grief of a young man whose fiancee has died.

Kathleen's heart went out to the tragic young man, and even more to his lovely young fiancee, and as the poem ended she was dabbing her eyes.

EARLY IN THEIR RELATIONSHIP, Omar and Kathleen spent as much time as they could together. This was often interrupted, though, when Kathleen was traveling on IRA business or Omar was sailing off somewhere in pursuit of his dreams of empire.

And every night that they were not in each other's arms, Omar thrashed in his bed, struggling with his green-eyed demon.

Kathleen knew, but kept a discreet silence on the subject. Through many nights of bleak uncertainty, her mantra was, *This is his battle to fight. He's either going to die on that hill or he's not; but he's got to climb it alone.*

AS THE MONTHS SLIPPED BY, there were far more good times than bad, and their relationship blossomed as it grew deeper roots. Marriage was talked about, but always as something for later; when they both felt ready. Each had their own issues to resolve, goals to achieve.

Nevertheless, less than a year after they met, Kathleen and Omar had their first child. A son. They named him Shafi, after Omar's father. The following year, their second child was born; another son. They named him Michael after Kathleen's grandfather.

In the last weeks of her first pregnancy, Kathleen found a new dimension to Omar's love. In the night, with only candles lighting their bedroom, they would lie side by side. Omar would press his lips softly against her womb. She felt his lips barely touch her skin, as he sang old ballads to his unborn child. Kathleen's favorite was *Misirlou*, a Greek song whose title means Egyptian Girl. Omar would open his mouth slightly against her skin and hum its haunting tones into her womb. The sensation of his hot breath thrilled her as the vibrations of his deep, rich voice sent shivers of delight through her entire being. A great desire would well up inside her. She would reach for him. She always found him ready, as she gently prompted him to move his head lower.

Even decades later, Kathleen would remember the way she and Omar learned about her body together. She relished each moment as his mouth and lips searched for what gave her the most pleasure. At first she didn't know, couldn't direct him when he asked her to. Little by little, she became sensitive to her own most responsive places, learned to know where they were and where they were not. When she grew tense, about to climax but didn't want to yet, she would feel him savor her with his tongue and she would relax, slip into another zone in her mind for a different kind of release. She thought of this special place as her "Panorama," where her sensations could spread out, give her a broader wave of ecstasy. They both learned. He would tease, torment, touch with his tongue for just a brief moment, ever so lightly, move away, and come back again. Once in a while, she would feel him place just the tip of a finger at her nether opening, pressing ever so slightly, never entering. She would whisper, begging him not to penetrate her there, yet begging him not to take his fingertip away. She would long for release. The flow of feeling would start from somewhere deep inside. The skin on her inner thighs quivering, her stomach muscles tensing, she would feel an undeniable rush. Never, as she soared upward, would Omar stop. Never did she feel him change his pace; not until she was over the top, not until after she moaned, or screamed, not until she reached down to grab his head and pull his mouth up to hers. Then they would rest, wrapped tightly in each other's arms.

In this way did Kathleen welcome Omar to share each of her pregnancies, safely, right up through the last days. In this way did Kathleen blend the miracle of new life with the miracle of love.

Years later, as the boys began to move from infancy to childhood and started to show their many natural talents, Kathleen would say to Omar in the privacy of their bedroom that *this* is what sparked genius in the boys before they were born. The singing, she meant.

4

Sea of Tears

1990

The Christmas Rose had put out a large yield this year of its characteristic cup-shaped white blooms along the path leading to the front door, and Omar had explained to Kathleen that this ancient flower was known to keep evil spirits out of the house. The flowers had been begging for a good spring mulching since more than a week ago and now, finally, while Omar was away on business, Kathleen was getting to it. The weather man had threatened rain, saying a cold front was on its way in from Scandinavia, but the erratic London sky had shown its typical vagary and a spring sun was pouring down a pleasant warmth. There might not be too many days like this one, Kathleen decided, until the heat of summer would make London gardening uncomfortable for a woman of Northern Ireland.

"Ma, where do I cut these?" Michael called out from the other side of the garden. He was determined to cut the Cotton Lavender at the perfect length, as his ma had told him to do, so that the shrub would sprout new growth and thicken up during the summer. Omar had planted two kinds, the Neapolitana for its lime green flowers and feathery leaves, and the Virens because he liked its bright yellow flowers and aromatic leaves.

"Well let's see now," Kathleen said, walking quickly over to where her son was working. The clippers he was using were old and rusted, too stiff for Michael's young hands, but when he saw his ma use them with ease he insisted he could do it too. His hands were aching, but he would not let on.

"If you just leave the newest bud on the stem, I think that will be fine. Cut just above the newest bud, where the wood turns from brown to green, and when you . . ."

"Ma," Shafi called out from the front door of the house. He had been excused from gardening this day because he was wanted to finish building his Marconi coil radio receiver before his dad returned.

"What is it?" Kathleen called out.

"Da's on the phone," Shafi replied.

Kathleen went in and picked up the phone. "Hello?"

"Hi," the familiar voice replied. Kathleen suddenly had a total recall of the first time she had heard Omar's voice on the telephone. *Could it be that was more than six years ago?* she marveled, as she remembered the day he had phoned to invite her to London. She shivered at the realization that after all that time his voice—even just one word—still gave her goose bumps.

"Hi, darling," she replied. "Where are you?"

"Still in Marseilles, I'm afraid," was the weary reply.

"Problems?"

"Yeah, 'fraid so. These people want to lease the Desert Star, but they don't want to pay enough to fuel the ship for crossing the Atlantic. With what they want to pay, I wouldn't cover my costs."

"Then why go on talking with them? Come on home," Kathleen said.

"I'd like to, but the ship needs ocean time. She hasn't been out in almost a year. Not good for a big freighter like the Desert Star to sit at dockside for this long. Right now, this bunch is the only prospect I have for leasing the ship. I may have to sign with them, even if I do lose money on it. Better to lose some money than lose the ship," Omar said, but Kathleen thought he sounded bitter.

Kathleen sighed. She didn't try to hide her disappointment. "I understand," she said.

"Why don't you take the boys and go ahead on up to Glenarm for a visit with Tom and Peg?"

She sighed again. "I don't know, Omar. I wanted this to be a family time."

"And it will be. I'm not going to stay here one day longer than I have to."

"How much longer?"

"I don't know. These guys play a waiting game, hoping to wear me down, but while they're doing that I'll be looking for another client to lease the Desert Star, and then I'll tell these . . ."

"Can you give me any idea how long it will be?"

"I can't be sure. Several weeks at most."

"Several weeks! That puts us into summer!" Kathleen complained.

Omar was silent for some moments before he said in a soft voice. "Darling, this is the best I can do. Take the boys and go to Glenarm. I'll come up for long weekends as often as I can. But you go now. Spring in Ireland is lovely. You'll have a great time. All kinds of places to show the boys. Okay?"

"All right," Kathleen said. At first she felt disappointment, but then she felt a sudden lovely anticipation rising in her breast.

"You're right about springtime in Ireland, Omar. It is lovely. I'll miss you, and the boys will too. But we'll have fun. And you come up as often as you can, okay?" Her voice sounded hopeful.

"Okay. I promise."

THREE DAYS LATER, after the London house was closed up properly and the garden put to rights, Kathleen and the boys arrived at Tom and Peg's house in the evening. At breakfast the following morning, Grandpa Tom mentioned the great stone pathway built by the giant of Antrim, an Irish myth Kathleen had told her children long ago. The boys wanted to see the stone wonder so a day's outing was planned. Tom and Peg were invited, but shortly before it was time to start out Tom said he wasn't feeling well. Peg insisted he stay home and rest, and she with him, so mother and sons went alone.

They reached the top of the cliff, and now the beach lay far below where the bright blue Irish sea glittered to the horizon. Kathleen's pulse was racing from the climb, and the boys were breathing a little hard. They had left the tourist path high on the ridge to get away from the noisy throng, most of them from overseas. The mob came, as Ireland's visitors had come for more than three hundred years, to marvel at the 40,000 white and black columns, some as tall as a football field is long, that seemed to rise up out of the sea at land's edge all up and down the coast at county Antrim.

Scientists of today say these chalk and basalt columns are a geological freak caused by volcanic eruption. The ancients knew differently, and whispered with pride: *this is the Giant's Causeway!*

A winding path of stone—an easy safe descent bordered by sturdy railings of wood and rope—led Kathleen and her boys down the tower face of the great highroad, then up again until they emerged on a promontory far from the passing crowd. Now their only companions were the noisy kittiwakes as they flitted through the air making their piercing cry. The hard rock of the little family's climb had been replaced at the top by a meadow of soft heath and silverhair grass that invited them to sit, or lie down, and rest. Large patches of wildflowers waved their small bright heads of blue, pink and yellow in the gentle breeze, their roots embedded deeply in their rocky home.

Kathleen stole a peek at her two little boys standing beside her. Shafi would start school in the fall; Michael a year later. They had grown so fast and Kathleen's heart ached at how much of that growing up she had missed because of her work—her endless travels, her tireless forays on behalf of the IRA.

The Irish sea seemed in a generous mood this early spring day. Its light wind was warm, and scented with a gentle tang that was stirring to the spirit and almost sweet to the nostrils. The sea always gave its distinctive salt aroma, Kathleen reflected, but today it bore the special scent it saved for those rare days when it decided to charge the air with magic. Kathleen smiled as she saw both her young children sniffing eagerly at the aroma she had recognized immediately to be not of this world. They were her children through and through, all right, and they belonged to the same mystical Ireland that claimed her own heart and soul.

"What is that nice smell, ma?" Shafi said just above a whisper, his voice showing he was in awe.

Before Kathleen could reply, Michael said, "Salt" in his matter of fact way as he folded his arms across his chest. He looked at his brother—one year older than he—and at his mother, quite determined to show them both how smart he was. "It's the salt in the water," he added with a nod of his head. "Same as any place near the sea."

"Ah, well now," Kathleen said as she sat down and patted the earth beside her in an unspoken invitation that her boys should sit with her. "Don't be so sure," she chided playfully with a smile at Michael. The boys sat. It was time for a story, they knew.

"Do you remember when I showed you the bees in the honey-suckle behind grandpa Tom's shed?" she asked as she lay back in the grass and gazed up at the heavens. Immediately the two boys did the same.

"Yes," they said in unison. She reached out and took their hands in hers.

"And do you remember what I told you gives the honey its deep rich smell?"

"The tears of the bees," Shafi answered.

"Yes. And there are other tears you need to know about. The lovely smell of the Irish sea also comes from tears."

Shafi came up on one elbow to look at his ma. "Whose tears, ma?"

Michael frowned. He wasn't sure he liked stories about tears. Tears were for girls.

"Now you both lay back," Kathleen said softly, "and keep looking up at the clouds, because some of what I'm going to tell you is up there. You can see it, if you look."

Shafi eagerly lay back down and reached for his mother's hand. Michael, on his side, also held his mother's hand tightly in his own. For a brief moment he wished his da could be there with them. He thought da's stories were the best, though he'd never let on that he thought so.

"Before I tell you about the tears of the sea, I want to find out how much you remember of what I told you about our town. Can you tell me what our town's name means?" Kathleen asked.

"Sure. Glenarm means valley," Michael said quickly to cut off any reply his brother might have been about to make. Shafi might be a year older, but Michael was determined he wasn't any smarter.

"Aye," Kathleen said. "That it does. But you know there are nine such valleys here in our Antrim county, all beginning with

Glen. There's Glencloy, Glenariff, and six others besides ours. What does our Glen's name mean? Our Glenarm?"

"The valley of the army," Shafi shouted, pleased for once to get the jump on his little brother.

"Aye. The valley of the army. And what was the name of the giant who led that army?"

Neither of the boys could remember.

"He was a famous giant," Kathleen coached. "And very big." Still no reply.

"Why, it was the giant Finn McCool, general of the great king of Ireland's grandest army. I've told you this before, I think," Kathleen said with a laugh as she gave her boys' hands a little shake in mock rebuke at their having forgotten.

"Is he the one who could pick thorns out of his feet while he was running?" Shafi asked.

Kathleen noted with a certain pride that her Shafi's verbal and imagery skills were years ahead of his age. It was true of both her boys. She wondered where they inherited that. It had to be from Omar, she decided. No one in her family, including herself, was particularly gifted in that way, she thought.

Her boys had showed her the joy of teaching, and she often asked herself what life might have been like if she'd had the opportunity to be a schoolteacher—or anything other than an IRA warrior. She wished there was some escape from the life. Her rightful place was with her boys and Omar, not traipsing the world for a cause she sometimes wondered if she still believed in.

Michael laughed. "He picks thorns out of his feet while he's running! That's funny!" With that he jumped up and began hopping along on one foot while picking at imaginary thorns in the bottom of his other foot, then switching feet, all the while, shouting, "Ooh! Ouch! Ooh! Ouch!"

Shafi rolled with laughter. He loved his brother's silliness, and knew he could always depend on it. Every day, in some way.

Kathleen was laughing too. "Now you get back here, General McCool!" she yelled.

"I'm General McCool, and I'm a great fool! I'm General Mc-Cool, and I'm a great fool!" Michael repeated as he hopped on one foot back to his mother's side and plopped down beside her.

"What else can you remember about the giant Finn McCool?" Kathleen asked.

"Oh, I know!" Shafi said eagerly. "He tore up a big piece of . . . of *dirt* . . . to throw at some guy he was fighting, because the guy was running away, and the dirt landed in the sea, and it made an island. And it left a hole that made a big lake."

"The Isle of Man, and the lake is Lough Neagh," Kathleen added. "Very good, Shafi."

Not to be outdone, Michael scoured his memory for details of this story. "Didn't he build this place?" he asked with a wave of his arm at the surrounding giant domain.

"Aye," Kathleen affirmed. "Can you remember why?"

Both boys shrugged.

"Well, it seems our giant Finn McCool—"

"How big's a giant, ma?' Shafi wanted to know.

"Ten times taller than anything. When he walked, Finn McCool had to brush the clouds away from his eyes so he could see where he was going."

"Wow!" Michael said. "Did he live in a house?"

Kathleen knew if she let them, her boys would keep asking questions until the sun went down. She wanted to get back to the story. "Any-*way*," she said with a certain emphasis that signaled question time was over for the moment, "our giant Finn McCool fell in love."

"Aw, ma," Michael said. Love stories were so boring

"Who did he love, ma?" Shafi asked.

Kathleen grinned and twisted her knuckles sharply into Michael's ribs. He jumped and yelled, laughing, "Okay, okay! I'll listen!"

"Giant Finn McCool fell in love with a lady giant who lived on an island called Staffa."

A soft voice and a wavering image from long ago brought a sudden warmth to Kathleen; she was four and Tim was eight. They sat before their mother's lap and listened as she told them about Finn McCool's great love. Sharp pain rose from her breast as Kathleen thought, *Oh, my Tim! Ma! Da! I'm so sorry I made you all die!* In the same moment she felt an intense desire—it had been growing lately—that she could escape her dead family. Today that desire was anguish.

Shafi caught the pain that flitted across his mother's face.

"Ma?" he said.

She shook her head and cleared her throat. "Well, Finn McCool wanted to bring his lady giant home with him. He built this place so she could walk away from her island without getting her feet wet. And that's why it's called Giant's Causeway." She smiled but both boys saw it was a thin cover for pain.

"Why are you sad, ma?" Shafi asked, his voice mirroring what he saw in his mother's eyes.

Kathleen smiled again as she shook her head. "Come here, my darlings," she said and gathered her boys in her arms.

"What's wrong, ma?" Michael wanted to know. Tears were forming in his own eyes at seeing his ma in pain.

"When I started this story, I said I was going to tell you about the tears that give our sea the lovely smell it has this day."

"Yes, ma," the boys said in unison. They had both forgotten about that.

"But what about *your* tears, ma?" Shafi wanted to know.

"Hush," Kathleen replied. "Listen and you will hear." The boys sat close to their mother and gazed out at the sea as she told the story.

"Long ago, when Ireland was filled with demons and heroes, there was a spirit man named Oengus. One night, he dreamed of a beautiful maiden named Caer. He searched for her everywhere. Finally, he found her chained to a rock that rises high in the air from the middle of the sea. In those days, the sea water had no salt in it and it had no smell. Caer warned Oengus that if he kissed her they would both be turned into swans. Oengus loved Caer so much that all he wanted was to be with her, so they kissed. Immediately, they were both turned into great white swans. But Oengus could not take Caer home with him because she was chained to her rock. They soon discovered that on this cold dead rock the only way love could be shared was through tears. So Oengus and Caer wrapped their big wings around each other and started to cry. They have been crying on that rock for nine hundred years, and they are still out there crying right now. Their tears have filled the sea water with salt, and their tears smell sweet like their love. Sometimes, like today, you can smell the sweet love of Oengus and Caer on a breeze from the sea."

"Why doesn't Caer just break her chain, ma?" Shafi said, sadness brimming in his eyes. "Can't she just break her chain? And go be with Oengus?"

Kathleen hugged her boys tightly. "Yes," she said in a thin voice, a far away look in her eyes and a faint hope in her voice. "Maybe some day she will."

"Does the story make you sad, ma?" Michael asked in a hush.

"What makes me saddest, my dear darlings," Kathleen said, holding her boys close, "is that my tears for my ma and da and brother have made it impossible for me to give you all the love you should have gotten from me. I'm afraid the best I have ever offered you is the lovely smell of the sea. A sea of tears."

Shafi and Michael looked at each other. At the level of words and thoughts, they understood none of what their mother had told them about her pain, about her chain. At another level, somewhere far deeper than words or thoughts, there was a dim glimmer of understanding. It would become brighter over time.

"Tom, I need to talk with you," Kathleen said that evening. The boys were in bed and Peg was visiting friends. Tom was entering the kitchen just as Kathleen was finishing up the dishwashing.

Tom fixed Kathleen in a searching look. He saw resolve in her eyes. "Aye? What's on yer mind, child?"

He pulled out his briar and his tobacco pouch. He opened the pouch and sniffed the tobacco, as he had done for more than fifty years, but he was doing it automatically, out of habit, and this night he smelled it not at all. His mind was on his stepdaughter, the daughter he and Peg had never had. He loved her as though she were of his own blood, but there was more. Kathleen was his most important commando trainer and the IRA's most valued purchaser of guns and bomb parts.

The look in Kathleen's eyes was unyielding, disturbing. She slid quickly into a chair at the kitchen table, and appeared to settle in for what might be a long siege. "It's been more than ten years, Tom." Her voice was quiet, low and steady.

"What's been more than ten years?" Tom asked in his most basement-like bass. He knew.

"That I've been serving the IRA," Kathleen replied. Her voice had come up a semi-octave; still quiet and steady.

Tom sat opposite her. He took a wooden match from the dispenser that always stood at the center of the table and made a quick ripping motion with it against the table's underside. The match head burst into noisy blue flame as it reappeared and Tom brought it slowly, studiously, to his pipe's rim the way a surgeon might bring a scalpel to bear.

"I thought . . ." he paused to suck the flame down onto his tobacco ". . . ye might say it's been ten years, since . . ." he sucked again, three times, and found the wad lighted to his satisfaction "yer family was *murdered.*" He shook out the match and tossed it lightly into an ashtray. The word 'murdered' had been drawn out, and he had rolled the 'r'. Both times.

Kathleen sighed. She hadn't known what to expect from Tom when she broached the subject, but she hadn't thought it would go like this.

"What's your point, Tom?" she asked, her arms thrust out toward him on the table top, palms up, in a gesture that might be seen as supplication or defiance, or both.

"Me? My point?" Tom replied, looking innocent and offended. "I don't have a point. I thought ye were making a point here." He locked the pipe stem between exposed clenched teeth, sat back in his chair, and blew a thin stream of smoke out through both nostrils. He searched Kathleen's face.

"All right, then," Kathleen said, just above a whisper. She fixed Tom in a level gaze for a long silent moment before she said, "I want out."

"Out?" Tom asked, pulling his pipe abruptly from his mouth and springing forward in his chair as though hearing something unbelievable or beyond understanding.

"Out of the IRA, Tom," Kathleen said with impatience at Tom's game-playing. She knew that he understood very well what she wanted, and he was not making this any easier. "It's time my life was about my children. And my . . . their father."

"I see," Tom said with the air of tolerance a parent might use toward a child who is trying to defend a bad decision. "Is Omar pressuring ye into this?"

"No. It's my own idea. My family needs me and I need them." Kathleen leaned back in her chair.

Tom studied his pipe sternly, as though he'd never seen one before. His eyes did not look up as he said, "Ah, yes. I see. Yer family." He fixed Kathleen in an iron gaze that came from just beneath his furrowed brow. "And what about yer *first* family, then," he asked in a voice both slow and hushed. "What about yer murdered parents? And yer murdered brother Tim? Do ye just walk away from *that* family?"

"No, Tom. But I—"

"It's a time of war, child!" Tom interrupted, coming forward in his chair. "If ye turn your back on Ireland now, what legacy do ye leave yer sons?"

"I wasn't going to turn my back. I would train someone to take my place," Kathleen said in a voice that wavered a bit.

"Ah yes, train someone. Fine," Tom said with a wave of his arm. "Ye train well. Go ahead and train. But not someone to *replace* ye, Kathleen. Ye can't *be* replaced, child."

He got up and walked around to Kathleen's side of the table. He placed his hand lightly on her shoulder as he continued in a gentle voice, "I need ye by me side to win this war. Remember yer oath to free Ireland. Ye can't turn yer back on us whene'er ye take a fancy to it! Ye must set aside these foolish thoughts."

Kathleen looked up at her stepdad, her eyes brimming. She loved him as her own father, and she felt a strong loyalty to him as his chief lieutenant. She had made an oath to Ireland. An oath was not to be taken lightly. Her guilt that she was alive while her parents and brother were dead—that guilt was strong as ever. To expiate that guilt, the murder of her family must be avenged. And God had killed them for her sin.

Loyalty, oath, guilt, vengeance, sin: they swirled together in her heart and her head, sucking her into a vortex of confusion. *Where does loyalty to Tom end, and loyalty to Ireland begin? The enemy: Great Britain, or The Order of Orange; or herself? Where does guilt and a thirst for vengeance become the same thing? How much penance must be paid before the sex sin of a fifteen-year old is forgiven? At what point does "family" stop being only the dead; when does the word start to apply to the living?* Kathleen wished she knew the answers. Even one.

She sighed. Her children and Omar would have to wait a bit longer.

"All right, Tom," she whispered sadly. "For a little longer. Only a little, though. Only a little."

5

Mulcahy and the Monsignor

Summer 1990

Mulcahy was pushing the idea, and it was making Omar uncomfortable. He wished Kathleen were here to help him navigate this discussion, not off on another damn IRA run.

"I know it's not easy for ye to be here, yer not bein' Irish and not Catholic, and all," Tom said. "Still, this isn't such a bad place."

Tom drummed his fingers on the table. Peg looked like a balloon about to burst. Omar waited.

"I'm sayin', me and Peg would really like to have the boys livin' here, Omar. We're feelin' like they're our own grandchildren, though of course we're not Kathleen's real parents, and all."

Omar wasn't sure he liked the idea. The boys loved Tom and Peg, and of course Kathleen would like being here. Still, he had reservations.

Mulcahy reached for his Meerschaum and went through the ritual of packing and lighting it. He looked up several times at Omar.

Peg was impatient and wanted to get to the point. She said, "Would ye be willin' to make a home here, then, in Glenarm, with Kathleen and the children?"

Mulcahy said, "We're walkin' distance from a good school, yet secluded enough." He drew a long puff, and the pipe glowed red. "And it's a big place, this."

Peg was excited and said, "There's plenty of room for—"

"Let me tell it, then, sweetheart," Mulcahy interrupted and patted her on the hand. "There's a good lass." He turned to Omar and continued, "I'd like to add a wing to this house for ye and yer family. Bedrooms, baths. Maybe an office or two. Whatever ye and Kathleen want. Yer own entrance, of course. Ye'd be livin' here with us, but ye'd have yer privacy. Yer own home."

Peg sighed with relief. Tom had finally gotten to it.

"Live here with you in Glenarm?" The idea was strange.

"Aye."

"Tom, I thank you for the offer, but we could never do that. The locals wouldn't hear of it."

"Oh, they'll hear of it, all right. From me. And there's not a man Jack among 'em will dare say me nay. That I'll promise ye," he said with a severe nod.

"And Kathleen? What does she say about this? Wouldn't it put her and the children at risk? Her being IRA and an unmarried mother, and the children . . . born out of wedlock?"

"Bastards, ye mean?" Mulcahy said with a heavy voice.

Omar sighed. "That's not a word I like to use, Tom. But that is what people think of them. You're right to point it out."

"'Tis a word I hate meself, Omar."

Omar's face showed his frustration. "I don't want my boys to grow up under any prejudice I can help them avoid. In London, they can—"

"Face the same curse," Mulcahy interjected. "People are prejudiced everywhere, or I'm damned!" Peg patted his hand.

"Have you spoken to Kathleen about this?"

"I wanted to speak to ye first. *Will* ye make a home here?"

Omar sat back in his chair and took a deep breath.

"Tom, do you think you can really protect them? I mean, I don't know anyone here. All I could do is start shooting people, and only after someone hurt one of mine. I'd a damn sight rather no one got hurt at all."

"I believe I can protect them, Omar. I've been in the IRA a long time."

"Yes, I know, but—"

"No buts about it. I've got a fair amount of say-so in these parts. And friends with guns, comes to that."

Omar didn't need another house to live in, but for the sake of his family he decided to give it a try.

"Only if you let me pay for the construction," Omar said.

"Only if ye let me supervise the construction," Mulcahy said with a broad smile. "I've too little to do."

Omar laughed. "Of course, Tom."

Mulcahy rubbed his hands in glee. "Let's sit down and draw up some plans. Peg, will ye fetch some paper and pencils? There's a good girl."

Soon a crew was trucking in building materials for the additions to the Mulcahy residence.

"Omar, it's wonderful! Tom has hinted at this, but I never brought it up because I didn't think you'd want to," Kathleen said.

"You don't expect us to give up our home in London, do you?" he asked.

"No, of course not. We'll live in both places; part of the year there, part here."

"And we'll always have our home in Florenza," he added, more for his own reassurance than anything else.

"Of course we will, darling," Kathleen said, holding him tight. "Always."

Omar built a garage large enough for not only two cars but also his helicopter and, behind the garage, there was a helicopter pad.

A simple, typical, Irish country home; one that people from miles around drove by to gawk at. The helicopter pad raised many an eyebrow and started a variety of rumors about the Arab that lived there with old Tom and Peg Mulcahy. Some had him as the runaway Sultan of Araby in hiding, some an oil baron or the owner of a country somewhere—probably Africa. About the woman, a native of this very town, living with the foreigner, and her two kids of mixed blood, there was mostly just a shake of the head and a murmur of disgust.

What the gawkers couldn't see was a treasury of sophisticated electronics and communications gear concealed behind a large bookcase in the master bedroom.

Shafi quickly took a rapt interest in the computers, the radios, all the electronics, and this is where he began to develop the talents that would later serve people he didn't dream existed.

Behind the bedroom bookcase, with an uninterruptible power supply that could last for months, Omar maintained contact with his ships, the *Thea*'s six moorings, and special persons on his payroll around the world. Also behind that bookcase, he kept a small arsenal.

There was one threat, however, against which guns could not prevail: the Holy Roman Catholic Church, Northern Ireland style.

SIX WEEKS AFTER THE JABRI family moved into their new home, there was a knock Saturday morning at the Mulcahys' door. Peg answered it.

"Oh!" she said with a curtsy. "Monsignor Ryan. Please, Yer Holiness, do come in!" Behind the pleasant greeting, her heart sank.

"Mrs. Mulcahy," the Monsignor said with a nod and a stern look as he walked in. "Is Mr. Mulcahy at home?" He knew that he was.

"Please, Yer Holiness, do sit down. I'll fetch him, then. Cup of tea?"

"Thank ye, ma'am. That'll be nice. No trouble?"

"None at all!" Peg ran off to the kitchen where Mulcahy was preparing a fresh leg of lamb. His Kathleen and family were expected for dinner.

She gulped and said, "Tom, ye have a visitor." He was turned to his work, so he didn't see Peg's expression.

"If it's the devil, tell him I died and went to heaven an hour ago."

Mulcahy turned and saw Peg was wringing her hands. He frowned.

"Who is it, darlin'?" He saw big trouble in Peg's manner.

"Monsignor Ryan," she whispered, her voice shaking.

Mulcahy's face turned cold as steel. "It *is* the devil, then. In me own house!"

"Now, Tom, let's see what he has to say, and all."

"I'll handle this. And don't bring tea, woman," Mulcahy said in a voice dark as a storm.

The monsignor stood as Mulcahy entered the room.

No greeting. "We'll sit here," Mulcahy said and pointed to two straight-back wood chairs which stood alone, inhospitable, in one corner of the room.

The monsignor perched on the edge of his chair, sitting only on his tailbone as though ready to leap. Mulcahy turned the other chair around and straddled it, the back of the chair at his chest, up close to the monsignor. Mulcahy leaned forward, as close as he could get to the prelate's face, his hands resting lightly on his chair's curved top. He stared hard into the prelate's faded blue eyes, mere inches away.

"Tom, I've come on a grave matter."

"Get on with it," Mulcahy growled. Behind the kitchen door, Peg strained to hear. Her hand-wringing got worse, and her eyes showed pain.

The monsignor fidgeted. He never allowed anyone to talk to him this way, but he knew Mulcahy carried an anger that was decades deep.

"It's about the O'Toole woman, Tom."

Mulcahy let the words sink in. "Her name's Kathleen O'Toole, not *the O'Toole woman* I'll have ye know. In this house ye'll watch yer mouth, mister."

The monsignor's eyes flared. "Mulcahy, my name's not *Mister!* I'm Monsignor Ryan!"

"And I'm *Mr.* Mulcahy to ye. And the door's over there!"

The monsignor took a deep breath.

"It's come to my attention, then, *Mr. Mulcahy*, then, that yer *Miss* Kathleen O'Toole is livin' here on this property with a heathen. And they have two children, and them not married, and all."

A moment of silence. In a quiet voice, his words spaced, Mulcahy said, "*So . . . what?*"

"She'll have to *leave*, then, *Mr. Mulcahy! That's so *what!*"

Mulcahy got up, made a short circle. He stopped before the monsignor and said with a low snarl. "Ye've got one hell of a nerve, then, Ryan. Comin' to my house and pissin' at me with this." Mulcahy sat again in his chair, exactly as before.

Defiant, the monsignor resisted pulling back from Mulcahy's face.

Mulcahy leaned forward even more. His voice was menacing, and his eyes flashed with challenge. "How *the feck* do ye plan to *make* them leave, then?"

The monsignor's anger rose. "I can have that woman off to the Laundries tomorrow, and the two bastard kids with her as well. *And ye know it!*"

Fast as a dog on a rat, Mulcahy grabbed the monsignor's testicles and held them in a crushing squeeze. The prelate blanched and gasped. His instinct told him to resist, to fight, to get up and run, but the pain paralyzed him. He was sure he would lose his scrotum, that it would be ripped off, if he so much as twitched.

Mulcahy growled, "What if I just carry these to mass this Sunday, then, all nicely wrapped in wax paper. And I'll go up with ye in yer pulpit, too. And there ye'll tell yer congregation what happened. Tell them these are the rotten balls that made me sister pregnant. Back when ye were a young priest. Long before ye became *Monsignor Ryan!*" He added with a sharp twist to the prelate's testicles. With a grimace of hate, he snarled, "And then ye got 'er locked up in the Magdalene Laundries. To die there with *yer* child, ye *sonofabitch!*

The monsignor tried to speak, to yell, but agony gripped his voice. His eyes bulged and his mouth was frozen open in the shape of the letter "O" while his head shivered violently.

"Will it be all right with ye, and all, *Monsignor Ryan*, ye prick, if I just tell the world what ye did? *What ye are?*" He gave the monsignor's scrotum a harder twist and held tight.

"I'll have ye arrested for this!" the monsignor squeaked.

"Do that, Ryan. And I'll have a long rifle shoved up yer arse. They'll find bits and pieces of ye in the treetops." Mulcahy gave the monsignor's testicles a final twist, a crushing squeeze, and let go.

The prelate made a long yelp. His face was gray with pain. He groaned as he pushed himself up out of his chair and limped, bent over, away from Tom. Peg ran into the room.

"What's happenin' here, then?" Peg whispered in alarm.

"What's happenin' here, dear Peg, is the good monsignor is just leavin'. Perhaps ye'd be kind enough to show our honorable guest the door." Mulcahy went back to the kitchen and washed his hands.

From that time on, there were none in the county who spoke aloud against Kathleen or her little family. The subject never came up. Never in public, that is; behind the hand, tongues wagged—as tongues everywhere always have and always will.

6

At the Gilded Lily

Omar Jabri was born a pirate. Fated to it. Destiny took a hand when, many centuries ago, the Jabri people came upon an uninhabited island in the Persian Gulf about seven nautical miles off the coast of present-day Iran. The Jabri clan took the island for their own since there was no one else there, and they called their island home Jabrin. Some years later, as a reward for special service to the king, the Jabri clan was given permanent dominion over the island. It was to be the Jabri home forever.

Born in 1959, Omar was far too late to be the bearded kind of freebooter who wears a sword on his hip and a parrot on his shoulder. But he was as much a pirate now as his Jabrinian ancestors had been for centuries. He served a pirate's apprenticeship with his grandfather and father on their ships, and was well on his way toward graduation to a ship of his own when Jabrinian rule of the island came to a violent and bloody close.

On his eighteenth birthday, Omar was given a black stallion. He named it Nime Shab, which in Persian means Midnight.

One day, Omar rode Nime Shab on a wild boar hunt, alone in the mountains of Jabrin, far from his village. On that day, the Shah of Iran sent an army west over the Zagros Mountains, down to the coastal valley of Shtb Kuh, where the soldiers boarded ships at the port city of Bandar-Makam and sailed into the Persian Gulf to take the island of Jabrin.

The sun was touching the highest peaks when Omar turned his horse for home. He'd found nothing to shoot that day, and he was looking forward to dinner at the family table.

Long before he could see his village, he saw smoke rising above the treetops. At first he thought it was a lightning fire, but he'd heard no thunder. Omar spurred his horse. As he broke through into a clearing, he saw the horror. Most of the houses were burnt to ashes. He ran his horse to where his home had stood. There in the charred remains he found the bodies. His father and grandfather were shot through the head. His mother and two young sisters had met a worse fate. Their clothes were ripped off. Their throats slit. A quick look around told him death had met everyone, their bodies left where they'd fallen. Of the community's more than two hundred souls, he was the only survivor. The Shah's marauders left not even a dog alive on Jabrin. They did, however, leave their flag proclaiming that this island had been conquered by the Shah of Iran.

A great rage filled Omar with strength and resolve. First, he buried the five members of his immediate family in a common grave. He used his horse to drag all the other bodies into one great pile, and set it on fire. Last, he set his horse free to forage for survival in the island's rich, grassy plain.

On the shore Omar found the ships and boats of the island had all been stove in or set afire except for one large motorboat hidden by the low branches of a tree at the water's edge.

He gathered up a supply of gasoline and set off with his boat into uncertainty.

He knew only that he would return. The Jabri scion would take his vengeance against the Shah of Iran some day, and reclaim his family's dominion, but for now his only home was the sea.

And this was why Omar Jabri maintained, angrily, he was not Iranian. He was Jabrinian. And he was a pirate. His plan was simple: get so rich, so powerful, that no one could ever take anything away from him again.

This same rule applied to women he would come to know.

Would-be master of the seas at age eighteen, Omar didn't have an effective pirate ship like the ones his father's fathers had once captained, and it turned out the old motorboat leaked a lot.

He didn't crew the best ruffians in the world, either. But across the Gulf in Ad Damm (which means to sacrifice blood) and Al Khubaf, and later in Qatar's Al Fuwayrit, he did manage to assemble a gang of minor thugs from various dark corners of the world who were willing to sail with a pirate younger than themselves.

He did have a motor boat, after all. And these reprobates all held the same vision of their skipper's immediate future: He would be killed for his share of the loot.

On their first sortie, under cover of night and with more luck than skill, Omar and his gang managed a successful attack on an oil tanker en route to Japan from Saudi Arabia. They motored up alongside the heaving vessel under a moonless sky, pitched muffled grappling hooks high up onto her deck, and climbed aboard. Before the crew knew what happened, the machete-wielding invaders were threatening to cut off the captain's head if he didn't open the ship's safe.

The job netted the gang only about thirty thousand dollars, but it was more money than Omar's ruffians ever expected to see in their entire lives. Their appetites were whetted and an unspoken agreement was born among Omar's hooligans: Their leader would be allowed to live for at least one more run.

On their second mission, the take was a lot higher. Omar studied the shipping news where he targeted a brand new freighter, the *Nalaba*, loaded with aluminum ingots going from Sumatra to Japan. With a phone call to a metals broker, Omar learned the *Nalaba*'s cargo was worth eleven million dollars on the open market. Next, he found someone that would buy what he intended to steal. He replaced the old speed boat with a newer one that didn't leak as much, and he bought his crew guns. Big mistake, those guns.

Four hours after she left port, the *Nalaba* was reported lost. Omar and his gang had boarded the vessel and put the crew in life boats on a calm sea about thirty miles from shore. Out of the boat's sight, Omar's crew steered the freighter into a cove at the mouth of the Sampit River in Borneo.

There, black marketeers out of Banjarmasin awaited Omar's arrival as arranged. They paid him a half million dollars, U.S. cash, for the entire load of ingots, plus the freighter, with the pretty-good speedboat thrown in. Omar knew they were cheating him grossly but he didn't care. A half million dollars in reliable cash, divided ten ways, was still a lot of money for one day's work.

Later that night, Omar and his band gathered in the back room of a bar called The Gilded Lily. The name didn't help the place's appearance at all. It was a filthy dive on a back street of Sampit, and featured the usual assortment of drunks, unconscious or on their way. Only worthless scum ever went into the Gilded Lily. For anyone else, it was dangerous to walk through the front door. Even the hookers stayed out. All the money in all the pants in the Gilded

Lily wouldn't buy twenty minutes with a good hooker anyway. Besides, the clientele were most often too drunk to do much with a woman, assuming they ever did find the money to buy one.

A pinball machine blinked in one corner of the back room trying to attract a few coins. Near another corner, a door tilted out on its bottom hinge, and beyond it in deep shadows there was a naked toilet bowl. No one could remember how the seat and cover disappeared. The rim of the bowl bore scratches from the shoes of users who stood on it and squatted—a bit risky, especially for a drunk.

Near the middle of the room, a dim yellowish light came from a single bulb at the end of a frayed electrical wire. There was no switch. Tighten bulb for light; loosen bulb for no light. The cracked and rotted plaster walls told the room's sordid history: bullet holes, knife marks, the occasional dent showing browned traces of blood where a head had gotten bashed. In one corner of the room, there was a chair with a leg gone—probably taken as a club.

Under the lightbulb there stood a decrepit pool table that hadn't hosted a game in years. The leather pockets of the table had decayed away long ago, and there were small piles of termite droppings on the floor near three of the table's legs.

Nowadays, when the bartender wasn't vigilant, the pool table served as a bed for some sleepy drunk. Most days, the table stayed empty. The bartender prided himself on being vigilant.

But on this day, the bartender was paid to stay out, and the door separating the back room from the main bar was closed. Two of Omar's gang were posted to keep wanderers away. One of the gang watched the street for trouble. This left seven men in the room with the money, including Omar. The beer they drank was warm, flat, and tasted a bit sour. But it was beer.

This was a multinational set of brigands. Two of them, half-breed Bornean and Botswanese, agreed to look out for the guards' interests when the money got divided. And there was Omar, a Jabrinian he insisted, and the other four gang members who were Ethiopian.

The Ethiopians and Omar gravitated into one camp within the gang, the rest into another. No one in either camp trusted Omar, but all of them began to think they could do worse than stay with him. Omar would live, at least for a few more jobs.

The half million dollars was tied in bundles. Each bundle held five hundred dollars. Omar repeated this several times.

There were thin bundles of twenties, thicker bundles of tens, and the thickest bundles were the fives.

When the gang received the money, it was stuffed into a great steamer trunk. Now the trunk was open and Omar told the two literate Ethiopians to sort the bundles and stack them on the pool table. Everyone else watched like jackals at a kill, and there wasn't a sound in the room.

Each man had a seabag to hold his share.

Omar stepped up between the two money sorters.

The sea bags stood open like the mouths of hungry sharks. There were three extra bags, two for the guards at the door and one for the guard out in the street. He was called Big Emil.

"Now, listen," Omar said. "Me and Fahed, and Abu, here, will pass around the money. Everybody gets the same number of bundles. Each man gets the same number of twenties, the same number of tens, and the same number of fives. This way, we all get an equal share."

The four Borneans looked lost. Fresh out of the jungle, they had years of missionary English taught them by the Holy Biddites an anti-technology religious sect from England. They understood guns. Bigness they understood, also. But number words, like "twenties," "tens" and "fives," they were never taught because the Holy Biddites believe numbers are tools of the devil.

The missionaries had taught them mistrust, too, in abundance, and this was now bubbling to the surface.

Omar was about to begin the distribution when one of the Borneans, the one called Bonk, pulled out his pistol and aimed it at him. He held the gun out at arm's length where it shook a little.

"Hey! We not stupid!" Bonk said. "We got brains!"

Oh, shit, Omar thought. He was fed up with Bonk. "Tell me your problem!"

"Them bundles is bigger than the others," Bonk said, pointing to the fives.

"Yeah!" echoed the other Bornean, the one called Rasta. He, too, was schooled by the Holy Biddites. He pulled his gun. "Maybe you think we—"

"All *right!*" Omar said. "All right, damn it! You want the *big* bundles. *Fine!*"

These two were dumb as planks. They'd been a pain in his ass since the day he met them. When they learned they were going to sea in a boat, they argued no boat should ever be pointed toward the horizon because the devil waited out there to suck sailors over the edge of the world, a flat world, and throw them into hell.

When Omar asked them how the Holy Biddites managed to travel from England to Borneo and not fall off the horizon, they couldn't cope with the question. They were taught that questions were another tool of the devil and should never be asked or answered. A question, any question, did not compute well in their Holy Biddites minds.

"*Fine!*" Omar repeated. He pointed to the twenties. "Will you be happy if we get two *thin* bundles of twenties for every *thick* bundle of fives you get?"

Bonk and Rasta didn't seem to quite get his meaning. Omar tried again.

"Okay, now. This is for me," he said holding up two thin bundles of twenties, "and this is for you," he said, holding up one thick bundle of fives.

Bonk and Rasta understood this. They looked at one another. Rasta shrugged. His eyes told him it was a good deal. Thick and thin he understood.

"Look okay to me," Rasta said to Bonk with a conspiratorial grin.

One of the Ethiopians, a short round man who understood basic numbers, started to laugh. In a few moments, he was laughing so hard he had to support himself on the edge of the pool table. Soon he was laughing so much he had to sit down on the floor. His name was Jesso, and he was called Fat Jesso. Sitting on the floor didn't seem to help much because, in seconds, Fat Jesso was lying on his back and roaring at the ceiling. His dark brown face turned purple, his eyes were squeezed shut, and his laughs were coming out in wheezes and snorts.

The hilarity was infectious. The others laughed even though they weren't sure what set off the one on the floor.

Omar suppressed the urge.

Bonk figured they were laughing at him, though he could not imagine why, and he got insulted. He fired a shot into the ceiling and shouted to Omar, "You make him shut up! Everybody shut up! I kill everybody!" Bonk pointed his gun at Fat Jesso.

Fat Jesso tried to stop laughing, and managed to say, "No! No! I ain't laughing at you, man!" He rolled over on his side and went into a fetal position, laughing hard as ever.

Bonk fired his gun again. Big Emil must not have heard it because he didn't run in from the street. If anyone in the bar's front room recognized the shots, it didn't seem to make any impression. When a gunshot rang out in the Gilded Lily, anyone awakened by the noise would check themselves for a bullet hole. If they didn't find one, they'd put their head on the table and go back to sleep. Or put their nose back in their beer.

Bonk's bullet tore a hole in the wood floor about two inches from Fat Jesso's nose. He wasn't being temperate; he was just a lousy shot. But it got Bonk what he wanted.

All laughing in the room stopped as though a switch was thrown. Fat Jesso struggled to his feet, his eyes wide with terror. "Okay! Okay, man! No more laughing!" This time he meant it. Or wanted to.

Omar rested the heel of his hand on the butt of the gun tucked into the front of his pants, and drummed his finger tips on the weapon as he said to Bonk, "Now it's time for you to put that gun away."

For a moment, with Bonk's gun pointed straight at him, Omar thought he might have to dive for the deck and try to snap off a quick shot on the way down. But he decided to try to lighten the moment with his big movie-star grin, and this seemed to work.

Bonk grunted and jammed the gun into his belt.

Omar squinted a mean look at Fat Jesso. *You start laughing again and I'll shoot you myself!* Fat Jesso pinched his lips together. He managed to keep a straight face, but the shiny black cardboard belt that cinched his big belly kept bobbing up and down and he kept snorting, but softly.

The distribution of the money got started.

Soon, of course, there were no more twenties on the table. Half of the fives were remaining, and all the tens were there as well.

"Here's how we'll divide the rest of it," Omar said to Bonk and Rasta. The others at the table looked amused. "We get this," he said holding up two bundles of tens, "and you get this," he added, holding up one bundle of fives next to the tens to show they were of the same thickness. "You can see they're the same."

"Good!" Bonk said, willing to be generous and accept an even split on this go-round because he was convinced that he and Rasta had swindled Omar and the Ethiopians on the last go-round.

Fat Jesso's belly was still bobbing, and behind his clamped lips, his brown face still wore a light shade of purple. Bonk snarled at him.

When all the bundles were gone from the table, Omar told Bonk to call in Big Emil. Bonk opened the door and let out a loud whistle that made most of the unconscious drunks sitting at tables in the next room shift from one cheek to the other. Big Emil swaggered in.

Bonk chuckled as he pulled Big Emil aside to explain how he bamboozled Omar in the money distribution. He spoke in a language not many in the room could understand, but the gist was clear enough from Bonk's facial expressions and hand gestures.

Big Emil let Bonk's words sink in for a moment. He turned to Bonk with a look of disbelief and asked him something. Because it was a question, Bonk was confused, but still looked amused. Big Emil recognized his error and rephrased from question to statement. The laughter on Bonk's face died and was replaced by a hint of fear as he confirmed what Big Emil suggested.

Big Emil, who was far from stupid and known to be hot-headed, asked Bonk another question, but put as a statement. Bonk's confirmation was brief and now he looked worried. There was one more brief statement and an even briefer confirmation. A look of terror crossed Bonk's face.

Big Emil slapped Bonk with the back of his hand, pulled out his gun and shot him in the head.

The other Borneans pulled their guns and started firing. At the same time, the Ethiopians and Omar pulled their guns, and fired as fast as they could keep pulling the trigger.

The shooting, though it lasted only a short time, got complicated and, pretty much, before it was over, everybody was shooting at everybody else.

Rasta shot at Emil because he shot Bonk. Fat Jesso shot at Rasta because he figured Rasta was about to shoot at him. One of the guards at the door got his gun hung up on his belt when he tried to pull it out of his pants, and he got shot by one of the Ethiopians. The other guard exchanged shots with another Ethiopian and went down for poor marksmanship. Fat Jesso sprayed bullets in every direction and connected a couple of times. Omar shot him and then somebody shot Omar.

In the space of about eight seconds, more than twenty shots were fired. In the brief silence that followed, a cloud of blue smoke rose to the ceiling and the air was sharp with sulphur.

When it was over, Omar was on the floor. He squirmed and gasped with pain. Three of the Ethiopians were on the floor alive and unhurt. Everyone else was dead, including Fat Jesso, Big Emil, Bonk, and Rasta.

Omar was hit in the lower abdomen. The bullet, small in caliber, exited through his back. The bleeding was minimal but scary. Omar knew he would need to find medical attention, fast, to avoid an infection that would kill him.

His mind flashed back to the slaughter of his family on Jabrin Island. *I escaped that. I'm not going to die now in the back room of a filthy bar!*

To control the bleeding, he tore his shirt in three pieces and folded two of them as makeshift bandages. He considered pouring a shot of whiskey over the injury but he knew the pain of the alcohol on his open flesh might knock him out, and an unconscious man is easy prey. Besides, he suspected the polluted rotgut sold in the Gilded Lily might increase his chance of an infection, so this made two good reasons to abandon that idea.

Pain spread throughout Omar's torso, but he did carry his own money. The four slipped out the back door as sirens were heard coming close out front of the bar.

With that many gunshots fired, someone had decided to call the police. It was probably the bartender being vigilant again.

After Omar found a doctor to sterilize his wound and dress it properly, the money was re-divided. Omar and the three surviving Ethiopians each got a big hundred and twenty-five thousand dollars, much better than the fifty thousand they had expected before the guns started to blaze. The Ethiopians had no idea how much could be done with the amount of money they carried, and they would lose it quickly to women, gambling, and swindlers.

FROM THIS SHAKY START, Omar Jabri became a wealthy ship owner before he was thirty. But not without some changes to the way he did business.

He and his crew, with replacements, did hijack a few more ships, but soon the old ways became too risky. Piracy was on an upsurge worldwide, and merchant ships were more careful. Armed seamen stood watch, and when an alarm was sounded, the entire ship's crew broke out guns while the radioman sent an urgent call for help from the nearest navy.

Some merchant ships and cruise ships, and some luxury yachts, went far beyond carrying hand guns. Machine guns were a common installation, concealed from cruise ship passengers' eyes but instantly put in service when needed, and some ships also installed sonic cannon. This gun emits an ear-splitting sound aimed narrowly at approaching attackers. A large sonic cannon can cause deafness and the largest will cause blood to flow from orifices. Pirates everywhere quickly came to regard the sonic cannon as the most dreadful weapon on Earth—worse than any machine gun or conventional cannon, and most often when they saw one being uncovered on a ship they were attacking, they would duck their heads, do a quick one-eighty, and run like hell.

The International Piracy Alert System (IPAS), dormant since the 1920s, was revived to locate pirates and forward the data to appropriate authorities. Omar's marauders, like many other pirates, got chased by every navy from Japan to Italy to Uruguay and back to Japan.

Omar realized to survive he would have to work smarter. That's when he graduated from thuggery to trickery, and no longer needed a gang of dangerous hoodlums. His most lucrative enterprise was a strategy IPAS coded as CADI. The four letters stood for CARGO DIVERSION. Omar learned some fast stepping. He posed as an international trader and bought goods discounted for sale in third-world markets. Omar reported the goods stolen, collected on the insurance, and sold the merchandise in Europe or America for top price. At a fancy resort in Bali, or some such paradise, he stayed underground while insurance detectives searched for him. A few weeks later, he'd surface in another Western country with a new identity and repeat the dance all over again. It was a tango Omar loved.

It made him rich fast. But more important was the sense of power and control he got from it. The money was attractive, but knowing he held his own destiny was what gripped him.

He was smart enough to invest his ill-gotten gains in legitimate maritime businesses. With most of his millions, he bought ships. And much of the time those ships carried legal cargo.

Owning ships made Omar's games at sea much easier and, though part of him wanted to convert all his assets and activities to legal enterprise, another part of him, the generations-old part that resided in his blood, wanted to remain a gunrunner, smuggler, and pirate. There was no way legitimate enterprise could ever give Omar the sense of adventure he craved.

7

The Scarring of a Child

1993

When he was nine, Shafi decided to build a tree fort in grandpa Tom's old apple tree. Looking for the right spot to build, he climbed about halfway up the ancient tree. He wrapped his arm around the trunk and bounced up and down on a limb to test its strength. At this time of summer, the apples were still green and tight to the tree, but several did shake loose, and Shafi heard them hit the tin roof of Grandpa Tom's shed. He grinned because they sounded like gunfire. He told himself he must remember to tell Michael about it when he came home from camping with Da. Shafi was looking forward to his turn at camping.

Two more apples smacked the tin roof.

The main thing was to build his fort in thick foliage so no one could find it. This was the best spot, Shafi decided. He couldn't see the ground, so it was sure that no one would be able to see his secret fort.

"What you doing?" a voice called. Shafi froze. It was either a girl's voice, or a real young kid. The voice sounded weird. Maybe it would go away.

"Hey, you up there. What you doing?" It was a girl. *Bloody hell! Girls! This fort is for guys only!*

"You aren't very good at it," the voice said, teasingly.

"At what?" Shafi said aloud before he could stop himself. *Bloody hell! Now I've done it! She knows where the fort is going. Damn!*

"You're not very good at hiding. I see your legs," the voice said with a giggle.

Shafi reached a foot onto a higher branch. *She won't see me up this high.* Shafi heard a loud crack. His foot was in the air. His hands slipped. He grabbed, but all he got was a handful of leaves. He hit the shed roof. All went black.

"You okay?" the girl whispered. She sounded worried.

Shafi's eyes fluttered open. He found himself looking up into blue eyes that were wide with concern.

"Sure, I'm okay," Shafi replied with a gruff manner. He found himself on his back on the ground next to Grandpa Tom's shed and realized he must have landed on it pretty hard and then rolled off.

"Can you get up?" the girl asked. "Do you want me to get somebody?"

"I don't need anybody," Shafi replied. He wasn't sure that was true.

The girl knelt next to Shafi and slipped her arm along the ground under his shoulders, her face next to his. "Here, I'll help you sit up," she said as she urged him to a sitting position. Shafi caught her scent. *She smells like flowers.*

"There. That's better," she said. Shafi didn't enjoy being treated like a baby. *She's not my mother.* But he was sorry her face wasn't close to his again. The scent of flowers was almost too far away.

"You sure talk funny," he said.

The girl shrugged, a look of disappointment on her face. She stood up, turned with a shake of her shiny brown curls, and began to walk away.

"Hey! Wait a minute! I didn't mean nothing!" Shafi jumped to his feet. He noticed she held an apple in her hand.

The girl stopped and turned. "*Je suis Française.* That means I'm French. I live in Paris."

Shafi forgot her voice sounded funny. It was music. "You from France? I don't know French."

"*Oui,*" she said. "That's yes. You from here?"

Shafi nodded. "What's your name?" Might as well be polite, even to a girl. Besides, she sure was pretty.

"Dadou. What's yours?"

"I never heard that name before. Mine's Shafi."

"I never heard that one, either."

For an awkward moment, the two stood facing one another in silence, toes digging into the soft earth. "What were you doing up there?" Dadou asked with a glance up into the tree.

"Building a fort," Shafi said enthusiastically. "You can help if you want to." He figured it didn't *have* to be not for girls.

Dadou shrugged and said "Maybe," in a careless way. "But I got to go now. *Au revoir,*" she added lightly with a smile. She turned and started to walk. Shafi rushed to her side. "Where you going?"

"Dance class. Ballet."

"What's ballet?"

"Like this," she said and twirled. The edge of her skirt flew and shafi saw pink panties. He laughed.

"I saw your underpants," he said, pointing.

"Stupid!" Dadou said and ran.

Shafi let her go. But the next day he was there again when she walked by on her way to ballet class. He saw she carried an apple again. He stepped out in front of her. She started to walk around him.

"Hey, wait a minute," he said as he took her arm. "I didn't mean to make you mad."

Dadou shook her curls and said nothing.

"Can I walk you to school?"

Dadou looked into Shafi's eyes for a long moment. "Say you're sorry for yesterday."

"I'm sorry. Cross my heart, I am."

THAT EVENING AS HE was going to sleep, Shafi thought about the girl. She said she was here only for the summer. That meant weeks. More fun than building a fort. He could do that any time.

He decided he wanted to join the ballet class. It would mean being with mostly girls, but that was a price he could pay if it meant being close to Dadou. Without his brother around, he was bored with summer. Most of the kids from Glenarm never invited Shafi to play, and how much time could a guy spend in the company of his mother? Except for the occasional hike to see the Celtic ruins with Grandpa Tom, Shafi was on his own.

Kathleen was surprised when Shafi asked to join the summer school ballet class, until she uncovered the real motive: boredom ten percent and the French girl ninety percent. She was amused and decided it would be fun to watch her little boy's first case of puppy love.

Not one to waste time, the next morning Shafi met Dadou outside her house and walked with her to ballet class, where he promptly enrolled. The only other two boys in the class were brothers. They didn't seem to like Shafi, and he didn't care. He wasn't there to make friends with them.

One morning, as Dadou came out of her house, Shafi didn't see an apple. He asked, "Where's your apple?"

"Oh, I have it," Dadou said with a toss of her curls.

Shafi could see her dress had no pockets.

"You do not," he said.

"Do, too!" she said and stuck out her tongue at Shafi.

"Where?" he said. *Could she have it under her clothes?* he thought. *Why would she do that?*

Dadou made no reply. She tossed her curls again and continued walking. Neither spoke for a long while.

"Where's your apple, if you've really got one?" Shafi said. By this time, they were in front of the school.

"If I show you, do you promise not to tell? Not ever?" she said, her eyes wide, as she placed her hand on Shafi's arm. The touch of her fingers on his skin sent a shiver through him. Shafi swore, *I'll never wash that arm again!*

"Cross the old ticker." Grandpa Tom had taught him that.

"All right, then," she said in a stage whisper. "Come on! I know a place!" She ran up the steps to the school door.

Shafi felt lightheaded as he followed Dadou up the stairs, her sweet scent in his nostrils.

Inside the front door of the school house and to the left was a large storage room. Dadou opened the door, and Shafi followed her in. As he closed the door behind him, she turned on the light.

"Now you promised!" Dadou said softly and shook her finger at Shafi.

He nodded but didn't try to speak.

"You have to sit down," the girl whispered. "On the floor." Shafi would have sat on nails if she had asked him to.

Dadou walked up close to Shafi and pulled up her dress.

Shafi saw her blue panties were pouched out in front.

"Here's my apple," she said.

Shafi thought this was the funniest thing he'd ever seen. He knew he shouldn't laugh, but he couldn't help it.

"Now you stop that! Don't laugh!" Dadou said as she stamped her foot, hard, on the floor, which made the apple fall out of her panties; on reflex, Shafi reached out and caught it in midair.

The door opened. Dadou's dress was up. Shafi was sitting in front of her, the apple in his outstretched hand.

It was the janitor. "What the bloody. . . . "

The children were marched down the long hall to the headmaster's office, one in each of the janitor's big hands. The kids didn't know what was happening and they were frightened by the man's angry face. They cried and begged to be let go. The janitor wasn't having any.

"Now ye wait right there, young man!" the janitor said as he pushed Shafi onto a hard yellow bench.

Shafi heard a chair scrape as the summer school principal got up and said, "Well, what's this, then?" Dadou snuffled as she went in, and Shafi hoped her tears would win sympathy. The door slammed. Now that he was alone, Shafi turned off the crying. It hadn't worked as a bid for freedom.

He needed to hear what was said on the other side of the wall. He wasn't sure what he'd done wrong, and he needed to be prepared for when he'd have to face his mother about this. Below the ceiling was a vertical glass panel the entire length of the room. In three places, the panes of glass could be slid open for circulation of warmth between the two rooms in cold Irish winters. One of the panes, the one nearest the tall empty bookcase, was open a little.

He tested the bookcase for sturdiness and found it was fastened to the wall. He climbed up onto the third shelf with no trouble. After this, it got tricky but, bit by bit, he got up on top of it and crawled to the window, careful to not make a sound. He slid it open a few more inches. Now the voices were clear.

"He was offering her an apple?" Mr. Covington said. "To go further?"

"Aye, that he did. Saw it with me own eyes," the janitor said. "And her with her dress already up, and all."

"What on earth were you thinking of, child?" Mr. Covington said in a voice of concern. "Don't you realize what almost happened?"

"*Non*, Monsieur," Dadou wailed.

"Well!" Mr. Covington said, "You might've . . . he might've. . . ."

He cleared his throat. "Whose idea was this, anyway?" he wanted to know.

"I don't know," was Dadou's singsong reply.

"Well, I'll wager I *do!*" Mr. Covington said in an angry voice. "Now you go on to class, Miss Cantenot. Your mother will hear of this."

"*Oui, Monsieur,*" Dadou said and came out of the office alone. She looked around but didn't see Shafi up on the bookcase. Dadou ran out of the antechamber. Shafi turned back to the window.

"You can't trust these dirty Arabs!" Mr. Covington said.

"Ain't it the truth!" the janitor said. "Regular sex fiends, them Arabs is! Even the young ones!"

"Filthy animals," Mr. Covington said. "Filthy, disgusting animals! Why the poor child, she could have been—"

"Yes, sir. Nearly was," the janitor said. "When I came in and stopped him, the Arab boy was trying to get her to. . . ."

"Yes?" the Headmaster said as he leaned forward.

"Well, sir, ye know," the janitor said as he twisted his cap in his hands and hung his head.

"Yes. I can just imagine," Covington said softly. A thin film of sweat glistened on his brow. A long silence passed as he seemed to be watching a movie in his mind.

The janitor cleared his throat. "What shall I do with the Arab boy, sir?" he asked. "Want me to call his mother? Have her come in?" He was fond of big doings, liked to be part of them, and didn't have many in his life.

The janitor's voice popped Mr. Covington's private movie. "Eh?"

"The boy's mother, sir. Want I should have her in?"

"What good would it do? She's Arab, too, isn't she?

"Uh, no, sir. Begging yer pardon, sir, but I believe the mother's Irish. It's the father what's not Irish, as I'm told, sir. They aren't married, sir."

"Not married? Well, that's it, then, isn't it? The mother's a whore with an Arab stud and a bastard kid!"

"Two bastard kids, sir."

"Two!"

"Aye, sir. Two."

"Well, then, what can you expect from the likes of that?"

"Can't expect much, I'm afraid, sir."

"Yes," Mr. Covington said. "Well. Let him go. We can't do anything with him. And I don't want to talk with his mother. The bloody ballet classes will be over in another week. Let sleeping dogs lie. We'll be rid of the lot soon enough."

Shafi hopped down from his perch and was gone before the janitor came out to release him.

What's a bastard kid? he asked himself. *What's a sex fiend?* Shafi didn't know. He only knew the words were said with hate—that, he heard clearly.

A FEW DAYS LATER Shafi was laying on top of Grandpa Tom's shed, thinking about Dadou and what the principal said, when he heard his father's car. He leaped to the ground, fell, and rolled in the dust. Before Shafi could recover, Omar was out of the car, arms open, a warm smile on his face.

"You ready to do some camping?" Omar asked Shafi.

"You bet!"

"Great! We leave tomorrow for the Canary Islands."

"How do you know this place, Da?" Shafi asked as father and son were backpacking their gear up the side of Calle Mountain.

"My grandfather Atash used to come here," Omar said. He puffed from the climb. The load on his back was heavy. "Built himself a wood cabin on this mountain."

"What does Atash mean?"

"It's an old Persian name. It means fire."

"Wait a minute! Isn't your middle name Al-Atash, Da?"

"Yes. I was named after him."

"Then you've got fire in your name, too!" Shafi laughed.

"I think all the Jabri men have fire in them. Including you."

"I thought all your ancestors stayed on ships in the ocean, Da."

"Mostly, grandfather Atash *did* stay on his ship. But sometimes he needed a place to hide. When the Spanish navy chased him too hard. He built a hideout up here."

"Are we going to see it?"

"No. It's gone now."

"What happened to it?"

Omar was thinking as fast as he could. Atash's house. What happened? Atash. Fire.

"He burned down his cabin. But we're going to camp right where it used to be. About a thousand years ago."

Omar looked sideways at Shafi and waited for his son's reaction to the start of a story. He didn't have long to wait.

Shafi stopped and put down his knapsack.

"Why did he burn down his own house?"

Omar sat and removed his heavy backpack, glad for a brief rest. "No choice. He saw some thieves coming up the mountain. They were going to steal his treasure map." Omar was making this up bit by bit. Parts of it weren't easy.

"Why didn't he just burn the map? Or grab it and run?"

Omar thought a moment. "Couldn't. He couldn't grab it, and he couldn't burn the map without burning down the house." Now Omar was sure of where this story was going. The next question was going to be the clincher.

"Why?"

"Because the map was chiseled into the bedroom wall."

How much was Shafi buying? Omar wasn't sure. He needed time to think of more details.

"I'll tell you all about it tonight. Now pick up your gear, and let's go."

After half a day of climbing and resting, they reached their destination, a bluff overlooking the town of Calle. The face of the bluff was broad and steep, a cliff actually.

"Is this the place, Da?"

"Hmm?"

"You know. Where Grandfather Atash built his house and then burned it down. Tell me about it."

"Oh, yes. But, you know, a story like that has to be told under the stars. You'll have to wait until bed time."

On a clear day, Calle could be seen from this bluff, its streets full of color. But on this cloudy day in Calle, the town beneath them lay blanketed by a cottony mass tinged with gold, while on the mountain, Omar and Shafi stood in bright sunshine, a world of calm and solitude.

With their tent pitched and the campsite put in order, father and son rested again. They lay side by side on their backs, gazed at the heavens, and discussed the animals and monsters that drifted in the clouds above.

The afternoon drew to a close and Omar built a small fire to prepare their evening meal. The fire burned low, and Omar stoked the coals while Shafi tried to roast two fresh goat meat sausages on sticks.

"I don't know, Da. I think we might have waited too long to cook."

"Well, that's easy to fix. We need a few more pieces of wood for the fire."

"I'll get some!" Shafi said. "I saw some good branches when we came up!"

"Okay," Omar said. "But don't go near the edge."

Soon Shafi was back with dry sticks, and in a few minutes, the sausages were ready.

"Are we higher than an airplane?" Shafi asked as he gazed down at the cloud cover below them.

"Higher than a small airplane, maybe," Omar said.

"If we stayed up here, I bet no one could ever find us," Shafi said.

Omar smiled and said, "And your mother? And Michael? Wouldn't you want them to find us?"

"Oh, sure. They could come up. It's those others I'm talking about. They could never find us, I bet," Shafi said.

"What others, son?" Omar asked in a gentle voice.

Shafi was silent a moment before he said, "I don't know if I should talk about it, Da."

"You don't have to, unless you want to." Omar could see he did.

Shafi shrugged. "Okay, then. The ones who hate you. And ma. And me." He said the words in a dry and unemotional way, as though this were a simple problem in arithmetic.

"They hate Michael, too, even though he looks Irish. They hate him when they know we're his family."

Omar saw his son was hiding pain.

"Come here, son," Omar urged gently as he pulled him down so they could sit face to face on the grass. "Who hates us?" he asked as he looked into Shafi's sad eyes.

Suddenly Shafi burst into tears, crying as though his heart would break. Omar held him against his breast, his arms close around the boy. He was shocked. There had been no hint that Shafi was in so much pain.

"Shh, now. Shh," he whispered, and put a few light kisses along the side and top of Shafi's head. His son's natural scent came up from the boy's hair and filled Omar's heart. *He's so much like his mother, yet he's the mirror image of me.*

"Do you want to tell me?" Omar whispered.

"No," Shafi sobbed. "Yes."

"Now what's this all about? Hmm?" Omar smiled at his son to encourage him. He was pretty certain he knew what this was all about.

Shafi shrugged his shoulders, as though in despair. "I don't know. It's just people. The way they are, sometimes."

Omar waited.

"Do you know what I mean?"

"I think so. But why don't you tell me."

"They say things. They call a person names."

"Who do they call names, son?"

"You." Shafi started to cry again. "And me. And Michael. They call us bastards. And filthy. And sex fiends."

Omar stroked Shafi's shoulders and gave the boy time. Shafi's crying slowed to a pattern of infrequent sobs.

"It hurts," Omar said. "I know." He was determined to hide his rage. *That's not what Shafi needs to see right now,* he resolved.

"I want to kill them!"

"Shafi, if you kill the people who hate you, you are no better than they are. Worse. You'd be a killer."

Shafi nodded and said, "I wouldn't like to be a killer." He looked at his father for hope, a tentative smile on his face.

"No, you wouldn't like it. You know what I think you'd like to be, when you grow up?"

"What?" Shafi was starting to feel better.

"I think you'd like to sail big ships across the ocean. Just like me."

"Oh, yes! That would be fun!" The ugly people were forgotten for now.

"Maybe you will. I'd like you to. You know what I'd like you to do right now?" Omar asked playfully.

"What?" Shafi asked with a big smile, eager to have a game.

"Go get some more wood! This fire's about out!"

"Okay!" Shafi yelled and ran off.

COMING HOME FROM camping, Shafi slept most of the flight from the Canaries to Ireland. This gave Omar time to reflect on their conversation on Calle Mountain. With his dark skin and Middle Eastern features Omar had tasted prejudice throughout the Western world, but the Irish kind was the most poisonous he was ever forced to eat.

Shafi's right. These people even turn against Michael's Irish face when they know I am his father.

In Michael's eyes, Omar saw Ireland's ancient history; in his smile he saw the curious light that gives the country its lustrous green. In Michael's laugh, Omar heard echoes of his child's Celtic and Viking origins.

Yes, Michael is the image of Kathleen, as much as Shafi is the image of me.

For one brief moment, Omar considered leaving Kathleen and the boys. *They might suffer less prejudice without me around. But Shafi has my looks. I could take Shafi and leave Michael with her. Michael's got a tough skin, a hide like mine. Shafi's the sensitive one. Like his mother.* Omar's heart threatened to pull him apart. *Yes, I could leave Kathleen,* he sighed. *It would be like splitting myself down the middle with an ax. I would go away with one half, leave the other half with her. Stupid idea.*

No way I'll ever leave Kathleen. Or either of our boys. We stay together. After a pause he added, *but in London.*

WHEN THEY ARRIVED FROM the airport, Kathleen saw something was troubling Omar from the moment he and Shafi walked into the house. His hug lacked strength, his kiss seemed distracted.

"What's wrong, dear?" she said as soon as she could get him alone.

"Shafi told me about something that happened at summer school. About prejudice. You know this isn't the first time. It's just another example of how our family is treated here. Kathleen, I really believe we have to leave Glenarm, leave Ireland. For the boys' sake."

Omar saw Kathleen's face turn to granite. He mumbled, "We'll talk about it later."

8

Love at the Academy

1989

The U.S. Naval Academy at Annapolis accepted female candidates, and first-semester plebe Capper Harris noticed the pretty blonde. She was hard to miss: tall, moved with the ease and grace of an athlete, golden skin, dark brown eyes complemented by dark lashes and brows. The kind of creature who gets admired even in simple clothes, little jewelry, and no makeup. Naturally pretty. The kind other girls don't want to like, but do. The girl noticed Capper. He was taller than she and looked rugged, like a guy who'd be at home in the outdoors. She saw he laughed and smiled easily; probably not a deep thinker, she decided. More like what you see is what you get. Friendly.

She and Capper shared some classes, and he learned her name was Ivy Rhodes. Capper thought the name was just about classy enough to wear the girl. It wasn't only that she was good-looking, but she had a way about her, a manner that said a guy would be damn lucky to get anywhere near her. It wasn't about being aloof or looking hard to get, exactly. She gave the impression of confidence, a woman secure enough to know she simply didn't need the basic hassle of guys hitting on her, one of the little games college boys and girls play on their way to maturity.

She did seem a bit arrogant; almost as though she were too strong. Maybe too independent. But, somehow, this only made her seem like a safe harbor to Capper.

He had to find a way to reach her. He discussed it with his roommates. They approached the problem as a military exercise, and the group consensus was to baffle her with bullshit. Capper would use the time-honored gambit of showing high intellect. It always leaves a girl stumbling for a reply, and a girl who is stumbling always appreciates the gentle strong man who restoreth her balance by wrapping an arm tenderly around her mid-section. After that, it's anchors aweigh.

Going in to Naval History 101 one day, Capper took the plunge. "So what do you think," he asked the lovely blond as he held the classroom door open for her, "was Thayer right about Farragut?"

"I think Suffren said it better," the pretty girl said, tossing her words carelessly and pronouncing the French name precisely right, as she walked on by into the classroom. "And Thayer is a pain in the ass," she flipped back at Capper over her shoulder.

Yes, Capper decided, there is a certain arrogance to the woman; this was clear. But the important thing was, he thought later as he tried to reassemble the pieces of his ego, she *did* toss him his opinion with a bright smile. Wasn't this a good sign?

Capper caught a whiff of her scent as she walked by, and it made him a little dizzy. Reminded him of mountain air in spring.

Ever the persistent warrior, Capper decided (with encouragement from his roommates) to try one more sortie using the same armament. At the next meeting of Naval History 101, he waited again at the door. She saw him as she turned the corner down the hall, and Capper thought he saw her suppress a small grin.

Ivy approached the door without looking directly at him. "Yeah, well *Suffren,*" he said, emphasizing the accent, but poorly, "didn't practice what he preached. He called tactics the veil of timidity, yet he used them every time he sailed into battle."

She breezed past him into the classroom and said, "Huh?" as though she'd no idea what the young man was talking about. But about halfway through the class, when the instructor asked if there were any inconsistencies in Suffren's history, she stood up and said, "It seems Suffren didn't practice what he preached. He calls tactics *the veil of timidity,* yet he. . . ." She turned to Capper, two rows away, and extended him a graciously offering hand and a matching smile.

". . . used them every time he sailed into battle," Capper finished the phrase in a small voice, not sure whether to feel elated or deflated.

On the way out of class, he caught up with her in the hall and said, "I'll strike my colors if you'll agree to an armistice."

"Terms?"

"I take you to dinner."

"Unacceptable."

"Alternative offer?" Capper asked, his heart beginning to sink.

"I take you," she said with a seductive smile. "To dinner," she quickly added with a look of innocence.

"Wow!" Capper gulped. "I mean, yes! Deal! When? Tonight?"

The new rule at the Academy said a plebe got one weeknight off campus per semester, if his or her grades were right. Capper was more than willing to use his precious pass for a date with this lovely creature.

"Easy, skipper," she said, "you'll blow a boiler. Can't make it tonight. Can make Saturday. Okay?"

Saturdays were a little more liberal. With good grades, a plebe got three Saturdays per semester, from five in the morning until eleven at night. With this many hours, a person could accomplish a lot.

"Yeah! Yeah, sure!"

"Okay, sailor. Meet me in port." This was the name the cadets gave the nearby town of Annapolis.

She added, "Do you know a Cuban restaurant called *El Segunda Victoria*?"

"I'll find it," Capper answered. "What time?"

"Like Sassy Sarah said, I get too hungry for dinner at eight. Make it six. Dress code is civvies."

"Okay! Six. Who's Sassy Sarah?"

"Sarah Vaughan. Look her up under oldies but goodies in the music department. Bye. See ya."

Capper gulped and wrote down the name of the restaurant before he forgot it. With help on his spelling, he eventually found it in the yellow pages.

He looked up Sarah Vaughan that evening at the Academy's ship store and bought a triple album after deciding instantly (without listening) that this Sarah Vaughan person was the greatest singer of all time—past, present, and future.

"Hell, Capper, you'd love whatever that tall blonde likes, even if all the singer could do is snort like a pig," one of his roommates said later. "But play that last one again. What's her name? Sarah what?"

Two days later Capper found a note in his mailbox. It said, "Sorry, can't make Saturday night. Unexpected visitor. How about Saturday, breakfast, same place, 0700 hours?"

Capper didn't care about the time change, as long as he was going to see her. Be with her.

He thought about her unexpected visitor. *Some other guy with a higher priority?* he asked himself. That didn't feel good.

EL SEGUNDA VICTORIA was a simple place but large, noisy, and a favorite of the Cuban locals.

Capper got there first and was waiting just inside the front door when Ivy arrived. At their table, the waiter greeted Ivy by name and spoke to her in Spanish.

"I didn't know you speak Spanish. Are you from Spain?" Capper asked.

"No," she said with a laugh. "Cuba. I came to this country when I was a kid."

The menu was long—all of it in Spanish, to let the *Yanquees* know whose turf this was.

"May I order for both of us?" Ivy said.

"Sounds fine," Capper said.

Ivy ordered *huevos con almejas*—scrambled eggs with clams—and *café con leche*. The waiter brought them a basket of sliced *pan cubano*, the classic and unique Cuban bread with its pale gold crust, and a dish of soft *mantequilla*.

"You gringos are spoiling our culture here in the States," Ivy said with a smile. "Actually, that's not true. We're doing it to ourselves. It's more like we're diluting our culture with yours."

"How so?"

"Well, eggs for breakfast is one example. In Cuba, we didn't eat eggs at breakfast. We ate them at *almuerzo*, what you call lunch."

"Just eggs?"

"No," she said. She laughed again, and Capper thought it the most beautiful sound he'd ever heard.

"Actually," she continued, "lunch was our biggest meal of the day. Three courses. We'd spend the morning cooking. First the soup, then fried eggs and white rice, or maybe *picadillo*. That's ground meat with olives and spices. Avocado salad. And there's most always *platanos*."

"What's . . . ?"

"*Platanos?*"

"Yeah."

"Fried ripe plantains. A type of banana. They're black when they're ripe."

The waiter arrived with their food. Ivy ate with good appetite, but she could see Capper was mostly pushing the food around on his plate. "You don't like it?"

"Oh no, it's not that. The food's fine."

"Well then what is it? You're hardly eating."

"Your, uh, note. It said you have some unexpected visitor to-night. I was just wondering. . . ."

"Who my visitor is?"

"I'm sorry," Capper said, pushing himself back in his chair. "That was stupid of me. It's none of my business. I'm just glad you're here with me now." *Geez!* he thought. *I've really screwed this up!*

"Me, too. And about me having another date tonight, you were right. I do."

"Oh." Capper looked like he might be ill. *Could this get any worse?*

"Yes. With a nice—"

"I don't want to hear about him," Capper said, putting his hand up.

"Him? Who said anything about a *him?*"

"A *her?* Your date is with a *woman?*"

Capper's eyes went wide. He'd heard why some women join the military. *Could Ivy be . . . ?*

"Yes, a woman. And she's about seventy years old."

Capper felt like a dope all over again, and he was sure it showed in his face.

Ivy reached out and took his two hands in hers.

"Hey, sailor. Ease up on yourself, okay? My date is with a woman I correspond with. It's for a book I'm writing about life in Cuba before Castro. Now she has agreed to come visit me. Her name is Oliva Revuelta. But her stage name was Carmela."

"Her stage name?"

"Yes. A long time ago, she was a showgirl. So was my grand-mother. They dated some big-name American gangsters in Havana. I'll tell you about it some time."

"That does sound like it would make a good book. Your name; Rhodes isn't Cuban, is it?" Capper asked through a mouthful of eggs. In the words *I'll tell you about it some time*, he registered the implied promise she would see him again. His appetite improved.

"My mom was Cuban. My dad was Irish."

"When did you come to the States?"

"Nineteen seventy-four. If I'd come here a dozen years earlier, I'd have been a Peter Pan kid."

"What's that?"

"Between 1960 and 1962, the U.S. government flew more than fourteen thousand kids out of Fidel Castro's Cuba. They were called Peter Pan kids."

"Fourteen thousand? That's a lot of kids. Where did they all go?"

"They all landed in Miami, first. It was called Never-Never Land. From there the kids went everywhere in the States to Cuban families. When I came over, I lived with an aunt and uncle in Miami. Grew up there. Big family. What else would you like to know?"

"I don't know. Why are you at Annapolis?

Ivy shrugged. "I've given that a lot of thought. I don't think of myself as a warrior. I'm more the domestic type. But before I start having babies, I want to do my little bit toward making planet earth a safer place to *have* kids. And you? Why are you here?"

Capper grinned. "Same reason a lot of guys join. The adventure, the excitement." He laughed. "The uniform."

Ivy shook her head. "Men. Just big kids."

Capper shrugged. "How'd you get the name Ivy? Doesn't sound Spanish," He looked for the waiter. He'd never tasted bread as good as *pan cubano.*

"My real name is Ivona. My dad called me Ivy. When I was little, he said I smelled like the wild ivy that grew in the mountains near Killarney, in Ireland, where he grew up."

Capper snapped his fingers. "That's what it is! I knew it!"

"Knew what?"

"Your scent. It's the same today as when you were a little girl. Ivy. Just like your dad said."

Ivy lowered her eyes. She felt a rush of tenderness toward this brash young man.

"Did your parents come to America?"

"No. They were supposed to come later. But politics got in the way, and my dad died of cancer before he could get out. Mom never could get out. She lives with relatives out in the countryside."

"Do you ever see her?"

"No, we write back and forth, and I phone her, but until the laws are changed, there's no way for me to visit."

"Oh. I'm sorry," Capper said.

"We have a large family in Cuba. They all look after each other. She seems happy."

The bread arrived, and Capper extended the basket to Ivy. "More bread?" he asked.

"No, thanks. I'm satisfied," Ivy said.

Capper wasn't. He was searching for what to say next. He wanted to sound urbane, and the silence was starting to feel like a load of bricks.

"So what was life like in Cuba?" he tried. "I mean when you were a little girl."

Ivy smiled. Apparently he'd hit on a good topic.

"My favorite memory is fishing. Me and my cousins would get up early in the morning and walk to the pier with my uncle Diego, and he would line us up to sit at the edge of the pier with our fat little legs dangling over the side."

The mischievous little kid in Capper surfaced. "Do you still have fat little legs?" he asked, grinning through a mouthful of scrambled eggs.

"Funny," Ivy snipped. "Uncle Diego called us his seven little *calabazas*. I'll bet we looked like a row of pumpkins, too, sitting elbow to elbow and dangling our legs over the water."

Capper swallowed. This was fun. "I can just see you, a little pumpkin with fat legs sitting at the edge of the dock. Ever fall in?"

Ivy laughed. "No, I didn't. Now, what about you? For instance, where'd you get the name Capper?"

"From my great grandmother. She was half Dakota Indian. I'm fifth generation."

Capper ran his hand through his straight black hair as he spoke.

"I can see this, now that you say it. And what about your great grandfather. Was he Indian, too?"

"Actually, the story begins with my *great*-great grandfather. He was from France. Migrated to Quebec. He was what the Canadians call a *Coureur des Bois*. The *Coureurs* were French fur traders down from Quebec. They dealt peacefully with the Indians of what's now the North Central states, starting back in the late seventeenth century. When Lewis and Clark got to Missouri in 1804, the *Coureurs* were there to greet them. They all spoke *Chinook* and married Indian girls."

"Is *Chinook* the name of an Indian tribe?"

"No," Capper said, pleased to be able to instruct this bright young woman. "Actually, *Chinook* is a slang mix of several Indian languages, plus French and a little English."

"Oh," Ivy said. "Like Yiddish is a slang made up of Hebrew, old German, Aramaic and a bunch of other languages."

"Exactly." Capper said brightly, as though to acknowledge this yong woman's basic knowledge of Hebrew heritage. He hadn't known any of this about Yiddish, but he wasn't about to let on.

"So did your great-great grandfather marry an Indian girl?"

"Yes. She was a *Cicot* Indian. The *Cicot* nation migrated south from Canada into the States. In French they're called, *La Race Cicot*. This is how she got her name: *Racicot*."

"I've heard that name."

"It's pretty common. So, anyway, my French and Cicot great-great grandparents wound up in upstate New York. Somehow, as the story goes, she civilized him."

"She civilized him?"

"Yeah. The way I was told, he was the savage."

Ivy laughed.

"Turned him into a good husband. And eventually there were seven kids. My great grandmother was the youngest."

"Seven kids? Yeah, I'd say she turned him into a good husband!" Ivy said, laughing again.

"Great grandma died when I was five years old. She was a hundred and two. Not only that, but she was in perfect health when she died."

"What happened?"

"She climbed up into a big old maple tree to steal honey from a beehive. She lost her balance and fell. Broke her neck. Dead when they found her."

"What an incredible woman! Climbing trees at her age!"

"Yep. She was."

"So why did your great grandmother call you Capper?"

"She said it was because of the way I cried when I was a baby."

"I can't wait to hear this."

"If you ever tell anyone, I swear I'll—"

"You'll what?" Ivy said with a laugh.

"I'll tell everybody you have short fat legs," Capper said. It was lame, he knew, but it was the best he could think of at the moment.

Ivy laughed again and said, "Hey, I'm not going to tell anybody! Come on, now. Get on with it!"

"Well, she called me *Ká-ah-pwah.*"

"What the heck does *that* mean?"

"It means Gentle Thunder."

"So you cried like thunder?"

"I guess so."

"Gentle Thunder," Ivy said. "Nice."

"Great grandmother told me *Ká-ah-pwah* is the kind of thunder you hear before a spring rain. It's a soft, rolling sound everybody welcomes because it means new life is coming."

"That's beautiful," Ivy said softly.

"When I started school, the kids called me Capper. They couldn't say *Ká-ah-pwah.*"

Ivy touched Capper's cheek, smiled, and said tenderly, "Thanks for sharing this with me."

Whether it was the depth in her eyes or the touch of her hand or the curious little twist of her mouth when she smiled, Capper wasn't sure. But at this moment he fell in love.

Capper didn't merely fall; he went down like a giant sequoia.

Other than childhood crushes, this was his first time. Love covered him like a thick woolen blanket thrown over his head. For days, he wandered around on campus, bumping into walls, drifting in and out of classes. A constant vision of valentines danced in his head. His friends were annoyed but amused and tolerant. His professors, too, were annoyed. But they were not amused. And they were certainly not tolerant.

Eventually, though, with a lot of prodding by everyone including Ivy, Capper was able to put some order back into his life just in time to avoid academic disaster. When he finally shook off the blindness, he was amazed to learn how many days had slipped away in a fog.

"Whew! Where the hell have I *been?*" he asked his roommate.

"Not here, man. Outer space," his roommate said. "You gonna get your act together now?" He added in his best Edward G. Robinson snarl, "Or do I have to put out a contract on that dame?"

CAPPER DID MANAGE TO RAISE his grades, like a phoenix from the ashes, and four years later he and Ivy graduated side by side with honors. He even earned a special award in leadership and tactical planning.

The relationship between the two cadets deepened during that time, and long before their student career was over they were very much in love. A military academy isn't the most permissive place in the world for lovemaking, though, and finding a way to be alone was always a challenge. They made a game out of scouting for opportunities, and competed to see who could find the best ones.

"Let's grab a quick snack after this class," Capper said one day as he and Ivy went their separate ways to their next classes. "Meet me at the vending machines."

"Sure," said Ivy. *A quick snack, he says. I'll bet!*

Ivy sipped a cold orange juice and felt warm with anticipation as she waited for her Capper.

"Pssst," she heard, and looked around. She spotted him at the edge of a dark hallway that led to a storeroom. She was amused and felt excitement course through her.

Capper wore a conspiratorial grin as he signaled her to follow. They slipped down the hallway, muffling their giggles. At the end of the passage, Capper pressed Ivy against the door. He was randy as a billy goat, and Ivy was quick to reach orgasm.

As they casually walked back into the daylight, they laughed at their strange but exhilarating love life. The next time, Ivy found a spot. Then Capper again. And so the competition went.

A MONTH BEFORE GRADUATION, Capper got a call from the front office. Vice Admiral Wilfred Mandrake, the dean, wanted to see him. When Capper got there, he was surprised to see Ivy and some honcho.

"Ensign Harris, I'd like you to meet Marston Hardale," the dean said as he rose from behind his desk. "Mr. Hardale is from the National Security Agency. The NSA."

Capper shook hands with a large man in a dark blue suit. He had blond hair in a severe military-style crew cut and eyes the color of amber. His muscular build seemed to be threatening the seams of his suit jacket, and Capper thought he might have played college football ten years ago.

Capper sat down on the small sofa where Ivy had scooted over to make room for him. There was an extra chair in the room, but Ivy seemed to want Capper to be sitting next to her.

"Are you familiar with the NSA?" Dean Mandrake asked Capper as he sat back down at his big desk.

"Only what came up in our class on international accords in intelligence," Capper said, riffling as fast as he could through the note cards in his head. The writing was faded on the NSA card. "Something about keeping harmony among the nations of the Western intelligence community."

Mandrake said, "On your futures planning form, when you were freshmen, you both expressed an interest in working with intelligence. Still feel that way?"

"Yes, sir," Capper and Ivy said simultaneously.

"What do you know about MI6?" Hardale said. The question was directed at Capper, but with no hesitation, Ivy rattled off: "Security and counterintelligence for Britain. Formed in 1912 to cover all areas outside the United Kingdom. Originally an abbreviation for Military Intelligence, Section Six now has no military connection and is known as SIS, or Secret Intelligence Service. Its companion agency, MI5, was formed in 1909 to cover internal affairs."

Capper was reminded of the day four years ago in Naval History 101 when Suffren and Farragut brought them together. He liked the outcome, but he hadn't enjoyed the way Ivy torpedoed him in class that day. It looked like she was at it again. He loved the girl, but he did have some ego, so he decided this time he wouldn't wait to sink with Suffren or fail with Farragut.

"—and since the disintegration of the Soviet Union, both MI5 and MI6 have sought new roles, including the fight against organized crime," he said a little too hurriedly. As he finished his recitation, Capper glanced at Ivy and saw in her eyes the tiniest twinkle. It plainly said *What? No veil of timidity today?*

At that moment, if Capper'd had a tail, he'd have been wagging it. Hard.

Dean Mandrake's fatherly expression said he was pleased with his two young graduates.

Hardale said, "The NSA is working with the CIA in developing a new branch agency. Cooperation between those two agencies isn't all that common, truth be told, but in this instance it's absolutely necessary. The NSA will be the agency behind the scenes, but deniability will fall upon the CIA. This new branch agency will be small. I'm heading it up. It's called the Terrorist Tracking Team, or T3. We'll be working closely with the entire intelligence community in this country as well as SIS and the French Sureté and Interpol, and other such agencies throughout the world. We'll also be working closely with our own Department of Defense, and under some circumstances directly with the Oval Office."

Capper and Ivy stole a quick glance at one another. The excitement on their faces was plain. Was he going to offer them a role in this dream outfit?

He continued, "There's noise, again, from terrorist groups around the world, especially from the Middle East. The International Islamic Front for Jihad Against the Jews and the Crusaders—the ILF—is a particular worry. CIA's human intelligence and signal intelligence offices are picking up indications there may be a repeat of the attacks against American interests, either abroad or here at home."

Hardale stopped and pulled out a short briar pipe. He waved it in a half-circle before his audience and asked, of no one in particular, "Mind?"

"Not at all," Ivy answered.

Hardale frowned at Ivy as though she'd spoken out of turn. He looked at the dean.

"Please," the dean said. "Go right ahead. It seems no one

minds." Ivy could have sworn she saw the tiniest wink of amused complicity from the dean.

Hardale packed his pipe in silence, lighted it, and took a long puff. He kept glancing back and forth at Capper and Ivy.

"Well? Not curious why I'm telling you this?" His phrase was broken up into little parts as he was still sucking air to the flame in his pipe. The aroma of fruited tobacco followed.

Capper said, "Yes, sir. I'm curious. I just didn't want to interrupt."

"Ditto," Ivy added, and tacked on, "sir."

"Well, I'll tell you. I'm not outright offering you T3 membership. There's a training. You'll have to prove yourselves. But, based on your record here, I think you'll do just fine," he said like an encouraging uncle.

"T3 will have one major assignment. Find and stop terrorists before they can hurt us again. This assignment does involve the right to carry and use firearms. A concealed weapon. The work will be dangerous. Still curious?" The pipe wasn't working right.

Capper opened his mouth to reply, but before he could speak Ivy interjected, "More than ever." This time it was Capper who said, "Ditto," and a moment later, "sir."

"I don't want you to get the wrong impression, here," Hardale said, frowning as he studied the contents of his briar.

He mumbled around his pipe stem, "This isn't some kind of James Bond stuff." He tapped the failed wad of tobacco into an ash tray. He slowly rubbed the warm pipe bowl on either side of his nose to let the wood absorb oil from his skin, and then he slipped the pipe into a jacket pocket.

"Well, damn it," he said as he leaned back in his chair, "I suppose it is James Bond stuff, in a way. No point denying it."

Hardale leaned forward again and joined the fingers of his hands, saying, "Our first task will be to weld a tight partnership with MI6.

"We want to train some of our people to work with that agency in terrorism intervention and prosecution. The British have developed some expertise in this area because of their dealings with the IRA. Now they're offering to share their expertise with teams from the United States, Canada, Australia, and a few other friendlies. They've put together a six-month training in basic plot detection. I'm sending over a hand-picked group from various branches of our military. About twelve in all. That six-month stint will be just the beginning, though. Were looking for a long-term commitment eventually."

Capper and Ivy saw a lengthy trip to the United Kingdom on the horizon, and even though they wanted to appear sophisticated, there was no way either of them could hide the gleam of enthusiasm lighting up their eyes.

"There's one aspect of this opening which is, shall we say, peculiar," Hardale said, looking ill at ease.

"It was decided by the team who shaped this program that a couple is needed. A man and woman who can work together, travel together, posing as man and wife. We know you two are, uh . . . are, uh. . . ."

Ivy chuckled. With a wry smile she asked, "May I ask why?"

"Yes. Well, you'd be working undercover most of the time," Hardale said. "A married couple is less conspicuous than a man or a woman working alone."

"Well, sirs," Capper said to both Mandrake and Hardale, "speaking just for myself, and I know Ensign Rhodes may want to think about it, but speaking only for me, I'm ready to sign up right now. I think it's a great opportunity. That is, if Ensign Rhodes is interested, I mean."

Ivy took Capper's hand in hers and, looking into his eyes, she said in a low voice, "Ensign Rhodes is very interested."

"And, I might add, Mr. Hardale," Ivy continued, "you needn't worry about us pretending to be married. Right after graduation, we're headed down to Miami. My family is planning a big wedding for us," she said, flashing the diamond on her left hand at him. "You're invited."

The T3 training would begin Monday. Capper was just hooking up the stereo in their London flat when Ivy burst in waving a big envelope.

"It's from Uncle Ernesto and Aunt Tia. I bet it's the wedding pictures."

"Hey! All right!" Capper said.

They plopped down on the sofa and Ivy tore open the envelope.

"Oh, look at this," Ivy said. "You look hungry enough to eat the whole thing yourself." It was Capper turning a small pig roasting on a spit. Next to him were tubs of iced beer. Happy faces filled the photo.

Capper sighed and sat back. "I can close my eyes and be there. Smell the food, hear the music."

Ivy leaned her head against his shoulder and said, "Fun time. You didn't know you were getting into such a big, crazy family."

"Mmm," Capper whispered in her ear, "let's do something big and crazy right now," as he let his hand wander over her breasts. She slapped it away playfully.

"Look at the pictures!" she growled.

Capper laughed. "Look at all the kids in this one," he said. "They sure were a wild bunch."

"Capper, you sound like a senior citizen. Don't you like kids?"

"Sure. Bar-be-cued, deep fried, poached on toast. Taste like chicken."

Ivy grabbed Capper by the head and gave his scalp a hard nuggie.

"Yeow!" he screamed and tickled her ribs until she was screaming too and had to let him go.

"Well, you *better* love 'em! 'Cause we are gonna *have* a *bunch* of 'em!" she said, trying to tickle him back.

"I might help you *start* 'em, but you are gonna do the *having!*" he argued as the tickling contest got underway with yelps and screams.

Soon they were rolling on the floor, their laughing turning to lovemaking—the pictures quite forgotten.

Later that afternoon, Ivy managed to get Capper back to the neglected photos. "Listen to this," Ivy said. "Tia says the kids have formed 'The Capper Fan Club'. They sure did monopolize you." Ivy turned to look in Capper's eyes, as though searching, and said softly, "Were you okay with that?"

Capper laughed and tossed off his reply: "Oh sure. I had a lot of fun."

"I didn't think they'd ever let me have you back," she said, holding him tight, her face against his chest. "Capper, you're going to make a great dad," she said softly.

She didn't see his discomfort. "Me? I'm just a big kid myself."

Ivy heard Capper's words echo in her mind. She didn't like the sound, but she smiled at Capper and let it go.

ON THE FIRST DAY of T3 classes, a man walked into the room in a brown military uniform with creases that would cut a lumberjack's finger. The jacket bore a few ribbons and some brass. He had sharp blue eyes, a slim chevron mustache that was distinctly red, and he moved like a smoothly functioning windup soldier. He sported a riding crop under his right arm and wore his cap pulled low over his eyes. He stopped at the door to survey his audience, then walked to his desk with a military bearing that announced full control. Standing behind the desk he removed his cap to reveal red creases in an already ruddy forehead that yielded to an equally ruddy but prematurely bald pate. He checked his wrist watch, snapped to parade rest, fixed his eyes on some point at the ceiling near the back of the classroom, and waited motionless. There was not a sound in the room. Fifteen seconds passed. No one moved. The man glanced at his watch again, in an almost careless manner. He now was apparently satisfied that the time was right, for he slowly walked around to the front of his desk, and, in a low and booming voice, he intoned what sounded like funerary information.

"My name is Black Watch Captain Sean McGuire. I'm your T3 instructor. The name Sean is Gaelic for John. Gaelic is the language of Ireland. The Irish hate the Black Watch, whom they still call the Black and Tan. I'm Irish."

Capper nudged Ivy, sitting next to him, and whispered, "And this guy's gonna teach us about cultural harmony?"

"Good hearing is one the many blessings the Lord bestowed upon me," the Instructor muttered, glowering at Capper. "Please *rise*, sir!"

Capper stood and snapped to attention.

"Your name?" the Instructor droned in the same sub-basement voice.

"Ensign Tom Harris, *sir!*" Capper said in a loud voice, and ripped off a taut salute.

"Well, Ensign Harris," the voice droned with numbing slowness, "tell us something about Irish culture." Captain McGuire held his riding crop in his left hand, and with it he softly tapped the palm of his right. His voice could hardly be heard, and he spoke in a manner that might succeed in coaxing a fragile child to recite the days of the week. But the man's gentle way showed a hard edge that matched the steel in his eyes, and the quiet tapping of the riding crop shouted "danger!"

Capper hesitated a moment before saying, "Sir, I don't know anything about it, sir." This time Capper's voice seemed a little thin, not loud, and he didn't emphasize the "sir." But he did remain rigidly at attention.

Putting a long pause between each of his words, Instructor McGuire said, looking away from Capper, "Right. Sit down, Ensign Harris."

"And that," as Capper told it years later, ". . . was how, for the first and last time in the United Kingdom, I put my big fat foot in my big fat Yankee mouth."

After that somewhat dubious beginning, Capper actually did well in the training, and so did Ivy. Somewhere in the early days, Black Watch Instructor Captain McGuire did explain to his students that he had been chosen as a T3 instructor specifically because he was both a British officer of a special unit hated by the Irish, and yet he was Irish. This duality in their instructor, it was hoped, could help his students better understand the sharp passions that divide the Irish from the British—and, by extension, understand better the nature of the sharp cultural divisions between most other peoples of planet Earth.

The training material was presented in five units: Investigation, Martial Arts, Armored Vehicle, Hazmat, and Computer Forensics. The training pace was brisk and there was a demand for proper attitude. Survival in a firefight, the team was taught, included more than physical protection and deterrents. Survival required attitude, and that came from proper preparation.

The training day began long before sunrise with what the Brits call setups. Capper thought the instructor had said situps and he'd always included that particular exercise in his morning routine back at the Academy, so he wasn't too concerned. But setups wasn't situps. For setups, early each morning the group was brought by truck out to a quiet country lane on the outskirts of London where their instructor led them in a ten mile run—five miles out and five miles back. This was before coffee. The run began at a slow enough pace but then it speeded up. By the time they reached their turnaround point it was sheer hell. Team members were told they could finish at a walk if they had to, and the rest of the team would wait to go in for breakfast. And wait. And wait. For as long as it took the slowpoke to get in.

On the second day, two of the team got out of bed early enough to make themselves some breakfast at their flat before coming in for setups. They regretted that. Not long into the run, they both were seized with violent stomach cramps that felled them. The team had to wait by the side of the road until an ambulance came to get the two men, and then the run was continued.

The lesson being taught, one that most of the men had already learned, was that the unit did not leave anyone behind. It was a lesson worth learning, worth reinforcing. It made a big difference in morale.

Physical fitness was one of the many aspects of the training that carried a particularly British slant. The martial arts, which were to become an area of major achievement for both Capper and Ivy and remain with them through most of their lives, were taught with a sense of style or bearing that any Oriental practitioner would have found inhibiting but which the Brits found to be correct.

"Physical Confrontation," which the Americans—"Cousins," as they were known,—called street fighting, was a departure from the martial arts that emphasized injuring the opponent and learning to stay on one's feet during a fight. The focus was on causing pain. Eyes and genitals were prime targets; knee joints not far behind. But even in this no-hits-prohibited kind of engagement, the Brits found ways to formalize movements and ritualize procedure. This was annoying to those Cousins who had grown up on the mean streets of L.A., New York or wherever. One day, a lad from Detroit whose nickname was Hatchetface challenged Captain McGuire to his own kind of street fighting. McGuire agreed, and, in a flash, Hatchetface was flat on his back. And not getting up very fast.

It was early one evening about midway into training month number six, the last, that Marston Hardale knocked on the door of Mr. and Mrs. Tom Harris, where Capper and Ivy were known to the neighbors as that pleasant young American couple taking a summer seminar at a local college. Capper was busy in the kitchen, so Ivy answered the door and her mouth dropped open." Mr. Hardale, what a surprise! Please, do come in. Capper, look who's here!" she said. "You're just in time for dinner. We're having *rabo alcaparrado.*"

"It smells wonderful! I'm glad I didn't eat on the plane," Hardale said. "What is it?"

"It's oxtails with caper sauce," Ivy replied. "You're gonna love it!"

"Hey, Mr. Hardale!" Capper said as he came out of the kitchen wiping his hands on a towel. "What brings you to London?"

"To visit the two of you, actually. And my nose tells me I came at the right time!" Hardale replied.

Ivy laughed. "You sure did. As usual, Capper's made too much. We'll be eating this for a week."

"Capper made it?" Hardale said. "The name sounded like a Spanish dish. I'd have thought—"

"That Ivy would be making the Spanish dishes?" Capper cut in. "Cute trick she pulled on me. Got me *aplatanado*, as they say in Cuba. Turned me into a Cuban, and now I do all the Cuban cooking!"

"Oh, stop complaining," Ivy said. "You know you love it."

"Sounds like the perfect squabbling of an old married couple," Hardale said.

"Yeah, we're getting the hang of things," Capper said with an obvious leer at Ivy. She blushed and swatted him on the rear as she walked by into the kitchen to set another place at table. Capper invited Hardale to join him and Ivy while they finished up the cooking.

During dinner, Hardale explained why he had come, starting with a question:

"Have you two decided on being a permanent part of T3?"

"Yeah," Capper replied. "If you'll have us, we'd love to. Right, hon?"

"You bet. Are we in?" she asked.

"You've done well here in your six-month indoctrination. T3 would very much like to have you." Hardale said with a smile.

"Hey!" Capper said. "That's great!"

"Let's celebrate. I'll get the wine," Ivy said.

After dinner the three settled into the flat's tiny sitting room and Hardale broke out his briar again, looking at it dubiously before asking, "Mind?" with a wave of the thing. This time the question was directed at Ivy.

"Not at all," Ivy replied.

Hardale took particular pains to pack it properly and this time he got his pipe lighted well with no trouble at all.

Looking downright pleased with himself, he said, "We'd like you to make some new friends. A couple in Northern Ireland."

Hardale explained that this couple, Kathleen O'Toole and Omar Jabri, were of special interest to the American intelligence community.

"Omar is a privateer," Hardale said. "Sort of a modern pirate. He uses a fantastic warship built for stealth and speed. Also owns a small fleet of legitimate merchant vessels that carry freight around the world."

Hardale puffed on his pipe once, slowly, relishing the taste of his fruited tobacco, and then continued. "Now, the woman, she's quite different. Gun buyer. Combat trainer. Top quality warrior for the IRA. But holds no office there. Just a fancy grunt."

Hardale glanced over at Ivy, expecting her to bridle. She shifted in her seat uncomfortably, glanced for a moment at Capper, then looked at the floor.

Hardale seemed pleased at Ivy's apparent discomfiture. He continued: "Kathleen O'Toole is smart. Knows a lot about guns, bombs." Another puff on the pipe, this one brief, then: "You look at her story and you get real insights into the IRA system for terrorist recruitment." He paused a moment and then began ticking off on his fingers: "Find someone who's young and lost. Impressionable. A loner. Vulnerable. Imaginative. Someone whose family was the whole world. Lives in a war-torn country. Revolutionaries take that person in. Manipulate them. Take advantage of their vulnerability by promising them protection and a sense of belonging to something important, indoctrinate them into the cause . . ."

Ivy said with disgust: "Is *that* what she does?"

Hardale looked surprised, then amused: "What? Uh, no. That's what was done to *her*. She was fifteen when her family was killed. The IRA moved in and snapped her up. It's all here in the dossier." Hardale handed the envelope to Capper. The he looked at Ivy with a lame smile and said "Fascinating reading, really."

"What's our mission?" Capper asked.

"For now, your assignment is just to meet them. Draw them out. Get information that might help us recruit them. Of course, this is a covert operation. You will have a plausible cover. You're a young American couple looking at real estate in Ireland. You have a modest amount of money for investment, and because your father was Irish, Ivy, you might be interested in investing in that country. You might even consider moving there and becoming the owner-operators of a pub or other small business."

"You said you might want to recruit them," Capper said.

"Yes. These people are regarded as potential assets to our country's intelligence community; particularly Omar. You probably won't find it hard to strike up an acquaintance. I understand both are quite personable," Hardale said.

THE NEXT DAY Capper and Ivy flew from Heathrow to Cork International Airport.

About halfway through the flight Capper noticed that Ivy seemed withdrawn, moody. "What's going on, hon? You've hardly said a word since we took off."

Ivy lifted her eyes from the dossier she was reading about Kathleen O'Toole. She leaned her head against the seat back, closed her eyes, and sighed loudly. She snapped the dossier closed, turned to Capper and looked at him with angry eyes. "The rotten IRA deprived her of everything normal. Brainwashed her, for God's sake!" she added, as her voice rose in pitch and volume.

"Easy, hon." Capper looked around the cabin. A man across the aisle glanced sternly in their direction over the edge of his newspaper and then went back behind it.

"But she was just a kid!" Ivy hissed.

Capper placed his hand lightly on Ivy's. "Kathleen O'Toole may have been a kid when the IRA grabbed her, but she's no kid today. She's a dangerous woman. And don't you forget it."

Nothing more was said on the subject and soon the conversation between the two young lovers lightened. By the time the plane landed at County Cork Airport in Ireland, the issue had been closed and filed. Or so it seemed.

From there they set off in a rented car for the drive to Northern Ireland. To prepare for this trip, Ivy visited a travel agency and loaded the car with road maps, pamphlets and brochures showing every main road, side road and byway of the entire country. Every mountain, glen, bay, river, lake and island was included. She had a full description and history of each of Ireland's most noteworthy castles and cottages and even some of its stone walls. Before the pair reached their destination in Glenarm, she had recited aloud to Capper the names, descriptions, and behavior of every animal residing in Ireland's woods, the fishes in its streams, the birds and butterflies that occupy its skies; the names and seasons of its trees, shrubs, bushes, flowers, and grasses, as well as the Shamrock Isles' legends, history, stories, heartaches, dreams, and fantasies.

"Look! Look!" Capper would say to her repeatedly as he drove, to get Ivy to lift her eyes off the printed page and actually *see* some of the wonders and beauties she was describing.

She'd look and draw her breath in sharply with delight and exclamation at the sights. Then she'd dive right back into her reading, eager and excited, as though *the reading itself* created all the beauties outside their car window.

At one moment, as she was leaning her head against the car seat and gazing upward at the sky, Capper looked over at her and found tears running down her face. A moment earlier she had been laughing at the antics of a lark who seemed to be racing with their car.

He pulled over to the side of the road, turned to her, put his hands on her shoulders and asked, "What's wrong?"

"Oh, Capper!" she said, weeping, as she lay her face on his chest. "There's so much beauty in the world! More than enough for everyone. Why must people fight? Hurt one another?"

Capper had no idea what to reply and had the good sense to say nothing. He just held her and rocked her gently.

"This place is so beautiful," Ivy sighed. "If I could take everyone in the world on this trip through Ireland, I know there would never be another war. The world's too beautiful to fight in!"

Capper was overwhelmed by this new and gleaming facet of Ivy. He added it to the aspects of her he already knew, this person who could best him in the martial arts, this woman who was a wild and creative lover, this scholar whose intellect and capacity for learning were far greater than his own, this friend who understood his mood and his mind long before he did.

For a brief moment Capper feared the full power of his love for Ivy might be more than he could bear, might make him blind, or deaf, or turn him to stone. Or ashes. Surely, he suddenly realized, if he ever lost her he would not be able to draw another breath.

Capper wasn't given to easy tears. It just wasn't in his nature. But now, now with this sense of an overwhelming love covering him like a mantle of light, he felt big drops running down both his cheeks. And he didn't care.

9

The Meeting in Glenarm

1993

They called to say they'd arrive late, and at about ten that night they pulled in to Glenarm By The Sea. The date was June 21st, the longest day of the year, known as Summer Solstice. This far north there is no true nightfall at Summer Solstice. Instead, the countryside is bathed at night in an eerie pearl-gray that lasts until day.

The inn's owner and desk clerk, Mr. Joseph Moriarty, was a portly gentleman who made it his business to know something about everyone in town and to tell all he knew to every visitor. "Ye've come up for the Summer Solstice Festival tomorrow, have ye?"

"A festival? No, we didn't know!" Ivy's face lit up like a child's.

"Aye. We Irish are always lookin' for an excuse for a festival. This is goin' to be the year's biggest."

Mr. Moriarty's eyes reflected the gaiety in Ivy's smile. "There'll be arts and crafts and singers and dancers."

"It sounds fun! I can hardly wait!" she said.

Capper noticed Ivy was putting a slight lilt in her voice.

Moriarty beckoned to be followed as he turned away saying, "Come along now. I've saved ye a spot of supper."

"Wonderful!" Ivy said. "I am a little hungry. What are we having?"

Mr. Moriarty entered the dining room with his charges just behind him as he said, "Potato soup. I hope you like it."

The room, supper long over, was a quiet study in black and white with just a few splashes of color. Its windows reached almost from floor to ceiling and were framed by lacy white curtains, thin and translucent. They were tied back, letting in the strange light of midsummer's eve.

Moriarty was moving about the dining room, touching this and that as though things needed straightening, clearly looking for reasons to stay.

A woman in her mid-thirties entered the room with a determined air, and bearing a steamy tureen. A smile lit up her face as she set it on the table.

"Smells delicious," Capper said, as the woman ladled out the chunky potato soup.

"There you are," she said. "It's one of me favorites." Her girth suggested she had no shortage of favorites. "Make it meself, I do," she added proudly.

"Mmm," Ivy said. "Tastes good! What's in it?"

The woman smiled broadly at being asked. "Well, potatoes, of course, that we grow in our garden. And I use light cream and butter, and those are crumbles of Irish bacon, and I just now added in some bits of fresh parsley there, floatin' on top."

"Food's an important part of our festival," Moriarty said. "We have cookin' contests," he added with a sly smirk at the serving woman.

She giggled and blushed like a girl, then turned and fled the room as though unable to bear what Moriarty might say next.

"That's our own Jillian O'Shay," Moriarty said in a conspiratorial voice. "A bit of a sleeveen, I'm after sayin'."

"Sleeveen?" Capper asked.

"Do ye not know what is a sleeveen, then?"

Ivy and Capper shook their heads.

"Why, it means she's a sly type. Pinch the eyes out of yer face, as some would say. But not I. That's a bit much, I say. But a sleeveen she is, nonetheless."

He pulled up a chair, sat down, and leaned toward his two guests as they looked at one another with a quick grin of amusement.

"Let me tell ye what she's done, then, has our Miss Jillian."

"I thought I saw a wedding band," Ivy said.

Moriarty adjusted himself on the chair, rocking from one cheek to the other for a moment. His excitement was visibly mounting. He said in just above a whisper, "Aye, ye did! She be married, right enough. That's *part* of it!"

He went on tiptoes to the door and peeked around the corner. He came back to his chair, his eyes wide as he continued just above a whisper, "At the festival each year, we have a bake-off, ye see. Irish cakes."

"I'm looking forward to that," Ivy said.

"Aye, lass, so are we all. So are we all." He seemed a tiny bit annoyed by the interruption. "Well, let me tell ye, then, every year now for five years the cake bake-off has been won by Maggie Maguire's Black & White Plum Cake. But Maggie'll not be winnin' it this year," he said with a wag of his finger and a smug smile. He sat back in his chair and grinned like a man with a secret.

He leaned forward again and whispered. "This year, I'm after thinkin', it'll be our own Jillian O'Shay's Irish Chocolate Cake what's goin' to win, then."

"How can you be so sure?" Capper wanted to know.

"Ah, well now. They might as well not be havin' the bake-off contest *at all!* Just bring the prize here to our Jillian O'Shay and *forget* about it." He made a sage nod and grinned.

"And why would that be, now?" Ivy said. Capper wondered how she could suddenly be talking with a perfect brogue.

Moriarty replied, "Well, ye might say it's her secret ingredient." He pulled a big red handkerchief from his pants pocket and took off his glasses to polish them. Moriarty was playing for suspense. With a nod toward the door, he leaned forward in his chair and stage-whispered, "Jillian's been seein' Will O'Shaughnesy, the bake-off judge!" He nodded to confirm his own words and replaced the glasses and the red handkerchief.

"Seeing him?" Ivy said.

"In the biblical sense."

"Oh," Ivy said and glanced at Capper. Both were determined not to smile.

"Been goin' on a long time, has it?" Ivy asked. Capper noted she'd gone totally Irish; lilt perfect.

"Months."

"Big secret?" Capper asked.

"To just about no one but Jillian's husband and Will's wife. And Maggie Maguire, of course," Moriarty said with another sage nod. "Whole town talks about it."

Ivy couldn't suppress a giggle. "What if Will's wife finds out?"

"Word is, she'll kill our Jillian."

Ivy leaned way forward and with a guttural rasp she said, "Ye don't mean it!" Capper could have sworn she'd lived her whole life in Ireland.

"Aye, but I do. Hot tempered, is Will's wife. Whole town's keepin' it a secret. Even Father Flaherty."

"The priest?" Capper said.

"Aye. Afraid of a killin', he is." He glanced at his guests with a frown. "I'm sure Father's tried to make her stop, as I have meself. But it's no good. She's got her mind made up to win that bake-off."

THEY FOUND THE BEDCLOTHES turned down and a mint on each of their pillows. In a slender bud vase on the bedside table stood two delicate red roses.

Ivy managed to struggle out of her clothes, and the moment she laid her head on Capper's shoulder, she was asleep. Capper, though blitzed-tired, couldn't sleep right away. The gentle scent, sound, and feel of the woman lying in his arms was disturbing. He expected love to bring its benefits: good sex, companionship, sharing ideas, making plans. But he didn't bargain for a love that involved parts of his soul he hadn't even known he possessed; didn't expect this kind of thing to ever become part of his life. He'd read about ideal love, of course, and halfway believed in it, but. . . . Finally, he drifted off on dreams of wonder.

MORNING FOUND CAPPER AND Ivy back in the small dining room for breakfast, seated at a table by the window where they could see the ocean across the road. Last night's eerie whiteness was replaced with bright sunlight, and the room was lively with the merry laughter and chatter of guests becoming acquainted and the gentle tinkle of tableware.

"Look at that, Capper!" Ivy whispered. The wind was whipping off flecks of white foam from the incoming waves and flinging them against the huge black rocks that made up the beach. "It's like we're on another planet!"

On the other side of the dining room, the windows gave onto the inn's bountiful flower and herb gardens. These were bordered by trees at the edge of the forest that lay beyond. The dining room furniture was dark and heavy. Against one wall, a black walnut low-boy stood piled with fresh-cut flowers of yellow and purple. On it, amidst the flowers, was the hotel's pride and joy: a set of two silver candelabras and a large bowl of Waterford crystal. The candelabras supported a family of slender white tapers that were lighted just long enough to blacken the wick tips. The bowl was heaped high with fresh pears and oranges. A little paper sign said *Take One*. The room's five tables, each seating six, were round and covered with Ireland's own famous linen, heavy and white. It seemed to shimmer a soft gold in the morning sun. Set for breakfast, the tables were laid with bright white china edged in a lace pattern, gleaming table-ware, and polished crystal sprouting crisp fan-folded green napkins. Everything looked like it just came out of its packing for the first time.

Ivy wasn't very hungry and ordered just Irish coffee and scones, a biscuit-like pastry. Capper tucked into a traditional Irish break-fast, much like the ones he knew at home: bacon, sausage, eggs, pan-fried potato with toasted brown bread, and coffee.

Before long, the dining room filled. Guests were chatty, and some seemed in a jovial summer mood. At the table with Mr. and Mrs. Harris were two other couples. One was middle-aged, from Ohio, on their second honeymoon. The other was a couple from Germany. The German woman said they were in Glenarm to attend her uncle's funeral. It was being postponed, she was careful to explain, until the day after the Solstice Festival. The second-honeymoon couple, though they tried to conceal it, looked unhappy with one another. Apparently, the husband didn't share his wife's interest in Ireland, and he was missing some important college sports on TV back home in the States—which he wouldn't be missing, he explained, if they'd gone to Niagara Falls like he wanted. The German/Irish couple, though, laughed and joked throughout breakfast and seemed to be having a happy time on their sad occasion.

SHORTLY AFTER TEN THAT morning, the festival got started in earnest on the village green. In little tents scattered along the entire length of the midway, hungry visitors could buy bangers in a bun with onions, or on a stick. There were also scones, Irish stew in bread bowls, Irish soda bread, Shamrock shortbread, and chips—better known as french fries on the other side of the Atlantic.

This year, for the first time, in response to a vigorous and revolutionary demand by senior high school students, there was also American-style pizza for sale. Pizza Hut had come up to Ireland from London with a full kitchen—at considerable expense. All day long, they did a brisk business in pizza slices, with all proceeds going to the Starlight Foundation for kids with serious illnesses.

And there were soft drinks and water and a nonalcoholic ale for the kids. For the adults, there were several other ales: pale, nut brown, red, and another beverage called oatmeal stout.

For festival-goers with more sophisticated food tastes, there was a gourmet kitchen with covered seating where one could buy a complete meal that started with chicken liver paté laced with Bushmills Irish Whiskey, followed by a cream of parsnip soup, then a garlic roast sirloin of beef with butter sauce and ending on a sweet note with Irish mist souffle, apple cake with custard and a locally made vanilla ice cream.

In one corner of the green, along Main Street, tables were set up for the bake-off, scheduled to begin at 11:00 a.m.. Not far from those tables was an elevated stage, and toward its rear was a set of bleachers for the high school's symphony orchestra. High up behind the bleachers was a long banner proclaiming this to be The One Hundred and Fifty-eighth Consecutive Annual Glenarm Summer Solstice Festival. Down near the front of the stage was a line of twelve folding chairs, and, at the center of that line, a speaker's podium (very old) with a built-in audio system that, as often as not, failed to work.

The high school athletics and music director, Tommy Devine, was supposed to have bought a new podium (with audio) two years ago. He insisted, though, that the old one was just fine, and not used often enough to warrant replacement. Besides, he declared, every bit of his budget was needed for the new band uniforms, toward which Tommy had saved for five years. This was the year, finally, when the new uniforms were bought. The *Irish Times* newspaper had attended a full-dress rehearsal and reported the uniforms to be beautiful. Today the town would judge for itself. Tommy'd made a bags of purchasing football uniforms eight years earlier, got it banjaxed beyond all help, ordering the wrong sizes in the wrong quantities, and some townspeople were expecting to see the band come out in uniforms they were either busting out of or dragging on the ground. Truth was, a few of the good old boys, bold as barn owls they were, hoped he'd made a hames of it again, just so they'd have something new to slag old Tommy with.

The day's musical program included the Glenarm School of Irish Dance, Irish tales told by local story tellers of considerable repute, and a madrigal group from the high school singing old Celtic songs and lively Irish ballads in four-part harmony. There was also a talented group of senior-citizens called The Blarney Stone who played Irish tunes on the Celtic harp, uillean pipes (Irish bagpipes, mellower than the Scottish), tin whistle, the bouzouki (a Greek eight-stringed instrument resembling a mandolin), the fiddle, a guitar, and a bodhrán, which is a small Celtic drum.

The games of the festival covered a broad range of sports and contests. There was soccer, of course, with matches going on all day and into the night, and traditional games known in much of the world, such as three-legged sack races, tug of war, free the prisoner, red rover, and snatch the bacon. In snatch the bacon, two teams would line up facing one another with the bacon (a bunch of rags tied together) on the ground between the two lines. One member from each team would run up and try to snatch the bacon without being touched by the member of the opposing team. A lot of sharp slaps on the back and skinned knees occurred during snatch the bacon, and unless there were at least two beefy adult peacekeepers on hand the game could degenerate into outright warfare with all the members of both teams in one fist-swinging pig-pile.

There were many kite contests going on all day. There were parents and little children flying them together, some children flying them alone and in teams, some dancing their kites to music, some making their kites do acrobatics, others seeking altitude, and some just testing out new shapes.

One young boy was flying a simple diamond kite when it got caught in the branches of a tree. Ivy was standing nearby when it happened, and she offered to help get it down.

"I could climb up and get it," the boy said, "but our teacher told us never to climb up a tree to get a kite." The boy thought this injunction against kite rescue to be strange since he was always climbing trees for other important reasons of all kinds.

"Your teacher is right," Ivy said as she tugged on the line gently from various angles in an attempt to coax the kite down. "Kites get caught on weak little branches that wouldn't support you. You'd fall. Might get a broken leg."

Capper walked over to join the rescue effort. "Let's see if we can't get another line up to the kite, then we can tug it in two directions at once," he said.

"How you gonna do that?" the boy wanted to know. He was thinking maybe adults were permitted to climb trees to rescue kites.

"I'll show you," Capper said.

He emptied his key ring and tied a length of kite line to it. He slipped the key ring over the line that went up to the kite. Next, he told the boy to walk a good distance away, so that his kite line created a shallow angle to the earth. By tugging on his line, Capper coaxed the key ring up the boy's line, almost to the kite.

"Now watch my hand. When you see me tug, you tug. We take turns. Not too hard."

The boy understood, and after only two tugs from each direction the kite sailed out of the tree and came to rest on the ground as the excited boy ran shouting to retrieve it.

"Well done!" A man's voice came from behind Capper and Ivy.

Capper turned and smiled at the man. "I wasn't sure it would work."

The boy returned with his kite as the man extended his hand. "I'm Omar Jabri. This is my son Shafi."

Capper darted a quick glance at Ivy, and extended his hand as he said, "Name's Capper Harris. My wife Ivy."

"Pleased to meet you," Ivy said. "And Shafi the kite flyer," she added as she tousled the boy's hair while he stood looking up at his two new friends with a big smile.

Ivy extended her hand to Omar. He pressed it almost imperceptibly in his for a moment and said to them both, "You're American. What brings you to Ireland?"

"My dad was born here. Dad promised to show me his Ireland, but he died before he could. This is my first time here," Ivy said.

"Well, our Kathleen will have to show you two around, then," Omar said in his best imitation of an Irish accent, which he knew was comical.

"I'm sure we'd like that," Ivy said.

"Partly, we're here on vacation," Capper said. "Might be looking for investments, too."

Omar laughed and shook his head. "Investments. Americans start everything young." It reminded him that he was younger than these two when he commanded a gang of pirates in the Orient. "Ah! Here comes our Kathleen now, with Michael in tow."

The two couples and the boys walked together along the midway, and, as they talked, there was something about these two Americans Omar found almost magnetic. He wasn't a particularly social person and this young couple's attraction surprised him. He was sufficiently intrigued that, after clearing it first with Kathleen, he invited them home for dinner. Ivy, seeing a good opportunity to practice a bit of tradecraft, pretended she wasn't sure they should accept; after all, they had just met, and this might be an imposition on the family.

"Nonsense," Omar said. "If it were any imposition we wouldn't have invited you."

So it was agreed.

As the couples wandered among the displays of arts and crafts, Shafi and Michael begged to go off and play.

"Yes," Kathleen said after getting a nod from Omar. "But meet us at the main stage in an hour."

The boys agreed to be faithful about the time and ran off to find other kids to play with.

Soon they were in a game of four-way Frisbee with two other boys who were a bit older. Andy, the boy who owned the Frisbee, wanted to practice his Australian Boomerang Shot. The Frisbee glides up beyond the receiver, turns around, and comes down into his hands. Shafi agreed to be the receiver. It was a beautiful shot when it worked.

On one try, the Frisbee went way beyond Shafi, and came down the wrong way. He took off after it, running down the hill and into some tall bushes. The other boys didn't see which way Shafi went. "It went that way," Andy called out, pointing in the wrong direction near the roadside.

"Come on! Let's go find 'im!" yelled Andy. He didn't want that goddamn Arab kid to steal his Frisbee.

Shafi kept searching. He was getting close to some park benches on the other side of the bushes.

"No, we can't be after invitin' Kathleen O'Toole to no Christian weddin'," one lady was saying to another. Shafi perked up his ears when he heard his mother's name.

"And why not, I'd be askin'?" the second lady said.

"Ye haven't seen what she's got shacked up with her, then?"

"No! Some bleedin' jackeen, then, is it?"

"Hmm. Would that it were! Much worse, I'm after sayin'!"

"Oooh, isn't she the brasser, then! Tell!"

"It's an Arab, or I'm damned!"

"No! Right here in Glenarm, then?"

"Aye, it is. And those two children of hers she's always makin' a holy show of. They're his! And them not married, and all."

"Oooh, and wasn't I sayin' to Mary Cochran, and wasn't it just yesterday, that one of Kathleen O'Toole's boys looks like a bleedin'

Indian or somethin'. But I never dreamed the child was a bastard. I thought she was widowed or somethin'. What with 'er bein' off all over the world all the time, I thought she'd married somewhere else, in some foreign place, ye know, and then got widowed, all respectable like."

"Widowed me arse! She's in the bloody scratcher with a filthy Arab! Both of them boys is bleedin' bastards, or I'm damned! And him a comin' and a goin' right here in our town, and all!"

"Well, I never! And what's the likes o' him doin' in a Christian community the likes o' this in the first place, I'm after askin'? He'll be struttin' up and down the bleedin' town like a right gov'ner, and all the while him bein' a right old hoor, I'm thinkin'."

"He can strut and fooster about all he's a mind to. He'll never get inside this polite society, now I'm tellin' ye. Some might seem to take a likin' to the man, or to his two bastards, but it's only 'cause the gob's got a bit o' money, as I'm told. And that's the long and short of it!"

"Got a bit o' money, then, has he?"

"Oh, aye. He's into shippin', and all. Why else would a good Irish lass be after shackin' up with an Arab?"

Shafi was confused. *Why do people hate us?* He was angry and hurt, and tried not to cry. He spotted the Frisbee half hidden under some leaves and picked it up. Shafi felt a great weight in his chest. He just wanted to find his brother and go home.

The kids grew tired of searching in the roadside bushes. Andy was certain the Arab kid had run off with his Frisbee. He was angry and wanted to punish.

"Here, then!" he said, grabbing Michael by the front of his shirt. "You was with that bleedin' Arab, now wasn't you, then?"

"What?" Michael said, confused and unable to believe his ears.

Michael didn't see that one of the other kids got on his hands and knees behind him.

"Here, now," Andy said, "don't play the eejit with me!" and gave Michael a shove.

Michael sailed over the boy behind him and landed flat on his back. The boys started laughing. Andy was standing over him, hands on hips.

"Now, I'll be askin' ye one more time, ye right gobdaw! Where's that feckin' Arab ye brought 'round here? Where's he gone with my merchandise, then?" Andy hauled back and kicked Michael in the ribs, hard, as he yelled, "I want it back, see?"

Michael curled up in pain. He couldn't get a breath.

One of the other kids now became concerned. This looked like it was going to turn into a serious beating. He said to Andy, "Aw, come on, then. Lets get away from this bloody header." He put his arm around Andy's shoulders and pulled him away.

Michael finally was able to suck in a breath.

"All Arabs is feckin' thieves, they is! And ye're one too, if ye hang with 'em!" Andy yelled over his shoulder as the boys moved away.

A few moments later Shafi saw Michael lying near the street. He could see his brother was in pain. What could have happened? Was he hit by a car? Shafi came running and slid to his knees on the grass by his brother.

"What happened?"

"Andy. He pushed me down. Kicked me. I can't get up," Michael muttered between clenched teeth.

"Bloody hell!" Shafi said. He looked up and saw a man walking nearby. "Hey, mister! Help us here!"

The man walked over quickly. "Here, then, what have we here?"

"My brother's hurt," Shafi said.

"A kid pushed me down. Kicked me," Michael said.

"I'm a doctor. May I look at your injury, son?"

Michael nodded.

"All right, then. Let's just have you stretch out flat and straight, if you can. There's a good lad," the doctor said.

"I gotta go get my parents," Shafi said.

"Yes, you do that. Is it far away they are?" the doctor said.

"No. They're over at the main stage. I'll go get 'em."

When Shafi told his parents Michael got in a fight and was hurt, Kathleen felt her heart freeze. As often as she'd seen combat, seen the blood of others run free, this was the first time someone had hurt one of her children.

By the time Shafi and the adults got there, the doctor had finished his exam and was helping Michael to his feet.

Kathleen got down on one knee and wrapped her arms around her son, making the clucking and soothing sounds mothers everywhere make.

"I don't think there's any serious injury, Mr. Jabri," the doctor said after quick introductions.

"He's going to have some sore ribs for a while, but it's nothing, really, though I'm sure it hurts a lot. Give him some children's aspirin, not more than four in a day. But mostly, he's just got the wind knocked out of him and got plenty scared, too, right enough."

"You don't think I should have it x-rayed at the hospital?" Omar asked.

"You could. But I've checked him pretty carefully. Broken bones are my specialty." He fished a business card out of his shirt pocket and handed it to Omar. It identified the man as Douglas Lockwood, M.D.

"My advice to anyone is, stay out of hospitals. They're dangerous places," Dr. Lockwood said, looking over his half-rim glasses at Omar.

"Thank you, Doctor. I'll send you a check," Omar said.

"And I'll send it right back. There's never a charge for Good Samaritan work. The Bible forbids it. So don't make me waste a postage stamp returning your check," he said with a wink.

Kathleen wasn't sure the Bible did forbid the Good Samaritan from being paid for his kindness. She suspected the doctor's reluctance to being paid might have more to do with a proscription from the insurance company. But she wouldn't challenge the doctor. Besides, it was many years since she'd read her own Bible and didn't trust her memory on anything much beyond I-am-the-Lord-thy-God.

"Maybe we shouldn't impose on you this evening, what with Michael being hurt," Ivy said to Kathleen. This time it wasn't tradecraft.

Michael took hold of Ivy's wrist and in a plaintive voice said, "Please come. I want you to."

"We might be in the way," Ivy said.

"Nonsense!" Omar said. "You're not going to disappoint the boy, now are you? Michael's fine! We'll expect you for dinner at 6:30. Will that be all right?"

"Yes, of course," Capper said. "We're looking forward to it."

As the little family walked home, Shafi explained about the Australian Boomerang Shot, and about finding Michael by the side of the road.

Michael said the boy who kicked him called Shafi a bleeding Arab. Shafi repeated what the two ladies in the lawn chairs said. Kathleen was indifferent to the comments of the women, but she vowed to find the boy who'd kicked her son and have a talk with his mother.

Omar was tired of this small-minded town and all its prejudices. At the right time, he'd talk to Kathleen.

MICHAEL WAS RESTING IN bed with an ice pack on his ribs and Omar was reading the newspaper in his favorite chair. He said to Kathleen, "I rather like that Capper. Nice chap. Aggressive, too. Reminds me of myself fifteen years ago."

Kathleen laughed and said, "Well I'd a damned sight rather you take a fancy to him than to her!"

"I never said I didn't take a fancy to her, too," Omar said with a grin and ducked to avoid the small sofa pillow that went sailing over his head.

"Just wait until I practice my Australian Boomerang Shot!" Kathleen said. "See if you can duck that one!"

Omar laughed again, and Kathleen came to sit on his lap. She swung one leg over to straddle Omar and bent to kiss him. She knew Michael and Shafi were both taking a nap. Dinner wasn't going to need much preparation time.

THE LITTLE SOIREE went well for everyone. Michael was up but moving a bit stiffly. The Frisbee and the kite rested in one corner of the living room. The kite was not in quarantine, but Kathleen made it plain that the Frisbee was. If she could discover Andy's last name, she intended to deliver the toy to the boy's mother with a few choice words.

After dinner, Kathleen and Ivy accepted a challenge from Shafi and Michael to a game of Monopoly. Omar and Capper went out in the back yard to nurse a fresh bottle of Bushmills and admire the color of the long day's night. The conversation turned to the comments the boys picked up that day. Omar remarked he had no problem being mistaken for an Arab, though he wasn't one; it was the disparagement that went with it he objected to.

"Where are you from?" Capper asked.

Omar explained that his ancestors, going way back, were from Persia and his most recent ancestors were from the island of Jabrin off the coast of Iran in the Persian Gulf.

"Your people still live there?"

"No. I have no people, now. My family was slaughtered by the Shah when he stole our island. I am the only survivor."

"Sorry to hear it."

A look of angry determination clouded Omar's face as he said, "Someday, though, I plan to reclaim our family's island. Take it back. My home will once again be on the island of Jabrin."

"Jabrin. That sounds like Jabri," Capper said.

"Yes. The island was named by my people after the king gave it to them," Omar said.

"How do you plan to get it back?"

For a long time Omar did not reply. Finally, in a low voice, he said, "Any damn way I can."

Capper saw the tension. "Can you go back to visit if you want to?"

"There's a price on my head in Iran." Omar replied.

"Isn't Iran an Arab country?" Capper asked.

"No. Many people think it is, but it's not. It's Persian. Iran was part of the Persian empire and has a different language and cultural history than the Arab countries. My people spoke mostly Persian, which is also called Farsi. But not Arabic."

"Are you Iranian, then?" Capper said.

"No!" Omar's voice was harsh and his eyes flashed with anger.

"I'm not Iranian. I'm Jabrinian. Behind that, I'm Persian."

Capper thought it best to get slightly off center of that subject. "And where did the Persians come from?"

"This interests you?" Omar asked.

"Very much so," Capper said with a vague wave of his hand. "Some day I'm going back to school and study history. I never did study it the last time around."

"What did you study?"

"Civil engineering," Capper said, true enough because that was his minor at Annapolis, but before Omar could ask him what school he'd attended, Capper turned the subject back to origins.

"So, tell me, where'd the Persians come from?" Capper asked.

"They were Indo-European from central Asia. They came into Persia in the second millennium before Christ," Omar said.

"And who were the Indo-Europeans?" Capper asked. "Where did they come from?"

"Well, they come from a group called the Aryans who spoke a language similar to ancient Sanskrit. According to the Christian bible, if you go back far enough, we come from Shem, son of Moses. We are all, supposedly, the sons of Abraham. Jews, Christians, and Muslims. All brothers. All from the same father: Abraham."

The evening wound down, and so did the Bushmills.

The girls beat the boys at Monopoly. Shafi suspected his mother cheated. He wasn't sure how. Kathleen insisted she didn't cheat, but she laughed enough about it to appear suspicious.

Later that night, back at the hotel, as Capper and Ivy were preparing for bed, Capper said, "Mission accomplished. I found out something that might be useful to Hardale. Omar's got a price on his head in Iran."

"Really?" Ivy said, a look of shock on her face. "What did he do?"

"Nothing. It's what somebody is afraid he might do. The government wants him dead." Capper was about to fill in the details when Ivy interrupted him.

"Sometimes I wish we weren't involved in this sort of stuff." She kicked off her shoes. "Damn all governments, anyway! Kathleen and Omar are nice people."

"Yeah, but don't you want to know why he's got a price on his head?"

"I suppose so," Ivy said with a sigh of sadness. "But not now. I just feel bad that we've deceived them. They think we're their friends."

"Well, we are, aren't we?"

"Yeah. Friends with an agenda. Excuse me, Kathleen and Omar, but we made friends with you because the NSA told us to."

Capper put his hands on Ivy's shoulders. "We're still their friends."

"Yes, I know. It just feels funny, though. And they're great parents. You can tell just by watching how Michael and Shafi behave."

"Yeah, those are nice kids."

"They sure took a liking to you," Ivy said, searching Capper's face.

He said nothing. She took him in her arms.

"What is it about you? You attract kids like a magnet."

"Just call me the Pied Piper," Capper said with a big grin.

He changed the subject. "Yeah, Omar's all right. But I'm not so sure about Kathleen." He tossed his jeans over a chair. The Bushmills was starting to pound at the back of his head, just above the neck.

"What do you mean?" Ivy said. "I like Kathleen." She tossed her jeans on top of his.

"A mother who'll cheat on her own kids at Monopoly?" Capper

said, as he dropped his shorts. "The way she was laughing, I'll bet she did cheat, like Shafi said."

"Oh, you goose!" Ivy said and slapped Capper on the butt. She pulled off her shirt and slipped her arms around Capper. "She cheated, all right. But not to beat them. She cheated to try and help the kids win. I saw her do it several times. She just didn't do it enough. She couldn't do anything to hurt those boys. She'd give her life for them. So would he. I can tell; they're nice people."

"Mmm. So are you," Capper said as he undid Ivy's bra and kissed her shoulders and neck. That sent shivers down her spine. Her mouth sought out his, and Capper forgot about his headache.

At Kathleen and Omar's residence the remainder of the evening wasn't going so well. It was an old subject, an old argument.

"I'm fed up," Omar said. "Small-minded people. I'm sorry. You don't want to hear it, but it's true. Here in Glenarm. All of Ireland. Full of prejudice. I want the boys out of here. Out of the country."

Kathleen put her arms around Omar. Gently she said, "Omar, the boys have two identities. Yours and mine. Jabrinian and Irish. Just by living with you, anywhere, they'll grow up Jabrinian. But to grow up Irish, they have to live in Ireland. At least part of the time. And would you separate them from Tom and Peg?"

Omar sighed. "I'm sorry, Kathleen. It won't work. There's just too damn much prejudice here against Middle Eastern peoples. And that's something Tom and Peg can't protect them from. Nobody can. After what happened today at the festival, I should think you'd agree. The boys have got to be out of Ireland. Now."

Their conversation became stiff, polite, the stuff of détente. Neither wanted to be the one to yield, to be the first to break through the awkwardness, yet both were hating every moment of this trench warfare.

"You know, this isn't something of our making," Omar said, finally in a low and quiet voice.

"Beg pardon?" Kathleen said in a vague and airy manner.

When she was feeling pressured by Omar, she didn't understand much that he said. Omar often had to repeat things. He knew the game, had slogged through it with her many times, was weary of it.

He sighed. "I'd like to leave in the morning for Florenza. With the boys."

Omar had said he'd stay in Glenarm for two weeks at festival time because the boys enjoyed it and because Kathleen needed a few days for IRA business in Glenarm. Afterward, the family would go to Florenza together. Now it was all changing at the last minute, and Kathleen didn't like that one bit.

"Will you stop in London?" she asked.

"Maybe for a day or two."

"You know I can't leave right away," Kathleen said. It was almost like an accusation, but low key, with no heat in it. "It will be a few days before I can leave."

"Fine. That will give me time to put the house in order," he said. This was a thin recourse, and they both knew it. Omar wasn't the housekeeping type, and besides, the house in Florenza was always in tip-top shape. His staff saw to it with pride. Omar changed those peoples' lives, made them the best-paid campesinos on the entire Costa del Azahar, and they took care of him and his hacienda as though both were holy.

Not much more was said that evening. Whatever words did pass between them were like a fish talking to a bird. At the level below words, though, communication continued rich and full, as always. This quarrel about where they should live, where their boys should grow up, didn't alter their deep love for one another. This was why, perhaps, when Kathleen lay with her back to Omar and as far over on her side of the bed as she could get without falling off, and while Omar did the same on his side, she shed some quiet tears before falling asleep.

WHEN OMAR ARRIVED IN London with the boys to enroll them in school, the academic year was not scheduled to begin for another two weeks, but enrollment was in progress everywhere.

"Why are you putting us in a school here, Da?" Michael asked his father as they stepped out of the taxi at the first school on Omar's list.

"Because in London there are people from everywhere," Omar replied.

"Ireland has people. Spain has people," Shafi said.

"Ireland has almost only Irish people. Spain has almost only Spanish people," Omar explained. "But London has a lot of people who come from Africa, from the Middle East, from China and Japan."

"So?" Shafi wanted to know.

Omar squatted to be eye to eye with his boys. "Shafi, you remember what you told me, about how some people hate us because of our looks, and they even hate Michael when they know we're his family?"

Shafi glanced nervously at his brother for a moment and then nodded a reply to his father.

"And it hurt you, didn't it?" Omar said gently.

Shafi nodded again.

"Well," he said, wrapping an arm around each of his sons. "I don't like it when people hurt my boys."

"Nobody's gonna hurt us here?" Michael asked.

Omar sighed. "That kind of hurt could happen to you anywhere. But here in London, because there are so many different kinds of people from all over the world, I think it may not happen to you so much. Anyway, that's what I'm hoping. That's why I'm placing you in school here."

Shafi looked like he might cry. "But we're never gonna see you and ma!" he complained.

"Of course, you will!" Omar said. "Do you think we could live without seeing you?"

"Because you and ma are going to live all the time in your house here in London, right?" Michael said hopefully.

"No, not all the time," Omar replied. "Part of the time we'll be here, and part of the time in Florenza, and part of the time in Glenarm."

Now Michael looked as though he might cry. "Then Shafi's right. We never will see you no more. Or almost never."

"Not true," Omar said. "We'll be together every weekend except for the time me or your ma has to travel. You'll be with one of us, see?"

"But how about if you and ma are gone at the same time?" the boys chorused.

"I've made arrangements. On Friday afternoon, a car will be here for you as soon as school lets out for the day. Then you'll be on a plane to stay with grandpa and gramma."

"And if you're in Florenza or Glenarm?" Shafi asked.

"I know!" Michael said. "You'll come and get us in your helicopter!"

"Right. Or, if I'm off on a business trip, the car will take you to the airport where you will get on a plane. You'll see, we're going to be together on a lot of weekends."

"Well, okay, then," Michael said. "I guess that's all right."

Shafi shrugged and said, "I guess." But there was little conviction in it.

The first school Omar and the boys visited in London didn't have primary grades; the second one did, but Omar didn't like the neighborhood. The third was the one Omar chose. Called Brimbury Academy, it was a small, secular boarding school located in a good neighborhood, rather well thought of but somewhat impoverished.

A small amount of prejudice would only toughen his sons and inure them to the world they would have to live in as adults. But Omar wanted the prejudice controlled, kept to a minimum. He hoped his money could buy this for Shafi and Michael at Brimbury.

"YES, THE INFORMATION YOU picked up on O'Toole and Jabri is potentially useful. Good job," Hardale said. He had phoned Capper and Ivy at their London flat, using a secure land line MI6 had installed in the apartment at the CIA's request.

"We have a new assignment for you. How would you like to make London your permanent duty station? Back to the States for holidays, vacations, family things. And we'd send you off on special assignments in other parts of the world. But you'd be mainly in London. How's that sound?"

"Sounds great!" Ivy said.

"Sure. We love it here," Capper added, speaking on the extension. "What will we be doing?"

"Your first responsibility will be to maintain a friendship with Kathleen O'Toole and Omar Jabri. We will approach them, eventually, to work with us, and we want you to continue developing a personal profile on these two.

"But your main task will be reconnaissance. We've asked MI5 to vet for us some reliable persons—both men and women—from the Middle East. Iran, Iraq, Saudi Arabia, that sort of place. Muslims, all of them. Through them, we're targeting mostly the mosques.

We're finding out that some of their clerics are the radicals who organize. We are looking for money laundering, explosives deals, attack plans, recruiting. Anything like that. We'd like the two of you to be handlers. We need a couple—a man and a woman—for this, because some Muslims are sensitive about gender. Ivy, you'll work with the females, Capper you'll work with the males. MI6 will provide each of you with a safe house for meetings."

"What are we to do, exactly?" Ivy asked.

"You'll ask your people—your eyes and your ears—to report back to you anything they learn about terrorist plans. If it's a plan to attack in Great Britain, we'll turn the information over to the Brits. If it's in our interest elsewhere in the world, including here at home, then we'll handle it ourselves, of course."

"That's pretty straightforward," Capper said. To Ivy on the extension he added, "You okay with that, hon?"

"Sure," she replied.

10

Florenza

Florenza. A town along Spain's Costa del Alzahar on the Mediterranean, Florenza gazes east toward Majorca beyond its horizon. It's a sleepy village, about thirty miles north of Valencia and a long way from the modern world. Visitors to Florenza either love it so much they don't want to leave, or they hate it and run. The townspeople prefer the visitors who hate it and run.

Florenza got its name from the wife of a Jew named Estory, born in that town before it had a name, circa 1282. As a young man, Estory was sent by his father to explore Palestine. While there, he fell in love with a beautiful girl whose name was Petra, which means flower in Hebraic. After Estory completed his work in Palestine, he returned with his bride to Spain and his birthplace. Petra changed her name to Flor, which means flower in Spanish. Flor was a midwife. The women of the town grew to love Flor because of her gentle ways, and eventually the town name became an extension of her own.

The color of Florenza is white. The sand is white, the buildings are white, the sky is white, even the sun is white. A high bank of heat stands, always, over sand or asphalt. The heat bank is visible, dense, and near. An oncoming car remains a shimmering blur until the moment it rushes past, and then it dissolves.

Florenza has a contingent of expatriates, most of them habitues of the El Palacio hotel bar. Many are political or criminal refugees, or ex-military from some small republic that has chased them out, but not all, and each has a unique story.

Some doze on their bar stools and, when startled, reach for a sidearm that isn't there anymore. Some never doze, but keep a sharp watch over their shoulder for whatever they believe will soon catch up with them. Some search for their elusive nirvana or their lost muse. Some merely want to hold on to a stolen dream or the memory of a lover who has died or run away.

Some need Florenza for only a few days, some for the rest of their lives.

One young couple, much in love, will be in Florenza for a long time or until their money or their love runs out because, back home in the small German town where everyone knows them, there cannot be a passionate sexual relationship between a brother and sister.

The general store, reminiscent of wild west America, is a daytime gathering place for the locals. It has no air conditioning. No air conditioning is to be found, either, in the ramshackle houses and lean-tos that make up almost all of the village. Most residences also lack electricity, running water, and indoor toilets.

Florenza's population: 276 persons, 68 cows, and 1,104 goats. There are seasonal fluctuations among the livestock because some are harvested for food. Fluctuation among the human population is negligible because the birth rate is low and only Father Time harvests these.

There are a few fishing boats rotting at seaside. Commercial fishing petered out here long ago because the big seining trawlers overfished the area to extinction. The locals still do fish from the shore for their table with rod and reel, but nobody catches much.

The average wage of the townspeople, not including the few who hold the precious jobs in the El Palacio, is around 17,000 Spanish pesetas, or about 120 U.S. dollars, per annum. The average is low because most do not hold a job. They live off the land, much of it too poor to grow anything but goats.

Before Omar built his home here and hired locals to keep it spotless, cleanliness in Florenza always bore its own unique character. For example, after every occupancy at the El Palacio the sheets that aren't too soiled get hung in the sunshine to be freshened. After every third occupancy the sheets get washed whether they need it or not.

The only thing Florenza has going for it is the pretty sea. The broad white sandy beach and the azure Mediterranean are exquisite. The north-south highway in and out of Florenza runs west of the village, so there is nothing between the town and the sea. There is a craggy and inhospitable cliff to the north of the town and another one like it to the south, which is one reason the place has never grown or attracted investors. There is not much room to expand.

There is another reason investors and new residents never build in Florenza, and this reason is the more important one: An ancient civic code enforced by the policía, who have too little to do, forbids homes be torn down and rebuilt. It also forbids the sale of land to anyone not born in the province. The law is a reaction against modernity and outsiders, so there isn't much anyone can do to change the fate of these people. An ingrained cultural bias against such things as fertilizer and engine-driven farming tools helps to steel Florenza's paralysis.

IN 1982, AN EXTREMELY WEALTHY pirate (also gunrunner, also sea-merchant) of only twenty-three came to Florenza from the East.

This young man, mature far beyond his years, took great pleasure in finding a simple way to get around the stupidity of the law and the cultural bias that keeps foreigners out of Florenza.

His name was Omar Al-Atash Jabri.

Omar wanted a vacation home overlooking the Mediterranean. He decided secluded Florenza was perfect. Because this coastal town faced Majorca beyond the east horizon, he knew intuitively it was the perfect place for his already-troubled soul to find peace.

To get around the problems of law and bias, Omar leased the land with "qualified right of survivorship in perpetuity." This made everybody happy.

Of course, the attorney he selected to draw up the paperwork also happened to be the province's presiding senior judge, Señor Alejandro Penelas. He was the current judge in a long family line that had occupied that position since the office was created, and chances were the Penelases would continue to occupy it until the end of time. Omar paid him well, but only for his legal services, of course.

Omar selected a plot of two hectares, almost five acres, on a high hill behind the north cliff, where the offshore breezes were best. Staying within the law, Omar didn't buy the land from the five campesinos living on it. He leased their land. Forever.

The peasants' houses were all situated on the outside perimeter of the acreage, as though around the rim of a rough circle, the center being a high but poor pasture with an abandoned barn in the middle of it. In the center of this circle, at the barn, is where Omar wanted his home.

Following the agreement in the lease, Omar renovated and modernized the land owners' houses, at no cost to them.

Again staying within the law, nothing was torn down. The original structures became lost in the corners and room angles of the renovations that engulfed them. Repairs to old dwellings were not forbidden by the law, and the repairs sort of swallowed up the old houses. Omar's barn disappeared the same way. Now living in new and beautiful homes, the land owners were delighted, of course.

Omar's leases also established that the landowners would always have work, if they wanted it, as Omar's groundskeepers, gardeners, maids, cooks, and housekeepers at a wage pinned to the average income for those occupations in Spain's three largest cities. This made the five campesino families of Florenza the top earners of the entire region, a status which made them happy and proud. This was evident by their swagger as they paraded before their less-fortunate neighbors going in and out of church on Sundays. (A few of these good folk hadn't seen the inside of the church since they were married or since the last family funeral.) A few became downright snobbish. They were country gentlefolk who no longer needed to struggle, as other villagers did, with the barren land.

Omar wasn't exactly a modern day Robin Hood. His largesse was not what might be called charity. It was enlightened self-interest.

11

Keeping A Good Reserve

1993

The flight in from London to Valencia International was brief; not tiring, she supposed, but she felt tired just the same. The private aircraft service manager at the airport escorted Kathleen to a shaded waiting area where Omar's helicopter was scheduled to land.

Of course, he was late.

Where is that man? she thought, tapping her foot with impatience. It made her think of the night they met on the beach north of Glenarm, and she smiled inwardly. Over the years, she realized, he hadn't become more punctual.

Drop it, Kathleen! You're not going to change the man at this point in the game, now are you? Do you love him or not? Yes, you do. Well all right, then. Give over!

Kathleen needed to be with her family now, even here at what felt like the opposite end of the world from Ireland. Although the hacienda was beautiful, she doubted Florenza could ever feel like home to her. She was glad, though, that there remained two weeks of summer—two weeks of family time. She watched as Omar settled his Hughes 500 down toward the tarmac.

He waved out the window and smiled at Kathleen. She smiled and waved back, admiring his deft hand on the controls. She didn't see the boys.

The helicopter made a smooth descent through the last twenty feet. It came to a soft-as-velvet touchdown that looked like it wouldn't crack an egg. He retarded the rotor speed as a service tech drove up in an ATV to position a small stairway beneath the chopper's door. The tech offered a hand to help Omar down the steps, but the hand was ignored.

"Where are the boys?" Kathleen asked after she kissed Omar.

"Camping. They joined the Boy Scouts of Spain and they're off on a camping trip."

"But, do we know these people? Is it safe?"

Omar laughed and picked up her bags. "They'd be a lot safer if I kept them locked in their room." He slid the bags into the Hughes's capacious hold and walked Kathleen around to her side of the craft.

"Omar, I'm concerned!" she said as he helped her into her seat.

He walked around to his side and got in. "Buckle up," he said as he put on his earphones. He increased the throttle. The compressor whined, and the rotor began to revolve.

He turned to her and smiled. "My dearest, we can't keep them shut away from life. The Boy Scout troop they've joined is old, there's a companion troop of Girl Scouts going with them, which means there are both male and female scout leaders there."

"But do we *know* them?" Kathleen insisted.

He reached over and put a hand on her knee. "Please don't worry. I did a lot of checking before I let them go. The scout leaders are policemen, clergy, businessmen, teachers. A mixed lot. That's safest. There's never been an incident of any kind that I know of. It's an active troop. Big public profile."

It was obvious from the expression on her face that Kathleen wasn't satisfied.

"Being with local kids will be good for them. They're both still upset about what happened in Glenarm. This will be a good experience. They'll meet new kids they can have fun with for a change."

"You make a good point. It's just that I was looking forward to seeing them," Kathleen said sadly.

"And you shall. They'll be home in a few days, and that will give us all time together. Also, parents are expected to drop in at the camp grounds any time, unannounced. I kind of figured we could go up tomorrow if you want to. Make a day of it. How's that?"

Kathleen looked long at Omar. *Sometimes I get angry with him. But he does right by us. Brimbury. He was right to enroll the boys there. I've got to stop needing to have everything my way. My boys have a father who cares.* She smiled at Omar.

"I'll enjoy that visit tomorrow," she said. "And, Omar . . ."

"Mmm?"

"Thank you."

"For what?"

She said with a smile, "Just for being a good man."

Am I ever going to figure this woman out? he asked himself.

He took a northeasterly course along the shore. The sea was calm today, not a wave in sight. Brilliant teal under a sunny sky, it gleamed and shimmered as a breeze ruffled the surface. "Let's go up higher and look around," Kathleen said. "It's so beautiful."

"Sure," Omar said with a smile. He checked his fuel gauge. They had two hours' worth.

Omar cruised in a big lazy circle, climbing slowly above the rolling countryside at the edge of the Mediterranean. As they climbed, and as the white beach shrank far below, Kathleen imagined the sea had painted for itself a thin white line of demarcation called beach.

Everything on my side of the line belongs to me, the sea told the land, *and everything on the other side is yours.* She wondered who had more to keep or lose, the sea or the land. The question seemed personally threatening, somehow, made her brow furrow, and she didn't know why.

Kathleen looked for distraction. She smiled with pleasure at seeing the brown and green landscape unfold beneath her, with twisty rural roads meandering off in all directions. Most of the solitary homes she saw were small, appeared well kept, and nearly always had an orderly patch of something growing alongside. A few homes also had a child or two playing nearby, lines of laundry drying in the ever-blazing sun, the occasional man walking slowly behind his horse-drawn plow, here and there a few goats, or a couple of cows. Quiet dogs.

Kathleen pointed down at a farmer plowing his field and asked, "What do you suppose he's planting at this time of year? It's late."

"Don't know," was Omar's reply. "Alfalfa, maybe. Or field corn. Some winter crop for animals." After a pause he added with a smile, "I guess I know more about navigating the sea than cultivating the land."

There's that contrast again, Kathleen thought as the furrow returned to her brow: *the sea and the land.*

Omar saw it. "Something wrong?"

She shook her head in reply and went back to studying the landscape. There were abrupt little hills everywhere, steep bumps not much higher than a person stands, dotting the earth meaninglessly. Many had lost a side or two to erosion, revealing a reddish interior—like a gaping wound that would never heal. Here and there stood one that had been stripped of all its sides, and now brooded, alone, like a wounded and solitary sentry, while its stubborn head continued to maintain its long green tuft of wild grass, its only enduring identity. As the helicopter passed one of the naked hills, Kathleen turned abruptly in her seat, with a sense of wanting to help, to heal. It was fast receding in the rear when her mind called out to it, hopefully, *It's going to be all right!* The instant the thought was formed, Kathleen saddened, fearing it wasn't true.

Wild trees were not plentiful, most of them old and gnarled, nearly useless to man except as fuel, the good ones having been harvested long ago as building material and never replaced. There was an abundance of huge citrus and olive groves, though, all owned by corporations abroad, and for a few moments Kathleen made a mental game of pretending she could tell what kind of fruit each grove bore. Soon the game paled.

"Look!" Omar said, pointing upward.

"Oh, my! Beautiful!" Kathleen said, as she watched a flock of some twenty geese flying in perfect formation, north along the sea at an altitude higher than their craft. "Out of Africa?" she asked.

"Probably. Though it's far too late to be going home for the summer," Omar replied.

"Yes, they're late," Kathleen said. "They should have started home long ago," she said sadly. Omar looked at her intently for a brief moment and then turned his eyes away to check his instruments.

"We'd probably better go in. Still have plenty of fuel, but don't want to run past a good reserve," Omar said, and put his helicopter on a southerly course, high above the white line of demarcation.

"Yes," Kathleen sighed. "Must always . . . keep a good reserve."

Soon the town of Florenza glided into view beneath them. Omar telephoned the house that he was landing. Kathleen thought the call made the flight official, made it real, putting an end to her growing fantasy that as soon as the craft touched down, all that she had seen and thought would become only chimera, a dream that had never happened. He approached their home from the north and settled the machine to a landing.

As the rotors drifted toward a stop, Omar hopped to the ground and went to Kathleen's side to help her down.

It will be nice to see Marilia and Jacinta again, Kathleen thought. She had come to think of them as friends, not household staff. They, in turn, had become relaxed with her. When they first met, they were so stiff and uncomfortable with the Irish lady that Omar had to laugh.

Marilia, the housekeeper, and Jacinta, the cook, walked out to help with the luggage. Marilia was a small slender woman. Her pinched face looked like it had never worn a smile. Jacinta was a large, round woman who found reason to laugh at everything. They made a good pair, except for one thing: Jacinta's cat. It was a large gray female that Omar had found on the streets of London, half dead of starvation, and brought home to give Jacinta after her first cat died.

Jacinta named her new cat Shasha. The animal did not like Marilia. Whenever it got the chance, Shasha tormented the housekeeper. The cat was brilliant. It knew how to invent tools and could use ordinary things as weapons.

One of Shasha's favorite tools was the small herb garden behind the kitchen. Herbs flourished there because of the garden's bed of rich black loam which Omar had imported. The cat waited until Marilia finished washing the kitchen floor, which she did every day because the floor was white and the kitchen was the most popular gathering spot in the house. Before the floor was dry, Shasha went outside through her cat door and traipsed around in the herb garden, then marched back into the kitchen, and left a trail of black footprints on Marilia's white floor.

This was a deliberate act on the part of Shasha, Marilia was sure.

Another of the cat's favorite games of torment was to lie still, unseen, on the fireplace's gray stone mantle—the same shade of gray as the cat's fur. Sometimes, when Marilia walked close by, Shasha would leap to her feet and hiss in Marilia's ear. The poor woman's face would go ashen. She would stagger across the living room, one arm flailing the air for balance and the other clutching at her breast, as she wailed to the ceiling that she was having a heart attack. The cat was smart. It didn't try to scare Marilia every time she walked by. Shasha waited, sometimes many days, until Marilia's guard was down; and then she would strike again.

Marilia was certain the evil cat wanted to kill her, and she suspected the demon of being Satan's personal succubus.

AFTER SHE UNPACKED THE clothes, Marilia came to Omar. She was wringing her hands and looked upset.

"What's wrong, Marilia?" Omar asked.

"Ah, Señor Jabri," she said in a plaintive voice. "Something bad has happened while you were gone today. Some neighbor children were playing near the house and I offered them lemonade. It was so hot outside. After they went away, I saw that the dish for the chocolates near the front door was empty. They took all your chocolates, Señor Jabri. There are no more in the house."

Omar laughed. "Well, I don't think we should have the children shot for that. I must say, though, they have exquisitely good taste. Never mind, Marilia. Call Hakim at my home in London and ask him to buy some and ship them here by overnight express. Tell him to be sure it's Butlers."

"Yes, of course, Señor Jabri. Butlers. Right away, Señor Jabri."

BEFORE THE BOYS returned from camping, Kathleen and Omar decided to take a long walk through the hills surrounding their hacienda. It was late morning and the heat of the day was building.

"Let's walk east and catch the ocean breezes." Said Kathleen, as she took Omar's hand.

Omar stopped and pulled Kathleen to him. She looked at him quizzically.

Omar threw down the gauntlet. It had been on his mind non-stop for days. "Why do you continue on with the IRA?"

Kathleen stiffened. She had been expecting this. "I owe them everything."

"You do?"

"Yes. Of course I do. They took me in. I was alone. Unprotected."

Omar placed his hands on Kathleen's shoulders and looked deep into her eyes. "But now," he said in a quiet voice, "you don't need their protection. You're free to choose."

"Choose?"

"Yes. Choose to live your life the way you want."

Kathleen shrugged Omar's hands off her shoulders and turned away. "But you're forgetting something. If it wasn't for. . . ." She didn't want to go there. She'd never told him that God had killed her family with the fire bomb to punish her for having sex before marriage. It wasn't something she wanted to say.

"If it wasn't for what?" Omar asked.

Kathleen looked at the ground before her feet. She felt like a fool. "I'm alive and they're dead."

"Yes," Omar said. "That's true."

"And I'm the only one who can make things right."

Omar looked up at the sky, as though searching. Kathleen saw the gesture and was annoyed.

She grabbed Omar's arm, just above the elbow, and held it in a tight grip. "You don't understand. You don't *want* to understand!" She was squeezing as hard as she could, digging her fingers into his flesh. She wanted this to hurt.

Omar looked at her hand on his arm, then at her eyes. His own eyes were sad. Kathleen's grip felt like a steel clamp, tightening, hurting. He placed his hand lightly over hers; not pulling, not prying, just letting his palm lay across her fingers, now white at the knuckles as she continued to squeeze as hard as she could.

"I feel pain," he said just above a whisper. "Is this what you want from me right now?"

Omar's words hit Kathleen hard. She let go his arm and threw her hands over her face. She sobbed hard. Omar pulled her gently to him. He wrapped his arms around her and gently rubbed the black hole between her shoulders. Kathleen put her arms around Omar and held tight.

In a few moments the sobbing subsided. "I'm sorry, Omar. I'm ashamed. I wanted to hurt you. I did it on purpose. Forgive me." She pulled her head back to look up at his face.

He smiled. "I'm glad it was on purpose. If that was by accident, you'd be dangerous."

"I do wish you would try to understand, Omar," Kathleen said, now feeling herself freed from the unreasonableness of her little attack on Omar's person. "Please try," she added in a hushed voice.

"I do understand. Tom took you in. He protected you. After your parents and Tim were killed, Tom and Peg became your da and your ma. You needed family, and *there* they *were*," Omar said. "But *we're* your family too," he added. "Shafi, Michael, me. Why can't you *see* that? The past is over. You can't change it."

Kathleen sighed and pressed her lips together hard to prevent herself from responding. After a long pause, Omar took her hand and said, "Promise me you'll think about it, okay?"

Kathleen nodded with a sad smile. Then the pair bounded up the final hill to catch the full impact of the Mediterranean winds.

ON THE FINAL EVENING of the family's stay in Florenza, after dinner when the house slowed down and Marilia and Jacinta had retired, and even Shasha was still, Omar put on some soft music and invited Kathleen to dance. She blushed at the invitation. It had been a long time. She was surprised. Flattered.

Omar selected music he knew she liked. He wanted everything to be right.

"Very seductive music, sir," she whispered in his ear, intentionally tickling him with her breath.

"For a nice lass," he said in his typical attempt at an Irish brogue.

Kathleen laughed. The first time she'd heard his false brogue, many years ago on a cold Irish night, she was offended. But now she enjoyed Omar making a bags of the Irish accent. It was a humorous hallmark of their relationship.

Omar can be fun when he wants to be. Her next thought was a deliberate, and honest, modification. *Omar is fun, when I let him be himself.*

The music cast its spell and before the last tune was finished Omar said softly, "I didn't realize how much I'd missed you."

"Mmm," Kathleen whispered. "I'm so glad to be in your arms again."

"To a lovely future together," Omar offered as a toast over their champagne.

To Kathleen the words sounded like the prelude to something she wasn't ready for. She had an unfinished commitment to complete, like a soldier who must leave his loved ones, pick up his rifle, and return to the battlefield where his buddies died.

She sipped her champagne and said nothing. For a long time she would not meet Omar's eyes. A sense of guilt tormented her. The old rage that once had fueled her life, given it meaning, had decayed to putrescent guilt. Was it guilt that her life was about buying weapons that kill? Was it about holding back a part of herself that belonged to Omar and her children? Or was she guilty of just being alive, while her family was dead? That she could never do enough for them? That she didn't deserve to live? She didn't know which it was. All?

Omar had intended to say more. He had intended to ask her to marry him. He wasn't insensitive to Kathleen's prepared reply: Her refusal was already in the air.

12

The Mullah

1994

About midway through their first year, life at Brimbury took a sharp turn for Michael and Shafi.

It was spring holiday, and Brimbury would close. At Christmas break, Omar had taken the boys skiing while Kathleen was on a gun buy in Russia, and now she was supposed to pick up the boys for Easter break. She was to collect them at the school for a visit with their grandpa and grandma, and Omar would join them later in Florenza.

But Kathleen was delayed, nowhere near a phone or radio.

Omar was in a similar fix. His ship was adrift without power in the middle of the Indian Ocean. A massive electrical storm had caught the *Thea* somewhere southwest of the Cocos Islands near the Tropic of Capricorn. The radio was fried.

There was no way for either Kathleen or Omar to communicate with the world or each other.

On the following day, Shafi and Michael were the only two boys left on campus. Headmaster Forsyth was concerned because his own plans for the spring break didn't include having these two underfoot. He tried to call their grandparents in Glenarm and got no answer. The previous day Tom Mulcahy was rushed to the hospital. In one of the first operations of this type in Ireland, a stent was put in his neck to open a clogged artery. Peg stayed with him day and night.

The staff at the family's London home had standing instructions: Only callers with the proper password were to be given the where-abouts of Omar or Kathleen. Not hearing the password from Mr. Forsyth, the staff regretted to say they were unaware of the couple's location.

He got the same regretful response from the Florenza staff.

What was the headmaster to do, poor man? His head was begin-ning to throb. This Arab and his two kids represented a small for-tune to Brimbury. The boys would have to come home with him to his wife. He knew the dear woman wouldn't like this. She would have a problem, especially, with having the dark one in her home. No, Clive Forsyth would have to find somewhere to deposit these two headaches.

Though he had never spoken to anyone there, he knew there was a Muslim school at a mosque in Ferndale. He found the phone number and called.

"Yes, hello," he said. "My name is Clive Forsyth. I'm headmaster of Brimbury Boys' Academy over here in Walswerth. May I speak to the person in charge at the mosque, please?"

"Yes, I am Mullah Ispahani. What can I do for you Mr. Forsyth?"

"Well, I have this situation, you see, awfully awkward, and I'm afraid I'm in need of a bit of assistance."

"I see," Mullah Ispahani said, though he didn't have the foggiest notion what the English gentleman was talking about.

"It's these two boys, you see. The Jay-bree brothers. Father's Eye-ray-nian. He can't come pick up his boys for the holiday, and the mother is I don't know where, and the point is, you see, there is absolutely no one to care for these lads the next two weeks." Headmaster Forsyth stopped and took a breath.

"Yes, I understand." Mullah Ispahani hoped the caller would get to the point.

"Well, you see. The thing is this, I wondered, what with the boys being from your part of the world, you see, that is, I thought perhaps, if it isn't outright too much to ask, you or someone from your mosque might be able, be willing, to sort of *take* the boys. For two weeks, I mean." Headmaster Forsyth cleared his throat. "I'm sure the parents would compensate you."

There was a pause as Mullah Ispahani put this together. "You say you have two students at Brimbury who are from where? Did you say, Iran?"

"Oh yes, I-*rahn*," Headmaster Forsyth said, a light sweat along his brow.

"And you can't find their parents?" The mullah was trying his best to understand.

"Well, you see. It isn't so much we don't know where to find them, after all. I've called the mother's office. She was supposed to pick up the boys yesterday. But they say she's out of the country on business. And the father seems to be out of reach as well. Do you see?"

The mullah now understood. "And you want someone to take the boys for the duration of the time the school is closed. Two weeks, you say?"

"Yes, now you have it!" the Headmaster sighed with relief. This might work out after all.

"I see. Are the boys Muslim?"

This gave Headmaster Forsyth pause. As far as he knew, the brothers didn't practice any religion at all. Was the mullah saying he would not take them unless they were Muslim? "Oh yes, of course they are. Devout, too!"

"Hmm." Mullah Ispahani was asking himself why these devout Muslim boys were not enrolled in his own school. "What are their names?'

"Shay-fee and Michael. Jay-bree." Headmaster Forsyth pronounced it carefully, and wrong as always.

"Do you mean . . . Jabri?"

"Yes, well I am sorry, you know. These for . . ." he forgot for an instant who was on the other end of the line.

"Is it spelled J-a-b-r-i?"

"Yes, that's it! Do you know the name?"

"Ah, Mr. Forsyth, the name Jabri is well known by my people. It would be a pleasure to make the acquaintance of Mr. Jabri's sons."

"You'll take the boys?" Headmaster Forsyth was almost unable to believe his good fortune.

"Yes, of course, Headmaster Forsyth. Allah tells us we must take care of one another. Will you bring them here? I think Ferndale is about a thirty minute drive from Walswerth."

"Oh, by all means, Mr. Mullah, sir! I'd be delighted!" It occurred to Headmaster Forsyth he might have set up the loss of the Jabri endowment. This mullah, he reflected, also ran a private school. Probably needed money.

Hmm. Bad mistake to call him, possibly. Must shore up my relationship with this Jay-bree gent. Must begin to do that the next time I see him!

ISPAHANI HUNG UP AND rushed to make arrangements to receive his two guests. He was eager for the opportunity to have these children of wealth at his school.

His objective would be simple: get these boys to trust him, to like him. As the headmaster of a school for boys, Mullah Ispahani understood male adolescence. He knew some boarding school boys needed to bond with an adult male to fill the void left by a father who is only part-time.

HEADMASTER FORSYTH PULLED his car to the curb in front of the huge plaza of inlaid tile in intricate patterns of red, gold, blue and silver. People walked in all directions, most of them wearing the standard Muslim garb.

Standing at the rear of the plaza was the Ferndale Mosque and School, a residential Islamic academy. The mosque was imposing, with its large onion domes of gold sitting atop a building of many dimensions and many colors, and its tall minaret, from which the faithful are called to prayer five times a day.

The three passed through a covered arcade where the poor are traditionally allowed to beg while sheltered from the sun, and at the front door Forsyth rang the bell. He glanced down at Shafi and tucked a bit of hair in place behind the boy's ear. Michael's hair was wild, as always, and there was nothing that could be done about it—or nothing Michael would allow.

The door swung open and there stood a portly gentleman in what appeared to be a thin white lab coat, revealing at the knee the white trousers he wore underneath. Over his coat he wore a short vest of dark brown. All three of his visitors were awed by the man's face, almost tripled in width by an enormous black beard that had a wide red smile in the middle of it. The gentleman peered out over tiny square glasses, rimless, and on his head he wore a black round cap with a flat top, which Shafi was later to learn is called a kufi. Michael would refer to it as a "goofy."

He brought his two hands together before his breast, as though to pray, and the two boys, told to make a good impression, hastened to do the same, but then the strange man made a shallow bow and said, "Welcome." His smile broadened and he added, "I am Mullah Ispahani. You must be Mr. Forsyth?"

The mullah extended his hand to Headmaster Forsyth, who shook it nervously and stumbled with the words, "Yes. Thank you. Pleased to meet you, sir . . . er . . . I mean, mullah, sir."

"And these two young men," the mullah said, smiling down at the boys to Forsyth's sides, "must be Michael and Shafi. Yes?"

"Ah yes! Please meet Michael Jay-bree," Forsyth said placing one hand on Michael's head, and Shay-fee Jay-bree," he said, placing his hand on Shafi's head.

"Welcome," the mullah said. "Welcome to Allah's house. Please, do come in."

Forsyth had rehearsed his reply. He had it honed to a simple: "I'm sorry. I'd love to stay. Another time. I must be off. An appointment." With that, he backed away a few steps, calling out, "Just for a fortnight. Either I'll come get them, or their parents will. Many thanks. Goodbye, then."

He turned and fled to his car. He started it noisily, ground the gears putting it in first, and had the gas pedal much too close to the floor as he let up on the clutch, so that the car roared as it moved slowly away, a thick blue exhaust showing the engine had suffered this kind of regular abuse for a long time. "Come with me, Shafi and Michael. I will introduce you to some of the boys."

The mullah led his young guests to a large recreational center. Several boys were playing board games. In the corner some others were gathered to watch a lively game of table tennis.

After introducing Shafi and Michael to the group, Ispahani beckoned to one of the older boys. "Yusuf will show you to your quarters. You will be staying in his dormitory section," he said with a broad smile.

As the three boys walked down the hall to the dormitory, Michael said to Yusuf, "This is a lot like Brimbury." Under his breath he muttered to Shafi, "Not as weird as I thought it was going to be."

After the boys had put away their things, Mullah Ispahani appeared at their door.

"Would you like to see our mosque?" Ispahani asked his two charges. The boys shrugged careless agreement.

Ispahani first took them to the prayer room. The walls were ornate, with small shapes repeated in endless patterns of mosaic, and many scrolled messages in the ancient lettering of Islam's culture.

"What's that?" Shafi asked, pointing to the writing on the wall.

"Hmm," the mullah said, more to himself than to his guests. "It would appear you are not Muslim after all. No matter. Allah is great." In response to Shafi's question, he said, "Those writings on the wall are prayers. Later on you might like to learn what they say."

Shafi was intrigued but Michael was bored. He could hear boys at play outside. "Can I go out and play?"

"Yes, of course. Just don't leave the school grounds," Ispahani said. "The other boys will show you what to do at prayer time." Michael walked quickly to the door and went out. The closing of the door reverberated through the large empty room.

Shafi felt a little uncomfortable, alone with this odd-looking stranger in a place unlike any he had ever seen before. Yet, he was interested. "What are those lines for?" he asked, pointing to white lines that extended clear across the floor.

"Allah does not like disorder," Ispahani replied, "especially not in His house. So when we gather to pray, we kneel in straight rows along these lines, facing Mecca. The men at the head of the room, the women to the rear. Those who arrive first take the front lines, and they have the greater reward."

"Why?" Shafi asked.

Ispahani smiled. "You ask excellent questions, and we have two weeks to get them all answered. I promise you, you will learn. Come, let us see more." And with that, he led Shafi out of the prayer room and down a long corridor. "Would you like to see our classrooms?" he asked.

"I guess," Shafi said, again with a shrug.

The halls were quiet. "There are no classes today," Ispahani explained. "Here we are," he said simply as he stopped at a door and pushed it open. He reached in and clicked on the light. "Come in."

"Wow!" Shafi said as they walked inside.

The mullah looked pleased. "This is our science wing," he said. "We have all the latest equipment."

Shafi walked among the tables and examined various items. "We don't have anything like this at Brimbury," he said. Ispahani watched Shafi for a moment and said, "We also have a computer room."

Shafi's mouth fell open. "I love computers!" he said. His eyes were wide with excitement.

A male voice rang out from somewhere. It echoed through the halls and outside in the gardens. The mullah said, "Quickly, come with me," and motioned Shafi into the nearby teacher's bathroom.

The mullah closed the door. "Sit," he said gently. "Be relaxed. You may sit down."

"Where?" Shafi asked. He was not feeling relaxed; this was starting to feel creepy.

"On the toilet lid, or stand if you wish. It doesn't matter," Ispahani said.

Shafi chose to stand. The mullah turned on the tap in the sink and with plain water he quickly washed his hands—his right hand first—then his mouth, nose, face, and arms to the elbow, again starting with the right. Shafi was shocked when the man next removed his shoes and lifted his right foot into the sink to splash water on it, and then the left. Taking a small towel from a shelf, he dabbed himself dry and then slipped on his shoes.

For a long moment, neither spoke, the mullah studying Shafi silently. Shafi started to fidget.

Ispahani smiled and said, "Aren't you the least bit curious about what I just did?"

Again Shafi made his noncommital shrug.

"That was a ceremonial washup. A good Muslim does that to be clean each time he prays. If he has no water at prayer time, he simply makes the motions. Allah understands."

Shafi said nothing. He was wondering if he might go out to play with his brother and the other kids, but he was embarrassed to ask.

"Come," said Ispahani. "It's time for the prayer we call Maghrib."

They approached the prayer room along with about two hundred boys and several men. Everyone walked in a quiet purposeful manner. The mullah stopped to take off his shoes and put them on a long rack. He motioned to Shafi to do the same. Ispahani said, "Shafi, I have to get ready to lead the prayers. Go in with the other boys and just do what they do. If you have questions, I will answer them later."

In a few moments Michael came up to Shafi's side and whispered, "You should see what I just saw! Some guy was up on the roof, and he started singing. I thought he was a nut. I was waiting for him to jump. And when this guy started to sing, all the guys stopped in the middle of the soccer game. Then they took me to this room, and, I swear, they started washing themselves! But they weren't dirty! They even washed their *feet*, Shaf! They wanted me to do it, too, but I said 'no *thanks!*'."

After dinner, Shafi and Michael joined the other boys in the recreation room. At Brimbury, they had learned what it's like to live with a large group of boys. There, Michael had fit in well. He was good at soccer, quick to make friends, and he got decent grades. Rarely was he in a fight, and when he was he usually won. For Shafi, life at Brimbury was a standoff. His grades were good, but he tended to be shy, and he felt that others didn't like him. He suspected it was because of his dark coloring. Here, everybody had the same look.

The evening was interrupted by another loud chant from the man on the roof. Just as before, all activity ceased and everyone made their way first to the "ablution room" and then to the prayer room.

Michael found the ceremonial washup routine ridiculous and, again, refused to do it. He also refused to join the others in the customary praying position: down on both knees, face to the floor.

At next morning's assembly for prayer, the Jabri brothers were the opening topic of discussion on Mullah Ispahani's list, with Michael the main focus. With all the boys and instructors seated facing Mecca, the mullah stood on a prayer rug at the front of the room. First he begged Allah for His blessing, and everyone made the proper response. Then he began his sermon.

"As you know, we have two guests with us while their own school is closed for holiday. Michael and Shafi Jabri, will you please stand?"

Michael and Shafi looked at one another. Michael looked angry at being singled out for whatever it was. Shafi was confused. They stood.

"Michael and Shafi are our guests, and we are pleased to have them. Their father is of Persian descent, and their mother is Irish. The boys and their parents are not Muslim, not believers in Islam."

There was a low murmur in the room. Shafi and Michael looked at one another anxiously. What did this mean? What was about to happen?

The mullah held up his hand for silence. "Allah has provided us with an opportunity," he said in a kindly voice and with a smile. "The Koran tells us to be compassionate, and in so doing draw non-believers to Allah, may His blessings be upon us."

"Our word for today is 'compassionate'," the mullah said. "Find it in the Koran. Study why Allah tells us to be compassionate. Discuss it among yourselves. Come to me with your questions. Above all, you must apply the word to our guests during their visit with us."

The mullah paused a moment, then said, "Michael, would you please raise your hand a moment?"

A chill went through Michael. *What now?* he thought. He raised his hand.

"Thank you, Michael," the mullah said in a friendly way. "You may put your hand down now. And you may both be seated."

To the assembly, the mullah said, "Some of you have come to me and asked why Michael Jabri sits when the rest of us, even his own brother, go down on our knees to pray. Some of you have criticized, have called him infidel, have said he must be punished."

There was another murmur in the room, and again the mullah held up his hand for silence.

"You are wrong to think so, may Allah forgive you," the mullah said in a gentle voice. "In this school, we do not use the word infidel. We say non-believer. And we do not criticize those who are not Muslim, not believers in Islam."

He paused for effect. There wasn't a sound or a movement in the room. "I know, even better than you do, that the Koran says there is only one Allah and all must believe in the one true God.

But remember this: Allah is eternal. Allah created time. Allah is not in a rush. Only we mortals get in a rush." He paused again. "My point is, we must be patient. When one sits among us, while all the rest of us go down on our knees and lower our faces to pray, we must be patient. By kindness and good example, we will draw our brother down on his knees beside us, and he will lower his face to the earth in humility, to worship Allah."

Michael smiled broadly at the whole room, turning this way and that, nodding his head in agreement to everyone, and feeling wonderful, as he said to himself, *"In a pig's arse, you will! Not me, brother! Not on the longest feckin' day of your feckin' life!"*

"And so," the mullah went on in his gentle manner, "when Michael Jabri chooses to not join us, not join his brother Shafi, when we all pray together, no one of us shall criticize him, or even think ill of him. Michael Jabri is our guest, just as we all are the guests of Allah here on Earth, may He make us truly grateful. We will treat our guest with respect, with tolerance, and above all with compassion."

"Now let us pray."

Later that day Ispahani sought out Shafi and invited him to his quarters. Shafi felt proud when he saw what looked like envy on the other boys' faces. He rose quickly and turned his flushed face away from them.

Shafi walked with the mullah to a far end of the dormitory building. They stopped at a door while Ispahani reached in his vest and pulled out a key. "Here is my apartment," he said simply. "Come in."

The mullah's front room was simple but elegant. Books covered one entire wall. The opposite wall contained a window that overlooked the extensive lawns and large trees that were part of the campus.

"Please, my dear young Shafi, come and sit here and we'll have some tea." They sat at a small wooden table that had deep carvings around the edge and on the legs. The chairs were covered in a fabric of intricate design and bright colors. While the mullah poured tea, Shafi looked across the room to study the books. Ispahani said, "I have collected many holy books. Some are quite old and are historically important. Another time I will show you some, if you are interested."

"Yes, Mr. Mullah. I would like that."

Ispahani chuckled. "To call me Mr. Mullah would be like me calling you Mr. Sir. Just call me Mullah Ispahani. That will be fine." He paused. "Mr. Forsyth says your parents couldn't come get you from school."

"Yes, Mullah Ispahani."

"Are they often away, your parents?"

Shafi nodded, and Ispahani thought he saw sadness in the boy's eyes. "Which do you miss the most, your mother or your father?"

Shafi shrugged, and said. "Both. My father the most, I guess."

"Of course," Ispahani said gently. "That's only natural. A boy would miss his father the most."

"He's very busy. He has to travel a lot." Ispahani noted the boy's deep sigh.

"Does he go to the mosque? Does he pray?" Ispahani wanted to know.

Shafi shook his head. "He's not religious. He's a businessman. We can't really see each other that much. He's got a lot of important things to do."

Ispahani sighed and looked up at the ceiling. "It must be nice to be important. Maybe I could learn how from your father. But," he sighed again, "my devotion to Allah fills my life." He looked over at Shafi for a reaction.

"Oh, no, sir! I think you are important. I mean, what you do is important," Shafi said.

"Do you think so, my son?"

"Yes. I mean, you help people with their life, and problems and stuff. Right?"

"Well, yes, Shafi. I suppose you are right. But don't judge your father harshly for being away much of the time. He is an important man. And I, though a simple man, can be your friend. I will always be ready to help whenever you need me. Now, are you finished with your tea?"

"Yes, Mullah Ispahani. Thank you."

Ispahani walked across the room and removed two books from the shelf. "I would like you to have this copy of the Koran, my son. This other one is for your brother. It's written in English, so you will be able to read it. Open the book whenever you feel alone. It will help you. While you are here, you are invited to pray with us, study Islam with us, and in every sense be part of our community."

"Gee, thanks, Mullah Ispahani!" Shafi said and took the book.

"Come, now," said the mullah. "Let's go find Michael, shall we?"

Michael declined politely when the mullah offered him the Koran, and over the next several days, he became more and more miserable. At the same time, Shafi became immersed in his study of the Koran and life at the academy.

Frequent praying was, for Michael, a test of his endurance, and for Shafi a flight into another world. The boys were each given a little prayer book to carry with them. In it were listed the times of day for mandatory prayers, the position to be taken after the proper washup motions, and the prayers themselves, in English.

"This place is so boring!" Michael said one evening as the boys were getting into bed. Michael had the top bunk and Shafi the bottom, in a dormitory with more than a hundred other boys. "I wish ma and da could come get us."

"Well, they can't!" Shafi snapped. "They're not home!"

"Then why can't we call Grandpa?" Michael whispered. He didn't want the boys on the neighboring bunks to overhear. "We could go stay with them."

"The mullah says he got their number from old man Forsyth," Shafi whispered. "He calls all the time, and they're not home either."

"I think he's a liar," Michael replied. "He's just trying to keep us here on purpose. It's not fair!" he said as he punched his pillow.

"He is not a liar!" Shafi said, as if his own father were being insulted. "He cares about us! You'll see!" To himself, he added, *Besides, I like him.*

"You really want to be here, don't you?" Michael said. "Why?"

"I . . . I like studying the Koran. It means something to me."

Michael lay his head back on his pillow. *I wonder what it's like to have faith in God?* he thought. He was pretty sure his ma and his da didn't have any, though he'd never asked.

IT WAS A TIME OF INTENSE focus for the mullah. He had many talks with Shafi, and he made certain the boy was well regarded by the students who lived at the school. In Shafi Jabri, Ispahani found a serious boy, quite intelligent too; the kind he was always looking for. With Michael, he made a far smaller effort because he realized he had little hope of converting him. In spite of Michael's religious intolerance he was well liked by the boys, and Ispahani was concerned that Michael was setting a bad example for the other students.

The time went by much too fast for Shafi. He and the mullah

became friends. While this happened, the mullah gave Shafi a thorough introduction to a boy's life as a Muslim, and Shafi showed signs of becoming an avid student of Islam. He turned to the mullah again and again for help with passages from the Koran. Shafi found the empty places in his heart started to be filled, and by the end of their stay at Ferndale he was a believer.

Now Shafi's challenge became how to continue these studies. Of course he had his copy of the Koran, but he wanted more than the Holy Book to read. He wanted to be part of the Muslim community at Ferndale.

Would his mother and father permit it? He was nine years old now. This was old enough, he resolved, to make his own decisions.

WHEN OMAR WAS FINALLY able to make contact with the outside world he called the Mulcahy home to talk to his family.

"Hello?" Peg whispered into the phone.

"Peg? It's Omar." Something in her voice alarmed him. "Is everything all right?"

"Oh, Omar, I'm sorry for the confusion," Peg replied, still in a soft voice. "I guess Kathleen and the children are with you?"

"With me? I'm in the middle of the ocean! They are supposed to be with you and Tom!" He felt anger rise, and with it fear.

"Dear God! Oh, dear God!" said Peg. "We've been at hospital. Just got home yesterday." Omar heard the panic in her voice. "Tom's had surgery. I thought I was goin' to lose him. I kept callin' home, thinkin' Kathleen must be here worryin' and wonderin' what's happened to us. But there was never an answer. Now you're sayin' she's not with you? Where are they?"

"Now Peg, I'm sure everything is fine. Just some kind of mix-up. I will get this sorted out today." He tried to sound calm and reassuring. "You must not worry. Take care of Tom. Is he okay now?"

"The doctor's say yes, but we'll just have to see . . ." she trailed off. Omar could hear her shallow quick breaths.

"Now you must think only of Tom. He needs you now. I will take care of everything and call you later when I have word of Kathleen and the boys. Goodbye."

Omar called Hakim in London. "Get the headmaster of Brimbury on the phone immediately. Find out if he knows where Kathleen took the boys. You'll probably have to reach him at home. His name is Forsythe."

"Yes, Mr. Jabri. I will handle it immediately."

Omar contacted the few IRA operatives he knew. Within the hour, after applying the right combination of threats and incentives, he was told that Kathleen was stranded somewhere in Afghanistan. She was supposedly making her way to Kabul. She would be asked to call Omar as soon as she was heard from.

With that information he knew whom to contact, and using the correct code to go through a series of cutouts, he was able finally to speak with him directly. "Massoud, old friend. Jabri here."

"Hello, Omar!" Massoud said in a warm enthusiastic way. "What are you up to? Staying out of trouble?"

"I should ask that of you! Have you been able to keep those Red madmen out of your country?"

"Yes, we're rid of the Soviets. But now a new group is trying to rise up. Call themselves the Taliban. A nasty bunch. But, Allah be willing, we will prevail. Now, what can I do for you, old friend?"

Omar explained that he needed help finding a woman who was in Afghanistan on business. "She's a patriot, like you, but for Ireland."

"I understand," Massoud said. "But something tells me your interest in her doesn't involve Ireland. Is she your woman?"

Omar laughed. "You read minds well, Massoud. Even over the telephone. Yes, she is, as you put it, my woman. And the mother of my two sons."

"Ah, well now. That makes all the difference. How can I help?"

"Her name is Kathleen O'Toole. She could use your protection right now. Can you *find* her, Massoud, and help get her to Kabul, and out of the country?"

"Consider it done," said Massoud.

Omar took his meal in his cabin. He needed to stay on the phone; to get this situation under control.

The phone rang at his desk. It was Hakim.

"Mr. Jabri. I phoned Mr. Forsyth. He says Miss Kathleen—"

"Yes, I know. She didn't pick the boys up at Brimbury."

"Is she all right, Mr. Jabri?"

"Yes, she's going to be okay. We know where she is. She'll be home soon. Now tell me, what about Shafi and Michael?"

"The school is closed. Mr. Forsyth said he found a Muslim boys school, and he took the boys there for a fortnight."

"What?" Omar roared into the phone.

"He couldn't keep them while the school was closed. He said he was sure you'd be pleased.

"Pleased?" said Omar. "I'd like to wring his neck!"

"Well, sir, in all fairness to Mr. Forsyth," Hakim continued, "He did call here asking for you or Miss Kathleen, and of course I had to tell him we had no idea where you were or how to contact you."

"Yes, you're right," Omar said, his anger dissipating in the face of reason.

Hakim added, "Then we lost touch with your ship, and we had to wait for you to get back in contact with us."

"True," Omar said. "All right then, let's move on. I'm making arrangements to get home immediately. Get me full information on this Muslim school. I'll phone you tomorrow. I'll go pick up the boys myself. They must be confused and worried."

Omar said to Wessam, his ship's second in command, "If . . . no, *when* . . . Miss O'Toole calls, tell her I'm on my way to London. I'll meet her there. Tell her to call her mother as soon as possible."

"Yes, sir," said Wessam.

"One more thing, tell her the boys are in London. Don't go into details."

"Of course, sir. I'll berth the ship at Singapore and wait there to hear from you."

"Good man, Wessam," said Omar. "I'm off."

From the *Thea,* Omar flew his helicopter to Jakarta, and then on to Singapore where he caught a commercial flight for his first leg to London.

"EXCUSE ME FOR DISTURBING YOU," said Dr. Nimer in his rich, melodic voice.

"Yes, what is it?" Ispahani asked as he looked up from his Koran. He had found a quiet spot in the garden and was enjoying the fresh spring air. He felt slightly annoyed at the interruption.

Dr. Nimer, one of Ferndale's most respected teachers had become the mullah's trusted advisor. Ispahani saw a look of urgency on Nimer's face.

"Yes?" said Ispahani as he closed his book to give Nimer his full attention.

"It's about the Jabri boys. Their father is here to collect them."

"Allah be praised!" said Ispahani as he jumped to his feet. "I must greet him properly. Where is he now?"

"Mr. Jabri insisted on seeing his sons at once. I took him to their classroom. The boys were very excited. I escorted the family to the meeting room."

Ispahani smiled. "I can always count on your good judgement, my dear friend. Please have refreshments brought to my office where I will visit with Mr. Jabri while the boys pack."

Ispahani could hear much laughter as he approached the meeting room. *I can see where Michael gets his boisterous ways*, he thought. "Ah, Mr. Jabri!" exclaimed the mullah as he approached Omar with his hands extended. "It is an honor to meet the father of such fine young men! I am Mullah Ispahani."

Omar stood to shake hands with the mullah. The boys clung to their father's sides and looked up at him, all smiles.

"Thank you for taking my boys. They seem to be quite well. I think they're eager to go home and see their mother, though." Omar looked down at his sons with a big smile and tousled their hair. "Would you like to come with me to London? You still have a few days' vacation before school starts. And your mother will be home tomorrow."

Ispahani said to the boys, "Go and pack up your things. Your father and I will be in my office. You can meet us there."

Mullah Ispahani used his private time with Omar to ramble on about the many fine advantages his school had to offer.

Finally, Omar had a chance to break in and said, "Of course I want to compensate you for taking in my boys." He reached in his pocket. "Here is a check. It should more than cover their stay here."

"My dear Mr. Jabri. I cannot accept your kind offering. It was an honor and a pleasure to have your sons at our academy. I only hope that we will see more of them in the future, may Allah be praised."

A school that refuses money? thought Omar. *What is this fellow's game?*

Soon the car was packed, and after several more thank yous and well wishes, father and sons were on their way home.

It took a couple of days for the family to get settled. The major concern on everyone's mind was grandpa Tom's surgery. Kathleen planned to go visit him in Glenarm right after the boys went back to school.

Michael was his usual rambunctious self, and full of stories about the mosque that made his parents laugh.

Shafi had stories, too, but they were mostly about the great things he learned at Ferndale.

Kathleen noticed that Shafi seemed more confident, less shy, than usual. *Was it Ferndale that's done it?* she wondered.

"Shafi, you seem to like this school, and Mullah Ispahani," she said.

Shafi looked off in the distance to avoid his parents' eyes. *Now's my chance*, he thought. "I want to go to the Ferndale school. It's really good. Everyone there is nice and . . . and it's better than Brimbury."

Michael said, "Not me! Not in a zillion years. The school's okay, but all that praying and stuff is boring."

Omar wanted to be fair to both boys. He was not in favor of a religious school, and he didn't think much of that mullah. *Come to think of it, Forsyth is no prize either,* he reasoned.

"Tell me, Shafi, what is it about Ferndale that you like so much?" Omar asked with a smile.

"Well, they have all kinds of stuff for science. You can do experiments and things. And they have a computer lab. That's the best part. It's really interesting!" He sensed it best to avoid mention of his studies of the Koran.

"That sounds wonderful," said Kathleen. "And Brimbury doesn't have these things?"

"No, they don't. They don't have anything!" Shafi said.

"What about it, Michael," asked Omar. "Do you agree that Ferndale has better science equipment?"

"Okay, it's true. But it's the only good thing they have. Please don't make me go there, da."

Kathleen raised her eyebrows and looked at Omar. Her face said, *Well?*

"Let me think about it," said Omar. "And I want to discuss it with your mother."

DURING THE FIRST WEEK that Brimbury was back in session, Headmaster Forsyth called a special assembly of everyone in any way associated with the academy.

The happiness on his face was apparent and unusual. "Parents, teachers and students," Forsyth began, sounding almost giddy. "Thanks to the generosity of an anonymous donor, I have the great pleasure to announce that Brimbury will be adding a state of the art computer and science program." He stopped to catch his breath, and he gave a nearly imperceptible nod to Omar.

Forsyth continued, "A new science wing will be added to the school. Computers, electronics, all the latest in communications technology. New equipment will be purchased, and an extensive library will be added to our school. Three new teachers will be hired."

The audience broke into applause, and stood to cheer the school's good fortune.

On cue from Forsyth, the music teacher rose from his seat to lead the singing of the school anthem, and Forsyth, all red-faced, took a seat next to his wife. He leaned close to her ear and whispered, "I certainly did the right thing bringing those Jay-bree boys to Ferndale. And here I was worried about it. I need to learn to trust my own good judgement more often."

ONE SATURDAY, A FEW WEEKS LATER, the news surfaced.

"Shafi says he's studying the Koran," Omar told Kathleen one night as they were getting ready for bed.

"I know," Kathleen said. She continued brushing her hair. Seated at her dresser, in the mirror she could see Omar standing behind her. He looked troubled.

Before he could speak again, she said, "Did he tell you he wants to go to the Saturday school at the mosque?"

"Oh, so he asked you too. What did you say?"

"I told him to ask you."

"Oh, great. Thanks a lot."

"Omar, you know you wouldn't want me to approve of something like that without it going to you first. So I told Shafi to ask you. He's got to learn to fend for himself."

She was right, of course. As usual. He walked up behind her and placed his hands gently on her shoulders. Softly he kneaded them with his strong fingers.

"That's nice." She turned her face to kiss the top of his hand. She was wearing a peignoir she knew Omar particularly liked and she saw him eyeing her in it with obvious interest. He removed his hands and turned away.

"Kathleen, there's something about Mullah Ispahani that I don't like. That's why I tried to talk Shafi out of this, but he can be just as stubborn as—"

"Me?" Kathleen said with a chuckle.

Omar smiled. "Yes. Sometimes. You can be stubborn."

"And you know what happens when you try to make me change my mind."

"Oh, it's not too hard. Like pushing a barge with a row boat," he said as he walked back to the dressing table and put his hands on her again, but this time he slid them down over her breasts. A light rub with his palms made her nipples hard.

"Mmm," she whispered. "That's nice too." She lifted his hands off and stood up to turn down the bed. Omar followed her movements with his eyes, and he appreciated—as he always did—the soft curves and taut muscles of her youthful physique. Having two children added a softness, a lovely maturity, to her body.

"What are you going to do?" she said.

"I suppose we can let him give it a try. I think he'll soon find better things to do with his Saturdays than sit around and listen to that bag of wind spout off about Islam," Omar said as he slid into bed from his side.

Standing on the other side of the bed and smiling, with one hand on the light switch, Kathleen used her other hand to pull a little string-tie at the neck of her peignoir. A slight shrug of her shoulders started the filmy garment down her body and in that moment she flipped the switch that plunged their bedroom into darkness.

She turned on the soft light of the bedside lamp, crawled under the covers, and pulled herself up tightly to Omar. She reached down and found he was halfway ready.

"Mmm," she murmured as she nuzzled his chest. "And that's *very* nice."

At family breakfast the next morning, Omar studied his two boys and reflected on what the headmaster at Brimbury told him and Kathleen at a recent parent conference:

"Michael puts ideas together in the way of someone ten years his senior. And he has the social skills of a much older boy. He has a good head for business.

"Shafi," Forsyth continued, "is quite different from his brother. Shafi has a strong interest in computers and electronics. His test scores all say so, and I believe he has read every book in our library on these subjects. He should be encouraged to go into mechanical design, or communications technology. Scientific research, possibly."

Omar had hoped Shafi, his likeness, would some day be his successor in his maritime enterprises—the legal ones. If this man were right, that position would default to Michael.

Over his scrambled eggs, Shafi kept glancing up at his father. Omar said Shafi would get an answer at breakfast.

"You still think you want to attend Saturday school at the mosque?" Omar asked.

Shafi nodded enthusiastically. "Can I?"

Before Omar could reply, Kathleen said, "And you, Michael? Are you going to become a Muslim too?" Her voice, matching her smile, was sad.

"No," Michael said. "I don't like that stuff."

"Well, I like it. Can I go, please, da, can I?"

Omar and Kathleen exchanged glances that showed their shared concern. But there comes a time in the life of every parent when letting go is the only option, and this was the time for Shafi to be let go.

"Yes, all right," Omar agreed with a sigh of reluctance. "Go ahead and study the Koran on weekends with Mullah Ispahani."

Shafi was all smiles. "Thanks, Da! Ma!"

This was to be his first step in a long journey.

13

Two Can Play That Game

It was a beautiful spring morning, and Capper and Ivy had decided they would explore more of their new surroundings in London. They walked the streets hand in hand, stopping to look in shop windows and discussing where they would go for lunch.

"I'm kind of leaning toward Indian food," said Ivy. Capper agreed that something spicy would be nice. *I'd love to learn how to make papadum,* he thought.

"Hey," said Ivy. "Let's go into that old book shop across the street."

The tinkle of the little bell hanging just above the door announced them. "This place is right out of Dickens," Capper said softly. The first thing they noticed was the aroma of antique books: the earthy scent of old leather and the spice of aging paper.

"Smells like fresh crushed black pepper," Capper whispered, as though in reverence.

Ivy laughed, "I think the day you walk into hell, you're going to find that the place smells like food cooking."

Capper made a face. "You are macabre!"

The walls were covered in dark green paper with thin vertical gold stripes. There seemed to be endless rows of shelves jammed with books of all sizes, only a few young enough to still wear a dust jacket, and most with bindings that were tattered from many thousands of page turnings.

Overstuffed chairs of faded colors dotted the room, each with its own floor-lamp and low table beside it. The tables were loaded with books and magazines, some in haphazard piles that seemed about to teeter over. The lamps linked the room in a mosaic of soft yellow light, no two lamps the same, each with its shade of amber or gold and all of them looking as old as the books they illuminated.

Everything about the shop said *Stay a while,* and invited book lovers to hunt for hidden treasures.

Ivy found the military warfare section and dove in. Capper headed off in another direction, and spotted Kathleen in children's books. "Hey, Kathleen, how are you doing?"

"Oh hi, Capper!" Kathleen replied. "Good to see you," she extended him her hand. "Ivy here?"

"Yeah. We just walked in."

"I want to thank you again for having me and Omar over last week. We had a great time . . . and the food was delicious! I've never had a Cuban dinner before."

"Thanks. I love to cook for company. Now that we're all living in London, I hope we can get together often," said Capper.

"Absolutely," Kathleen said. "We were planning to invite the two of you to dinner, but on a weekend so Shafi and Michael can see you again."

"That'd be great! You want to work out the details with Ivy? Last time I saw her, she was headed that way," he said pointing to the back of the shop.

"I'll find her," said Kathleen. "You go ahead with what you were looking for."

On the other side of the shop, Ivy pulled down a copy of *Jane's Guns Recognition Guide*. She flipped the cover open to the copyright page.

Look at this! she thought. *First edition. What a find!* She became so lost in the pages that she jumped when she heard a voice from behind say, "Hello, Ivy."

Ivy turned to see Kathleen looking up at her with a smile. "Hi, Kathleen," she said brightly, trying to appear calm. The book in her hands was like an announcement. *Have I blown my cover?* she thought.

"What's that, a book about guns?" Kathleen asked in a warm voice. She knew the Jane's library of books well, for she had used them often when planning gun buys. She was curious why Ivy would have an interest in such a book.

"Uh, yes. For my nephew's birthday. He's a military history buff," said Ivy, now fully recovered.

Hmm . . . I wonder if that's all it is. Being a soldier, and having trained many, Kathleen sensed that Ivy was a kindred spirit somehow.

Ivy decided to turn the tables and have some fun. *Tit for tat* she thought. She handed the book to Kathleen and said, "What do you think? Is this a good book?" Ivy studied Kathleen flipping through the pages. *She's so petite,* thought Ivy. *But tough as nails, I bet. She'd have to be, in her line of work.*

Kathleen handed the book back to Ivy. "I wouldn't really know. I'm not into that sort of thing," she said in an offhanded way. "But it looks like something a military buff would enjoy."

Just then Capper came into view, arms loaded with books. When Ivy saw the covers, she said, "Oh, lord! More cookbooks!" which made the three friends laugh.

14

Peace Talks

1994

In August, Kathleen brought Shafi and Michael to Ireland for a visit with Peg and Tom. It would be a week of fun for the boys and a time for Tom to burn off some of his newfound energy.

"He's a new man," Peg said to Kathleen as they stood at the window and watched the boys roughhousing with their grandpa out in the back yard. "Will ye just look at 'im, then?"

"Aye. That stent they put in his neck sure has made a difference," Kathleen said as she shook her head and smiled.

"Gave me an awful scare, he did," Peg added. "Thought I'd lost 'im the day he went down. A mini-stroke, they calls it. Wasn't gettin' enough blood to his brain." She chuckled and added, "Do ye know what he told me next day in hospital, then? Said he didn't know he had enough brain to be *needin'* any blood."

Kathleen said, "I can't believe he's come over the surgery so fast! He's like it never happened."

Peg said, "Mmm. Says he never realized just how poorly he'd been feelin', and all. A changed man, 'e is."

"You'd better watch out," Kathleen said, laughing. "He'll be chasing you around the table, and all."

Peg giggled and her face turned red. "Ooh, he has done, and more!"

Kathleen wrapped an arm around Peg's shoulders, more like a girlfriend than an adoptive daughter, and said, warmly, "Some people. The older they get, the more like kids they become."

She added, "Long may it last!"

"Thank ye, child. Ye've been a wonderful daughter to me and Tom. Filled out our life, ye have."

"And you mine. The best parents any girl could have. I love you."

"Aye, be off with ye, now," Peg said in embarrassment. "I've dinner to prepare."

"Shall I help you, then?" Kathleen asked.

"No," she said, laughing. "You go out and play with the other children."

That evening, Michael and Shafi were in the parlor with Peg. They had persuaded Grandma Peg to tell them one of the stories about ancient Eire. Tonight it would be their favorite about brave Oisin who lived with the beautiful Niam of The Golden Hair for three hundred years in Tir na nog, the land of never-ending youth.

On demand, Peg had told and retold the story of Oisin many times, until if she left out any detail either boy could provide it— and did. For Michael, the next best story was the one about the four Children of Lir, who were turned by their evil stepmother into swans for nine hundred years. For Shafi, the best was the story of Cuchulain, the little man who could swell up and become huge with anger when provoked.

While the ancient myths of Ireland were being told in the parlor, Tom and Kathleen sat together on the front porch rehearsing a modern myth called The Unification of Ireland. The main fairies in this myth were Northern Ireland and the Republic of (southern) Ireland. The hobgoblin was Great Britain. There were lots of minor characters in the story who aspired to greatness; among them, the Royal Ulster Constabulary, which sought greatness in law enforcement; and Sinn Féin, the parent of The Provisional Irish Republican Army, with its tedious history of violence, and its desire to be the one legitimate political power in unified Ireland—possibly the greatest myth Ireland has ever known.

WHEN THE BOYS WENT BACK to school, Kathleen decided to stay in Glenarm rather than return to London. She wanted to help with the peace talks, which were nearly stalled.

"The sides are no closer now than they were months ago," Kathleen said in disgust. "This may well be all a waste of time."

"Aye," Tom replied. "It's one thing for us to call a ceasefire, but when the Brits ask us to give up our weapons, that's a bit much."

More than three tons of Semtex plastic explosive and hundreds of automatic weapons were concealed in the basements of safe houses everywhere in Ireland. Machine guns, rocket-propelled grenades, and even a SAM-7 surface to air missile, were carefully wrapped and put away in hay lofts and behind false walls. Months of wrangling followed, and not much was accomplished. There would be no disarmament, and Sinn Féin would not gain Ireland's political authority.

"You know, Tom," Kathleen said, "this may sound like sacrilege to you, but I'd a damn sight rather there were no Sinn Féin at all."

Tom's face showed his surprise. He'd never heard his Kathleen talk this way, and it certainly was politically sacrilegious. "What on earth are ye on about, child? Sinn Féin is God's own great gift to Ireland. Where would we be without it, I'd like to know?"

"I'd like to know that myself. Probably we'd be better off. When Sinn Féin started, it was only supposed to be a loose propaganda machine for passionate young men and women who wanted to celebrate their Irish roots."

"That's not true, child, and ye know it. Arthur Griffith wanted a monarchy for Ireland. If that's not political, then I don't know what is."

"No, Tom. It was those who came after Griffith wanted that. And some of his followers wanted a republic, not a monarchy. And others just wanted to kill."

Tom scratched his head vigorously. "Ye confuse me, child. Ye really do, and all. Wasn't it I who swore you into Sinn—"

"Yes, Tom. You did. But I was never interested in the party. The whole idea of politics makes me sick. Look at what politics has got us into. We're at the bargaining table with the Brits. The *bargaining* table, for the love of God!"

"And what would ye have us be doin', then, I'd be after askin'?"

"Tom, we're like people who come to Sunday mass wearing no clothes. Our nakedness shames us."

"I don't understand."

Kathleen took Tom's hands in hers and shook them as she answered, "We're naked at the table, Tom. We're at the table having nothing to bargain with, Tom!"

"But we have weapons! And they know it. We've Semtex, and bombs, and guns, and—"

Kathleen laughed. "Stop it, Tom! You're preaching to the choir. It's me who goes out and buys those guns and those so-called bombs. Petty things, they are. Little more than children's toys. We're never going to impress the Brits with those. What we need is a show of real strength."

"And what real strength would ye propose to show, then?"

"I'm thinking about it, Tom. I'm thinking about it."

Next afternoon Kathleen saw on Tom's face a strained look from the incessant meetings. The twinkle was gone from his eye. She knew this must be taking a toll on his health—probably defeating all the good the stent in his neck was doing. He and Peg were planning their annual berry canning, and Kathleen was glad the talks had been called off for a month. The distraction of canning would be good for him.

As Tom and Peg chattered away about the wild strawberries they would be putting up, Kathleen's mind drifted to Omar and the special week she had planned for them.

I'm so looking forward to that. The kids at school. A whole week alone together in London. Every year, just like the first time. Her mind had a problem with the word "anniversary." She tried to apply it here. It wouldn't stick; didn't fit somehow. Her next thought was a longing, a hunger. *I wish we could just be married and be done with it.* She shook her head. *Nonsense! Later for that!*

That trip to London would be a blessing, though, and she realized she needed a few things.

"Well!" she announced brightly to Tom and Peg. "I've just decided to trip off to Belfast for a couple of days. I've got some shopping to do and a gift to be buying. It's our . . . anniversary . . . coming up. Eleven years! Can you believe it?"

Tom and Peg saw Kathleen's broad smile and realized it had gone missing for months. "That's a lovely idea, Katie" said Peg.

"Well, times a wastin'," Kathleen said as she gulped down the last of her coffee and ran out of the room to start packing. Mulcahy winked at Peg and smiled.

Kathleen drove down to Belfast with the windows open. The scenery and the cold air cleared her head. Omar was on her mind. *Why do I let my work dominate my life so?* she chastised herself. She realized that somehow the intense attention her IRA work required made the time with her children and with Omar all the more precious.

Kathleen checked into a lovely old hotel, right in the heart of town. In addition to finding a special gift for Omar, she wanted to buy some things for herself that Omar would particularly enjoy. She gathered arm-loads of dresses and tried them all on. The touch of the fabrics and the sight of herself in the mirror drew her away from her work.

Look at me, she laughed to herself. *I'm as giddy as a schoolgirl.*

"Oh madam," the sales girl gushed at everything she tried on, "you look beautiful in this." She wasn't lying. Kathleen's figure made the most of each dress. She finally settled on a few very soft, very feminine outfits, in shades that particularly showed off her creamy skin and her luxurious auburn hair.

Kathleen saved the best for last. She went to the finest lingerie shop in Belfast and selected a few very seductive items. Her favorite was an off-white teddy with rich, heavy lace. Omar's favorite, she knew, would be the sapphire blue bra and panties with the matching kimono.

Next, she would find something unique for Omar. *What do you give a man who owns a battleship, a helicopter, three homes, and a bloody fortune?* she wondered. It would have to be something totally unexpected. Unique. Something intimate he would consider his. Or theirs.

As she passed a chic little gift shop she saw the words Tantra Chair on a sign in the window. She associated the word Tantra with mysticism and magic. But a chair?

"Good morning." The dignified-looking young woman smiled as she approached Kathleen just inside the door.

"Good morning," Kathleen replied.

"May I help madam?"

Kathleen smiled at the exotic woman, dressed in a sari and wearing numerous gold rings and bracelets. "I'm curious. What is a Tantra Chair?"

"This is the Tantra Chair, madam," the woman said, pointing to a chaise lounge with no arms. Its seat had two pronounced curves, one higher than the other, and it was padded and covered in oriental silk.

Kathleen was puzzled. She ran her hand along the sensuous curves of the Chair. "But . . . what's it for?"

The woman's eyes fluttered a bit. "That depends on the user. For some, it is a comfortable seat in which to meditate. For others, it is a wonderful way to achieve . . . well, let's just say it elevates love."

"*Really?*" Kathleen thought the chair reminded her of something. Then she saw it. It had the likeness of herself in silhouette, lying on her side.

"Would madam care to watch a video on the subject?"

Kathleen was led to a small desk at the back of the shop. On it was a video player. As Kathleen sat, the woman clicked the player on and discreetly moved across the store.

The first image Kathleen saw gave her a start. It was a still picture of the Tantra Chair, this one apparently upholstered in gold velvet, and straddling it was a smiling woman with long blonde hair. She was wearing no clothes.

That scene quickly faded to another photo of a dark-haired woman, also nude, lying on the lower part of the Chair, with her legs up on the high curve. Her smile suggested she was very happy.

A short movie began. It showed a series of graceful action scenes depicting a woman and a man using the chair, intimately, in a variety of positions. Watching, Kathleen felt a rush of warmth. She began to imagine herself and Omar by their bedroom window, overlooking the garden. They were inventing new pleasures on their Tantra Chair. Kathleen's delicious reverie was interrupted by a woman's voice on the video. Her testimonial said, ". . . its sexy yet discreet design is nothing short of an invitation to lovemaking."

Kathleen's face felt hot and flushed. She looked up at the shop-keeper across the store. The woman smiled, her raised eyebrows clearly asking, *"Well?"*

"How much is it, and how soon can you have it delivered to London?"

KATHLEEN HAD AN INNER SENSE that was like the rearview mirror on a car. She knew she was being followed.

The little man darted like a ferret from one doorway to the next as he tagged along behind her. His long iron-grey hair hung straight down in all directions from a point at the top center of his head, and he moved with surprising agility for a man obviously in old age. He kept his hands shoved deep into the pockets of loose-fitting trousers, wore a dull brown jacket that drooped from his shoulders and the lower half of his face was wrapped in a black scarf. The weather was cool, but not cold enough for the scarf.

Kathleen nonchalantly made a left turn. Her tail hurried to regain visual contact.

As he started around the corner, he nearly ran head-on into his quarry.

"Well?" Kathleen said, her eyes flashing anger.

"Sorry, mum," the man muttered as he wiped a finger under his nose. His mouth was pursed and his brow raised like a man whose life is about apologising. The raw-looking skin on his forehead was permanently creased in worry lines, and his face was engraved with: *Oh, pity me!*

"No offense, mum," he said in a fearful way.

"I'll decide if there's offense," Kathleen said through clenched teeth. "Start talking."

"Yes, mum. I was hired by Cramwell and Bromwell, mum. Law firm." He wasn't paid to lie. Not this time. "Mr. Cramwell said to find ye. He wants to see ye. It's something about yer work. That's all I know, mum."

"Beg pardon, Miss! You can't go in there! Stop!"

Kathleen didn't slow down or even look at the secretary. The door was marked Alexander Cramwell, and she pushed it open hard. It hit the wall with a bang.

The man at the large desk looked up, startled. "What the—" The secretary followed Kathleen into the office, saying, "She wouldn't stop. Shall I call the police?"

"Do that, my dear," Kathleen said, turning to the nervous woman. "And maybe your Mr. Cramwell here can explain to the coppers why he has people followed in the street."

"Ah!" Cramwell said with a grin, understanding now what was afoot. "It's all right, Janet," He rose and buttoned his tweed jacket. The secretary backed out of the room and closed the door quietly behind her. "Please, Miss O'Toole. Be seated."

"I'll stand," Kathleen replied. "Now what the bloody hell is this all about? Start with why you had me followed."

Cramwell laughed. "I didn't. Not actually. The chap you met is Homer Blunt. Homer's a former private detective. His specialty was shadowing unfaithful spouses. I didn't tell him to follow you around the city. I told him to just find you, and give you my message. But he can't help himself. Still thinks he's supposed to be shadowing. Not quite right in the head, I think, but I like the old man."

Kathleen asked, "How did you know I was in Belfast?"

"I phoned your home in Glenarm," Cramwell replied. "Your mother told me you were here for a couple of days."

"How did your Mr. Blunt identify me?"

"He got a photo of you from police files. He probably found your hotel by paying the desk clerk, and then waited for you in the lobby."

Cramwell saw Kathleen relax just a little. "I'll get right to the point, if you will please be seated." He resumed his seat at the desk and removed an envelope from a folder.

Reluctantly, Kathleen sat in one of the two overstuffed chairs in front of the desk. The cushion sank deeply beneath her. She noticed she was looking up at Cramwell. Against the wall was a sofa with several large throw pillows. Kathleen got up from the chair, picked up two of the pillows, piled them on her chair and sat back down. Now her head was slightly higher than Cramwell's, though her feet barely touched the floor. She felt a little silly, but she wanted to make the point that his game of superiority by position was blown.

"You've got three minutes," Kathleen said.

"I know that you are a munitions buyer for the IRA," Cramwell said without preamble.

Kathleen sat back in her chair, her practiced manner a facade of calm and control.

"I have no political position in this matter. I'm merely offering you information."

"I'm listening," Kathleen said with exaggerated politeness.

"We're talking arms and armament."

Kathleen knew the room could be bugged. This Cramwell could be working with the police. Yet he might not. She reached across his desk, tore a piece of paper from his note pad and picked up a pen. On the paper she scribbled, *The tea shop across the street. Now.* She showed Cramwell the note, then crumpled it and dropped it into her purse. She gestured to Cramwell to go out ahead of her. As he did, he picked up the envelope from his desk.

"Mr. Cramwell?" the secretary said in bewilderment as the boss and his visitor walked by.

"I'll be out for a while," Cramwell said without turning his head. "Take my calls."

"YOU ARE WISE to be cautious, Miss O'Toole," Cramwell said as he stirred his tea. "I can see why you are still alive in your dangerous business." He put down his spoon.

Kathleen sipped her tea. She put down the cup and said, a bit icily, "Mr. Cramwell, if you have anything for me, I am grateful. Now, shall we get down to business?"

Mr. Cramwell laughed. "Yes, of course. Do you know anything about the politics of Zimbabwe?"

"No. The politics of Ireland and Great Britain are more than enough for me, thank you." She paused. "And your question is relevant to what?" she added in her trade-speak manner.

Cramwell continued, "Many years ago, I went to school in London with a fellow from Zimbabwe. Name was Umbatwa. When he returned home, he joined the army. Rose to the rank of general. Then, five years ago, he led a revolution to topple the government."

"I don't recall reading that the government of Zimbabwe was overthrown recently." Kathleen said icily.

"True. It wasn't. It seems my friend—General Umbatwa—was a better student than a rebel. His revolution has failed, and he is being offered the chance to get out of the country alive. Exile."

"And this should interest me because?" Kathleen asked, beginning to see where this might be going.

"General Umbatwa would like his exile to be luxurious. He wants to sell his arms cache. The entire lot."

"Do I take it you are his broker?" Kathleen asked.

"No. He's a friend." Cramwell sounded defensive. He sighed. "Well, yes, I am being paid to put out the information. But I'm doing it mostly out of friendship for my old classmate Umbatwa."

"Right," Kathleen said wryly. "And you have told who else about these arms that you're not brokering?"

"No one yet. But I will be sharing the information with one more munitions buyer. A dealer who sells in South America and the Middle East mostly," Cramwell replied. "Not a lot of people have the kind of money this purchase would require."

"Would that be a wealthy ship owner?" Kathleen asked.

"No, it is not Mr. Jabri." Cramwell paused for a moment to let that register. "May I continue?"

Kathleen nodded.

"The asking price is three million dollars U.S., or its equivalent in any Western currency," Cramwell said.

"That *is* a lot of money. What's he selling?"

"Here's a list," he said and handed Kathleen the envelope. She opened it and scanned. "You'll see there, he's selling some of the same stuff your people already have a lot of, I would imagine. With one exception."

"And that would be?"

"Last item on the list. Three light fighter bombers. Late model, Chinese. And a large supply of bombs for those planes. And that, I believe, is something you do not have. The British have bombers. You don't." He paused. "Right?"

Kathleen smiled as she got up. She slipped the list into her purse, put money on the table to pay for their tea, and said, "This will take some time."

As she left the coffee shop, a man watched over the top of his newspaper. He was sitting in a distant corner, careful to not be seen. He had watched her open the envelope Cramwell gave her, and judged by the way she scanned the paper that it was a list.

That night he used a professional lock pick to slip into Cramwell's office. He wasn't sure what he was looking for, and he searched through files for hours, always careful to replace them neatly. Shortly before daybreak, as he was almost ready to give up, he came upon a list. It identified guns and airplanes for sale by some General Umbatwa in Africa. He knew he'd struck paydirt. He made a copy of the list on Cramwell's office copier, put the original back in its folder, and left quietly after re-locking the front door.

In a short time, the list was in Marston Hardale's fax machine, and later that day a small sum of money was wired from Washington DC to a bank in Belfast where it was deposited into the account of Homer Blunt.

15

The Bank Robbery

Richard Murry was a staunch—no, *passionate*—member of the Protestant Grand Order of Orange. He had only one passion that was greater: his thirst for money. Murry was also a loyal member of Sinn Féin, or so he pretended so that he could spy on them for the Order of Orange.

The saddest thing in Murry's hidden life was that he could not march in the annual Orange Walk, a parade to celebrate Protestant William of Orange's victory over Catholic King James II at Ireland's Battle of the Boyne in 1690. He especially regretted that he wasn't among the brave and hearty souls who walked the Orange Walk routes that just happened to pass near Nationalist (Catholic) areas. The Orange Walk was never intended to be contentious, though somehow, as if by miracle, along those routes the bloody street battles between Catholics and Protestants happened every year.

Murry was a pharmacist by vocation, and a spy by avocation. There was nothing he liked better than playing people off against one another. Murry was not a double agent; that term applies only to serving two masters and deceiving at least one of them. Murry did not limit himself as to quantity, and he deceived everyone he could as often as he could. In one of his enterprises, Mr. Murry ingratiated himself with a small and shadowy element within the Royal Ulster Constabulary, the Protestant and unionist law enforcement agency of Northern Ireland since 1922; hundreds of its members killed by the IRA.

From his apothecary, Murry's Pharmacy on Beale Street in Belfast, Richard Murray enjoyed watching the comings and goings of the armored trucks that served the largest bank in Ireland, the Bank of Éire, right next door to his shop.

It was a typical dank January day for London: no rain, but everything felt damp and cold. Sir Andrew Talingford, minister of defense for Great Britain, called a meeting for seven in the morning.

"Gentlemen," Talingford began. "As you know, the IRA ceasefire is breaking down. Sinn Féin feels that negotiations with Her Majesty's government are too slow, and nonproductive. And now we have word that the IRA may be looking to increase its munitions."

"But where's that supposed to come from, then?" asked Mortimer Montrose, personal secretary to the Queen of England. "All their munitions sources are shut off. Qaddafi, Walden Scott. All shut down."

"Sir Corbin can speak to that," Talingford replied. He gestured to Corbin.

"Gentlemen," Corbin began, "MI5 has found a member of the Order of Orange who has infiltrated Sinn Féin. He is willing to work with MI5." With a mischievous look covered poorly by his straight face, Corbin said, "His code name is Agent Orange." Appreciative guffaws went around the room.

Corbin continued, "This agent informs us that someone in the

IRA, acting independently, intends to rob a bank in Ireland. The leadership of the IRA doesn't know anything about her plans."

"*Her* plans? A woman?" Montrose asked. He had a rushing sense of foreboding. It could only be one person.

"Yes. Bank robbery is a little out of her line. She's the IRA's munitions buyer," Corbin replied.

"Why is she acting outside the chain of command?" Montrose said.

"Not sure, and that's troubling," Corbin replied.

Montrose asked, "Can't we just nab her in the act? Make a bloody show of it in newspapers everywhere! Better yet, we'll arrest her live on the telly!" he added with youthful enthusiasm.

"Not quite," Corbin replied with a look to the others in the room that said Montrose might be not only young but perhaps also just a bit daffy. "Better to handle these things quiet like, you know," he added in a condescending way.

"Well, what then?" Montrose asked.

"Our agent in Sinn Féin will inform my office of any bank robbery planned. And if this woman acts on her own, Agent Orange will know. Our agent has already gained her confidence. If a robbery is going down in Ireland, we will send in the British Army. Agent Orange will be on the scene, as our informant, and we will be guided by his advice."

"But that's what I just said!" Montrose complained loudly.

"No, what you suggested was that we make a holy show of the arrest. What we intend, instead, is that we nab the perpetrators in the act and then invite Sinn Féin to come collect them from the police, quiet like. And, in exchange for no prosecution, Sinn Féin is to get back to the negotiating table with Her Majesty's government. Keep the ceasefire undisturbed, like."

A few days later Sir Corbin's faith in his Agent Orange bore fruit.

BELFAST'S FINEST low-class watering hole was Doyle's Pub. Richard Murry was the only one in the gent's loo, so after he tipped a kidney he decided to take a moment and freshen up. His four colleagues waiting for him at the table could damn well wait a bit longer. He dampened only the tips of his fingers and, squinting into the blistered mirror, he slicked down his hair. There wasn't much of it left, but it was important to Murry that order be maintained among the few long black strands that lay from left to right in splendid solitude across his pale white scalp. He wiped his fingertips on his pants and made his way back to the table.

"What the hell kept ya?" Finian Daly asked. "We thought ye'd flushed yerself down the shitter, me boyo!" The others laughed.

It was pub owner Ross Doyle himself who brought a dirty rag to the table and wiped it vigorously. The five men had to snatch their glasses or they'd have gotten dashed to their laps.

"Hey!" Daly yelled. "Watch it, ye blitherin' eejit!" Doyle gave Daly a dirty look and walked off. It was past closing, and they were keeping him from it.

Murry leaned in toward the table and said in his best conspiratorial tone, "It's done, then? We're all agreed?" He glanced around the table at his four conspirators, but his eyes stopped on Daly.

Daly shrugged and said, "Sure. If it's all the way ye say it is. Right, lads?" There were murmurs of assent.

Murry sighed and scratched his chin. "Now all I have to do is convince that IRA woman."

"What's she for, anyway? We could do the job ourselves. No need of her."

"Ye got no brains at all, Daly. I told ye, she's gonna take the rap. The law needs someone to pin this robbery on, now don't they?"

"And who's supposed to do the pinch? Surely, not the Royal—"

"No, ye fool. The British Army is what's gonna do the pinch.

It's plenty solid at the top," Murry replied. "I went meself to Sir Thomas Corbin, head of MI5. And I told Sir Corbin that the IRA is gonna be hittin' Belfast's Bank of Éire."

"Are ye daft, man? The British army?" Daly protested. "They'll be all over this!"

"Exactly. But only when I tell Sir Corbin to send them," Murry said with pride. It's not everyone who can tell a British lord what to do and when to do it. "And I won't be after doin' that until I know ye've wrapped up the O'Toole woman and hopped off with the cash."

"Wrapped 'er up?" someone at the table asked. "Ye mean kill 'er?"

"No, ye bleedin' eejit!" Murry replied. He was starting to feel in control of this crew. "We want her framed! What good's it do to frame a dead person? Hold 'er at gunpoint, ye see. Two of ye takes off with the money, the other two stays behind with the prisoners. When the army gets there, O'Toole is gonna yell that she's been framed, but no one's gonna believe her, because Sir Corbin, actin' on *my* instructions, is gonna tell his soldiers to ignore whatever the robbers say. Got that?"

There was a long silence while all this sunk in. One of the four asked, "What about the bank's alarm system?"

"I've got someone inside who is gonna turn it off."

Someone else asked, "And how does O'Toole get into the bank?"

"I've started to knock a hole in the wall between the basement of my pharmacy and the bank's vault room," Murry replied. "The buildin's a hundred years old. The concrete's gone soft, it has."

"No iron bar reinforcement in it?" someone else asked.

"Sure there is," Murry answered. "But there's water seepage inside the wall. The iron's gone rusty. Cuts easy and bends easy, it does."

"How does she get inside the vault?" someone else asked.

"I've hired a cutter to do the vault. He's a throwaway. Shoot him."

Another silence. Daly said in a respectful voice, "Looks like ye've handled everythin', me boyo."

Murry said, "Ye know, it's a good thing to be gettin' Miss O'Toole out of circulation, but it's even more beautiful that the money's goin' to some hard-workin', loyal, deservin' souls—"

"Namely us!" Daly said. Enthusiastic murmurs of consent came from around the table.

"Have you heard the latest, then?" Bridie said to Kathleen. They were sitting together on a park bench, eating the fish and chips they had just bought for their lunch. "The bloody ceasefire is already in the bogs!"

"Aye," Kathleen responded. "Tom told me this morning. That damned truce doesn't have a snowball's chance."

Bridie sighed, "Looks like it's back to making bombs, then."

"Not necessarily," Kathleen said.

"What do you mean, then?" Bridie asked.

"We have more than enough stuff to make bombs for the next hundred years, but that doesn't get the job done. Doesn't make a big enough bang," Kathleen said.

"What are you getting at?"

"I know where to buy some airplanes. Fighter bombers." Kathleen looked at Bridie for a reaction. "And the bombs for them."

Bridie stopped in her tracks. "Good lord!" she whispered. "What's the Army Council say, then?"

"They aren't gonna know. Not until I tell them the ship is on its way with the goods. Then they'll have to start planning around it."

Bridie let that sink in. It was a tall idea. "And where would you get the money to make such a purchase, then? It's got to cost a bloody fortune."

"Aye. More money than I've ever seen."

Bridie's eyes lit up. "Why don't you ask Omar for the money? He's got plenty."

"That he does. But I think Omar would like me to quit the IRA. He's not likely to help. And I won't ask," Kathleen replied with a smug nod.

Bridie sighed, "Then ye'll not be buying your airplanes any time soon, I'm after saying."

"True enough, Bridie. True enough. Unless. . . ." Kathleen smirked and raised her eyebrows.

"Unless?"

"I had a visitor. Fella name of Richard Murry. He's IRA in good standing. I checked him out. The man's a pharmacist, owns Murry's Pharmacy in Belfast."

Bridie's eyes grew big. "Jayzus! We're not gonna sell drugs, are we?"

"Oh, sure. Heroine, cocaine. The works. Dirty needles, too. No, ya gobdaw. It's what's next door to the place that is of interest. In the same building," Kathleen said with a mischievous smile.

"What is it, then?" Her excitement was plainly visible.

"A bank. The Bank of Éire, if you please," Kathleen said with a playful grin.

"Is it a deposit that you have in mind, then?" Bridie asked.

"No, Miss Bridie, as you might guess, damn good and well," Kathleen replied with a gentle elbow in her friend's ribs. "It's a withdrawal I have in mind. Of everything in the vault. "

Bridie got a worried look.

"Hey, now. You don't have to be in on this, and all," Kathleen said. "I just thought you might, well you know, want to."

"Aye, I do. I would, and all," Bridie replied, but the worried look persisted.

"Well then?"

Bridie shook her head. "Never mind. I'm in."

Kathleen demanded, "There'll be no 'never mind,' and all. What is it?"

"Well, it's just that, I'm after asking if we really should. I mean, you don't have anyone's blessing on this."

"Right. No one knows. It's my own plan. If we tell them now, they'll just say no. They say I'm past it. Too old! Can you imagine? I think someone on the War Council is just jealous. And I don't care. Richard Murry doesn't care either. For a pocket full of money, he's willing to do it my way."

Bridie thought a moment and broke into a smile. Quietly she said, "All right, then. Let's do it. Tell me the plan."

"Here, now! Be careful with that one," Mack said. "It's got dynamite in it."

"Dynamite?" Kathleen said as she handed him the bag through the hole in the wall. "What the hell for? We aren't using any bloody dynamite! Are you daft, man?"

"I didn't say we was using it. I carry it for luck. Always have, always will."

Kathleen looked at Bridie and rolled her eyes. *A kook, this one!*

Together the girls lifted Mack's oxygen tank in to him. "Be careful with that acetylene tank, too," he groused. "It'll go off like a bomb."

Mack grinned as he glanced over at the vault. "She's an old McKenzie. Stopped making these more than a hundred years ago.

Cheap. Doesn't even have its own alarm. And it'll cut like butter." He lit his torch. "We'll be inside this baby in minutes."

Kathleen spoke into her radio. "Still quiet out there?"

In his car parked across the street from the bank, Murry replied, "You're fine. Nothing moving." That was true. His people were in position since before midnight. "Are you through the wall yet?"

"Yes, we just got through. We're inside the vault room." Kathleen checked her Beretta to make sure it was loaded. Bridie did the same with her sidearm. The chance of needing weapons on this job was slim, but it paid to be safe.

Murry glanced at his wrist watch. Two a.m. Everything was on schedule. He took his penlight from his shirt pocket and flashed it once toward the window up above his pharmacy. Two flashes came back. They were ready.

"This old Mackenzie is made of soft stuff. Shouldn't be much longer now," Mack said to the women as they watched the blue flame eat away at the metal.

Twenty minutes later Kathleen radioed Murry again. "We're into the vault. We're filling our bags with currency. My guess is there's a bloody fortune here."

"All right," Murry said. "All's quiet. Plenty of time. Just come on back out through the pharmacy when yer ready. Through the front door, as planned. I'll be right here waiting for ye." He pulled his penlight out again and signaled once more to the upstairs window. He drove around to the back door of his pharmacy.

We already know to exit by the front door. Why is he emphasizing it? Kathleen asked herself. *Aw, you're just paranoid. No time for that.*

In the dentist's office above the pharmacy, Murry's four accomplices checked their weapons. They were not wearing their police uniforms, as arranged, and as they moved toward the door they pulled dark stocking masks down over their heads.

"Let's go!" Daly said quietly as he went out the door with the other three in tow.

Quietly, the four rogue policemen made their way down the stairs to the back of the pharmacy. The basement door was ajar. Daly gestured toward the open door and signed his men to be quiet. With more hand gestures he positioned the three behind cabinets and packing crates. Daly got down behind a long desk with a kneehole where he could see the open door to the basement.

Kathleen, Bridie, and Mack started up the basement stairs. The women were laboring with the two duffel bags of money, while Mack was toting his heavy tanks and his tool bag. One of Mack's tanks clanked against a pipe on the wall.

A voice rang out: "Police! Stop right there! This is the police! Throw yer weapons up here! Do it now, or ye're dead!"

The three robbers turned and ran back down the stairs. "Bloody fucking hell!" Mack said. Kathleen and Bridie pulled out their guns. They chambered the first round.

"Where can we go?" Bridie whispered. "No way out! We're trapped!"

Mack pulled open his tool bag. "Wait!" he said. "I'll fix those sons o' bitches!" Mack didn't like cops very much. He pulled out a stick of dynamite, lit the fuse, and threw it up into the room above, yelling, "See how ye like this, ya cop bastards!"

The dynamite stick hit the floor and rolled through the kneehole of the desk where Daly was concealed. He saw it coming straight at his face, the wick throwing loud sparks.

His eyes bugged out with terror as he yelled, "Dynamite!" and dove for cover. The other three also dove for the deck. Moments went by. The wick fizzed loudly. Then silence. Daly dared a peek at the dynamite. The wick was expired. The thing lay there, harmless as a stick of sausage. He picked up the explosive, dead of old age, and tossed it back downstairs. "Is this the best ye can do, asshole?" he yelled down.

Mack saw the dead stick bounce down the stairs. *Sons o' bitches must have pulled out the fuse!* he thought. He gabbed another stick out of his bag and lit it. He held it while the fuse burned briskly. Kathleen yelled, "Throw it! Throw it!"

The men upstairs, about to charge the basement door, heard Kathleen's words and dove for cover once more. It wasn't until Daly was back behind the desk that he asked himself, *Why the feck didn't I shut that feckin' door?*

When Mack judged the fuse had only one or two seconds left, he pitched the dynamite up the stairs. It landed on the floor just as the fuse expired. Like the first one, the thing rolled to a stop and did nothing.

"Hit them!" Daly yelled, and the four men charged the door as one.

As soon as their heads appeared in the open doorway, Kathleen and Bridie opened fire. Three of the men jumped back, but Lynch tumbled down the stairs to Kathleen's feet, his eyes open in death.

Mack saw the stocking-covered heads and civilian clothes and yelled, "They're no fucking cops!" A roar came from his throat as he picked up his acetylene tank. He held it over his head and charged blindly up the stairs in an unthinking rage, intending to smash some people's heads with the heavy cylinder. In the doorway, Mack made a target hard to miss. All three of the men fired repeatedly, and Mack was dead before he hit the floor.

As he fell, a bullet hit his acetylene tank and it exploded with a deafening bang. Shrapnel flew. Daly shook his head to clear it. "O'Doherty, Byrne, ye guys okay?"

O'Doherty's head came up as he replied, "I'm okay. Byrne took a hunk of steel in the face. He's dead."

Downstairs Bridie turned to Kathleen and said softly, "I think Mack's gone!"

"Come on! We're out of here!" Kathleen replied.

"Where? There's no way!"

"Yes, there is! Come on!" Kathleen ran to the hole in the wall and quickly climbed back into the vault room, Bridie right with her. They dragged the duffel bags of money through with them.

"Now what? That gate's alarmed!" Bridie said.

"Good! That'll bring some real cops!" Kathleen answered. She shot out the lock and the gate swung open. No alarm was heard.

The women hefted the heavy duffle bags onto their shoulders and ran into the bank lobby. The night lights threw a yellow sheen that made the place look unreal. The ceiling was low over half the lobby area. The other half of the ceiling was made of glass, and it was six floors above. The two women looked up, and through the glass they could see the black night sky. Neither was ever in the Bank of Éire before, and they quickly looked around for any door that might lead out. "The front!" Bridie shouted.

"No!" Kathleen replied. "The real cops could be waiting out there! We need a back door!" Kathleen realized as soon as she'd spoken that if there were police at the front of the bank, they would be at the back as well. *Start thinking!* she chastised herself. She saw a large door under the low ceiling, in the side wall, and ran for it. It was locked; Kathleen put a shot through the doorknob and it blew apart. The two women stepped gingerly into a long hallway leading to a large circular flight of stairs. To their left was a door leading out to the street. "Let's go up," Kathleen said. Always the soldier, Kathleen was thinking of holding the high ground: the roof.

A shot. Kathleen and Bridie spun around and saw O'Doherty and Daly running across the lobby. Another shot. Bridie yelled and grabbed her arm. "I'm hit, damn it!" she said to Kathleen who was returning fire. O'Doherty and Daly dove for cover and kept popping up to shoot.

"How bad?" Kathleen asked, watching for a chance to get off a shot.

"Not too, I guess. I can use it some. Hurts, is all."

"Can you run?" Kathleen asked.

"But the money!" Bridie complained.

"We can't! The hell with it!" Kathleen replied. "Another day, another bank! Let's go!"

Bridie followed Kathleen up the stairs, still holding her wounded arm.

The stairwell wound through the core of the building to the roof six floors above. Around the stairwell were offices, all of them closed on Sunday. Daly and O'Doherty were thundering up the stairs behind them. Daly looked up the stairwell to see if he could locate the two women, and as he did Kathleen fired down at him several times but missed.

At the top of the stairs, Kathleen was relieved to find the door she had hoped would be there.

Out on the roof they saw a square shed with a sign that warned of high voltage. One side of the shed was built right up to the edge of the bank roof. Kathleen leaned out and saw that a ladder went from the top of the shed down the bank wall. *Our ladder to freedom*, she thought.

Bridie and Kathleen looked for a way to get on top of the shed roof. "It's on this side!" Bridie said.

The ladder rose up just a foot away from the glass skylight they had seen from below.

"Can you climb?" Kathleen asked Bridie.

"Yeah. I think so."

"I'll go up first." Kathleen raced carefully along the narrow space between the shed and the skylight.

From the top of the shed Kathleen reached down to help Bridie.

She was half way up, when the stairwell door banged open; O'Doherty and Daly rushed out, looking in every direction.

Kathleen fired and O'Doherty went down hard.

Daly spotted Bridie struggling up the ladder. He fired and she pitched over backward, sailed away from the ladder and crashed through the skylight, screaming all the way to the lobby floor six stories down.

Unthinking, Kathleen jumped to her feet and yelled in horror, "No!"

A searing pain ripped at the top of her head, followed by the sound of a gunshot. She saw her Beretta fall in slow motion, endlessly, to her feet, and she felt herself slip down into unconsciousness.

Kathleen woke to a short shoving motion. She was on her back. Her eyes wouldn't focus and her brain wasn't working well. The shoving kept repeating, getting faster. Her arms were pinned; her wrists were squeezed hard. She heard heavy breathing. She tried to see, but there was blood in her eyes and she remembered having been shot. Through her dimmed senses she felt her assailant on top of her, lodged inside her. She struggled to gather up enough strength to pull her arms free, to plunge her thumbs into the man's eyes, to kill him. He moaned in satisfaction and the shoving stopped. The sound of sirens came from a distance. Daly grinned and said, "That was lovely, darlin'. Got to run. We'll do it again some time." He slammed Kathleen across the jaw and she went out again.

Daly flew down the stairs, snatched up the two duffle bags where Kathleen and Bridie dropped them, and ran out the back door.

"What the hell happened? What took you so long up there?"

Murry yelled as Daly pitched the duffle bags into the back seat and jumped into the front.

"Drive! Drive!" Daly screamed.

WITHIN THE HOUR, MI5 had located Omar at his London residence. They told him Kathleen had been shot and was in Holy Cross hospital, expected to survive. They were about to go into the details when Omar hung up. "Hakim, wake up," he called out into the darkened house. "I need a jet to Belfast." He gathered a few things and raced out to his car.

By the time Omar got to the airport, he was already cleared for take off.

"YES, MR. JABRI," said the nurse at the reception desk. "The doctor has asked to see you as soon as you arrived."

"Please, where is her room!" Omar said.

"Kathleen O'Toole is in 14B, but you can't—"

Omar took off down the hall and called out over his shoulder, "Tell the doctor to meet me there!"

The police officer standing in front of 14B held up his hand as Omar approached. "I'm sorry sir, you can't go in there."

"What? My wife's in there. She's been shot. Why are you—?"

"Mr Jabri?" Omar turned to see a doctor walking quickly toward him.

"Doctor, I insist on seeing my wife! Now!"

"Your wife is unable to have visitors," the doctor replied as he put his hand on Omar's shoulder. "Please. Come with me, where we can speak in private." The doctor's calm voice and demeanor had its intended effect. Soon they were seated in a small room two doors down from 14B.

"Mr. Jabri, your wife is conscious now, and under mild sedation.

She has a gunshot wound on the right side of her head. The bullet cut a shallow swath in the skull but did not enter the brain cavity. However, there is a chance of contusion, swelling of the brain, and we have ordered a scan. A full neurological workup is underway."

"When can I see her? And why is there a policeman at the door?" Omar demanded.

"Mr. Jabri there is more . . ." He glanced down for a moment and continued. "Based on information from the police who found your wife, and on the . . . physical signs on her person. . . ." The doctor cleared his throat. He was obviously nervous.

"Yes?"

"Mr. Jabri, we suspected your wife had been raped. Since she was unconscious on arrival, and there was no family member available to sign a consent form, it was decided, in the patient's best interest, to perform a physical examination."

"And?" Omar asked.

"We found fresh semen. Severe bruising in the area. And bruises on the wrists, where she was held while . . . held against her will. It is certain that your wife was . . . raped."

Omar felt something well up inside his chest. He didn't know whether it was mostly rage or mostly grief. He only knew that, in that moment, he felt raped himself.

"I demand to see her," he said.

The doctor got to his feet and replied in an officious manner, "I'm sorry. You can not. She must be kept calm. Speaking with you would likely be emotional, and that would be dangerous if there is brain damage. No, sir, your wife can have no visitors at this time. Contraindicated."

"Contraindicated?" Omar rose to his feet. "Are you out of your mind? I'll tell you what's contraindicated! Your arrogance is contraindicated, you pompous ass! I will see my wife!" Omar demanded loudly.

The doctor signaled a hospital guard standing nearby. The man came over, one hand resting lightly on the top of the club at his belt. "Something wrong here, then?"

"Mr. Jabri," the doctor said. "Even if a visit with your wife were not medically contraindicated . . ." he emphasized the word by dragging it out.

Omar felt his anger rising.

"You would find that you would not be allowed to see her because she is under arrest. The charges, I am told, involve murder and attempted bank robbery." He paused to let that sink in. "Four of her accomplices were killed. Others got away with the bank's money." Still seeing no reaction he continued. "Now will you leave the hospital quietly, and at once, or shall I have you evicted? Or arrested."

Omar spun on his heel and stormed out of the building. At the first corner he saw a telephone booth. In his address book he found the home phone number he needed. It rang a long time.

"Yes?" the sleepy voice of a woman answered.

"Sir Clifford Stringwell, please. Omar Jabri calling."

"The Minister is still sleeping. My God, man, this is Sunday. Do you know what time it is?"

"Yes, I know what time it is," Omar said, barely able to keep his anger under control. "This is a matter of life and death. Tell him Omar Jabri, is on the line."

Omar heard the phone clunk down on a table. Someone spoke in the background.

"Mr. Jabri!" the sleepy voice called out, trying to sound friendly.

He thought of the time Omar's boys bailed him out of a tough spot in Soho three years ago. "How can I help you?"

"I'm calling in a favor."

"Yes, of course, old chap. Of course," Stringwell said.

"My wife . . . Kathleen O'Toole is being held—"

"Yes, I'm aware of all that mess. MI5 notified me. I had them call you."

"I want her out of police custody, Clifford. Today!"

"Yes, I understand. Not sure what I can do on a Sunday, but I'll give it a go."

"I expect my lawyer to meet with me here in Ireland tomorrow," Omar said.

"I see," said Stringwell. *Oh God, I can't have Jabri mucking this up,* he thought. "Give me a couple of days to get things straightened out. I know it seems like an awful long time. But if lawyers and the like get involved it will just complicate matters. Will you give me a chance to work through my channels?"

There was a long pause, then "All right," Omar said in a reluctant voice.

"There's a good chap. You will hear from me no later than Wednesday morning" Stringwell said with relief. "Where will I be able to reach you?"

"I'll be staying with Kathleen's parents in Glenarm," Omar said, and gave him their phone number.

"Now try not to worry. Oh, and listen: please don't go trying to get in and see her."

"Why the hell not?"

"I've got some sensitive egos to deal with at the police. They need to feel in full control, right up to the . . . uh . . . end. I know I'm asking a lot. But go with me on this one, Omar. I'll have you and your lady together as soon as possible. All right, old chap? And keep the family away, too. The quieter the better, you see."

Omar didn't like it. *Kathleen's going to hurt when no one comes to see her,* he thought.

As if he could read Omar's mind, Stringwell added, "We'll send a message in with a nurse. Your wife will understand." Stringwell paused to take a breath. He had pressed Omar hard. "Okay? Do I have your word you won't try to get in to see her? Or go public?" *If the press gets wind of this, we're sunk!* he thought. "I'm pretty sure I can have her out in not more than two days. Are you with me?"

Omar grumbled, "Yes. All right. Thank you. Goodbye."

OMAR PHONED Peg and Tom. They were both up, and Mulcahy answered the phone on the first ring. "Yes?" he said. Omar could hear Peg weeping softly in the background.

"Tom, it's Omar. I hear Peg crying."

"Yes, as well she might," Mulcahy said. "The police were here. They told us almost nothing. Only that Kathleen's hurt and she's in hospital. And there are criminal charges. They wouldn't say what. What's happened, Omar? Where are ye? Have ye seen Kathleen? Have ye—?"

"Kathleen will be okay. I'll be home as fast as I can. I'll explain everything. See you soon. Goodbye." As he drove, Omar asked himself if he *could* tell them everything. He could hardly cope with knowing Kathleen was raped, and didn't know how he could begin to tell Tom and Peg about it.

They were in the living room when he arrived. "Me doctor refuses to let me travel," Mulcahy complained. "He says this thing they put in me neck—"

"Yer stent, dear," Peg interrupted officiously. "Ye're still recovering. Too much excitement, and it could come undone."

"Hmpf," Tom said. "Weren't for that, I'd be at Kathleen's side right now."

Peg patted Tom's hand consolingly. "How's our girl?" she asked.

"She's going to be fine," Omar replied.

Peg said, "Is it true, Omar? Are the police holding Kathleen?"

"Yes, for now. She's being held at the hospital. I'm working on having her released, charges dropped. You said the police were here?"

"Aye," Mulcahy replied. "Wouldn't tell us anythin'. Just asked a lot of questions we couldn't answer. And some we wouldn't."

Omar looked around the room. "Did they search? The place looks untouched."

"No, they didn't," Mulcahy said. "Wanted to, but they started their investigation too fast. Didn't take the proper steps. The fools had no superintendent with 'em, and they were in civvies. I told them to go to hell. Right pissed they were, and all, but I know the law. To search a house, they have to be in uniform, and they have to—"

"Yes, Tom. All right," Peg said, trying to shush him before he blew out his stent. She turned to Omar. "Are ye all right, then?" Peg asked. She saw something in him that needed to come out.

Omar looked at Peg in a way that clearly said, *Help me!*

She placed her hands on Omar's shoulders and, looking deep into his eyes, said in her gentle way, "There's more to tell, isn't there?"

Omar nodded. He thought if he tried to speak of it, he would choke.

"Come, sit down here beside me, then," Peg said just above a whisper as she sat on the love seat.

"Tom, maybe ye'd better be goin' upstairs to bed now, dear. It's been a long night," she said solicitously to her husband.

He didn't bother to answer her; just pulled up a chair. "What is it, Omar?" he asked. "Is Kathleen all right?"

"There's more than the gunshot wound," Omar said, fighting to keep his feelings under control.

"What do ye mean, lad? What more?"

Omar's head twisted from side to side. He spit it out like a mouth full of poison. "She was raped."

Peg's hand flew to her mouth. Mulcahy leaped to his feet, rage on his face. "Who did it?" he thundered. The veins in his neck bulged.

Peg whispered in alarm, "Yer stent, Tom!"

"I don't know. I intend to find out," Omar replied.

"I'll kill 'im!" Mulcahy said.

"No, I intend to do the killing," Omar said. "I'll find him and—"

"What a fine pair!" Peg shouted through tears. "Our Kathleen needs her family more than ever before, and all the two of ye can talk of is *killin'!* Shame on ye both!"

Mulcahy started to say, "Now, Peg, I don't think—"

"Smartest thing ye've ever said, Tom! Ye *don't think!* And neither do *ye*, lad!" Peg said to Omar. "If ye, either of ye, can't handle a problem by using a gun, ye're lost! Well here's one time yer guns won't help. Won't help our Kathleen, that's certain!"

"Now, Peg," Omar said. "I understand. You're saying Kathleen needs care and attention. I'm planning to bring her home to me as soon as I can, where I can take good care of her, and—"

"No! Not with ye likely to show yer murderous feelins' from one moment to the next. She needs calm. Ye'll bring Kathleen here to me, Omar. I'll be in charge of her recovery. She's goin' to need ye, Omar, that's certain. But she'll be goin' to need a lot of her ma, too. Agreed?"

There wasn't much that either man could say. They saw that Peg was right.

Mulcahy rubbed his chest and looked faint.

Peg rushed to his side. "Come, then. It's off to bed with ye. I'll get yer medicine."

"Can I do anything?" Omar asked and rushed to Tom's other side.

"Now stop yer nonsense, the pair of ye!" Tom complained, pushing himself free of his two attendants. "Ye'd think I was dyin' or somethin', the way ye carry on! I'm just tired, is all. I'm off to bed, now. Peg, if ye'll be so good as to fetch me a glass of water." Tom turned and started up the stairs to the bedroom.

"Let me help," Omar said.

"Try it, and I'll bust yer chops!" Tom said, but the threat had the sound of emptiness. Omar looked inquiringly at Peg.

"It's all right. Let 'im be," she whispered, and she went off to get his medicine and some water.

Omar went to their quarters on the other side of the house. He couldn't rest, so he began to search. He went through drawers, looked on closet shelves, even under the mattress. Nothing. He opened Kathleen's jewelry box, and there it was. A business card. *Richard Murry, Murry's Pharmacy*, and it gave the address and phone number. Kathleen's handwriting on the back of the card said, "11:30 p.m. at bank."

Monday late afternoon, the early darkness of January in Ireland was settling in when Omar parked in front of Murry's Pharmacy. Next to Murry's shop, as part of the same tall building, Omar saw the Bank of Eire. He fastened the silencer to his Beretta .45, pulled on a pair of tight-fitting leather driving gloves, and got out of his car.

The pharmacy door was strung with police ribbon that said,

SCENE OF INVESTIGATION. Omar looked around. Not a cop in sight.

About a block up the street, two men sat in a car belonging to the United Kingdom's MI5. One said into his radio, "Subject on site."

"Roger that," the radio replied. "Code eight." The radio squawked softly, then went silent. Code eight was the confirmation these two expected to hear. It was easy duty: watch and do nothing.

Omar looked through the window in the front door. At the rear of the darkened shop, he saw a backroom door with a large window in it, and through that window he saw someone move in bright light. Omar lifted the yellow tape and ducked under. The door was locked. He opened a small knife with a stout blade and, looking first in both directions, he jimmied the lock. Omar silently walked through the sales area. He saw a man going through papers, furiously, putting some in a shredder, throwing others in a wastebasket.

The phone on the desk rang.

"Yes, Grand Master," he said to his caller. "The Order of Orange was well served tonight. The O'Toole woman will go to jail for life. Yes. I'm just cleaning out my office now. All right. Goodbye." He hung up as Omar, Beretta in hand, pushed open the door.

"What the. . . ?" the man in the white lab coat said. He saw the gun. "Wh . . . what do ye want?" he asked, trembling.

Omar said, "Richard Murry?"

"Yes." Murry replied. The gun in the stranger's hand looked enormous, and the hand did not waver. Murry stood motionless.

"Please," Omar implored. "Go on with what you were doing. Fascinating work, pharmacology." He wanted the man's fear and tension to increase.

Murry suddenly knew how he might save himself. He had no gun nearby, but he had another weapon he could get to. He walked over to a cabinet and took down a bottle, careful to turn the label away from Omar's line of vision.

As he uncapped the bottle, a bitter almond aroma filled the air. Omar knew it: cyanide. *So*, he thought, *Mr. Murry wants to play.*

"What do you know about the robbery last night at the Bank of Éire?" he barked. In a louder voice he added, "And what do you know about my wife, Kathleen O'Toole?"

Omar saw the man stiffen. "I've never heard of her. I don't know what ye're talkin' about," Murry replied. He turned his back to Omar as he filled a syringe with the poison and fastened a stout needle.

"Last chance, Mr. Murry! My wife! Start talking!"

Murry spun around, the syringe held high, his thumb on the plunger. His eyes looked wild. He dove at Omar's face. Omar sidestepped, grabbed the man's wrist and twisted his arm in a half circle. Murry fought back, trying to break free, and he accidentally slammed the needle into his own face. The force of the lightning jab caused Murry's thumb to press down on the plunger. The syringe emptied into the man's flesh and he screamed, knowing he had just killed himself.

Murry fell to the floor. His breathing immediately became irregular. His hands shook badly.

"Sodium nitrite!" he gasped, pointing to the cabinet where the cyanide and its antidote were kept. "Blue bottle! Please!"

"This one?" Omar asked, holding up the blue bottle. Murry nodded. "Fill the syringe! Inject a vein! Please! If ye don't, I'll die!"

In a quiet voice Omar asked slowly, "Who were those people who ambushed my wife at the bank?" Murry watched hungrily as Omar filled the syringe with the antidote.

"Royal Ulster Constabulary," Murry gasped. His vocal cords were locking up.

"Bad cops?" Omar asked.

Murry nodded. He said in a fading voice. "Please! Hurry!"

Omar pulled up Murry's coat sleeve to find a vein. He saw the man's strength was nearly gone. Omar positioned the needle. "You want to live?" he asked the gasping man.

The man nodded briskly. "Yes! Yes!"

"Who raped my wife?"

"Finian Daly. Please! Inject me!"

Omar released Murry's wrist and stood up. With a small smile he said softly, "You've done this to yourself," and squirted the antidote into the air. Murry hadn't quite stopped twitching before Omar was out the front door with the Rolodex from Murry's desk.

He had driven only a short distance away when the two men from MI5 were inside the pharmacy and found Murry, dead.

"We have a code fourteen," one of the two men said into his radio. "It's Murry, the pharmacist. Our code eight subject has left the scene. Please advise."

"Ten four. One moment." A few seconds went by before the voice returned. "Come on in. A cleanup crew is on its way."

ADRIAN BURKE WAS JUST closing his tattoo shop, putting away his inks and needles, when Cedric Clarke walked in. "Cedric, me lad! Come on in! How long since I've seen ya?"

"About a year, I'd say. Closed up for the day?"

"Aye, just about," Burke replied. "Don't know why I bother opening any more. Seems everybody that might want a tattoo has already got two!"

"Well I know somebody what *needs* a tattoo, and he ain't gonna want one, neither."

"Huh?"

"Ye remember Omar Jabri, don't ye?"

"Oh, aye. Paid us well," Burke replied. He was referring to some adjustments Omar ordered made on a traitor's kneecaps with a baseball bat.

"Grab up yer needles and let's go."

"My needles? We're doing a tattoo?"

"Right. And be sure to take yer longest, strongest needles. We're going deep."

An hour later in a seedy district of Belfast, the thin wooden door to an apartment splintered as the terror company of Burke & Clarke smashed into the life of Finian Daly.

The shocked Daly dove for the gun under his pillow but he never had a chance. Some time later, the bound and gagged Daly was shown his face in a mirror. The bright green tattoo that covered Daly's entire forehead said RAPIST, and the needle had pushed the ink not only into the skin but into the bone as well. Burke and Clarke explained to Daly that the husband of the woman he raped ordered the tattoo done that way so that no skin transplant could ever hide the word completely.

Daly looked at himself in the mirror, heard the explanation, and passed out.

Twenty minutes later, Daly was slapped awake. He found himself in a car with his two assailants, his gag still in place, his wrists still bound behind him, but now something was missing: He was without pants; naked from the waist down, and this terrified him. Daly was seated in the middle of the back seat. Around each ankle was a cloth rope. The ropes went to the door handles to his right and left, pulling his two legs wide apart.

"We're at the hospital emergency room," Clarke said.

Daly was confused. *Emergency room?* He began to shake violently.

"Ye see, we want ye to live a long time with no cock and balls."

Daly passed out long before it was over, and was still unconscious when the emergency room staff found him at their door, a crude bandage on his crotch and the missing members of his anatomy nowhere to be found. Daly was rushed to surgery—which he came through just fine.

THE MULCAHY'S PHONE RANG and Omar answered it.

"Is this Mr. Jabri?"

"Yes, who's this?"

"This is Sir Thomas Corbin. I'm—"

"I know who you are. You run MI5. What do you want?"

Corbin understood the rudeness and paused a moment to let it pass.

Omar said in a subdued tone, "I'm sorry. These aren't exactly good times. What is it?"

"Mr. Jabri, it is not for you to apologize. It is for me to do so . . . in the name of the . . . British government."

"How can I help you?"

"I received a phone call from Sir Stringwell. Your wife is being discharged today, Mr. Jabri. Both from hospital and from police custody. The doctors are assured she's going to be fine, and . . . all charges against her are dropped.

"Officer Daly was interviewed in the hospital yesterday. He told us everything. He and three of his fellow police officers robbed the Bank of Eire. We've recovered all the money they stole."

"Then the police have no more interest in Kathleen O'Toole," Omar said.

Tom and Peg stared at each other, eyes wide.

"That's right, Mr. Jabri," Corbin said in a slow, deliberate manner. "The bank robbers have been identified. Officer Daly has confessed. The money has been recovered. All of the other participants in the robbery have been . . . accounted for." Corbin paused for a response.

He got none.

Corbin continued, "The entire affair is over. Kathleen O'Toole is free to go. And that is the end of it."

"When can I collect my wife at the hospital?" Omar asked.

"Why, immediately, sir. Immediately."

"Thank you," Omar said and hung up.

Corbin looked across the desk, waiting to know if his career was at an end.

"Sir Corbin," the woman said in a harsh voice, "we require you to get this foolishness set aside. All of it, and right now. We want everyone back to the bargaining table. Immediately. The IRA cease-fire must continue, at any cost."

After a pause, the voice continued in a more gentle way, but still bearing the ring of iron-clad authority, "You have done your duty, Sir Corbin. We are well pleased."

Corbin said with a sigh of relief, "Thank you, Your Majesty."

PEG PROPPED KATHLEEN up in bed with extra pillows and set the bed tray down over her lap. Five days of bed rest was prescribed, only as a safeguard against the possibility of swelling inside the cranium. Kathleen hated being confined, but she was not about to balk at Peg.

"I'll just sit here a bit with ye, child, if ye don't mind," Peg said as she pulled up a chair.

Kathleen did mind. Whenever anyone was with her—Tom, Peg, Omar—she immediately wanted to be alone; and when she was alone she was miserable.

Kathleen picked up her spoon and stirred her soup. After a full two minutes she was still stirring, her eyes vacant.

Peg's heart ached and she fought to hold back tears. "It's mushroom," she said, just above a whisper. "Yer favorite."

"Hmm?" Kathleen said, trying to focus on the face beside the bed.

"Try some soup, dear. It's not too hot."

"Oh, yes," Kathleen said. "I like mushroom soup." She sounded like a child rehearsing something that needed to be learned. She filled her spoon and lifted it toward her mouth. The spoon was shaking. As she got it almost to her lips, the spoon shook violently and flew out of her fingers.

"There, there, now," Peg said as she rushed to remove the tray from the bed.

Kathleen turned away from Peg, silent and staring at the wall. Peg waited.

Kathleen slowly turned her head to Peg. Her eyes were sunken.

Peg sat on the bed. "Would ye like to talk about it?"

Kathleen closed her eyes.

"Well, that's okay," Peg patted her hand. "Just know that I am here to talk or just to listen, any time. And know that I love ye . . . we all love ye very much."

Kathleen sobbed, "I feel so guilty. Like I've let you down."

"Oh, child, what can ye mean? That's impossible. It wasn't yer fault!" Peg felt as if her heart would break.

Kathleen felt anger rise up from her belly. "Oh, I've seen how it is! How it's going to be from now on! Omar feels sorry for me. And Tom won't look at me, can barely talk to me!" She almost screamed, "And I don't blame him!"

She fell into Peg's arms, crying hard. "It's not that way, Katie. It's not what ye're thinkin' at all," Peg said.

After a while, Kathleen began to calm down, and Peg even persuaded her to try some soup. "I'll just run down to the kitchen and heat it up. Be back in a minute."

Omar passed Peg in the hallway. "How's she doing?" he asked. Peg just fluttered her hand and shook her head.

Omar peeked his head in at the door. "Hello, darling. Want company?"

"Come in," Kathleen sighed. Omar sat on the bed. He reached out and touched her face. Big tears ran down Kathleen's cheeks.

"We're going to get through this," Omar said. "Together. You'll see. I know you. I know how strong you are."

Strong, sure . . . but still . . . damaged goods, she thought.

Omar tried to hold her, tried to kiss her. He ached inside, and wished he knew what to do.

"I'm very tired," said Kathleen. "Maybe I should rest."

"Of course. I'll go now." Omar stood and looked into her red, swollen eyes. "I love you," he said.

Kathleen said nothing.

AFTER SUPPER, TOM SAT VERY quiet and listened to what Peg had to say.

"Kathleen needs you now, more than ever. She needs you to love her, no matter what."

"Well, of course I love her. I can't stop thinkin' about it. What happened. I want to kill the devil that did this!" said Tom pounding his fist on the table.

"Ye've got to stop thinkin' about how *ye* feel, and think about how *Kathleen* feels."

Peg continued, "She told me that ye won't look at her. She

thinks ye don't love her . . . can't love her any more." Peg sobbed. "She thinks ye're ashamed of her."

Tom was shocked. He looked at Peg for a long moment, then buried his face in his hands. "Oh, God! What have I been doin'? Me poor Katie! Me poor, poor Katie! I'm goin' to talk with 'er right now."

He went to the sink and splashed some cold water on his face. "Thank ye, Peg," he said and walked in a deliberate manner up to Kathleen's room.

THERE WAS A LIGHT TAP on the door.

"Come in," Kathleen said. She looked up from her magazine and watched as Tom walked toward her. She had never seen such tenderness in his face.

Kathleen burst into tears. "I'm so sorry," she said.

Tom sat and held her in his arms. "There, now. There, now," was all he could say as they rocked gently and held each other tight.

After a while Kathleen reached for a tissue. Tom felt useless and confused.

"Ye know," he said, "I've never had to deal with this kind of thing. I don't know what to say."

Kathleen patted him on the hand. "It's all right, Tom. It's my problem. Not yours."

"Maybe so, child. Maybe so. But I feel as though I'm lettin' ye down. It's like I'm failin' me own daughter when she needs me most. More than ever before."

Kathleen threw her head on Tom's shoulder and cried. He stroked her back and said nothing.

After a while Kathleen's crying softened, and Tom said, "I think I'm sayin' all the wrong things." He looked into his daughter's eyes and whispered, "What are ye feelin' right now, then?"

Kathleen put her head back on Tom's shoulder. "I feel all mixed up. Sometimes I feel numb. All over. Other times I feel humiliated. And angry. Guilty." She shrugged her shoulders. "It keeps changing. Sometimes from minute to minute. It's like I don't know myself any more." She lifted her face from his shoulders and studied his eyes, waiting for a reply.

"Aye. A lot of feelin's. Changin'. One thing I learned when Colleen was taken away is that I had to let my feelin's be there. I couldn't change 'em. Couldn't chase 'em away. Oh, I tried. But that only made me feel worse. When I grew a bit older, I started to feel guilty that I couldn't have prevented what happened to her. Can ye imagine that? I was helpless when it happened. There was nothin' I could have done to prevent it. I had nothin' to feel guilty about." He stopped to see what effect his words might be having.

"Are you just trying to make me feel better, Tom?"

Tom sighed. "Lord knows, I wish I could. But I don't think anyone can make anybody else feel anythin'." He shrugged his shoulders. "Ye just have to feel whatever ye're feelin'. Yer feelin's are real. Ye mustn't deny them."

Kathleen smiled. "You sound like a doctor."

Tom's eyes watered. "No, child. Yer wrong about that. I'm yer father. I'm yer father what loves ye. Please don't ever forget it. I'll always be there fer ye."

KATHLEEN WAS DETERMINED. She was not going to appear weak—especially to Omar. She had given herself a good talking to: *Enough of this crying and carrying on. Get over it!*

"Well, now," Kathleen said to Omar in a bright tone of voice. She had given in to Peg's insistence that she remain in bed at least two more days, until the doctor came. Omar had brought her a new book to read.

Kathleen straightened the little rumples in the bedcover and composed her face to look pleasant. "Tell me what's going on in your world."

"Ah!" Omar seized the opportunity for a topic, any topic, of conversation. In fact there was something. "I'm off tomorrow. Been meaning to tell you."

"Oh!" Kathleen replied as though this were something new in their life. "Be gone long?" Her smile looked like it was made of candy.

"No. Only a couple of days, I should think. Arranging a pickup and delivery," he said, a bit too brightly. "I've been invited to deliver some stolen diamonds. I'm going to Africa to talk with the people who intend to steal them. I want to work out some details about the pickup."

A WEEK AFTER KATHLEEN's discharge from hospital, a local doctor removed the bandages from her head wound. Omar was there for the unveiling, and Kathleen requested a mirror. With a wry smile she said, "Well now, ain't I God's own great beauty!" as she looked at the long and broad patch of her head that was shaved clean for the surgery. The line of stitches zigzagged down the bare skin. "I've heard of some ladies getting a Mohawk haircut, but this is a bit over the top," she said.

"It'll grow back," Omar said as he pressed Kathleen's fingers reassuringly in his hand.

Kathleen sighed, "Yes, I suppose it will." She turned her head this way and that in the mirror. Her long auburn tresses always were her secret pride, the part of her appearance she valued above all others combined. Now her hair looked like a sad, cruel joke.

16

The Healing

1995

Kathleen covered her scar with a straw hat when she and Omar picked up the boys at school. They had never seen their mother wear a hat. Michael pointed and laughed, "What's with the hat, Ma?"

"You going to a fashion show?" Shafi wanted to know.

Kathleen smiled but said nothing. She got into the car first and immediately removed her hat. She and Omar had decided to let the boys see, and get it over with.

As he climbed into the back seat, Michael was shocked. "What happened to your head, Ma?"

"Did something fall on you?" Shafi asked as he followed his brother into the car. Omar got behind the wheel and looked over at Kathleen, waiting for her to start the prepared recitation.

"No. I was hurt in my work," Kathleen said.

"But how? What happened?" Michael wanted to know.

This was expected. It was Omar's turn now. "Come on, boys. What's our rule about your mother's work?"

Shafi hung his head in disappointment as he mumbled, "Don't ask, don't tell."

Michael found the "don't tell" rule hard enough, but the "don't ask" rule he found impossible. "Did some bad guys hurt you, Ma?"

"Enough, Michael," Omar chastised gently. This was part of the plan. Omar would hold the leash, and Kathleen would allow just enough slack to blunt their sons' natural curiosity.

"Yes," Kathleen replied. "They were some bad guys. But they're all taken care of. They are never coming back."

"Did you kill them?" Shafi asked.

"No, I didn't. But they're never coming back. That's the truth," Kathleen replied.

"Okay, boys," Omar said with a firm tone. "Subject closed." Kathleen and Omar exchanged glances that said, *Good job, well done!*

That evening as Kathleen and Omar were preparing for bed, Omar said, "I'm not very happy about what we did today with the kids."

"You mean the rule?" Kathleen asked.

"Don't ask, don't tell is very convenient for us. But. . . ."

Kathleen sighed. "We created it to protect them as much as ourselves."

Omar sighed, "I wish whoever invented parenting had written an owner's manual," and climbed into bed.

"Sorry you signed on?" Kathleen asked.

"Usually, no. But right this minute I am, yes."

"I know what you mean," Kathleen said as she slid in on her side of the bed. "I have moments, too. More often than I care to admit."

"I just think all the secrecy keeps us from being close."

"What's the alternative, Omar? Do you want to tell our kids that you're about to deliver some stolen diamonds?"

"No. I don't. Though I think one day soon they're going to figure it all out for themselves. We can't protect them forever."

"Are you more concerned with protecting them, or protecting yourself? Aren't you being just a little bit of a hypocrite?" Kathleen asked angrily.

"Hey," Omar protested as he propped himself up on one elbow. He was angry. "Where is all this soul-searching coming from all of a sudden? I don't remember you sitting down and telling the boys about how you robbed a bank. And got your friend Bridie killed."

Kathleen's eyes hardened. She turned to the wall. "That hurt, Omar."

Omar placed a hand on her shoulder. She pulled away.

"And, right now, I want to say you hurt me first." He paused, then added. "That sounds so childish." He lay back down and stared at the ceiling. "Have we come to this?" he said softly. "You hurt me, then I hurt you?" He turned to her and whispered, "Forgive me. I'm sorry."

Kathleen moved to Omar and he wrapped her in his arms. She cried softly for a long time on his shoulder, and Omar held her closely.

Both fell asleep that night vaguely aware that behind their seeming thoughtlessness, behind the hurting, lay the real problem—the real pain—that neither was ready to talk about. The healing would have to wait.

OMAR AND KATHLEEN found they could focus on whatever the moment happened to contain. This helped make the summer in Florenza bearable, but holding each rickety day together was exhausting them, and even the children sensed it.

On the surface, it was a time of family fun; a time of laughter and Sunday picnics at a small lake not far from their home, an outing that became a weekly routine.

One Sunday, Shafi was standing on the old dock. He was skipping stones across the water, trying to get two skips, but mostly he was getting only one.

"You'd better watch out," Omar said. "Old Whiskers will jump out of the water and get you."

Kathleen laughed. Another of Omar's stories was coming and she knew how much the boys loved that.

"Da, remember that story you told us when we were little?" Michael asked.

"Which one?" Omar replied as Kathleen handed him another hard boiled egg.

"My favorite was the one about the three brothers who skipped school," Shafi said.

"I think the last time I told you that, you were babies. You still remember it?"

"Sure," Shafi said. "Jeeper, Creeper, and Neeper skipped school and went to the zoo. They fed the elephant some pebbles because they didn't have money to buy peanuts. The elephant broke a tooth on a pebble. He got mad, and he picked up all three of the boys at the same time with his trunk, and he threw them in the river." He added, "That was some big trunk, that elephant had, to pick up three kids together."

"And what's the moral of that story?" Kathleen asked.

"Always have some peanut money when you skip school," Michael replied. Kathleen and the boys laughed.

"Doesn't anyone want to hear about Old Whiskers, the giant one-thousand-year old catfish?" Omar asked, pretending his feelings were hurt.

"Does he eat peanuts and throw kids into a lake?" Michael asked, teasing his dad.

"Hmph!" Omar said with a toss of his head. He turned his back and added, "See if I tell certain people any more stories."

"Aw, come on, Da," Shafi said from out on the dock. "Michael's just being weird." Shafi stood up to throw another stone across the water. He stepped on a loose board and teetered for a moment, flailing the air for balance. He prevented a dunking in the lake by grabbing at the loose handrail.

"Shafi!" Kathleen screamed. "Get off that dock this minute!"

The panic in Kathleen's voice froze Michael and Omar.

Shafi was shocked. He decided to try to make his mother laugh. "Ma, I'm okay! Look!" He put his hands in the air, stood on one foot and tried to look silly.

Omar saw Kathleen shaking. This was not like her. He said softly, "I think he's okay, dear."

"Okay, is it?" she screamed. "Shafi, get over here right now!"

Shafi walked slowly to his mother.

Kathleen looked from Omar to her sons and back again. She saw the confusion in their faces and realized her shouting had been unreasonable. She burst into tears and covered her face with her hands. "I'm sorry," she said through her tears. "I got frightened."

Omar took her in his arms. "It's okay," he said softly. "It's okay."

Shafi and Michael looked at each other. They shrugged their shoulders, totally confused.

"Boys," Omar said gently. "Better stay off the dock today."

"Aw, Da!" Shafi said.

Kathleen snapped, "You're to stay off that dock! Forever! It's too dangerous."

"Aw, Ma!" Michael said.

The family cut short their picnic. On the way home there was little conversation, and when they got to the house Kathleen went to lie down.

Omar put his hands on his sons' shoulders and led them outside. "Your mother is just tired. And a headache. Please don't worry. She'll be fine."

"What happened, Da?" Shafi asked. "Why'd Ma get so mad?"

"Yeah," Michael said. "We didn't do nothin'."

"It's not about you," Omar said. "Your mother has a lot on her mind."

"Ma ain't been the same since she got her head hurt," Michael said.

A jolt of surprise shot through Omar at hearing his son come so close to the truth. "Yes," he murmured. "A lot happened that day." He looked intently at his two boys and saw they weren't babies any more. He also sensed, though vaguely, that his sons weren't the only ones who were changing. Suddenly he realized how much Kathleen had needed him. Ever since the day that, as Michael had put it, she got her head hurt.

It was time, Omar decided. It was past time.

"You boys play outside for a while, but don't leave the property. I'm going in to talk with your mother," Omar said. "Don't come in 'til we call you."

The boys watched their father go in the house, then Shafi mumbled, "Don't do this, don't do that."

Michael put his arm around his brother's shoulders and said in a weary way, "Come on, Shaf. Let's go do *somethin'*."

Omar found Kathleen sitting in the swivel-chair looking out their bedroom window. "Feeling better?" he asked as he walked up behind her and placed a hand on her shoulder.

Kathleen took one of Omar's fingers in her hand and gave it a squeeze. She said no words, but to Omar the gesture meant she might be ready to talk. He turned the swivel chair around so that Kathleen was facing him and he sat on the floor in front of her. He lifted one of her feet, took off her slipper and began to massage.

Kathleen smiled and her eyes filled with tears. "That's so sweet," she said. "I don't really deserve a foot massage."

"Right," Omar said as he dropped her other slipper and began to massage one foot in each hand. "You deserve a two-foot massage."

Kathleen laughed and let a tear roll down her cheek. "I haven't been . . . very nice . . . lately," she said. "My mind's been . . . muddled."

Omar continued the gentle massage. "Want to talk about it?"

"Do you?" Kathleen asked.

"Touché," Omar said. He stopped the massage and sat back. "We both need to talk."

"Will you go first?" Kathleen asked. Omar thought she seemed like a small child afraid to take a chance.

"Well, I can," he replied pensively. He leaned forward and took Kathleen's hand in his. He looked up into her eyes and said in a low voice, "Raped."

Kathleen looked away quickly but didn't withdraw her hands. Her chin was trembling violently.

"Raped, Kathleen," Omar said softly. "Both of us were."

Kathleen tumbled out of her chair and into Omar's arms. She was crying hard now, and fell to the floor, drawing Omar down with her.

Omar was choking. He thought his throat would burst. Then he screamed, and his roar rammed the walls. It was pain, it was anguish, it was rage. Kathleen clutched him in her arms and kissed his face, his burning tears, a hundred times.

"Shhh, my darling," she said through her tears. "Shhh, now,

don't you cry," she whispered, still crying herself. "Shhh-shhh-shhh."

Moments went by. A small trembling voice said, "Da?"

Kathleen and Omar turned and saw their boys standing in the doorway of the bedroom, their faces full of fear and confusion.

"We heard you, Da" Michael said. "What's the matter?" he asked, his emotions overflowing.

Omar held an arm out to his sons, and Kathleen did the same. The boys ran to their parents, and slid into their arms. They still had no idea why their mother and their father were crying, but it didn't matter. They had never felt so safe.

Later that night when the boys were long in bed, Kathleen was in her nightgown and flipping idly through the pages of a magazine while Omar was trying to become interested in a novel. Kathleen looked up at Omar for a long silent moment, tears filling her eyes.

"What is it, dear?" Omar asked.

"I've made a decision. A hard one, but a good one."

"What decision, dear?"

"I want you to cut my hair off. All of it. Make it all the same length as what's growing back where they shaved me."

"What?" Omar was shocked. "Why?"

"Couple of reasons. First, I want to put the rape entirely behind me. Entirely." She paused. "Isn't that funny? I just said the word. Yesterday I couldn't bear to even think it." She sighed. "I've burned the clothes I was wearing that day." She paused again. "The day I was raped."

She looked at Omar. "Now I want to start over. My body wants to start over, too. As of today, I'm a new person. Stronger than before. Like the bone that heals stronger in the broken place. Thank you so much, my darling, for helping me get through this."

Omar shook his head. He asked himself, as he had so many

times, if he'd ever know even a tenth of this woman; but he was determined to pursue knowing her, pursue that knowing throughout his lifetime.

"Are you sure you want me to do this?" he asked. "We'll be returning to London soon, when the boys go back to school. You could go to a beauty shop. They would do a better—"

"No, Omar. Please. I want *you* to do it. This is hard enough. I don't want some stranger to . . . touch me . . . that way." She shuddered. "I want you to do it. Only you, Omar. Please."

"Okay. I'll do it. You said there were two reasons."

Kathleen opened her arms and said softly, tears in her eyes, "Come here, my darling."

Omar threw himself to her breast. She held him tightly. "Oh, my dearest," Kathleen whispered. "I haven't felt like . . . I'm so sorry, I've held you away . . . I'm ready now . . . to . . . be yours again."

Omar was both glad and worried. He was pretty sure he was ready, but not entirely certain. Part of him was eager to find out and part of him was not.

Kathleen sat at the dressing table and watched in the mirror as Omar took her long auburn tresses in his fingers. His hand was shaking. "This feels strange," he said.

"Feels strange to me, too," Kathleen said. "But it feels right. Cut it shorter, dear. Same length as what's growing back."

Soon Kathleen's long hair was in a pile on the dresser. She sighed, scooped it up and dropped it in the wastebasket. She roughed up her short straight hair. She thought it looked like matchsticks. "Looks good," she lied, bravely. "What do you think? Are you going to like me in short hair?"

Omar took Kathleen in his arms and held her close. "Long hair, short hair, or no hair at all. I wouldn't care if you shaved your head to look like a bowling ball." He grinned and added, "Come to think of it, though, I guess that wouldn't be my preference."

Several nights later Omar awoke to find himself alone in bed. Again. Kathleen had explained to Omar that she often wasn't able to sleep through the night and would get up to read for a while.

This night Omar decided to join her.

That's strange, no lights anywhere, he thought as he walked through the large hacienda. A full moon cast light across the living room through the French doors that overlooked the sea.

Omar saw Kathleen scurrying from door to door, window to window. "Darling, what on earth are you doing?"

Kathleen jumped at Omar's voice and turned to face him.

He crossed the room and held out his hands, while Kathleen stood silent. First she smoothed her robe, then she brushed her hair back from her face and let her hands clasp at the back of her neck. In the bright moonlight Omar could see that her eyes were closed.

She took a deep breath. "Well, I might as well confess," she said, trying to sound bright. She was embarrassed but felt relieved to have been caught.

I can't fight this by myself anymore, she thought.

She stepped forward to close the space between them. Her hands were outstretched and she placed them in his. "I'm afraid your Kathleen has gone a bit 'round the bend," she said looking up into Omar's face.

His eyes showed concern. "Tell me. You can tell me anything," he said.

She sat on the sofa, pulling him down beside her. "This is embarrassing," she said.

Omar sat in silence. He felt afraid, and was trying not to show it. Kathleen began again. "In the evening, before it gets dark, I make sure every door, every window, everything is locked. I even double-check for Chrissakes."

Omar shook his head, and said, more to himself than Kathleen, "We've . . . you've . . . never been one to be concerned about locking up."

"I know," she continued. "And a lot of times I wake up at night and worry about the locks," she said. "No matter how I try to reason with myself about it, I have to get up and check all the locks!" Kathleen sounded angry now. "It's crazy!"

So that's all it is. In spite of himself, Omar chuckled a sigh of relief. "I . . . I'm sorry . . . but, look at this place," he said sweeping his hand broadly in front of them. "It's all windows and glass doors! Our home is all glass." Kathleen stared hard at him.

"I didn't mean to make light—" he began.

Kathleen broke into laughter, and once she started laughing she couldn't stop. In between new bursts, she said, "And any simpleton could break in, if he wanted to."

Her face was red, and tears rolled down her cheeks as more laughter poured out of her. "Here I am protecting us from the big bad world out there . . . all night, every night, many times a night. . . ."

By now Omar was laughing too. They held each other and tried to suppress their giggles. But one of them would start up, and a whole new wave of laughter and tears would wash over them.

Omar stood and said, "I'll get us some tissues." He returned from the kitchen with two big bowls of vanilla ice cream. "I think it's time for a celebration," he said as he handed one to Kathleen. "I've put nuts on top—and chocolate of course."

Kathleen giggled, "Well, of course!"

They sat in the darkness and ate their ice cream.

"Better now?" asked Omar.

Kathleen thought for a moment. "Well, I do feel a bit foolish. And I have to admit I have been struggling with this a lot. And trying to hide it from you."

"Well, now we'll face it together," Omar promised. "And my darling, you may be struggling, but you know what? Tonight I see the light returning to your eyes."

It was almost dawn when Omar awoke and felt Kathleen's soft hand lightly touching his chest. He looked at her and smiled.

"I want you to know that you are the love of my life, and I trust you more than I ever thought I could trust anyone," she said.

Her whole body trembled as she slowly rose, and, with tears in her eyes, straddled Omar. Not sure what to do, Omar took a passive role while Kathleen made love to him.

Afterward, with Kathleen at rest on top, he vowed to always remember the tenderness and power Kathleen had showed him this morning.

AFTER THAT NIGHT, THE MAGIC was back into the love life of Kathleen and Omar, and in some ways sex was better than ever. One morning about a week after the breakthrough, Omar walked into the breakfast room and tousled Kathleen's pixie-like hair. "Good morning, Shirley MacLaine," he said with a grin.

"Oh, stop!" Kathleen laughed. "It'll grow long again, sure enough."

Omar poured a cup of coffee and sat down across from Kathleen at the breakfast table. "Oh, I'm not complaining. Kind of fun, actually, living with a famous movie star. Especially one that communicates with spirits." He tried to imitate the theme music from "Twilight Zone" but made a bogs of it, and Kathleen laughed—which is exactly what Omar was hoping for. "Let's take breakfast on the veranda," he said as he picked up his cup and walked outside, Kathleen following. "I missed our sunrise this morning," he called to her.

"Yes, you did," Kathleen said. "And it was a beauty. I saw you working at your desk and thought I shouldn't disturb. But we saved you some breakfast."

She turned and called, "Jacinta, Omar is ready for his breakfast."

"I'm hungry!" Omar said. "And I've got a big day. I'm driving up to Valencia on business. I'll be tied up most of the day." Omar paused between bites. "It's quiet around here. Where are the boys?"

"They're off fishing with the Molinaro kids. Be back for lunch. With fresh trout, I hope."

"I guess they want to pack as much as they can into this last week before school starts." Omar said.

He put down his fork and looked at Kathleen. He said, quietly, "It's been a wonderful summer. I've never felt as close to our two boys as I do right now." He reached across the table and took Kathleen's hands in his. "And I feel closer than ever to you, my darling."

Omar's eyes brightened. He smiled and added, "Hey, come up to Valencia with me! You can shop while I'm at my meeting, then we can have a late lunch at that restaurant you liked so well. What was it?"

"You mean the Tapineria?"

"That's the one."

Kathleen smiled, "I wonder if Manolo is still their chef. Yes, I'd love to go with you."

"Good! You'll have fun. You could go back to that flea market you enjoyed."

Kathleen grinned and said, "Remember the time I talked a vendor into swapping an embroidered robe for that beat up old purse I was carrying?"

"And *I* wound up with pockets crammed full of your stuff. I never knew a woman's purse could carry so much!" Omar said with a wry smile.

Kathleen's smile changed to a serious look. She turned her head and her voice hardened, "Omar, I got a call from the IRA."

Omar stiffened. "They phoned you?"

"Yes. But when I said I got a call, I was referring to more than the telephone. I mean, I got a call. The IRA is calling me in."

Omar got up from the table and turned his back. "No," he said in a low voice.

"Omar, the ceasefire is coming apart. They need me there."

Omar spun to face Kathleen. "I forbid it!" he said brusquely.

Kathleen blanched. "I beg your pardon?" she said as she rose from the table.

"Don't they have any feelings? After all you've gone through—"

"Omar, it's exactly because of all that. I'll be effective. They need me at the negotiating table."

He's forbidding me? she thought and turned her back.

Omar wrapped his arms around Kathleen from behind. "Darling, please," he reasoned. She felt his breath on her neck, and for a moment she wanted to give in to him.

Omar continued, "Think of your children. I was hoping we could make our permanent home in Florenza. Full time. Bring the boys to a good school nearby. Be a real family." He hugged her hard. "I need you. We need you."

Kathleen turned to him. Tears were running down her face. She hugged him for a long time, and Omar breathed a sigh of relief, thinking the crisis was passed.

She pulled back from him and said, "Omar, I've worked so hard to make Ireland whole. We all have. Sinn Féin has come so far. We're almost there. Omar, I can't turn my back on the movement now. Be reasonable."

Omar spun away from her. When he turned back to speak, Kathleen saw dark rage in his eyes.

In a voice of command, he said, "That's it! I forbid you to have anything more to do with Sinn Féin and the IRA! Do you hear me? It's over! Finished!"

After a pause he added, as afterthought, "I've got a few notes to get together before we leave for Valencia. I'd like to leave in about an hour." He saw Kathleen's familiar wall go up. *This is going to be a long uncomfortable drive to Valencia*, he thought.

He held his hand out to her. "Coming then?"

"No, you go on to Valencia. I have things to do here," she replied with her well-practiced nonchalance.

"Very well," Omar said, icily. "Then don't hold dinner for me." He turned and strode off.

An hour later, briefcase in hand, Omar walked to the front door. He saw Kathleen's back as she stood at the window, looking out at the sea. He knew she'd heard him walk down the hall, but she didn't turn to say goodbye. He almost said goodbye himself, but didn't.

LATE THAT NIGHT WHEN Omar returned from Valencia, he went to their room; Kathleen wasn't there. He looked on the veranda; she wasn't there either.

"She's gone, Señor Jabri." It was Jacinta coming out of the kitchen in her bathrobe. Shasha the cat hunched its back and rubbed against Jacinta's leg, its tail pointing straight up.

"Gone?" Omar was confused.

"The Señora took the boys and went to the airport. She said she has important work to do in Irlanda. I asked the Señora when she will come back. She said . . . maybe never. Do you believe that, Señor Jabri?"

17

The Door of All Subtleties

Tom and Peg were finishing a late supper when their phone rang. "Tom, is Kathleen there?"

"Aye, she is, Omar," Tom replied.

"Can I speak with her, please?"

"Ye could for all of me, lad, but our Kathleen's not havin' any. She doesn't want to talk with ye."

In the background Omar heard Peg say, "Here, let me talk to him."

"Omar, this is Peg. It's not that she doesn't want to talk with ye ever. It's just that she doesn't want to talk with ye right now, is all. What with the work she's doin', and all."

Omar paused before asking, "And the boys?"

"Yes, they're here as well, of course. Sleepin'. They leave for school in a few days."

Omar was silent.

"Kathleen told us what happened, what ye said to 'er. I know how ye must feel, Omar," Peg said sympathetically. "I wouldn't mind seein' 'er quit the IRA meself."

"Mind yer words, woman!" Mulcahy could be heard saying in the background.

"But, Omar, ye know our Kathleen. She can't be ordered to be doin' or not be doin'. Not even by ye."

Omar said nothing.

Peg sighed and continued, "Give it a rest, lad. Things'll turn around. Ye'll see. Don't try to speak with 'er just now. Don't even speak with the boys. It'll just upset things. Give it time. Ye can see the boys next week at their school in London, now can't ye?"

"Yes, well, I'm off on a business trip tomorrow. To Africa first, then to Taiwan. Kathleen knows about it. Be gone a while. I just wanted to say goodbye."

"Well do ye want me to wake them, then?"

"No, no," Omar replied sadly. "No need. Tell them I called. And tell Kathleen, too."

"All right, then. Bye-bye."

"Bye-bye."

OMAR CARRIED the heavy briefcase in his left hand as he and his three men approached the huge building. He felt nervous, and the palm of his right hand itched a little; it wanted to be wrapped around the butt of a gun. The instructions were explicit: *no guns!* On a delivery of thirty million dollars in stolen diamonds, Omar and his crew were too savvy, too acquainted with double-cross, to arrive without weapons, so their guns were concealed under their clothing. Quick shooting, were it called for, would be impossible, though; and this worried Omar.

They entered through a doorway wide enough to admit a large airplane. He glanced up at the overhead door and thought: *There is electricity here to operate that door, so why no lights?* His stomach tensed.

The air was stale; it reminded him of an Egyptian crypt he'd once broken into. The aluminum structure was unlike anything he had ever seen before. It was almost the size of a football field, had no windows, and rose the equivalent of a three-story building; but inside it was hollow, empty, seemed in disuse. The walls went straight up until they disappeared in darkness. Bright yellow light from the late afternoon sun poured through the doorway and threw long black shadows of Omar and his men across the white concrete floor. The harsh light from the door put them in sharp contrast to the gloom above. Near the top, in the murky reflected light, Omar thought he could make out the vague form of a wide catwalk along three of the walls.

Omar and his men walked about a third of the way into the building. They saw and heard no one. Nothing.

"Stop there, please." An amplified voice commanded from the darkness.

"What the bloody hell!" one of Omar's men said, just above a whisper. Omar's men ducked low and looked to him for direction.

"Steady on," Omar said softly.

"Put your weapons on the floor," the booming voice directed.

"We are unarmed," Omar shouted. *Can't they see?*

This was followed by silence. No one moved. Nothing happened. After a full minute, Omar started to walk forward again, cautiously, and his men advanced with him.

"Stop there, please." The four stopped again. Omar thought there was an unnatural sameness to the command voice. "I think it's a recording," he said quietly to his men.

"Put your weapons on the floor." Now Omar was sure the voice was automated. To his left, against the wall, he could see a short post, and at the top of it a small light fixture that seemed to emit no light. He looked across to his right and saw the same.

"Motion detector," he stage-whispered and pointed. "Infrared."

Laughter. It came from the open doorway behind them. Omar

and his men spun in their tracks. With brilliant sunlight at their backs, the new arrivals could be seen only as dark silhouettes.

"Welcome to Taiwan," the small man in the military uniform said as he approached Omar with his hand extended. "You are Omar Jabri, yes?" He was flanked by six soldiers in camouflage fatigues. They carried automatic rifles at hip level, and the guns were pointed at Omar's men.

"Yes, I am," Omar said as he shook the man's hand. He couldn't quite place the accent but thought there might be a thin Australian overlay on the man's Chinese-accented English.

"You were expecting General Zheng. The general sends his regrets. He is unable to be here today. I am Colonel Ying, General Zheng's second in command, at your service, sir."

The six soldiers were still pointing their weapons at Omar and his men.

"Your English and your manners are both admirable, Colonel Ying," Omar said in a low and menacing tone. "But your men's behavior leaves much to be desired. Why are your soldiers pointing guns at us?"

The colonel laughed. He barked a brief command, and his five men, moving in unison, pointed their weapons toward the floor as they snapped to parade rest. They were obviously still very much on guard. "Please forgive. These are troubled times," the colonel said, extending his hand toward the briefcase. "I will just relieve you of that."

"Not so fast, Colonel," Omar said, pulling the briefcase away from the man's reach. "I don't know you. General Zheng I know from a photograph. But you could be anyone; the general's second in command, as you say, or . . . someone else."

Colonel Ying pulled a pistol from its holster. "Never mind who

I am," he shouted angrily. "I'll take that briefcase now," he snarled. The soldiers whipped their weapons back to the hip position.

"You make a powerful argument," Omar said and handed the man the briefcase.

His gun back in its holster, the man opened the case and tilted it toward the sunlight. He looked inside, and his eyes grew wide; he emptied it onto the white floor. "Rocks!" he shouted. "Rocks! Not diamonds!"

"Did you think I was foolish enough to bring them with me?" Omar replied in a well-modulated tone and with a smile that showed not mirth but scorn.

Ying threw the briefcase on the ground and fumbled with his weapon's holster. He shouted something in Mandarin, and his soldiers started to raise their weapons to their shoulders. Omar and his men dug for their guns, as the colonel shouted again, "Do you think you can make a fool of me? Die!"

A single shot. A thunder of gunfire. It came from overhead. The six soldiers and their leader fell. Colonel Ying lifted his head weakly and started to raise his weapon toward Omar. A shot from above stopped him. Neither Omar nor any of his men had succeeded in drawing a gun.

"Mr. Jabri," a voice called from above. "Please wait one moment. I'm coming down."

Muffled boots running on wood echoed softly against the metal walls. A creaking came from a far corner. Omar strained to see through the darkness. A set of motorized steps was traveling down the wall. Omar dimly saw a figure high on the moving steps. Another, and another, until the mobile ladder was filled with the silhouettes of men descending. Soon the lead person stepped off the conveyor.

"Mr. Jabri," the man called as he walked quickly toward Omar.

"Good afternoon, sir," he said as he turned and nonchalantly put a shot in the head of one of Ying's men who was trying to get up. The newcomer was cloaked in black from the top of his head down to his boots. Men followed, also swathed in black, automatic rifles slung over their shoulders. Omar noted that all metal on the guns, where light could be reflected, was painted black.

As he approached, the lead figure pulled the cloth cover from his head, revealing an abundance of thick black hair that began as a straight line across the top of his forehead and swept back. He extended his hand. "I am General Zheng. Welcome."

Omar knew from the photograph that this was, indeed, the general. The two shook hands.

"That was some fine shooting, General," Omar said.

The general smiled and shrugged. "We do our best."

"It seems to me, General, that your *best* would have been to not expose us to this danger in the first place. Would you care to explain?"

The general smiled, put his hand on the back of Omar's shoulder and said, "My apologies, sir. Will you and your men accompany me for some refreshments? And I will answer your questions. Eh, do you have the diamonds?"

"Of course," Omar replied in a careless tone. With a grin he added in a conspiratorial way, "The diamonds are sewn inside the lining of our jackets. I believe we're wearing the most valuable jackets in the world."

"Indeed, you are," the general said with a laugh. "Worth many millions." He spoke briefly into his radio, and then said to Omar, "I've called to have this mess taken care of. Come, let us leave."

The general's small caravan of cars arrived after dusk at Taipei's Xinyi District. They followed the Xinyi Road to Lane 152 where the general directed his driver to pull in at a club whose large neon sign said *Crystal!*

"This is one of Taiwan's best clubs," the general said as he led his party into the nightspot. "Fine girls from every part of the country. Big band music. And the food is good too."

The doorman recognized General Zheng instantly. He bowed low, then snapped his fingers. A beautiful young woman appeared, bowed, and with a smile she led the general's party to a large private room, closing the door behind her as she departed.

An orchestra began softly playing *These Foolish Things* from somewhere beyond. *Remind me of you* crossed Omar's mind as he thought of the only woman who ever meant anything to him. *I wish I were with her now.*

A low table long enough to accommodate more than 30 persons occupied the center of the floor, and fat cushions covered in gold shantung surrounded it. The general bid Omar to join him at the head of the table. As soon as everyone was seated, a gong made a soft low tone, and the rear wall of the room slid away. From the adjoining space two women appeared. They were dressed in floor-length lucent gowns of gold and silver, with bodices that left little to the imagination. As the young women approached, slits in their gowns from floor to waist revealed their lovely long legs. Each was carrying a pink and white flower.

The women smiled at Omar and the General and set their flowers on the table beside the men.

General Zheng leaned toward Omar and said in a low voice, "The lady offers you her plum blossom. It means she offers herself to you, not only her body but her heart and spirit as well."

"That's quite an offering. I am honored. But I'm not quite sure what to do with such a gracious gift."

"You are not expected—certainly not obliged—to do anything

with it. It is merely an offering, just as this flower will offer you its fruit. You are not going to offend the flower if you do not take the fruit. But the offer is to be respected."

The general picked up his own plum blossom from the table and turned it slowly in his fingers, examining it closely. "This flower has great significance to our people."

"Oh?" Omar replied. "Why is that?"

"Because, like the plum blossom we are a gentle people, but also strong and resilient."

Omar picked up his plum blossom and sniffed its delicate fragrance. Other young women were entering the room, each with the same flower.

General Zheng pointed to the flower in Omar's hand and said, "You see these three stamens here? They represent Minzú, Minquán and Minshen, the Three Principles of the People."

"I'm not sure I've ever heard of that."

"I think you have. The three Principles are Government of the People, by the People, and for the People."

"Wasn't that from Abraham Lincoln's Gettysburg Address?"

"Precisely. And the great Dr. Sun Yat-sen brought Mr. Lincoln's three principles to us in the early twentieth century."

"Fascinating. And do the five petals have a special meaning as well?" Omar asked.

"You are observant, sir. Yes, they do. The five petals of the flower represent the five branches of our government. For these symbolic reasons, the plum blossom is Taiwan's national flower."

By this time, there was a woman standing behind each of the men seated at the table, and each had made her own plum blossom offering.

The women sat on the floor, one beside each diner, and filled the men's glasses with wine. The young woman filling Omar's glass lifted it to his lips.

"Thank you, my dear," he protested, "but I am perfectly able to—"

"Ah no, Mr. Jabri. You must not stop her, or she will be humiliated. It is our custom."

Omar was embarrassed. The woman smiled warmly as she lifted the glass to his lips. Her eyes and her smile were lovely, captivating. He decided to allow this lovely creature to continue catering to him.

The gong sounded softly again. The music came back up, this time with another familiar big band tune.

Servers entered carrying large trays filled with a variety of steaming dishes, which they placed in front of the men. The seated women began to feed the men, and some of Omar's crew complained but only laughingly that they were not babies to be hand fed.

"Before the evening is over," the general said to Omar, "I think we need to talk."

"Good idea," Omar replied.

"Yes. First, I wish to apologize for endangering you and your men."

"Apology accepted. It was no more than I've done to myself a number of times," Omar said. "But what was that all about?"

"It was all about betrayal. My messenger explained, I believe, that the diamonds would be used to help finance a revolution."

"Yes. But I wasn't told who or where. Or why."

"Let me explain. The grandson of Chiang Kai-shek intends to make his grandfather's dream come true. He is going to declare war on mainland China.

"Good Lord! Taiwan and China at war! In this day and age?"

"Yes," the general said, a light in his eyes. "I am to lead the troops in battle."

"And the diamonds I am delivering?"

"They will finance the start of the war. We expect the United States of America will come in on our side."

"That's a large expectation, I think."

"Not really. The United States learned in 1941 the price of not controlling this part of the world. If the United States were to win a war with China—and there can be no real doubt America would win—that country would never again fear the Far East."

Omar was becoming intoxicated by the young woman's tender touch as she fed and catered to him. But when she moved her hand to his thigh Omar gently brushed it away. Twice. She did not shy away when they made eye contact. It seemed to Omar that she was genuinely fascinated with him. He enjoyed it, was flattered, but it made him uneasy.

"The young lady seems taken with . . . her work," Omar said to the general.

"I believe the young lady is sincerely taken with you," the general said. "Her name is Miao."

The girl blushed and lowered her head.

"Her name means wonderful, excellent, clever, subtle," the general explained, a certain pride in his expression.

"I'll go along with the first three, but subtle?"

"I can be the door of all subtleties," Miao said in perfect English, still gazing downward.

Omar turned to her in surprise.

The general smiled and said to Miao, "'The door of all subtleties.' Isn't that from Lao Tzu?"

She nodded, "*The Way of Lao Tzu*, as translated by Wing-tsit Chan."

The general looked into the distance and added, "'The gate of the subtle and profound female is the root of Heaven and Earth. It is continuous, and seems to be always existing. Use it and you will never wear it out.'" He added with a modest inclination of the head, "Also *The Way of Lao Tzu.*"

Miao looked at the general during his recital. Her smile was broad as she complimented him in a cheery voice, "Your erudition is exceeded only by your rendition, General."

"And your modesty only by your beauty," the general said with another slight bow of the head. Miao returned the bow.

"And my surprise only by my delight," Omar added. "You both are amazing."

"But I have interrupted," Miao said softly. "Forgive me. I shall . . . keep my lips and my hands still, though not my heart," she added again looking deeply into Omar's eyes.

The general said, "You are truly gracious, Miao. You do honor to your given name." To Omar he said, "Where were we?"

Omar found it difficult to take his eyes off Miao. Her beauty was melting his resistance.

The general continued, "Your reward for delivering the diamonds is this: From this day forward, you provide all shipping from this part of the world." The general handed Omar an envelope. "Here is a letter signed by the thirty-seven men who control nearly all shipping from Asia and Africa. This is their letter of guarantee."

Just what I was hoping for, thought Omar as he pocketed the document without opening it. "Thank you. I shall honor this trust."

The general continued in a low voice. "Would this be a convenient moment for delivery of the diamonds?"

"Of course." Omar said as he stood and removed his jacket.

The general laughed. "Please, relax. You are my guests. Miao will collect your coats and return them in short order."

Miao and two of the women collected the jackets from Omar's men and carried them out of the room.

A few minutes later, the girls returned with the jackets. Miao also carried a small wooden chest, which she put in front of the general with a slight nod of her head. General Zheng sighed with satisfaction, knowing his lieutenant had correctly estimated that the entire shipment was here, as expected.

Miao stood in front of Omar and held his jacket up to him. He turned slightly to slip his arms into it, then turned back again to face her. Smiling seductively, she drew the jacket closed over his chest and slid her hands up his chest, to his head, then brushed his cheeks lightly with her fingertips. Omar's feelings stirred him deeply, making him slightly dizzy.

"Beautiful chest," Omar said, looking at the wooden artifact. "Is that teak?" The question was directed to the general, but it was Miao who replied.

"Yes," she said. "Fifteenth century. The carving was done by a blind Buddhist monk, Yun Shan. It took him fifty years. The chest is priceless."

Omar studied the carving. It showed two male images: one a youthful man wearing a fierce expression on his face, the other an old man with a serene look.

"Both are Genghis Khan," said Miao as she managed to brush her breast against Omar's arm while turning the chest to face him. Her perfume went straight to his head.

"Khan was both warrior and wizard," Miao continued. "He brought our little island out of obscurity in the thirteenth century when he made it a protectorate of China's Yuan Dynasty."

Omar was intrigued. He thought, *There are so many sides to her. Educated, charming, beautiful. And the general trusts her.*

The general peeked into the chest, turned to Omar and shook his hand. He stood and said to the room, "Gentlemen, our business here is concluded. I hope you are pleased by our simple food and entertainment half as much as I have been with your excellent company. And now it is time for me to say goodnight. When you are ready, your hostesses will accompany you to your rooms. Enjoy the rest of your evening." He picked up the chest, bowed deeply, and left.

Miao took Omar's hand in hers and said, "Will you come with me to your room, Omar?"

The sound of Miao saying his name brought a delightful quiver to Omar's stomach. The woman's scent was intoxicating him, and he sensed he might go with her anywhere. He turned to Miao, gently placed his hands on her shoulders, and looked deep into her eyes. The slightly dizzy feeling was still there, and he was enjoying it. Omar smiled and said, "Is there a terrace or garden where we can walk?"

"Walk?" Miao said with surprise.

"Yes. I would like to talk with you."

"All right," she added with a shrug. Disappointment showed in her eyes. "Come."

Miao led Omar out through a back door of the nightclub and onto a veranda overlooking a large garden area. They walked, hand-in-hand down a broad stairway of pink coral. From inside the club, the sound of laughter mingled with a sentimental trombone as the orchestra played Tommy Dorsey's *Street of Dreams.* As they walked, Miao wrapped her arm tightly around Omar and pressed her head against his shoulder. From where they stood together, the bright moonlight revealed a garden of ornate design, with shrubbery and beds of tall flowers intermingled with lacy trees. Omar saw at the extremity of the garden a stone wall more than three meters high. The wall was lined with ancient wisteria taller than a man.

As they reached the pendulant wisteria, Omar tenderly turned to Miao, and she held her face up to his. Omar kissed her on the forehead. Miao's eyes flew open. "Miao, you are a truly lovely woman, in every sense of the word. Any man would be honored to have your love. But I have another—" The sound of a machine gun split the night. Voices shouted something in Mandarin that sounded like a war cry. Screams, more gunshots, people running.

"Oh, no!" Miao said. "My general is betrayed! I must help him!" A figure appeared on the the veranda. It was General Zheng. "Miao!" he shouted. "Run! Save yourself!"

Omar and Miao saw the general fall as a volley of gunfire cut him down. Miao suppressed a scream. A man in a military uniform ran onto the veranda. He called out a command to his soldiers, and with his arm he made a sweeping gesture of the garden.

Miao grabbed Omar by the arm. "He's ordered a search!" she whispered. She pulled Omar with her through a small opening in the bushes to what appeared to be a bas relief in mosaic in the flat surface of the wall. "It's a door." She slid her fingers into a crevice and pushed the stonework open. Omar looked through the doorway into another hedge on the outside of the wall. "On the other side of those bushes is the street," Miao whispered.

The leader shouted again. Omar saw him pointing to where he and Miao were concealed.

"He's heard us!" she whispered. Three soldiers moved in a crouch in their direction, wary of being shot at.

"You must escape!"

"No!" Omar whispered loudly. "I can't leave you here!"

"You must! I was the general's lieutenant. But your life is not here!" She touched Omar on the lips. "I understood. You have another . . . life."

Omar tried to speak, "But—"

She placed her fingers on his lips again to silence him and whispered, "Take this ring. It will open many doors." She took a ring from her thumb and pressed it into Omar's hand, and then ran along the wall toward the enemy, staying out of sight behind the bushes.

"No!" Omar called softly to her. "Wait!"

Miao looked back at Omar, still at the wall opening. She smiled tenderly at him for one brief moment. She blew him a kiss, and stepped out from behind the bushes. The soldiers ran toward her.

Miao walked forward, her hands by her sides and her head high. She stopped in front of the one who seemed in charge. Omar could hear the man bark something at her. She replied in an angry tone, and the man slapped her across the face, knocking her to the ground.

Miao slowly got back to her feet, advanced to her assailant, and spit in his face. She turned and walked away, her dignity in full evidence. The leader shouted once more, which Miao ignored. He shot her in the back and she slumped to the ground.

She chose to be with General Zheng in death, Omar thought. *She chose that I should live.* Tightly clasping Miao's silver ring, he went through the opening in the wall and ran into the night.

YEARS LATER:

Omar rubbed the silver ring on his right hand. Sometimes he rubbed it absently; sometimes with reverence and a sense of loss. The ring saved his life long ago, and now it brought him brief but poignant memories and questions that could never be answered. The lady of Taiwan said the ring would open doors, and she was right. He showed it as he approached strangers for help that night. Some took a quick look at the ring and ran away, but offered him no harm. Others beckoned Omar to follow, and they led him to safety. Without the ring, Omar was sure he would have been killed. Others had. Including a woman he imagined was much like himself, a woman he cared about. He found little consolation in reminding himself there was no way he could have prevented her death. He never took the ring off, and Kathleen sometimes saw Omar become lost in thought when he rubbed it.

Often at night while he slept she studied the graven beauty on his finger, but she never asked.

18

The Secret of the Straws

1995

Michael bit into his apple. "First time we've picked apples before going back to school," he said to Shafi. The boys lay on top of the shed and gazed up into grandpa Tom's old apple tree. The apples were early this year. Spring thaw arrived the first week of April, summer was wetter than expected, and the trees bloomed sooner than usual.

"Ma taking us back to school?" Shafi asked and picked his second.

"Yeah, I guess," Michael said with a sigh. "Da sure ain't."

A long moment of silence passed.

"What do you make of it, then?" Michael asked his brother.

"Make of what?" Shafi replied.

"You know. The business with ma and da."

"Damned if I know," Shafi said and immediately felt a twinge of guilt for having used a word Mullah Ispahani did not approve of. Shafi was looking forward to being back in the Saturday study group of the Koran.

"They're split up, and that's for sure," Michael said.

"Aye. That's for sure. Did you see the way ma was crying when we left Florenza?" Shafi asked. He had eaten his apple to the core. A core needed to be thrown at something. He sat up and looked for a target. With an imitation of a baseball pitcher's windup, he threw his core in the general direction of a squirrel climbing a tree. Long before the missile neared its target, the little animal darted sideways around the thick tree trunk, and chattered as though scolding the boy. Shafi knew he'd never make a hit. The fun was in throwing things *at* squirrels, not in hitting them.

"I don't think I'll ever get married," Michael said.

Shafi grinned, "And who'd have you, then? She'd have to be fat, blind, deaf, and dumb!"

Michael gave his brother's shoulder a friendly shove. A silence followed. "Girls are stupid," Michael said. Another silence, this one longer.

"What is it that ma *does*, then?" Shafi said.

Michael sighed. "Da says it's government work. I asked Grandpa and he told me it was none of my business. I asked Grandma, and she just got all sad like."

"She didn't say nothin'?" Shafi asked.

"Nope. Just mumbled something about all the saints in heaven couldn't sidetrack our ma." He threw his apple core at the same squirrel, and got the same score. This time the animal didn't even scold.

KATHLEEN FELT ESPECIALLY lonely at Bridie's grave, as she always did. She visited almost every day since returning to Glenarm from Florenza. She had refused all Omar's calls. Now he was off to Taiwan. She missed him; wasn't sure when he would return. The boys were back in school in London; visiting arrangements pending.

Kathleen was talking in part to herself, in part to Bridie there in the ground beneath her feet. *I miss Omar so much, but he isn't going to run my life. He was totally out of line. Tells me I must quit the IRA. Not bloody likely! He knows how much I want Ireland united, the Brits out. You died for that, dear Bridie. So did Ma and Da. And Tim. If Omar can't understand what that means, can't accept it . . .* here her thought brought tears . . . *then he can't have me!* Her heart ached, but her head ruled.

The negotiations between Sinn Féin and the Brits were still in a slide, and it looked as though the ceasefire would end soon. Kathleen knew the only way to win in talking with the Brits was to show enough military power, and that meant planes and bombs. She also knew she would never get the Sinn Féin War Council to see it her way. Kathleen regretted very much the loss of the money from the bank robbery, and she began to think that soon another robbery would be necessary.

Could she take that risk again?

Bridie! Oh, my dear Bridie! I'm so sorry! I killed you! Kathleen knelt at the grave and arranged the new flowers she brought her friend. Part of her knew it wasn't true that she killed Bridie. The other part kept racing the thought, *If I had asked Omar for the money, maybe we wouldn't have needed any bank robbery and Bridie would still be alive.* The next thought was *Who am I kidding? Omar certainly would not have given me money for IRA weapons.*

After the tears stopped, and following a long meditation, Kathleen turned slowly away from the grave to walk toward her car. Her thoughts were on the part of Bridie's life—the largest part—that her friend never got the chance to live. Tears were starting again when she saw a man standing by the road. He seemed to be waiting for her. It was no one she knew.

"Miss O'Toole, I'm Liam Connors," the man said as Kathleen approached him. "My sincere condolences on the loss of your friend Bridie." He saw the tears on Kathleen's face and said, "Forgive me if I'm speaking to you at an inappropriate moment. Would you prefer another time? I didn't want to approach you at your home because I felt it might be . . . indelicate."

He sounds American, but what's the accent? Kathleen asked herself. "Indelicate? What are you talking about?" she asked, annoyed with this stranger's intrusion. "Who are you, Mr. Connors? What do you want?" *Is he police?* crossed her mind.

"I'm a lawyer. Originally from Boston. I live here in Ireland now. Belfast. At your service, ma'am," he added with a slight bow of his head. The Old-World mannerism reminded Kathleen of someone else. Connors opened his briefcase wide and tilted it so that Kathleen could see inside. "Letters," he said. "Written by your mother. They belong to you now." He took out the letters in a bundle thicker than a fist and handed them to Kathleen.

She flipped through the first few envelopes. Each one showed the same recipient: Mr. Tim Riley who resided at Louisburg Square on Beacon Hill in Boston, Massachusetts. "What are these letters? Who is Tim Riley?"

"Your mother wrote them to Mr. Riley. They cover many years. I hope you will read them." Kathleen could not help but notice that his eyes seemed sincere, eyes that could be trusted.

"And who are you?" Kathleen asked, but without the sense of distance she felt before.

The man slipped a business card from the breast pocket of his suit coat and handed it to Kathleen. It said that Mr. Connors was an attorney with the law firm of Chandrasekhar, Wilson, Lopez, and Gilmore. The address was on Newbury Street, Back Bay, Boston, Massachusetts. She turned the card over and read that the firm's Ireland office, in Belfast, was run by Mr. Liam Connors, Attorney at Law.

Kathleen looked up into Mr. Connors's face. "What's this all about, Mr. Connors?" she asked in a subdued manner.

"Mr. Tim Riley is deceased. Died only days ago. The law firm of Chandrasekhar, Wilson, Lopez, and Gilmore is handling his affairs, his will. You are mentioned in the will," Connors said.

"Me? But why? I don't know the man." Kathleen asked.

"True. But your mother did. She knew him . . . very well," Connors said. He cleared his throat.

Kathleen needed to think. She turned away from Connors and began to walk toward her car, glancing through the envelopes. She confirmed that, yes, all of them were addressed to this Mr. Riley, and all the envelopes seemed written in her mother's hand. A huge question formed in her mind. It seemed there was a major side to her mother that she didn't know, and she was eager to read the letters. She had quite forgotten about Mr. Connors when he called, "Wait! Miss O'Toole, please!"

Kathleen stopped and turned back to him. "Yes?"

"As I said, you are mentioned in the will. I'm not at liberty to say the amount, but I guarantee this: It's more than enough to change your life completely," Connors said. "No kidding," he added with a grin.

In a small voice Kathleen absently repeated, "No kidding." Her eyes snapped and she barked, "You're out of your mind!" and turned to stomp away.

From behind her, a gentle hand took her arm; Kathleen stopped. "It's true, Miss. Scout's honor." He showed that grin again. Kathleen couldn't resist being drawn to the innocent humor there, and to those sky-blue eyes.

"But what does this mean? Why me? Why a substantial amount?" Kathleen asked.

"When you read those letters you'll understand a lot of it. My firm has instructions. We are to make the award to you, according to the will, only if you will agree to certain terms. This will be explained to you at our home office in Boston. All travel at our expense, of course." He smiled again, and this time Kathleen noticed it was with warmth.

"Boston? Terms?"

"Mr. Riley had strong feelings about the reunification of Ireland. He wanted that as passionately as you do, I believe. This is about all I'm permitted to tell you here. Please read your mother's letters to Mr. Riley. May I phone you tomorrow to ask if you will come to Boston?"

"Yes," Kathleen replied in a thin voice. Her head was spinning. "Of course."

That evening, Kathleen opened a cold bottle of Pinot Grigio and tucked up in her bed to read. She found the envelope with the earliest postmark. It was dated decades earlier, four years before she was born.

"My Dearest Darling Tim,

My heart is in yours, always. Every breath I draw is for you. My dreams are filled with you. I cannot bear our being apart. Sometimes I think I shall kill myself if I can't be in your arms again. But of course I won't. Please don't worry, my darling. Don't let me alarm you. I didn't mean to do that.

I felt the baby kick for the first time this morning! I wish I could put your hand there to feel the kick. I wish I could feel your hands all over me again. I shiver at the thought.

Of course, if the baby is a boy I shall name him after you, my darling Tim. I've already told Aidan my choice for the baby's name. And, of course, there was a bit of a row. He has never forgiven you for his brother's death, of course. And it's only natural he should want the baby, if it's a boy, to be named after him, believing the child is his, but I told him my mind is made up. Tim it shall be.

Thank God, the Church allows that in naming her baby a woman has the right to overrule her husband's preference! Ah, Tim, I hope this baby is not a girl!

Tim, you must write to me. Do you still have the address I gave you of my friend Maureen? I'll put it in this letter again. I've decided that unless you start writing to me again, this will be my last letter. I must either have you forever, and immediately, or I must put you completely out of my mind.

Please don't let our love end in silence. I love you with all my heart. I must be with you. I'll come the minute you say. You know I have never loved Aidan, and only married him because of the circumstances. That's all ancient history now. Please call me to you. I'll come!

Yours forever,
Cliona"

Kathleen filled her wine glass and drank it down at once. She refilled the glass and emptied it again.

She reread her mother's avowal of love for this stranger. *What about my father?* she thought as angry tears came to her eyes. *How could you treat him that way?* Her next thought was, *I don't know what her situation was. Who am I to say what was right or wrong for her?* She wondered, *Would I cheat on Omar in some situations?* She started to say *No, never!* but had to admit she didn't know for sure.

After a third reading the questions started to form a potpourri in her mind, with a different question taking dominance every few minutes. *Why did my mother throw her life away? If she loved another man, why did she stay with my father?*

Kathleen had to face the truth. *Because someone becomes a mother, doesn't make her perfect. I loved my mother, but she was weak and I have always known it.*

Another question came to mind, this one about the man her mother claimed that she really loved. Who was he? *If Liam Connors is right, that Tim Riley wanted the reunification of Ireland, why didn't he help his son with IRA work?*

She was sure her brother never knew about his real father. That brought up the third big mystery: *the death of her father's brother.* Kathleen never knew her father had a brother.

For many hours, Kathleen read and reread the entire packet of letters, searching for answers. She expected to find, at least, some reference to why her mother married a man she didn't love.

The thought hit her: *Did Tim Riley sire both my mother's children?* Nothing in the letters supported that idea, but it wouldn't go away.

With her questions unanswered, and as daylight crept through her bedroom window, Kathleen fell into a troubled sleep. She dreamed a man with no face was holding his fist out to her. Between the fingers of that fist were the tips of straws. He seemed to be inviting her to choose one. She wanted to, but she was terrified to know the secret of the straws.

The dream was interrupted by her telephone. Kathleen answered it sleepily, "Hello?"

"Miss O'Toole?" the male voice said.

"Yes." The wine and lack of sleep were rapping hard behind her forehead.

There was a pause. "You sound sleepy. Should I call you later?"

"Who is this?"

"Liam Connors, Miss O'Toole. About Tim Riley."

That cleared Kathleen's head. "Yes, Mr. Connors. Go ahead."

"You've read your mother's letters?"

"Yes. They raise more questions than they answer, but I am glad to have them. Thank you."

"I regret that I'm not at liberty to answer some of those questions. Company protocol, you know. There is another letter. It is written to you. It's sealed. The letter is from Mr. Riley. He wrote it to you two weeks ago when he knew he was dying. His will says you are to be given the letter only if you will come to Boston. That is, only if you are interested in having your inheritance."

"My inheritance." The word sounded foreign, unbelievable.

"Yes. But you must come to Boston. Will you?"

Three days later, Kathleen and Connors were lodged at Boston's most elegant hotel, the Jurys. Kathleen occupied a luxury suite and Connors a more modest single, both courtesy of Connors's firm.

A short ride separated the hotel from the law office. Connors held the door for her as Kathleen stepped out of a taxi in front of a handsome two-story brownstone on Newbury Street in Boston's stylish Back Bay. The black iron sign built into the cut-glass door was engraved with gold lettering that proclaimed the building was occupied by, probably owned by, Chandrasekhar, Wilson, Lopez, and Gilmore, Solicitors at Large.

At the head of the long conference table sat a little man with shiny black hair, black eyes, and brown skin. Connors showed Kathleen to the seat at the far end, and took his seat with the others, seeming to Kathleen about fifty feet away.

The man at the head of the table stood and said, "Welcome to Boston and the United States, Miss O'Toole. Permit me to introduce myself. I am Kollagunta Chandrasekhar, or Sekhar for short. Think of salt shaker. Or pepper, if you prefer," he added with a laugh. Kathleen noted the man's bright white teeth that showed in his playful smile, his musical accent, and his coloration.

"Thank you, Mr. Sekhar," she said. She felt slightly out of place in the opulent surroundings. Wealth she knew because Omar was far from poor, and his homes reflected his new-age wealth, as did his cars, ships, helicopters—his entire big-money accouterment. But this law firm represented old wealth, and the office showed it.

"Would you care for tea, Miss O'Toole?" Sekhar asked.

"Thank you, yes," Kathleen replied.

"May I propose India's finest? It is grown high in the Himalayan range. We prize its delicate Muscatel flavor. The champagne of tea."

"I'm sure it will be delicious," Kathleen replied with a nod of courtesy.

Mr. Sekhar pressed a button on the telephone at his side, "Please bring our guest Darjeeling." Kathleen noticed tea was ordered only for her. She sensed it was typical strategy to distance any stranger in this way; a courteous old-money way of saying, 'Until you are known to us, we cannot eat or drink with you.'

Mr. Sekhar continued speaking to Kathleen, "While I am the senior partner, I am, nevertheless, new to this firm. The late Mr. Riley was a personal friend to our Mr. George Wilson, so I have asked him to present the matter to you," Mr. Sekhar said and resumed his seat.

Wilson, a tall thin man with a head of thick white hair, stood showing a bit of arthritis, bowed slightly toward his boss, and said in a faltering old voice flavored with a Back Bay accent, "Thank you, Mr. Sekhar." He turned to Kathleen, bowed again, hooked his thumbs in the armholes of his vest, and with his chest slightly outthrust he began. "This law firm, Chandrasekhar, Wilson, Lopez and Gilmore, has the honor and privilege of being trustee to the estate of the late Timothy Riley." Wilson flipped open a manila folder in front of him.

"And now, Miss O'Toole, we come to the purpose of your visit." From the folder he lifted an envelope and walked to Kathleen with it. He laid it down on the table in front of her in a way that almost made Kathleen giggle because his manner seemed sacramental. "This is the letter our young Mr. Connors told you about. You see it is sealed. May I suggest that you avail yourself of our guest office where you can read the letter in privacy? Mr. Connors, will you show Miss O'Toole the way?"

Connors led Kathleen to a small office just off the meeting room and closed the door behind him as he left. Kathleen had the choice of sitting at the desk, a chair, or a sofa near the window. She chose the sofa, opened the envelope, and began to read.

"My dear Kathleen,
I trust you will permit me to address you by your first name, as I am your father."

Kathleen was shocked. The hand that held the letter slammed down to her lap and tears burst from her eyes. A few moments passed. Her hand shaking, she resumed enough composure to continue reading.

"Your mother and I met when we were little more than children. She was seventeen, I was eighteen. I'd left my home, here in Boston, to join the British Royal Air force. I wanted to fight the Germans. The United States had not yet declared war on Germany. My British air fighter squadron was stationed in Ireland, and I met Cliona at a dance. It was love at first sight.

We were never destined to have a life together, yet we shared unforgettable moments of love. Our 'affair,' if it must be called that, lasted more than twenty years.

Unfortunately, when we met, your mother was already promised to another. It was a match arranged by the two families. They wanted to merge their business interests and thought that having their children marry, even though they didn't love one another, was a good idea. As it turned out, during the war the families lost everything. Your mother's fiancé was Oisin O'Toole. Oisin's older brother was the man you knew as your father, Aidan O'Toole.

Oisin found out about me and your mother, and he challenged me to a duel with pistols. I was stupid enough to agree. Oisin fired first and missed. I didn't miss. Oisin died instantly.

Under an ancient Gaelic law about dueling, I was not prosecuted. Cliona didn't get off so easy. Her parents were determined, and she was forced to marry her dead fiance's brother, Aidan. The alternative for her was the Magdalene Laundries.

I begged Cliona to run away with me, but at that time of her life your mother was obedient to her parents—and to the Church. I left Ireland in disgust. We exchanged letters. We got together on several occasions, in great secrecy, when I came to Ireland expressly to see her. Each time, I begged her to leave with me, and each time her sense of duty prevented that.

She wrote me passionate letters, swearing she would come away with me, but always at the last minute her sense of obligation—her fear of the Church, really—kept her from doing it. We were often 'together,' if I may use that euphemism, and the results were two children—you and Tim. My daughter and my son.

I am always quietly surprised at how long we were together when I reflect on the fact that your mother was 36 when your brother was born, and she was 40 when you were born. It wasn't a whirlwind romance!

Your mother ended our relationship by a letter that I destroyed in anger after reading it, and I never wrote to her again. What I didn't know was that she was pregnant with you at the time. It was many years before I knew of you.

The murder of my son and his mother, your own dear mother, nearly killed me. I watched how you responded to that murder, how you devoted your life to the IRA and the unification of Ireland. I must tell you, my daughter, I am proud of you. I say 'proud' only because I don't know a stronger word."

Again Kathleen had to stop until her tears subsided. She continued reading.

"I was the stranger at the back of the room at the funeral. I saw you staring at me. Forgive me for running. I didn't want to cause an upset. I doubt I could have lied about being your father. It was hardly the time and place for you to learn that.

That was the only time in my life I have ever seen you. Was the pride of a father clouding my eyes, or are you really so beautiful?

Aidan always believed you and Tim were his children, and I'm glad of that. He had done nothing to deserve grief. I'm sorry your mother and I deceived him as we did, but such is often the way of love.

I hope your own love life turns out better than ours did.

On the subject of how things turn out, I never did marry. You are my only family.

My father was an attorney, but he made his millions smuggling whiskey into America during Prohibition. When I inherited my father's ill-gotten gains, I invested in legitimate enterprise, and I was fortunate. It seems ridiculous how money sometimes does multiply itself. Almost like a virus.

In any case, the money is now yours, my Kathleen.

Take care of your personal needs first—yours and the children's.

I hope this man you've taken up with, Omar Jabri, turns out to be a worthy husband for you and a good father to your two boys—my grandsons, whom I shall never meet. And why haven't you married this Omar fellow by now? Perhaps you're not going to.

Follow your heart, girl!

I said to use the money to take care of yourself first. Also, I want you to use some of this money to help with the unification of Ireland. Although I left Ireland in disgust, one never does entirely leave the land of one's ancestors.

Mr. Liam Connors will be the administrator of the funds. I'm sure you can trust him.

All my love,
Your father"

There was a gentle knock on the door. "Yes?" Kathleen said. Connors poked his head in. "Need more time?"

Her voice faint, Kathleen replied, "No. I'm fine. Let's get on with it."

The stately Mr. Wilson resumed his presentation: "Do you have any questions about the content of the letter from your father?"

Kathleen shook her head.

"You understand that your father intended that you shall use part of your inheritance to further the cause, the unification of Ireland."

Kathleen nodded.

"And that Liam Connors, serving from his office in Belfast, will represent this law firm as the executor of the estate, meaning that he will invest your money in safe bonds and allocate the interest. If any of the capitol is needed for the unification, that can be arranged. All clear?"

Again Kathleen nodded.

"In that case, there is nothing left for me to do but inform you of the amount of the inheritance your father has left you. The amount is . . ." all eyes at the table turned to her ". . . fourteen . . ."

Kathleen waited to hear the word 'thousand.'

". . . million dollars."

"What?" Kathleen gasped as she sucked in air.

With a voice that sounded almost funereal, Wilson repeated, "Fourteen million dollars, Miss O'Toole." A moment of heavy silence followed. Kathleen sensed herself drowning in space, or perhaps, she thought, struggling for breath at the center of the Earth. She didn't know where she was. People spoke to her. Papers were pushed in front of her to sign. At some level, she understood all of it; at another, she understood none of it. She was aware of Liam Connors at her side most of the time, and once or twice during a transaction their hands brushed together. She found his touch comforting, electrifying, terrifying.

By four o'clock, the paperwork was done and everyone said their goodbyes. Kathleen realized she was exhausted and felt overwhelmed.

She could barely get out the words, "Liam, please take me back to the hotel." It was the first time that Kathleen addressed him using his first name. Connors sensed it was probably because she was too tired to maintain formality, but he was hoping it might be something more.

The taxi was crawling along in heavy afternoon traffic. Kathleen was feeling cranky and anxious to get to her room and collapse. They sat quietly together in the back seat. Kathleen was deep into herself trying to get her mind around the idea that she was wealthy, and that the person she always thought her father wasn't. Not actually. Connors glanced at Kathleen, saw her discomfort, and felt it himself. The silence was stifling. He groped for a way to open conversation on any subject other than the inheritance.

Their taxi moved only a few feet at a time. "Good lord!" Kathleen muttered. "This traffic is slower than molasses in January."

Connors jumped on the opportunity to lighten things. He pretended to be shocked. "Miss O'Toole, you must never say that in Boston!" The cab driver chuckled.

"Beg pardon?" Kathleen was drawn out of herself. She looked at Connors curiously. "And why not?"

"Because it was . . . molasses in January . . . that killed more than twenty Bostonians and injured a hundred and fifty. Killed a lot of horses, too."

Kathleen laughed and said, "That's absurd! You can't mean it!"

"Cabbie," Connors said. "Help me out here, am I making this up?"

"No, sir," the cabbie said enthusiastically. "You are absolutely right. My grandparents used to talk about it, come every January fifteenth. They were young at the time. Terrible thing."

"Not far from here is where it happened," Connors said.

"Right again, sir," the cabbie said. "Commercial Street, under the El, to the foot of Copp's Hill. It was in nineteen-nineteen."

"As I've read it," Connors said to Kathleen. "More than two million gallons of the stuff flooded the neighborhood and crushed houses. It rolled through the streets like a choking brown wave. More than fourteen thousands tons of it. It moved with the force of a thousand army tanks."

"You talk about it the way my grandfather did," the taxi driver said, glancing at his passengers in the rearview mirror.

"Was he there?" Connors asked.

"I'll say he was. He was a fireman on a fireboat. The molasses was stored in a tank twice as big as a house. He saw the tank go. First, he said, there was a muffled roar. Then the tank just kind of rose up, my grandpa said, and then it split. The rivets popped out of the steel and made a noise like machine-gun fire. Some said a terrorist blew the tank up. My grandfather said that moving wall of molasses pushed trucks through buildings, crumpled houses like paper, almost tore down the elevated railway—a train almost dove right into the stuff—and people got frozen in that sticky muck, like it was ice."

"My God!" Kathleen said. "That had to be horrible."

"Kinda gives a whole new meaning to slow as molasses in January, doesn't it?" Connors suggested.

"Sure does. I apologize for laughing about it before," Kathleen replied.

Connors took Kathleen's hand in his. "That's okay," he said. "Beantown traffic *is* slower than molasses—"

"Beantown? Why Beantown?" Her hand was still in his, and she made no effort to withdraw it.

"That sort of brings us back to molasses again," Connors replied.

"We Bostonians used to eat a lot of beans back in Colonial times—around the time *we* were trying to dump the Brits, like some other folks I could mention," he added with a grin. Kathleen was starting to look forward to that smile.

"We baked them in molasses for hours."

"The Brits?" Kathleen asked with a mischievous grin.

Connors laughed.

"Touché!" he said. "No, we never baked our Brits. Our beans we baked. Seems as though back then Bostonians lived on beans baked in molasses. Hard to find today, though. Few restaurants serve them. Best place to find beans baked in molasses today is in a can at the supermarket."

"Interesting," Kathleen said. She turned slightly to face this unusual person beside her and rested her head on the seat back. She was tired, and his personality seemed to encourage her to relax. "What's the big deal about molasses in Boston, anyway? Seems the history of your city is written in the stuff."

"Some of it was. Molasses was part of Boston's triangular trade."

"Triangular?" she asked, looking up at Connors.

"Yep. Slaves in the Caribbean grew sugar cane. The cane was shipped to Boston. Here, we made the sugar cane into molasses, and the molasses into rum. We sent the rum to West Africa to buy more slaves to send to the West Indies to—"

"Grow more sugar cane. Triangular," Kathleen interrupted. "Are you sure you're not a history teacher?" she tilted her head up to look at Connors again.

"Nope. Lawyer," he replied. "History's a hobby." His face grew serious. "Since this is your last night in Boston, I'd like to take you to dinner and introduce you to some of my Beantown. Will you join me?"

Something in Kathleen's heart said, *Careful!* "Yes, I'd enjoy going to dinner with you."

"Wonderful," Connors said. "And I'll tell you more Boston stories." He looked out the window of the cab as it pulled up at their hotel. "Ah, we're here," he said.

As Kathleen stepped out of the cab, she looked at the impressive façade of the building. "Something about the front of this hotel looks familiar," she said. Connors pocketed his change from the cabbie and turned toward Kathleen. "Got anything to say about it, Mr. History Teacher?" she asked.

"A little," he answered, smiling. "You may have seen façades like it in Ireland. The building was designed by an Irish architect."

"Really? Any special reason for an Irish architect?" she asked.

"Yes," Connors replied. "The Jurys Doyle hotel group is owned by two old Irish families. It's headquartered in Dublin."

"Ah yes. Now you mention it, I remember hearing of them. Big company?"

"Yes. And getting bigger. Going public soon. They're in partnership with Aer Lingus. That's why we flew Aer Lingus coming over. Package deal. Rooms and tickets at one reduced price."

"Liam, you are just no end of information," Kathleen said cheerfully. She was grateful to Connors for lifting her mood. He thought his name sounded new when she spoke it.

"I'll meet you in the lobby for dinner. Is eight o'clock okay?" Connors asked.

"Fine. It'll give me time for a rest."

"We'll go down to the wharf and have some of the best seafood you've ever eaten."

Kathleen left word at the desk to be called at seven. She fell into bed and promptly went to sleep. After her nap, as she was getting ready to go out she saw herself in the mirror and laughed at her funny short hair. She thought about the man who raised her as her father and decided that she would always think of him as her da because he was good to her, loved her, and cared for his family as best he could.

To the dresser mirror in her room she mocked, *Look at you! A multimillionaire! Hah!* She didn't see a wealthy woman. She vowed she would never change. She thought of Omar; *Is my great fortune going to matter to him?* She didn't want it to hurt their relationship—if ever they were going to have a relationship again. She wanted that. She thought of Connors. He was comfortable. Smart. Attractive. She shook her head: *Get out of there, girl!* She realized she'd never called herself 'girl' before; she remembered Tim Riley used the word in his letter to her. "Follow your heart, girl!" he wrote. She told herself she would. If she could find it. She thought of the money. *I'd give every penny of it right now if I could buy back Bridie's life.* She would tell her family about the money, of course. They were to be trusted and would never tell anyone.

I want to use a lot of this money to help unify Ireland. But I don't want everybody to know I have a huge fortune. How can I manage both?

I'll leave that up to him, she thought. She realized Liam Connors was going to be in her life forever. The fact of the money wasn't making her nervous; the fact of Liam Connors was.

THE RESTAURANT CONNORS chose was Anthony's Pier 4. As a first course, they both ordered Andalusian gazpacho, and for a second course, Connors ordered the grilled sea scallops with blood orange vinaigrette, while Kathleen selected the striped bass Provencal. For dessert, Connors chose the chocolate cake with raspberry sauce and Kathleen ordered the blueberry pie.

As they left the restaurant, Connors suggested, "What say we go for a walk along the wharf? It's a beautiful night. Shame to end it early." The sky was full of stars, a gentle breeze came in from the harbor, and somewhere in the distance music could be heard.

"I love that tune," Connors said. "What's the name of it? Do you know?"

"What?" Kathleen asked with an impish grin. "Something the encyclopedia man doesn't know? Well let me just show off a little, then. The song, sir, is called African Echoes. And the group is Ferranti and Teicher."

"I'm impressed," Connors said. "Are you a music buff?"

"Right at this moment," Kathleen whispered, "I'm not too sure what I am."

Connors stopped and placed his hand lightly on Kathleen's shoulder. "Kathleen, when we get back home, I'd like to see you again. . . ."

Kathleen moved away slightly. She kept her feelings from showing in her face but her insides were shaking.

They began to walk again, in silence. Connors pressed on: "I mean, it would be nice if . . . we can get to know each other . . . outside of business, I mean."

Kathleen looked at him. "I think that would be nice. I'd like to get to know *you* more. From the moment we've met, everything's been about me. It's all been so overwhelming, and you have stayed by my side, rock solid. I guess what I'm trying to say is, thank you for being so kind."

"Kathleen, I . . ." He took her in his arms; their lips brushed, touched again more surely, and they kissed tenderly. Another awkward silence followed.

Kathleen stepped back and encouraged them to resume walking. "Liam, you do know I have two children, and then there's . . . their father."

"Yes. I know. My office gave me a brief about you and your family, to prepare for meeting with you in Glenarm." Kathleen studied Connors's face. "Of course, I know very little about him. I do know, though, that you've taken the children, and that you're separated from Omar."

The sound of Omar's name shot through Kathleen. Suddenly she wanted him there with her. She missed him. She felt confused. Kathleen looked at Connors and thought, *What the hell am I doing? I just kissed him. I'm leading him on . . . making him think . . . making myself think. . . .*

"Liam, this is a mistake. Please take me back to the hotel."

Connors saw the change in her face, the distance.

What went wrong? he asked himself. He realized it happened when he said the word "Omar." It was clear that her relationship with him wasn't over. Not yet, at least. He could be patient. Time and circumstance were on his side.

Kathleen said, "I'd like to call it a night. I think I must."

"Oh . . . of course," Connors responded. "You must be exhausted. And we fly back to Ireland at eleven tomorrow morning. Let's catch a cab."

On the way back to the hotel, they chatted about the dinner, the restaurant, the weather—anything and everything to keep the mood light. They said goodnight in the lobby and agreed when to meet in the morning. Kathleen was grateful to be in her room. She tore off her clothes and crawled into bed.

In the morning, while packing, she thought about Liam and Omar and all that had happened. She scolded herself for being a silly woman and decided she must tell Liam that their relationship could be nothing but platonic.

They met for a light breakfast in the hotel dining room as planned.

As they finished their coffee, Connors asked, "All set to go?"

"Yes, indeed," Kathleen replied. "I've enjoyed Beantown, largely thanks to you, Liam, but I'm ready to . . . get back to reality." She looked meaningfully into his eyes. It was a stern look.

Connors got the message, and tried to hide his disappointment. "Me too!" he said a bit too enthusiastically. He took her hand across the table. "I meant what I said about getting to know you more. It's a standing invitation. I'm only a phone call away in Belfast."

"Thank you, Liam. You are truly a dear man." She withdrew her hand gently and said, "I'm sure we will stay in touch for the rest of our lives. About business, anyway."

Connors wasn't sure what the word "anyway" was supposed to mean. He decided it could go either way.

Mulcahy was there as arranged to meet Kathleen at the airport in Belfast. He saw her walk down the off-ramp with a young man at her side, a stranger.

At the foot of the ramp, Kathleen and the man shook hands and then she reached up, impulsively it seemed to Mulcahy, and lightly bussed the stranger on both cheeks. For a moment it appeared to Mulcahy that the man wanted to kiss Kathleen, but she turned quickly away. The man looked after her, with a longing in his face, Mulcahy thought. The stranger turned away, slowly Mulcahy noted, and walked away with his head down.

"Hello, Tom!" Kathleen said with an air that he thought just a little too light. "Good to be home. Did Peg come with you?" It was obvious she wasn't there.

"Who was that, then?" Mulcahy asked, his head back and his eyes looking sharply down his nose at his adoptive daughter. They walked together to where his car was parked.

"I'll tell you all about Mr. Liam Connors, attorney at law. But first tell me, how are the negotiations going? I got no news at all about it in Boston. Still think war is inevitable?"

"I'm not sure any more. Maybe you were right. We don't have the right armament. If we could show the Brits that they're dealing with a major power, they would have to listen. But as long as we're just throwing our little homemade bombs, they will see us only as a minor political aggravation. As ye have said, we'll never gain our independence. Makes me feel my life's a waste. And so's yers, or I'm damned."

"Not so fast, dear Tom," Kathleen said as they got into the car. He headed out of the parking garage and toward the road to Glenarm. "What if the IRA could get its hands on some airplanes?"

"Airplanes?"

"Right. Light fighter bombers. Chinese made and late model. And lots of bombs to go with them."

"What are ye talkin' about, child? Ye sound daft." Mulcahy negotiated traffic and got out onto the main highway. "Is that what this Boston trip was about, then?"

"I know where to get them, all nicely disassembled and crated, if you please, and I have the money to pay for them, too," Kathleen said, hardly able to contain her excitement. "I can buy three bombers to start with, and more as soon as I find them. The point is, dear Tom, I have the money. More than enough."

Kathleen filled Mulcahy in on the details of her inheritance. The news that Aidan O'Toole was not Kathleen's real father, and that some millionaire by the name of Tim Riley who died in Boston was her blood dad, made Mulcahy a little dizzy. *What does this mean to her?* he asked himself.

Kathleen saw pain and concern in Mulcahy's face. "My dear

Tom," she said tenderly as she placed her hand lightly on his shoulder. "You are the father of my life. The one who made me who I am, what I am. I love you with all my heart, my dear Tom—my dear Da."

She saw tears come down Mulcahy's cheeks, but he was smiling.

Kathleen also explained about the young man Mulcahy saw her kiss briefly at the off-ramp. She made a large point of saying he was only her solicitor, nothing more.

Hmm. She sounds a mite defensive about that, he thought.

"The Army Council will have to know about your bombers. They will have to approve, and all."

"No, Tom. Not this time. This is my money, my buy. I'll tell the Army Council about it only when the ship carrying the airplanes is about to dock here in Ireland."

"Are ye daft, child?"

"Not daft, Tom. Determined," Kathleen replied. "You heard how they went on after the bank robbery fiasco."

"No, child, nobody's blamed ye for that. Gave ye an award, and all, for yer years of service," Mulcahy offered reassuringly. "They wanted ye to know that ye shouldn't be sent out again, after all ye've sacrificed, all ye've done for the cause."

"Oh, and you think I didn't see through that?" Kathleen said with a huff. "They think I'm too old, and all. Well, we'll just see about that!"

19

Trouble in Zimbabwe

1996

Señor Alonzo de Quesada arrived in Al Khobar, Saudi Arabia, on his birthday, May 18th, about five weeks before the bombing of the Khobar Towers—which no one saw coming, other than the intelligence sources reputedly ignored. Marston Hardale had sent de Quesada to Al Khobar because part of his duties for the CIA involved putting an ear to the ground whenever and wherever there were terrorist rumblings.

The Khobar Towers qualified.

As he walked the streets of the city, speaking in Arabic with clerics and with folks in coffee houses and shops, the elderly man knew he made an impressive figure. He showed his advanced age, yet he didn't. He had a wide flat face; and his papery skin—astonishingly wrinkle free—was pulled tightly over prominent cheek bones. His broad square jaw looked like it had never needed to be shaved. Ears the size of a little child's lay flat against his skull, and his small eyes were set so far back under his brow that their color could only be guessed at behind oval rimless glasses that were tinted blue. For lips he had two thin grey lines that rarely curled into a smile outside his living room on the other side of the world, where privacy permitted him to engage in his only softness.

He was more than six feet tall and shadow thin. His clothes, though finely tailored, seemed to hang a bit loosely. He stood bent forward a little, as though to be ready for any ill breeze that might dare try to blow him down, and despite his apparent age there was something about him that advertised power.

After ten days of snooping in the city, the only thing de Quesada had learned was that maybe the Saudi Hezbollah was planning something in Al Khobar, and maybe they were not. His contact in Riyadh, nearly three hundred miles to the south, was less than help-ful this time. The contact claimed Riyadh had no connection with the Saudi Hezbollah, and he reminded de Quesada that Riyadh was counting on him to produce a certain outcome for them in Zimbabwe. Soon.

On a secure phone line, he passed his imprecise information about Al Khobar back to Hardale, along with the fact that the U.S. military local area threat condition in Al Khobar (THREATCON) was now at its highest level.

"Yes," Hardale said impatiently. "I would know what the local military threat level is in Al Khobar, wouldn't I?" He paused to take a deep breath. No point in alienating their man on the scene.

"All right," Hardale said. "Something new has come up. I want you to get on over to Zimbabwe."

"Oh?" de Quesada asked. He gripped the phone a little tighter. "What's going on in Zimbabwe?"

"We think we're about to learn the identity of someone who intends to buy a retiring rebel's entire arms cache, and deliver it to Riyadh," Hardale said. "It includes airplanes, bombs, a lot of stuff we don't want in the hands of the ILF."

De Quesada's eyes narrowed. "You don't know who the buyer is?"

"Not yet." Hardale thought that an odd question. "Why? Do you know something?"

"No," de Quesada said hurriedly. "Nothing." There was a pause, then he added, "What's my assignment?"

"We've sent some people in from London. They have a good lead on the ILF merchant's identity. If they can find out who he is, we will have some SAS people parachute in to arrest him. Your job at that point will be to get the perp on a plane to our black site in Romania."

"Do I work with your people from London?" de Quesada asked.

"No. We're going to use a cutout," Hardale said.

"Why?"

"Because," Hardale explained as though he were talking to a child who keeps forgetting, "by using a cutout, if there's a flashback we don't lose you, the senior agent. The worst we would lose in a flashback are the junior agents, our London couple."

De Quesada reflected: *A couple. A man and a woman. Not much to go on, but something.* "Who's the cutout?" he asked.

"Her name is Sumitra Tendai. I don't believe you've ever worked with her."

"Right. Never heard of her." That was a lie. The London couple could be a problem, and he needed to find out who they were. Fast. Sumitra Tendai, though, surely would not be a problem. They had worked together before, many times, in ways the CIA had no awareness of, and he knew her well.

WHEN OMAR got home to London from Taiwan, Hakim met him at the door. "Miss Kathleen called. She hoped to talk with you before she left."

Omar's heart sank. "Did she say . . . where she was going?"

"No, Mr. Jabri," Hakim replied. "I asked, but she wouldn't say. She left you this."

He handed Omar a package and a card. On the front of the card were flowers much like the ones that grew in his garden. He opened it and read Kathleen's note: "My dearest. I must be off."

Omar frowned. *She's gone on another IRA mission. Probably a gun buy.*

He opened the package. It was a box of Butlers chocolates, assorted. Kathleen included another note: "This is just to say I hold no harsh feelings about what was said. Where I am going and what I must do has nothing to do with us. Enjoy your chocolates, and remember, darling, what you taught me so long ago on our first evening in Glenarm: Good things should be savored. It makes the pleasure last. I love you with all my heart. Yours. XXXX."

Omar smiled. He knew that, once again, he had a clear road ahead with Kathleen. Everything good was still there. It could all work out. He would not tear it up again.

THE FOLLOWING MORNING when the phone rang Omar rushed to answer it. He was sure it was her. "Kathleen?"

"Hello?" a male voice said.

"Oh, sorry," Omar said. "I was expecting someone else. May I help you?"

"Then she isn't there?" the man said.

Omar paused. His stomach clenched. "Who is this?"

"My name is Liam Connors. I'm an attorney. Is this Omar Jabri?"

Omar reasoned quickly: *This man called to speak with Kathleen, so he couldn't be calling with bad news about her.* That was a relief, but his next thought triggered an old fear. *How is it he's familiar with my house?*

"What do you want?" Omar asked.

"Well I wanted to speak with Kathl . . . with Miss O'Toole before she left," Connors said. "I take it she's gone, though. Already left?"

Omar was annoyed. *Who the hell is this? What's his connection to Kathleen?*

"What do you want, Mr. Connors?" Omar said, his anger showing in his voice.

"It's a business matter, Mr. Jabri. Personal business. I'm not at liberty to say any more," Connors replied, growing a little annoyed himself.

"You have personal business with . . . my wife . . . and you can't say what it is?" Omar said, now almost shouting.

"Begging your pardon, sir," Connors replied in a low tone full of heat, "but unless you were married yesterday, Kathleen O'Toole is not your wife. And this is a personal matter which I am not at liberty to—"

Omar slammed down the phone. His pulse was racing.

IVY WAS STRUGGLING with the Sunday London Times crossword puzzle when the phone rang. Capper called out from the kitchen, "I'll get it," and grabbed a dishtowel to wipe his hands.

"If it's for me, I'm not here," Ivy mumbled, only half focused on her own words. She was stumped on *aerie hatchlings* at 126 down; something in her previous answer, across, had to be wrong.

"Oh, hello, Mr. Hardale," Ivy heard Capper say. She dropped the newspaper and grabbed the living room extension.

"I'm on, too," she said. "Good morning, sir." Hardale wouldn't call on a Sunday unless it was important.

"Good," Hardale replied, "and good morning, Ivy." The words were pleasant, but the voice was all business.

He continued: "We've just finished reading your report. You've done a great job. I commend you both."

"Thank you, sir," Ivy said.

"This is undoubtedly a terrorist cell you've tapped into. Your report that an arms purchase is going down in Africa jibes with another report we've had for some time about a large armament cache for sale in Zimbabwe," Hardale said.

"Do you know who's buying them?" Ivy asked.

"No. All we have is what you put in your report, that it's going to be someone from the ILF, or for the ILF." Hardale said.

Capper said, "I'm sorry we couldn't get you any kind of ID."

"Yes," Hardale said. "That is too bad. You couldn't even learn whether the buyer is going to be a man or a woman?"

"No," Ivy replied. "All we know is that a sale is going to be made within a few days."

"Yes," Hardale said. "And we can't let that sale happen. We're going to stop the deal. I want you there as observers, and to report back to me later. On the scene, you are to stay out of harm's way. Others will make the arrest. You are there strictly as observers. Understood?"

"Understood," Capper said.

"Same cover we used in Ireland?" Ivy asked.

"Right," Hardale replied. "You're a young American couple looking for investments."

"Does Zimbabwe have anything left to invest in?" Capper asked.

"You'll say you're looking at land. You might want to build a small tourist resort at some scenic place in the countryside when the country stabilizes," Hardale replied.

"If we don't die of old age first," Ivy said sarcastically.

Hardale chose to ignore that. "A messenger from our embassy should be arriving at your flat within the hour," he went on. "He's bringing you all that you'll need—airline tickets, room reservation, city map of the capital. You're staying at the Crown Plaza, at Harare Gardens. You fly British Air out of Heathrow at one this afternoon arriving at Harare around midnight. Tomorrow morning, you go to the National Art Gallery right there at the Gardens. At ten-fifteen you're to be at the Cecil Rhodes commemorative on the second floor. There you will be approached by a black woman. Her name is Sumitra Tendai. Born and raised in Zimbabwe, her native language is Shona. She was educated at Oxford, and while she was there, I'm told, she was recruited by MI6. Her degree is in commerce, and she is doing real estate sales and promotion for the Zimbabwe Tourism Promotion Board.

"She's working on the identity of the ILF buyer," Hardele added.

"Coffee?" the stewardess asked with a practiced smile.

Ivy shook her head and returned the stewardess' smile. Capper said, "No, thanks."

"Dinner in thirty minutes," the stewardess said with the manner of a reassuring doctor. "We arrive at Harare Airport in under five hours. Need anything, just call," she added, pointing to the call button, then turned to attend to the passengers across the aisle.

Capper leaned back in his seat and closed his eyes. "I wonder who he is," he said softly to Ivy.

"We know of only two arms dealers," Ivy said.

"Relax," Capper said. "The Yellow Pages is full of illegal arms dealers. If this was a buy for the IRA, I'd say look for Kathleen. But it isn't. This is strictly ILF. That much we're sure of. And Kathleen's certainly not going to do a deal for the ILF. Omar might do an ILF deal, but I don't see him getting himself boxed in like this."

Her active imagination turned on, Ivy wouldn't let it go. "Here's one for you. Let's say the person in London was sent by Omar to negotiate with the ILF, and we find Omar is on the scene to make the actual buy. What are we going to do?"

Capper turned to look her in the eye. "Follow our orders."

Their orders from Hardale were clear: Part one, use the cutout in Harare to find out who the ILF broker is. Part two, call in an SAS team to make the arrest. Part three, turn the ILF broker over to a CIA cutout, who would then turn the perp over to a CIA agent at a safe house. The CIA agent would put the ILF broker on a plane either owned by or leased to the CIA.

Next stop: one of the CIA's black sites, of which there are many; or, of which there are none, depending on what one believes. A black site is said to be a prison cell, or cells, set aside for the CIA, usually in a country of the former Soviet Union. Here special prisoners of the CIA are held, and here waterboarding and other creative techniques are supervised by low-level CIA agents who have strong stomachs and who don't mind the sound of screaming. The purpose is the extraction of information. The hope is that the information might, in some cases, be useful. Usefulness is not guaranteed. The only thing that can be guaranteed at these black sites is that the extraction proceeds without any hindrance from the Geneva Convention, or quaint U.S. federal proscriptions against torture.

CAPPER AND IVY'S PLANE did not land at Harare until almost midnight. By then the storm was long gone.

Not so, though, when Kathleen O'Toole's plane arrived hours

earlier. It was then that one of Africa's freak sand storms popped up out of nowhere over Zimbabwe's Harare International Airport.

As Kathleen's Air Africa 707 approached the airport, it was greeted by sheets of blinding sand. The grit sliced out of the Kalahari on a wind that gusted up to thirty-two knots as it tore across Harare International. The plane made its final approach from the north on runway one-eight. Runway two-seven, the only other at Harare, was closed for repair of bomb craters made weeks earlier by General Umbatwa's airplanes. Runway two-seven probably would remain closed a long time, because repairs had been made by a refugee team under personal contract to a close relative of the airport manager, and that team had made a mess of the repairs, and correcting the work was tied up in red tape.

Kathleen was sure she had a buy all but wrapped up. She decided she would start the bidding at three million for not only the planes but for General Umbatwa's entire cache of weapons. She would go up to five million, or possibly more if needed. She knew the cache was worth more than that, according to Cramwell's list.

ONE JUNE 2, the day before Kathleen was expected at General Umbatwa's encampment in the forest, a tall elderly white man in an immaculate three-piece linen suit materialized out of the bushes with a guide.

The well dressed visitor had not relished his walk though the jungle. He never sweat, and didn't mind the heat, but the closeness of the thick undergrowth made him uncomfortable. He liked openness. To distract himself during his hour-long walk to Umbatwa's site, he thought about his spacious home in a faraway land. His condominium was on the top floor of a high-rise; and he imagined himself standing on his balcony enjoying the unbroken vista of the sky above, the beach below, and the bright blue sea that stretched to the horizon.

Though he enjoyed his home, he was often away on business. If his employer, the CIA, knew of the many secret trips and the nefarious deals he often made, it could cost him his life. Other CIA agents had disappeared for the same behavior, he knew.

It was all part of the double life of a renegade CIA agent, a person who puts money far ahead of loyalty. A week earlier he had been in London, talking with certain mullahs. Only days ago, he was in Riyadh talking with a gent about an arms cache that was for sale in Zimbabwe. Two days before that, he'd met with a Mr. Cramwell in Ireland. He was advised by the Belfast attorney to hurry if he wanted to buy those arms for the ILF.

"A Miss Kathleen O'Toole is also interested in buying that weaponry," Cramwell had told de Quesada. "Especially the airplanes and bombs. For the Irish Republican Army."

"What?" de Quesada exclaimed. "You've told someone else about this?"

"I don't work for you, sir," Cramwell replied. "Of course, I am going to give the information to more than one possible buyer."

TWO OF THE GENERAL'S SOLDIERS on guard duty intercepted the visitor and his guide approaching the camp. The guide, also translator, explained that the tall one was there to see General Umbatwa, and the guards escorted them in at gunpoint.

"Good afternoon, General Umbatwa," the stranger said. "Permit me to introduce myself. I am Señor Alonzo de Quesada, arms broker," he added with a bow.

"Yes?" the general said. "And how may I help you?" He thought maybe this foreigner was sent by the President. He was not going to easily trust anyone who walked out of the jungle.

"I will come straight to the point. I am informed by an old schoolmate of yours, a Mr. Cramwell, that you wish to sell certain merchandise. I have a list. I am prepared to offer you two million U.S. dollars for all of it. Guns, planes, everything."

"Yes, Señor," Umbatwa said cheerfully. "I was told you might be visiting. Welcome! Welcome!" the general added with a broad smile and a congenial slap on his visitor's back.

In the next instant the general's face changed from gentle to hard. In a voice like stone he asked, "Is two million your best offer?"

"Are you ready to close a deal?" de Quesada asked.

"I might be. But not for two million. The arms are worth five million, easily," the general said as he shifted his weight from hip to hip and back again, as though settling in for a contest.

De Quesada suppressed a smile. *Amateur,* he thought. "My best offer is three million, general. And that's final." It was final. Three million was the ILF maximum. "Will you sell?" de Quesada asked.

"Before I decide, may I know who will be getting my . . . merchandise?"

Thinking the general wouldn't care, de Quesada said, "Yes. Of course. My client is the International Islamic Front for Jihad Against the Jews and the Crusaders. The ILF."

General Umbatwa's face grew a big frown. He folded his arms across his chest and quietly said, "No."

"I beg your pardon?"

Umbatwa placed his hands lightly on the butts of the two pearl-handled revolvers he wore at his sides, cowboy style. This obviously was a signal to the soldiers standing nearby because they seemed to go on full alert.

Umbatwa's eyes narrowed. "I know the ILF and all that they stand for. They seek world domination. I don't approve of religious extremism. I don't approve of terrorism. Before I sell my weapons to the ILF, I will burn them. All of them."

De Quesada could hardly believe his ears. Was the general trying to up the ante? "My general," he said. "Forgive me for pointing it out, but you yourself are a terrorist by world standards."

The general folded his arms again. "I really don't care about world standards. I am no terrorist. I am a patriot," he said, throwing his head back slightly. "And tomorrow I will be selling my entire cache to another patriot, a Miss Kathleen O'Toole of the Irish Republican Army."

De Quesada laughed. "Another terrorist organization."

"Not at all, Señor. Not at all. The IRA is merely trying to rid its country of a foreign and corruptive influence, just as I have tried to do here in Zimbabwe. I will be quite correct in selling arms to the IRA." He neglected to mention that the message from Cramwell said the IRA offer might go higher than three million.

De Quesada sighed. He smiled graciously while he thought, *true believers are so tedious.* He was far from disappointed; de Quesada never relied exclusively on a frontal approach to any deal. "I'm sorry I can't change your mind. Would you be so kind as to have one of your soldiers drive me and my guide back to the airport?"

"Yes, of course." The general was already thinking about the money the IRA buyer was bringing; he was glad to be rid of this man. "These are hard times," the general explained to de Quesada. "If anything should happen to you while in my care—a kidnapping or something—well, I just wouldn't forgive myself."

If anything happened to de Quesada, Umbatwa reasoned, the ILF might turn his retirement-in-luxurious-exile into a mortal game of hide-and-seek. The ride to the airport had damned well better be a safe one.

"Yes," de Quesada said, "I see what you mean. A kidnapping

would be possible. Thank you for the idea—of protecting me, I mean."

To escort de Quesada and his guide to the airport, the general picked his first lieutenant, Katumbo, who was also his brother-in-law. Katumbo sometimes behaved in a rash manner, was somewhat undisciplined, perhaps even a little unbalanced in the head, but since he was family the general decided he was still the most prudent choice.

On the way to Harare, with the guide as translator, de Quesada engaged Katumbo in intimate conversation.

"You know, I offered your general a lot of money for his guns and his airplanes."

Katumbo grunted.

"He was wrong to turn me down," de Quesada added.

Again, Katumbo grunted.

High on de Quesada's list of things on which he prided himself—and it was a lengthy list—was his ability to draw people out. The only thing he was drawing out of Katumbo was grunts.

"The general should sell his arms to me. For one and a half million dollars," de Quesada said. The Señor had just decided he would be able to reduce his offer. He understood the law of supply and demand; and he was planning a radical drop in demand.

Another grunt from Katumbo.

"The general will give you and the other soldiers some of the money I pay him. You will all be rich," he added.

This got Katumbo's full attention. He turned to de Quesada and gave him a big smile, showing a large gap where three front teeth were missing.

"When that buyer comes here from Ireland tomorrow to buy the general's weapons for the IRA," de Quesada explained through the interpreter, "I want you to kidnap her. Do it before the general sells her the guns. The people who sent her will pay a lot of money to get her back. You and I will split that ransom money. With her out of the way, I will buy your general's guns. You will have your share of the ransom money, plus a share of the payment for the guns; more money than anyone else in your army. You may be rich enough to buy a small country. Agreed? Will you do it?"

Katumbo smiled even wider and shook his head in total agreement. He grunted again, but this time it sounded like a grunt of happiness.

"Good. Take her first to some place where she can be held a short time. Leave her there under guard and meet me at the big hill just outside General Umbatwa's camp. We'll go in together to see the general. After he has sold me the guns, you will bring the woman to the house at 150 Luwana Road where you will hold her. I will join you at that house with the ransom money. It shouldn't take more than a day. Two at the most. All clear?"

Through the interpreter Katumbo said he understood.

"One thing more, my friend," de Quesada added. "And this is most important. Don't let anything happen to the woman. You must keep her safe until after the money is paid. The people who will pay for her release will want to talk to her before they pay. They will need to know we really have her, and that she is not dead. Or hurt. If anything happens to her, we will not be paid. Understand?"

De Quesada was thinking, *I want her found, alive, by the CIA.* He turned to the interpreter and said, "You have done an excellent job, my friend. I have a reward for you." And with that, he slipped a long knife high between the interpreter's ribs. Katumbo understood perfectly. He was an expert in these matters. Together the two new friends stripped the body and dumped it in a thicket.

After changing his flight reservation from that day to three days later, de Quesada rented a room in what passed for a hotel along the airport service road.

KATHLEEN'S 707 acted like it might crash. Air traffic control waffled on whether to close the field due to weather. At the last possible minute, the Air Africa pilot was advised to use his own discretion. He could either fight the intermittent crosswinds at Harare, or go on to Johannesburg where conditions were more promising. He decided to try Harare. He had a standing date with an attractive Belgian brunette, a junior consulate official, who was creative in bed. This tipped the pilot's decision to land.

Coming off the desert to the west, the wind gusted with enough force to knock a man down. It blew upward one moment and downward the next. The pilot was unable to hold the wings to anything better than a fifteen degree variation from level.

As the 707 descended past 600 feet, it flew through a sand tornado. Pilots refer to this as being hit by the anvil.

First, tons of sand pour down with great pressure on the nose of the airplane. Next, the sand hits the center of the aircraft, then the tail. There's a 70-to-100-mile-per-hour headwind, followed by a tail wind of the same strength.

More than one jumbo jet has gotten slammed into the ground by this gargantuan force of nature.

Suddenly Kathleen heard the engines cut out. Too much sand had gotten sucked into them and they quit. The pilot brought the plane into a glide—not a brilliant strategy, but the only one. It began to look as though his girlfriend might not see him this night or ever again. He kept trying to restart his engines. It was only an outside chance that he could, but he didn't want to die.

Kathleen O'Toole had flown hundreds of thousands of miles in all kinds of weather, in all kinds of aircraft, with pilots whose expertise ranged from excellent to terrible. She had once flown bomb parts out of Kazakhstan in a crop duster held together by duct tape and baling wire—literally. She had flown a large shipment of Czech rifles out of Prague in a DC7 whose pilot was so drunk he had to be helped into his seat.

When confronted about his heavy alcohol consumption before flying, he defended his drunkenness, saying, "This goddamn plane is so severely overloaded, and in such rotten condition, anyone would need to be drunk to find the courage to fly the damn thing!"

On another occasion, Kathleen was secreting a small load of nitroglycerine out of Burma in a Cessna Caravan, a single-engine seaplane. The pilot took off from a lagoon, and just before the plane lifted off the water, it struck something below the surface. The impact ripped off the left pontoon, with its landing wheel, and nearly cartwheeled the aircraft. The plane still got in the air, but now it was fit to land neither on land nor on water. Either kind of landing was likely to kill the pilot and Kathleen, even if the nitro didn't explode on impact. In rough weather, the pilot never would have—never could have—done the thing he did.

First, he skirted the shore looking for Kentadi, a seaside village where the natives would recognize his plane because he regularly brought out their opium. When he found the village, he flew low over the huts and cut his engine off and on, twice, to draw attention. He saw some people pointing up at his left wing where the pontoon was missing. This was what he wanted.

He explained to Kathleen what he needed her to do as he got out over the water again, and powered way back to let the plane drop. Kathleen was ready for some rapid gymnastics.

Moments before the plane touched down, she climbed as fast as she could out onto the right wing—the one that still had its pontoon. She scooted along on her belly, looking like an inchworm in a race. Her goal was to reach the tip of that wing.

As she got past the pontoon, the weight of her body tipped the wing down. This raised the damaged wing up, and kept it away from the water.

The pilot landed into a stiff seaward breeze. With his ailerons set, he began to taxi upwind toward land with Kathleen out on the wing tip. With the wind threatening to whip her away, she splayed out her arms and legs and clung to the airplane's slippery skin like a motivated frog.

As the plane began to come toward shore, it was met by natives in a big war canoe. This was what the pilot was hoping for. He stopped, and the villagers lifted the left wing up into their boat.

With a grateful Kathleen back inside the cabin, and with the war canoe serving as the missing pontoon, the aircraft finished taxiing the last mile to shore.

In the years to follow, whenever she told friends the story, Kathleen took a generous amount of ribbing about how much weight it took to tip that plane.

This 707 landing was different. The plane was coming in with no power. Kathleen was frightened. She knew the axiom that even the best landing is nothing but a controlled crash. She sensed that with no engines the pilot couldn't control this juggernaut. The wings swayed up and down, the cabin of the plane rocked from side to side. It was going to catch a wing tip on the ground and flip, she was sure. There would be an explosion, a fire. And that, likely, would be the end.

As the airport buildings zipped passed her window, Kathleen felt her fear replaced by sadness. Now that her life seemed about to end, what had she lived for?

If she were to die today in this teetering airplane on this postage stamp of an airport in this third-world corner of humanity, would it matter at all that she had lived? She didn't think so. Not really. It wasn't so much the fear of dying that gripped her. It was the sadness of knowing she would not see Omar again; she would not be there to see her sons grow into men.

With a few feet remaining until the big 707 met the unyielding concrete, the engines suddenly cut back on. The pilot breathed again, and Kathleen thought the roar of the engines was the most beautiful music she'd ever heard. Several of the passengers cheered loudly.

The landing still had to be made, and in a severe crosswind. Kathleen felt the plane skew to the right, though she could tell it was continuing to move straight ahead above the runway. The aircraft was crabbing. Kathleen remembered reading about some new kind of landing gear that permitted a safer, not safe but saf-*er*, landing by crabbing in a crosswind, and this gave her hope.

There was a bump, another, the rumble of wheels on pavement, the sound of rushing air as the pilot dropped his forward speed, the slowing of the rumble while the pilot urged the airplane to give up crabbing and proceed straight down the runway, then a slight shudder from brakes being applied a little too eagerly, and finally a pinging sound that said seat belts could be removed.

A recorded female voice said, "Welcome to Zimbabwe. Please stay in your seats until the aircraft has come to a complete stop."

The nightmare landing was over. Kathleen drew in a deep breath, let it out. *I think I am getting a bit old for this,* she admitted.

She looked around at the other passengers. There were a lot of fists still clenched in terror. Some persons hadn't unclamped their eyelids yet.

The wind and sand continued to rage as the plane came to a stop.

"Ladies and gentlemen, Mesdames et Messieurs." This time the stewardess's voice wasn't canned but live. "There is a walk of about thirty meters, or one hundred feet, from the aircraft to the terminal. The wind is strong enough to blow all of you down the runway. You would be badly injured, possibly killed. To prevent this, you are to form a line, holding onto one another.

"Hold each other tightly by the wrist, not the hand. The crew will be in the line with you. In this way, we will all be able to walk from the aircraft to the terminal. Your luggage and carry-ons will be brought to you as soon as possible. Again, welcome to Zimbabwe." She said the last part ruefully.

A few persons were grousing about how the pilot should have landed elsewhere, but most were accepting the condition as a kind of game. The stewardesses passed out goggles.

When she was handed hers, Kathleen saw immediately the lenses had a lot of pit marks.

A wheeled stairway was rolled up to the aircraft. The door behind first class opened to admit a roar of wind and sand into the plane. That created a sobering effect on those who thought this would be a game. The procession of frail humanity began to creep down the stairway and into the teeth of the raging sand.

The force of the wind curved the line as it inched across the tarmac. The people walked hunched over from the waist, head down and into the wind, and legs hard to control. Everybody clutched their neighbor's wrist, like the welded links of a steel chain. The line made slow progress toward safety, arms outstretched to the maximum, hands barely able to retain their grip as the wind shrieked like a jinni hungry for human flesh.

A woman lost her hat. She had been advised in the plane to remove it but had declined stubbornly.

She shrieked and whipped her head around to look for her lost ornament, which, from the looks of her, probably was expensive. Before and after her in the line were two large men, one of them the captain of the aircraft.

The woman tried to wrench her wrists out of their hands, to break free, and go after her hat.

She shook her arms and upper torso, twisting her wrists violently, trying to pull away, screaming, "Let me go! Let me go!"

The captain bellowed over the howl of the wind, "Lady, if this line breaks, we all go flying! Now shut up, and walk!"

The man holding her other wrist, a stranger to her, hollered, "I'll buy you a new one!"

The idea that she was being held against her will, held tightly by two men who were strangers, made her furious.

"Fuck you!" she yelled at the captain.

"Fuck you!" she yelled at the man who'd offered her a new hat.

She was still in physical contact with the two persons she'd just cussed out, and this made her twice as angry—so angry, in fact, that her little bladder control problem kicked in.

The line did make it safely to the terminal and the hatless lady, now giving off a new fragrance, muttered something about suing everybody as she scampered off, a little stiff-legged, to the ladies' room. Two hours later, after the sand had stopped blowing, the luggage came in from the plane. The hatless lady never reappeared.

THE LITTLE MAN WAITING AT the bottom of the passenger ramp was dressed in a clean white shirt that had had the life washed out of it long ago. His pants, also white and threadbare, were a bit short and revealed black ankle-high shoes, the left one heavier than the right. He was thin to the point of emaciation. His head looked like a polished ebony egg, with not a hair on it, and his two thin white eyebrows remained arched, as though in permanent surprise. His shiny black face wore a smile that might be described, generously, as empty.

He was holding up a sign, a piece of cardboard torn from a box. It said *O'Toole*.

"I'm Kathleen O'Toole."

"Ah yes!" the little man said, wearing his blank smile as he took Kathleen's two pieces of luggage from her hands.

Kathleen almost took them back when she saw that, with each step, her porter's whole body bobbed from side to side, as though his left foot kept stepping into one hole after another. But something about his manner suggested a great deal of physical capability, in spite of the one short leg, and a pride that wouldn't yield the two bags if she did reach for them.

Her guide gave the taxi driver instructions in a language Kathleen knew to be Shona, and did not understand, and the taxi headed towards the outskirts of the city. Kathleen asked the old man where they were going.

"Ah yes!" he said with the same vacant smile.

As they left the industrial section of the city the road changed from concrete to macadam. After about five miles of blacktop the road changed again, this time to dirt.

Along the dusty road Kathleen saw refugees. Their gaunt faces showed starvation. Some moved with torturous step toward the city. Others moved away from it toward the countryside. Many just sat on their makeshift bundles. They seemed in despair, with nowhere to go.

They were all Blacks. Kathleen noticed the children didn't move with the freedom typical of a child. They hung close to their mothers, some sucking their thumb, some with their arms hanging limp at their sides, head slung forward. All were in rags; all were filthy. None seemed to notice the constant flies at the corners of their eyes and on their lips. A few cried listlessly. Most just stared out with huge dark eyes at a world they didn't comprehend and probably never would before their short lives came to an end. The mothers didn't stare. Mostly, they looked down at the ground. A few looked out about them with eyes that were shrunken with knowing, asking nothing, expecting nothing.

They understood that death had missed them and their children by chance. Now they were to wait in hunger and silence until death came 'round again. There were some few men among the women and children. They were old. They seemed not to see anything or anyone, their gaze empty and fixed on nothing. Some few of the old men walked with a stride that, though weak, was dedicated and constant. That deliberate stride seemed to suggest these few men believed that, somehow, they might be able to walk away, walk out of this. They were not like the women. The women knew.

"Who are these people?" Kathleen asked her guide.

"Ah yes!" he said with the same blank smile.

Kathleen was beginning to think maybe he didn't understand any English beyond "Ah yes!" The language barrier didn't bother her but the empty smile suggested the man was an imbecile. "Are you really a fool, or do you just look like one?" she said more to herself than to him.

"Do not toy with me, madam," the little man said just above a whisper.

Kathleen drew a sharp breath, greatly embarrassed. "Then you do understand!"

"Ah yes!" he said with the same empty smile. He turned to face her and gazed deep into her eyes.

Kathleen tried several more times to get her guide to speak. All she got was that inextinguishable smile as their driver pushed his taxi at breakneck speed for about twenty minutes.

The road they were on suddenly came to an end. The driver stopped his car, reached into the back seat and threw the door open. He muttered something in Shona to the old man and was paid.

"From here we walk. It's about an hour," Kathleen's guide said.

"You *do* speak English!" Kathleen said in astonishment.

The guide smiled. "I shall explain. All in good time. But, for now, we must walk. We have far to go."

Kathleen was dumbfounded. "Are we going to Umbatwa?" she asked, hurrying to stay abreast of her guide.

"Yes. And when we are in the presence of the general's soldiers, please do not speak to me. And don't expect to hear me speak English."

"Are you one of the general's soldiers?"

The man put down Kathleen's bags. "Permit me to introduce myself. I am Doctor Henry Mooshu, Ph.D., professor of structural engineering and hydraulics." He extended a hand and Kathleen shook it. "That was before the revolution. Before my family was slaughtered and my university put into ruins. Now I am General Umbatwa's errand boy," he explained.

"Pleased to meet you, Dr. Mooshu," Kathleen said and shook his hand. Though Mooshu didn't squeeze her hand, Kathleen found herself thinking, *He has the strength of someone half his age.*

She reached for her bags but Mooshu snatched them up before she could grab them.

As they walked, Mooshu said, "I apologize for the long walk

ahead of us. General Umbatwa would have preferred to send his truck to pick you up at the airport. But none of his drivers can be trusted with women. The General knows he can trust me to get you to his camp safely."

"Those people on the road. What happened to them? Who were those refugees?"

Mooshu was leading Kathleen deep into the woods, thick foliage closing in on them. "Workers from the big farms. White people's farms. President Mogumba ordered the white people off the land so Blacks could take over. But the Blacks were all laborers. They knew nothing about running a commercial farm," he said.

Mooshu's face showed his anger as he continued, "The president promised to provide training in agronomy and business. And money for equipment. He never delivered on any of it. With no one to run them properly, the big farms soon failed. Now many thousands are out of work and homeless."

Kathleen asked, "Is that why General Umbatwa led a revolution? To put the big farms back into production?"

"Yes. He tried for many years. Now he's given up. All the young men are killed. No more young men to be soldiers. Not even any boys left."

"Is that an end to it, then? No more farms? No employment? What will these people do?" Kathleen asked.

"All die, surely. Hundreds die every day," Mooshu said.

20

The Makombwa

They walked up and down low hills, fording shallow brooks, through what was becoming a thick forest.

It was late afternoon when Mooshu stopped and set the bags down again. He pulled from his pocket a small whistle that looked like bone. He blew a long shrill note followed by two short notes, and another long one. In a moment the call was answered.

Mooshu signaled Kathleen to be silent. She heard a sound behind her and turned to see two men in military uniforms. One of them flashed a big smile that revealed three large front teeth missing.

No one spoke. The soldiers began to move forward. Mooshu signaled to Kathleen that they were to follow.

In a few minutes the undergrowth parted to reveal a large clearing with thatched huts around its perimeter. One of the huts was larger than the others and it was to this one Kathleen and Mooshu were led.

The hut's occupant stood to greet them as they entered; or, rather, he stood to greet Kathleen. Mooshu he pretty much ignored.

Their host was a black man past middle age and at least a head taller than the others. He was dressed in khakis, starched and sharply pressed. The pant leg bottoms were tucked into the tops of his paratrooper boots, dark brown and gleaming. Pulled low over the left side of his head he wore a beret, also dark brown and trimmed in black leather. In the center of the beret was pinned a gold star. The same star adorned his shoulders. On his chest was a display of ribbons and medals in a profusion referred to worldwide among soldiers of the rank as fruit salad.

On each hip he wore a side arm. Their holsters of dark brown leather gleamed like his boots. But these were not military-style holsters; they were nineteenth-century U.S. Wild West.

Kathleen noticed the handles of his sidearms were white; probably pearl, she thought, and though she couldn't see them she was reasonably sure the guns were old fashioned revolvers, probably long-barreled Smith & Wesson .44s. They made her think of General George Patton, whose arrogance always amused her while his military genius always impressed her.

The man in charge walked up to Kathleen and extended his hand. In his eyes she saw a sadness that reminded her of her own.

"Welcome," he said in perfect English. "I am General Umbatwa."

"I am Kathleen O'Toole, of the IRA," Kathleen said, and took his extended hand.

"Come," the general said. "I will show you to your quarters. It's all a bit primitive, I'm afraid. It's the best we can do. There will be a guard outside your hut all night."

A soldier, a small boy of about ten, walked up to the hut with a pitcher.

"Ah," the general said, "here is hot water. You may wish to freshen up after your long journey."

Kathleen thought the general's attempt at civility was kind.

"Please, rest now," he continued. "You will be called for dinner at dusk. After dinner there will be music. Tonight we will ask our ancestors to preside when we talk business tomorrow."

Kathleen entered the hut, carrying with her the pitcher of water. Inside she found a rigid-looking bunk with a thin mattress, threadbare but clean. On the mattress lay a pillow and folded bed clothes. At the foot of her bed Kathleen was surprised and pleased to find a wash cloth, a bath towel that looked lush and fresh, and a new bar of scented soap. She realized that here in this jungle these were undoubtedly treasures, and this made her appreciate the trouble the general had taken to make her feel comfortable.

The good quality of the soap and towel made her wish she could stand for a long time in a hot shower. A porcelain wash basin, chipped but gleaming, stood near the bed on a small wooden chest. A reed mat covered most of the earth floor.

Over the bunk was a light frame made of wooden poles to support netting that could be lowered for protection against biting insects. The hut entrance's flap could be tied open from the inside, Kathleen noted. Another piece of netting covered the entrance when the flap was cinched back.

Kathleen loosened the laces on her boots and removed her belt.

She lay down on the bunk, not to sleep but just to rest her eyes. The next thing she knew, a black face that would not come into focus was hovering above hers. A hand was shaking her shoulder and a voice was echoing a whisper from some distant canyon. She recognized her name.

"Miss O'Toole! Miss O'Toole, please wake up now! Miss O'Toole!" the voice whispered loudly. The face came into focus.

"Oh, Doctor Mooshu," Kathleen said. "Did I fall asleep?"

"Asleep? I thought you were in a coma, Miss O'Toole," Mooshu said with a soft laugh. "I looked in on you an hour ago and you were snoring like an old rummy."

Kathleen rubbed the sleep out of her eyes. There was something she wanted to ask. "Why did you pretend you couldn't understand English? Your English is as good as mine."

Mooshu's face grew sad. He looked around as though afraid to be overheard, and said, "To these soldiers, the white man is the devil. The white man's skills and his language are the devil's tools. Only the general knows of my languages and education.

"If the soldiers find out, they will see me as a white man in a black skin, the worst kind of devil. To protect myself I pretend I do not speak English; just a phrase or two."

"But the soldiers know the general speaks English. Doesn't that make him a devil?"

"No. He is considered upper class. What applies to others does not apply to him."

"Ah, I see," Kathleen said. Then she asked, "Doesn't General Umbatwa control his men? Can't he protect you from them?"

"The general remains the general only by consent. And this consent is given almost hour by hour. His life is in danger from his own soldiers. Always."

"Being upper class doesn't really protect him, then," Kathleen said. "Do you think your life may be in danger?" Kathleen asked.

"Ah yes!" Mooshu said with his vacuous smile.

Listening through the thin back wall of the hut, one of the general's soldiers was surprised to learn that Mooshu could converse easily with the woman in what was apparently good English. This called for a change in plan. The devil Mooshu would not be killed; he would live to be an interpreter. The soldier smiled at his good fortune.

Moving quietly, he walked away.

THE SUN WAS sinking beneath the trees, and their cooling shadow spread over the clearing as Mooshu and Kathleen walked together to where the evening meal was ready to be served.

To one side of the clearing there was a low stone oven, and next to it an open fire. Split logs were set up as benches. The soldiers were all seated and waiting for their guest. An open space in the seating was reserved to the general's right, the place of honor. As Kathleen approached, everyone stood.

The guest took her place and the banquet began.

"We have killed the fatted calf in your honor, Miss Kathleen," General Umbatwa said.

He laughed. "I'm afraid it isn't really beef. We haven't seen a cow in a long time. But this you might enjoy. Hanga is a national dish, a casserole made with guinea fowl," Umbatwa said, lifting the lid of a large earthenware dish and releasing a rich spicy aroma.

"Where did you go to school?" Kathleen asked.

The general smiled sadly. "I was sent abroad. Arts and sciences, an assortment of colleges and universities. The British Isles and the United States. While I was gone, there was an uprising. My mother and father were killed. My education abroad cost me a lot. Only my sister and I are left. She lives in Rome now."

Kathleen felt as if an old wound was opened. She offered a condolence and changed the subject. "This dish is delicious. And thank you for the special little things I found in my hut."

"You're welcome. I was glad to do it. Here, try this," he said, handing Kathleen a small shaker bottle of green liquid. "Just a few drops on your guinea fowl. It is peri-peri. Very hot."

"Mm! This is good!" Kathleen said, allowing the food and the friendliness of the general to push her painful memories down below the surface.

"And here is some derere. You call it okra. We fix it with peanuts

377

and kovo. It's like cabbage, but sweeter and lighter. What do you think?"

"Mmm! I've never tasted anything like it," Kathleen said with obvious pleasure.

The general laughed in appreciation of her enjoyment.

After the meal, torches were lighted at the end of tall poles in a big circle. The light flickered and threw its warm tones into the night shadows, seeming to push them away.

Into the middle of the circle stepped four men dressed in loin cloths and feathers. Their faces were painted with big white dots, their arms with blue stripes, and their torsos and legs were a soft yellow, luminescent as it picked up the flickering torch light. For a moment the dancers stood still. Silence.

Out of the darkness behind the seated diners a drum sounded. Once. The dancers remained frozen, looking at the ground. Another deep drum beat. Louder. Now the dancers lifted their eyes heavenward and raised their arms. The drum beat again, louder still. Other drums joined. Together they made a commanding steady beat. It grew hypnotic. The dancers began to move. They drifted in a circle, their arms and hands moving in unison. Other musical instruments joined the drums. An old man with tight white curls and a slender body was bobbing and weaving—his hands slapping, thumping, teasing the beat out of the taut drum skins.

A child stood next to him extending the cadence with a pair of rattling hosho made of dried gourds. Another musician, face tilted to the stars and eyes open wide, played an intricate melody on a worn guitar. The fourth player's arms were deep inside a large dried calabash, something like a big pumpkin. At the bottom of this gourd was a hardboard where the musician's fingers plucked at metal keys made from sofa springs and a tightly strung wire loaded with bottle caps. The keys made clear tones while the bottle caps buzzed. It sounded like sad whispering voices at one moment, raucous wind and rain the next. The calabash was a modern incarnation of the mbira, the sacred instrument of Lemba musicians.

The music was a prayer to the collective soul of vadzimu, the ancestors. It was the ancient heart of the music that later became the calypso of the Caribbean.

The mbira's insistent buzzing wove itself deep into the mind, clearing it of worries. Its clarion tones filled the air like spirit birds.

The dancers in the circle bent forward, allowing the music to pour through their veins like an electric primer. Without signal, but as one, the dancers rose into the beat of the music and let it have them. Their heads shook like leaves in a storm, torsos trembling, arms akimbo. They flailed the air. Their legs flashed like pistons, their feet like butterflies that lightly touched down.

The pulsating commands of the music went on and on. Over and over the dancers wove their intricate pattern. They turned to face one another. They faced outward. They addressed the heavens and the earth. They remained synchronized with one another, though their concentration seemed rooted in another reality.

As they danced, the old drummer began to sing.

General Umbatwa said, "The drummer is our healer. He sings to the makombwa, our most powerful guardian spirits. He asks them to guide me tomorrow when you and I must talk about money and guns."

Kathleen felt the mbira vibrating in her blood. "The music is exciting," she said.

"Make a sound in your throat like the mbira," Umbatwa said. "The makombwa will hear you. They will come to you."

"To me? But why? I am not of this people."

"The makombwa make a distinction only where good and evil are concerned. Never race or nationality."

"Hmm," Kathleen said. "The whole world could use some makombwa."

Umbatwa placed his hand over the front of Kathleen's throat, his long brown fingers making only the slightest contact with her pale skin.

"Let the music rise from your blood," he said. "You will feel it here, in your throat, and it will become sound. Let it happen."

A moment later he saw the music begin to take effect in his guest. "Yes!" he said.

Kathleen thought she felt something stir in her beneath the large man's hand, something like a vibration, but she was conscious of making no sound; no muscle moved.

"Yes!" he repeated as he sensed the effect building within her. "Now let it come out!" he whispered.

A sound much like the vibration of the mbira began to resonate deep in her throat. She didn't recognize the sound as anything she could make. Her lips were pressed shut as though she wanted to keep the sound in—must keep it in, because letting it out might be dangerous.

The vibration rising up inside Kathleen was metallic, not from her vocal range. It moved with a life and power of its own and she was merely its way of passage.

"Yes!" Umbatwa said again, this time loudly. "Now let it out! It is the makombwa speaking!" he added with a laugh.

Kathleen felt her lips parting, though she wasn't sure it was she who parted them.

The general removed his hand from her throat, now that Kathleen no longer needed his help. She was connected to the spirits.

As his hand slipped from her throat, Kathleen felt as though she were being released from a tether, and might float away in the darkness. The sound rose from the pit of her stomach. She began to feel liberated. The sound, her sound, released all earthly bonds. At any moment, she felt, she might rise to the sky, and her alarm turned to thrill.

Kathleen went from sitting to standing, from standing to dancing, and in moments she was one with the others in the lighted circle, whirling in the torchlight and in intimate union, in perfect communion, with these dancers of old Africa.

An observer might have said she was possessed. But she did not feel that way; rather she felt *in possession*.

The dancing joined her to the spirits. She flashed in her mind on the Celtic tradition of anamcara, a cleansing of the soul, but this was not Celtic. This was here. It was now. The night was personally hers.

Soon everyone joined in the singing, each finding their own voice and their own song, and the music united the singers. The moon, full this night, rose above them, until, bit by bit, gently, the evening wound down to a pleasant hush, and, in its diminishing and quieting tones, Kathleen heard sleep softly whisper, *Come!*

It was good to know there was a guard outside her hut. It gave her the confidence to relax and get the rest she needed. She loosened her clothes and boot laces, but decided to leave the boots on.

AN HOUR LATER there was a movement under Kathleen's bed.

Quietly, a form appeared. It was a large man, and in his hand he held a small gourd with a rag stuffed into its neck as a stopper. He stood in a crouch over Kathleen, pulled out the rag, dampened it with the contents of the gourd, and clapped it over Kathleen's mouth and nose. She struggled for a few seconds. Not a sound was made.

Kathleen's assailant picked her up, limp, and carried her out of the hut.

The guard in front of her hut was gone. All was quiet.

As the man carried Kathleen across the clearing and toward the trees, there emerged from another hut a second man. He, too, was carrying someone.

Together they toted their unconscious burdens off into the forest. Just beyond the clearing they were met by two other men. The one with the missing front teeth seemed in charge.

The two unconscious victims were tied hand and foot, gagged, and laid on litters. The four men carried them off at a trot deeper into the forest.

After an hour of running with the litters, the men stopped under a big tree to rest. They ran for another hour and stopped again for a second rest.

They moved west southwest until they came to the banks of the Tokwe River where a lightweight flat-bottomed boat was concealed.

By this time Kathleen and Mooshu were awake. They were still gagged, their hands and feet bound. Kathleen's throat was raw; she desperately wanted water and she felt nauseous.

Katumbo and his men roughly laid their victims into the boat. As they slid Mooshu from his litter to the bottom of the boat, Kathleen saw him hook his cloth gag on a small cleat. Before he could be stopped, Mooshu yanked his head back and forth violently, and his gag came off. Kathleen heard him say something softly in Shona. They stopped. With a nod of his head, Mooshu gestured to Kathleen and said something else to Katumbo. He said a few words in response, then began to move toward Kathleen.

"Shhh! Be still! Be quiet!" Mooshu called out to Kathleen in a low tone. "He's going to take your gag off. I told him the drug has made us nauseous, that we will die if we vomit with our gags on.

"Thank you, Mooshu," Kathleen said in a raspy voice as soon as her gag was off. "Can you get them to give me some water?"

"Yes," Mooshu replied. He spoke to one of the men, and water was brought to Kathleen and Mooshu.

"If you must speak," Mooshu said quietly to Kathleen, "do it softly. We mustn't anger these animals."

"What's going to happen to us, Mooshu?" Kathleen whispered.

"We've been kidnapped. They're going to hold you for ransom. Katumbo told me he is keeping me alive as translator. He heard us talking English back at the camp," he replied. Mooshu spoke again to Katumbo, since he was obviously in charge. He got a brief reply and translated to Kathleen.

"He says we're going to be set free after we reach Cheredzi. He says the old white devil man wants you out of the way for awhile so he can buy Umbatwa's weapons."

"Old white devil man? Out of the way *for a while?*" Kathleen asked.

"I don't believe that either," Mooshu said. "They intend to kill us, I'm sure." He spoke a few more words to Katumbo.

"He won't say who the old white man is. Says to shut up or he'll put my gag back on."

Kathleen and Mooshu mostly remained silent in the bottom of the boat as it made its way quietly down the Tokwe. Katumbo and his men spoke a word or two to one another just above a whisper and only at rare intervals. The one persistent sound was the nearly inaudible gurgle of the boat slipping along the top of the water, being directed by the pole man. Once in a while, there was the sobbing sound of an animal—probably a hyena, Kathleen decided—crying out in the night.

Katumbo suddenly seemed eager. He studied the shore line on both sides of the boat, pointing to things he obviously recognized, and muttering to his men. He lit a small lantern and swung it back and forth high above his head, looking downstream and to his right. The pole man forced the boat to alter course and head inward toward the shore in that direction.

Kathleen dared lift her head to peek over the edge of the boat. From in the distance ahead she saw the return light signal Katumbo was waiting for. Kathleen ducked back down again, to avoid being seen looking. Katumbo extinguished his lantern and returned to his seat.

A few minutes later, the boat was beached in front of a shack on the shore. It was made of corrugated tin sheets, set into wood frames. From a window to the right of the rickety front door, a dim light shone. Kathleen and Mooshu were half carried, half dragged, up to the shack. The door was shoved open and the two prisoners were pushed in onto the wood floor.

Sitting in a rocking chair by a small fireplace was an old woman. On a table next to her was the kerosene lantern that gave the yellow light through the front window and dimly illuminated the small room. The woman got up and greeted Katumbo with great deference, showing a toothless smile. Katumbo spoke to her briefly, gruffly, then left with his men.

Mooshu spoke to the woman. She replied.

"He's paying her to keep us here until he comes back," Mooshu said to Kathleen. "She said he'll be back tomorrow."

"Tomorrow!" Kathleen exclaimed.

"She says Katumbo left food. I asked her if she'd untie us."

"Oh, God, I hope she will! My hands and feet are numb. I can't feel them at all," Kathleen said.

The old woman reached behind her and produced a shotgun. She aimed it in the general direction of Kathleen and Mooshu as she walked slowly to the center of the room, never taking her eyes off the captives. She bent over, placed her fingers in a hole in the wood floor, and pulled a door up and open. She spoke again to Mooshu.

"It's a cellar. She says she'll untie us if we agree to go down there," Mooshu said.

"Yes, yes," Kathleen said. "Agree to anything. We can't stay tied up until tomorrow. We'd get gangrene."

"I don't much care for dark, damp places," Mooshu muttered. He spoke again to the woman. From a pocket in her dress, she pulled a small knife and opened one of its blades. Stepping behind Kathleen, she cut her ankles free.

The old woman lit a second lantern and moved to the opening in the floor. The lantern revealed a steep ladder built between the shack and the earth floor of the cellar.

"I'll go down," Kathleen said, "as soon as I can get these feet to work again." She tried to stand, but toppled backward and landed on the floor hard. She tried to get up again, but let out a cry of frustration.

The old woman moved to Kathleen, and sat on the floor in front of her, the shotgun at her side. She began to massage Kathleen's feet, one at a time, and looked at her with a large toothless grin.

Mooshu laughed softly. "Just as I thought. She has nothing against us. She's just trying to stay alive. Katumbo has said he'll pay her to be our jailer until he comes back for us. And she said something about water for her village. I didn't understand much of that."

In a few minutes, Kathleen was able to get up on her feet.

"I think I can negotiate that ladder now," Kathleen said. "Tell her I said thanks for the foot rub," she added, smiling at their captor.

Mooshu translated, and the old woman laughed heartily as she explained that she was glad she could help a person who was not only of her gender but who was also the first white lady she had ever seen, and who had miraculous hair the color of fire.

The old woman motioned Kathleen to the cellar opening and cut her wrists free. With difficulty, Kathleen picked up the lantern in one hand and moved slowly, carefully down the ladder.

"Whew! It is cold down here!" she said as she held the lantern up for Mooshu to see his way down. "And damp, too. Just as you said it would be. I'm not surprised, though. We have the same cellars back home."

As soon as he was cut free, Mooshu, with great pain, went down the ladder. When he reached the bottom, the old woman started to close the door. Mooshu spoke urgently to her and she stopped.

"I asked her to please not close that door. I guess she isn't going to," Mooshu said.

A moment later, the old woman dragged her chair over to the edge of the doorway to the cellar and sat, the shotgun across her lap. She smiled broadly down at Kathleen and Mooshu, apparently content that this was a good arrangement.

Mooshu began to talk with the old woman, and soon she was telling him about her village and her life. He translated for Kathleen, and, as it unfolded the story revealed that the woman's name was Mbuya Nehanda. She said that among her people she was regarded a person of some stature because she was a spirit-medium who could call down upon her village the blessings of Mulungu, the high god of the Mwari religion. She could also call down the ngozi, the avenging spirits, to punish the men of the village if they became too demanding or too rough with the women whose lives they ruled.

Kathleen asked through Mooshu why this spirit-medium was in league with a man as evil as Katumbo, and how she had come to know him in the first place. She explained that her village was dying of thirst, that Katumbo had employed some men from her village as soldiers, and that he had promised two large drums filled with water for her people if she would be their jailer for one day. About the shack they were in she knew nothing, except that it was luxurious when compared to the grass huts of her village.

Mooshu explained that he knew how to draw water from the earth. He promised to bring water permanently to her village, put an end for all time to death from thirst, if she would help the white lady and him escape.

Mbuya Nehanda said a lot of water used to come out of the mountain, but now it was only a trickle. She told Mooshu that she wanted to believe him, but that she was old now and could no longer fully trust her instincts. No, he and the white lady would have to remain prisoners until Katumbo came for them. Furthermore, she knew, she had little time left on earth. Maybe days. Maybe only hours. This she knew.

Her mind seemed to wander. In the next moment Mbuya Nehanda was inviting the white lady and Mooshu to visit her village. To get there, she explained, one had only to go to the fork in two dry rivers, the Baba and the Amai, which means Father and Mother. There they would find Mombe, the name of her village, which Mooshu told Kathleen means cattle. There had been no cattle in Mombe for a long time, she explained, but the villagers waited patiently. The spirits had told her the cattle would return when the Baba and the Amai flowed again.

The white lady and the black man had only to go there, to Mombe, Mbuya Nehanda promised, and speak her name to be received warmly. She made Mooshu agree to say good things about her to her people, if for any reason she couldn't be there with them. A moment later, in her mind she was back in her village again, welcoming her two visitors.

21

New Beginnings

Later that day, the general was surprised when de Quesada walked back into camp.

"I thought you had left Zimbabwe," Umbatwa said. The general thought the Senor's smile looked treacherous. He didn't notice that Katumbo had quietly walked up behind him.

"Yes, I started to. But I heard the IRA woman won't be buying your weapons after all," de Quesada said.

The general was shocked. "It was you who took her? What did you do with her? She was under my care! She—

"Relax, general. This is a rough old world. Let us not become sentimental, and let us not ask questions which will not be answered."

De Quesada waited a moment for that to settle in. He continued: "I'm willing to pay you, in cash, one and a half million American dollars for everything you've got," de Quesada said. "The guns, the planes, the bombs. Everything. What do you say?"

The general's body went rigid. "I say what I said the last time you asked. Furthermore, you have all but admitted to . . . doing away with the IRA woman. That makes my position all the more rigid. I will burn my munitions before I let them fall into the hands of the ILF," the general said.

"That's too bad," de Quesada said. "One and a half million dollars would have helped you and your men start a new life. As it is, though. . . ."

De Quesada signaled Katumbo. The traitor reached around front of Umbatwa's throat with a large knife and sliced so hard and deep that he nearly decapitated him. Umbatwa was instantly dead.

Almost before the general's body hit the ground, Katumbo's three henchmen ran to his side and raised their weapons in defense of their new leader.

"I am your general now!" Katumbo shouted to the assembled soldiers. "Anyone who disagrees with this is free to leave. If you stay today but disagree tomorrow, you die!" Katumbo shouted. No one raised a hand or even moved.

"This man," Katumbo said pointing to de Quesada, "has offered us a great deal of money for our weapons. Umbatwa refused to sell. Now Umbatwa is dead, and *I* will sell. We will all have enough money for our families to live free of hunger for the rest of our lives! What do you say to that?"

A huge cheer went up from the soldiers and they began to dance around Katumbo, singing a victory chant.

The munitions were packed into the general's trucks and transported to Harare for shipment to Riyadh.

De Quesada and Katumbo went to the Harare National Bank to complete the financial side of the transaction. De Quesada had given his new translator specific instructions about what to say at the bank. De Quesada made it clear if the man followed these instructions faithfully he would receive five thousand dollars. If he failed, he would die.

In the bank, the trio found the bank president, with whom de Quesada had made prior arrangements.

The bank officer produced a money bag and handed it to de

Quesada who, in turn, handed it to Katumbo saying, "Here is the full payment I promised you. One and a half million dollars."

In the bag there were fifteen thousand one dollar bills. Katumbo took the bag and smiled gratefully; unable to count and terribly naive, he had no idea that he had been cheated out of one million, four hundred eighty-five thousand dollars.

That sum, minus the five thousand for the translator and another five thousand for the bank president, was shipped that day to de Quesada's bank account in Switzerland.

With the ILF gun buy accomplished, de Quesada instructed Katumbo to go get the IRA woman and bring her to the house at 150 Luwana Road where she was to be held, he told Katumbo, until he could arrange the ransom—only a day or two.

SHORTLY AFTER NINE THE next morning, the phone rang at Sumitra Tendai's desk. "Zimbabwe Tourism," she said in her practiced way.

"Good morning. This is Andy. Do you have time for a bit of . . . late breakfast? I know you never eat breakfast unless your . . . uncle Sam is visiting."

"Of course, Andy." Miss Tendai's education abroad made her a privileged employee of the agency, free to come and go as she pleased. "Five minutes. The usual place," she said and hung up.

The usual place was a coffee shop down the street from the Zimbabwe Tourism Promotion Board. The words "late breakfast" meant the meeting was considered urgent by "Andy," Señor Alonzo de Quesada, and "uncle Sam is visiting" told her this meeting would be about CIA business.

"Did Hardale call you?" de Quesada asked Tendai after the waiter had delivered his toast and coffee.

"Yes. He told me you'd be in touch. I'm to be cutout between you and the agents from London," Tendai said, stirring the sugar in her tea.

"Who are they?" de Quesada wanted to know.

"Not so fast," Tendai replied. "You know a cutout does not reveal identities," she added with a laugh.

"And you know that I know enough to have you put six feet under the ground," de Quesada replied in a quiet and threatening tone.

"That goes both ways, my friend," Tendai replied in the same tone. Then she lightened up, smiled, and added, "Let's get on with business, shall we?"

"All right," de Quesada said. "Why don't you start by telling me what you know."

Tendai's smile was wry. She sighed. "You never change, do you, Alonzo?" She put her spoon down noisily in the saucer. "All right. I know this. *You* are the ILF buyer the agents from London are here to identify. How's that for openers to the book of knowledge?"

De Quesada's jaw clenched. He quickly covered his shock, but not before Tendai had registered it. He sat back in his chair. "What makes you think I'm that agent?" he asked.

"Oh, please, Alonzo," Tendai said, her eyes almost shut. "Remember, I spent five years in England. I, too, have some connections in London's Muslim underground."

De Quesada had worked with Sumitra Tendai long enough to have learned that she hated the United Kingdom for the way that empire had raped her beloved Africa in the prior century. She had taken her degree at Oxford in order to learn her enemy's mind, and was now posing as a genuine MI6 operative only to wreak as much mischief on the Great Empire as she possibly could. She was, in effect, a terrorist—or a patriot, depending on point of view.

De Quesada leaned forward and placed his elbows on the table.

He cupped one hand over the other and leaned his chin on them. "Anything else?" The extent of her knowing would tell him what price he could expect to pay for her silence.

Tendai took a sip of her tea and signaled the waiter. It had grown cold. "Only this. You are here to buy an arms cache from a certain General Umbatwa. If you succeed, the arms will go to the ILF in Riyadh." She paused and smiled again. The waiter poured fresh tea and left.

"How'm I doing, Alonzo?" she asked with a victorious and nasty smile. She enjoyed playing the vixen.

De Quesada realized how much he hated this woman. Some day, he would. . . . This was going to cost him a lot.

Then an idea struck him. There might be a way to make this woman earn her money. "What do you know about the O'Toole woman?" de Quesada asked.

This put a crimp in Tendai's style. Her cup stopped in midair. Surprised, she asked before thinking, "What O'Toole woman?"

Score one for me, de Quesada thought. "Kathleen O'Toole is here to buy the same weapons for the Irish Republican Army," he said.

"Oh?" Tendai interjected. This felt like a ray of sunshine. "The greatest arms broker on planet earth has a competitor right here in little old Zimbabwe?"

"Did have," de Quesada said.

"What does that mean? You've killed her?" Tendai had seen de Quesada dispatch troublesome people with no more hesitation than he might show in smashing a cockroach.

"That would be a waste of resources," he replied.

Tendai suddenly saw it. "You've kidnapped her. For ransom?"

"No. Too risky. Remember, I need to maintain my cover with the CIA."

"And what does all of this have to do with me?" Tendai asked. She was starting to smell money. Possibly, real money.

"You tell the couple from London that the ILF agent is waiting to deal with General Umbatwa. Say the agent is holed up in the CIA's Zimbabwe safe house. Do you know where that is?"

"Yes, of course. You showed it to me last year. Remember? It's at 150 Luwana Road."

De Quesada spread some jam on a bite-sized piece of toast. "That's not such a big thing to do, now is it? How much do you want to be paid for that? A hundred dollars? Two hundred?"

"A quarter million dollars, American," Tendai replied. She knew she was being ridiculous, but reaching for the stars did sometimes mean you could touch the moon.

De Quesada laughed. "Why not ask for a million?" Then he leaned forward and said, in a serious voice, "I'll pay you one thousand dollars. Take it or leave it."

This was moon enough for her. "I'll take it," she said.

De Quesada leaned back in his chair, feeling proud. He'd been quite ready to pay up to five thousand.

"Explain one thing to me, Alonzo," Tendai said. "Where are you going with this? Why have the IRA woman arrested, when what the CIA is really looking for is . . ." She stopped and drew in a sharp breath. "Oh, I see!"

De Quesada laughed. "Right. Just be sure you do not tell the London couple who the agent is buying for. The CIA expects to find an ILF buyer. Instead, they find an IRA buyer. The CIA is left to believe there never was an ILF buyer. Bad information. Hunt over."

Tendai laughed softly. "You are a nasty bugger, Alonzo. But stupid you are not."

"Have some toast?" he asked with a self-satisfied smile. Tendai declined.

"How soon are you meeting your London agents?" he asked.

Tendai glanced at her watch. "Oh, my goodness! Ten fifteen. I'm going to have to leave, or I'll be late."

"WAS CECIL RHODES A THIEF, do you think, or the father of a nation?" the female British voice said. Ivy and Capper turned, pretty sure they knew who they would find standing behind them.

"Good morning, and welcome to Zimbabwe. I'm Sumitra Tendai," the woman said and extended her hand and a smile.

"Very pleased to meet you, I'm sure," Ivy said, taking the woman's hand in hers for a moment and returning the friendly smile. "I'm Ivy Harris. My husband, Capper."

"Capper." Sumitra said as she extended her hand. "What an interesting name."

Capper took the young woman's hand in his for a brief handshake and noticed it felt like cool silk. He found her eyes to be a problem: they seemed a deep brown pool he might easily fall into and disappear. He had forgotten to release Sumitra's hand.

"And your name." Ivy said a bit forcefully. "Does it have a special meaning?" Capper woke up. He released the hand, and glanced nervously at Ivy. She glared at him for split second, then looked back at the woman.

"My given name, Sumitra, means good friend," she said with a flutter of her eyes at Capper. "My family name, Tendai, means to give thanks." Her voice was soft, Capper noticed. And warm.

"And what was that you said about Cecil Rhodes being a thief?" Ivy said, stepping between Sumitra and Capper to advance toward the tall statue. As she passed close to Capper, she took his hand in hers. Thief and thievery suddenly were on her mind.

"Yes," Tendai said, now also looking at the statue. "Well, you see, Cecil Rhodes came to Africa in the nineteen century to expand British colonial rule. He wanted to civilize us. Mr. Rhodes quickly became a millionaire here. Some say he did it by cheating simple farmers out of their diamond-crusted lands."

"And what do you say. Was he a cheater?" Ivy asked.

"Do you have a special interest in Cecil Rhodes?" Tendai asked Ivy.

"I'm not sure," Ivy replied with a slight coolness. "My father's name was Rhodes. He was from the United Kingdom. Ireland, to be precise." Ivy did not like this woman. Capper noticed that, and for some reason it made him a little uncomfortable.

"How very interesting," Tendai said, in the same cool tone. She turned back to Capper and said in a voice that had nothing to do with business, "The ILF buyer has been identified."

"That's great!" Capper said.

"Who is it?" Ivy asked.

"I wasn't told that," Tendai replied to Ivy. "Only where this person can be captured late tonight. Mr. Hardale has told me you are to call in an SAS strike?"

"Yes," Ivy said. "When we are sure. How certain is your information?"

"I'd stake my life on it," Tendai replied.

KATUMBO WENT WITH TWO of his men to collect Kathleen and Mooshu. As he pulled the van up in the field behind the shack, he considered whether to kill the old woman here and leave her body behind the shack for animals to find, or dump her somewhere else. He had no intention of delivering the water to her village, as promised, and she was now useless because soon he would be a wealthy man who would never stoop to talk with such trash.

He decided, finally, that perhaps the old woman could be a load bearer, or do cooking at the house where he was to wait with Kathleen. He tied her, hand and foot, and tossed her into the van along with Mooshu and Kathleen, who were also tied, again, hand and foot. The old woman screamed when Katumbo started to tie her hands, but she stopped after he slapped her once, hard, in the face. To her confused questions he answered nothing.

The van, with Katumbo at the wheel and containing his two men plus Mooshu, Kathleen and Mbuya Nehanda, headed toward the house at 150 Luwana Road.

It had been a half-day since he had last seen de Quesada.

"Outpost One to Central," the radio voice said as he checked his wrist watch. It said midnight. The volume was turned down on the radio, and was so low it was almost inaudible to the five SAS team members listening.

"Go ahead, Outpost One," the young officer replied. From where he was situated with one of his snipers, Central could see only the front of the house, to the east across the road and at the head of a long uphill driveway. Two snipers were at the rear of the house, facing it from the west at the foot of a hill, while Outpost One was on the grassy hillside near the road some hundred meters north to watch for anyone approaching. North was always covered by Outpost One, the manual said. Outpost Two was about the same distance to watch for arrivals from the south. They had scouted the house and found it empty before Central had positioned his forces, but Central was worried. The north and south sides of that house each had two windows, and they weren't covered. This was Central's first time in command of a mission, and he didn't want to screw it up. The ops manual was clear: *two* fighters, not just one, cover front and back doors; and both road approaches were to be surveilled. That ate up the six men assigned, including himself. *Then why the hell don't they assign eight, instead of six?* Central wondered angrily. The ops manual covered that, too, as he well knew: the two men on surveillance were to be called in to cover the sides of the building as soon as an oncomer was sighted. *Yeah,* Central reflected. *That's if there's time.*

"Van. Estimated speed thirty-five miles per hour." With the night vision scope on his rifle, Outpost One was able to make out the van had three seats. All were occupied. "At least six inside."

"Roger that," Central responded. *Is this our oncomer?* he asked himself. *Or is it just a passer-by?* If he brought in his surveillance on a false call, the real oncomer's approach could be missed, Central knew. That could spell disaster. If he made sure this was his oncomer by waiting until the van actually stopped at the house, his two Outposts might not get in quickly enough, no matter how hard they ran. Once, when he was on Outpost duty, he'd run in at top speed only to trip on something, hit his head on a rock, and he spent the entire mission laying in a field, out cold.

And then there were the two civilians laying in the grass behind him. Their code names were Dick and Jane. CIA people, Central had been told—or "intel units," as all such operatives are called in the field. A man and a woman. Trained for field combat and armed, they were there only to observe, nothing more. *This is stupid,* Central thought. *If these intel units get killed, I'm in deep kimchee.* But there was standard ops procedure on this, too, and Central could have recited it: *intelligence ops are to be observed by delegates from the controlling agency.*

"Can we help?" It was the female.

"Yeah," Central replied brusquely with an angry glance at the woman. "Keep your goddamn head down. And shut up."

Ivy fought the urge to tell this punk kid off, officer or not. She shot a look at Capper, the insult showing on her face, and he motioned her to be quiet. The guy was right, Capper knew. Ivy shouldn't have offered to help. Ivy knew it, too, though at this moment she wouldn't have admitted it. Their only job right now, they both knew, was to stay alive.

Deadly force against the perp would be used if necessary, they understood; but it would be a bitter thing if the perp turned out to be Omar.

It made Ivy wonder if the word "friend" had any meaning at all.

"Outpost One to Central," the radio said.

"Go ahead, Outpost One."

"That van just turned off its lights. He's slowing down. He'll be visible to you around the curve any second now."

"Right. I see him. Looks like showtime! Outposts One and Two, get to your battle stations! On the double! Over and out."

The van had turned slowly into the house's long driveway, proceeded about fifteen feet up an incline toward the house, and then it was braked hard to a sudden stop. The van's gears complained loudly as Katumbo shoved the transmission into reverse and floored the gas pedal.

"What the . . ." Central said. Then he saw it. On the hill behind the house, a small lantern was waving back and forth.

"Enemy lookout on the hill to the east behind the house!" Central shouted into his radio. Several shots came from the snipers' position at the bottom of that hill and the little lantern fell.

"Van getting away!" Central yelled. "Close in! Take prisoners!" The van raced in reverse downhill, down the driveway, to escape.

Katumbo had broken into a sweat. He'd seen the warning light on the hill fall, and through his open window he'd heard the shots; he wanted nothing to do with these people, whoever they were. By the time it reached the end of the driveway, spinning rubber all the way, the van was traveling much too fast.

Where the driveway met the road, Katumbo swung his steering

wheel violently to make the hard curve. The van couldn't take the centrifugal force. It flew off its wheels on one side and flipped, then rolled over twice and came to rest upside down on the opposite side of the road, a few feet from the edge of a steep drop to bushes some fifty feet down.

"Subject crawling out the driver's side! Shoot only if shot at!" Central yelled into his radio. It was Katumbo, and when he heard the English voice somewhere in the dark he started firing in that direction with his automatic weapon as he ran. One shot from the sniper with the night scope killed him.

From the rear seat of the van someone smashed out a window and began firing.

"Fire!" Central yelled. "Return fire!"

A hail of bullets from the SAS team peppered the van followed by a loud whoosh. The vehicle was enveloped in flames. The shooter in the back seat was closest to the gas tank; he screamed only once. Mbuya Nehanda was laying across Mooshu. He moved her off his chest. There was a bullet hole in her temple. He saw her eyes were open, vacant, and he knew she was dead. He muttered the Shona equivalent to rest in peace, and as he closed her eyelids he reflected that the old woman's prediction of her imminent death had been accurate. This did not surprise him.

"Miss O'Toole!" Mooshu yelled. He was already out the door on his side, with the vehicle between him and the SAS. The long drop was inches away. "Miss O'Toole!" The fire was creeping toward her. Just behind him was his possible escape, down that steep incline into dense bushes. Beyond that was the river.

Mooshu saw Kathleen struggling. "Miss O'Toole! Come on! We've got to get out of here!"

"My leg!" Kathleen said. "It's stuck!" She felt the flames coming closer, and raised her arm to protect herself from the searing heat.

Mooshu looked down at the cool bushes below him. Then he climbed back into the van. In the third seat at the far rear of the van, he saw two dead men.

"I see it," he said. "The front seat's shifted." He pulled sideways on it to free Kathleen's leg. The seat made not the slightest movement. He pulled again, with all his might. Nothing. Mooshu could see the seat was tightly bolted to the floor. The seat frame had only bent in the accident, not come loose at all. The intense heat from the fire ignited his shirt sleeve. With his other hand he slapped it out.

"Get out, Mooshu!" Kathleen said. "You can't help me!" She felt her own shirt sleeve catch fire and the edge of her hair went with it. She screamed.

Mooshu tore at her sleeve and rubbed Kathleen's hair briskly between his two hands to extinguish the flame.

Outside the van, Kathleen's scream was heard.

"Hold your fire! Approach with caution!" Central said into his radio. "We have survivors. One of them may be female."

Mooshu was determined. He would not leave her to die like this. He focused on a place somewhere inside himself where he knew all his ancestors lived. Their combined strength, their total power, he knew was enormous. He had never called upon them collectively before, but he did so now.

Give me your strength to save this woman! he said to his heart, and yanked with his entire body and soul at the seat that was pinning Kathleen. There was a ripping sound of metal and the seat came up out of the floor. Her leg was freed. Kathleen swayed in her seat, semi-unconscious from the heat.

"Miss O'Toole!" Mooshu called, shaking her hard by the shoulder. "Come on!" She didn't move. Mooshu grabbed Kathleen under the arms and dragged her from the burning vehicle. As he pulled her free, he stumbled over the edge, pulling her over on top of him as he fell. Together they flew backward down the incline, rolling over and over as they slid.

Ivy had run toward the burning vehicle along with the SAS soldiers. "Get back!" Central yelled when he saw her. She ignored him. In the backpack of the SAS trooper crouched in front of her, Ivy saw a lantern. She snatched it and took off, running as fast as she could toward the burning wreck, the lantern in one hand and her gun in the other.

"Stop!" Central yelled at her. Again, she ignored him. Into his radio he yelled, "Hold your fire! All hold your fire! Intel agent in the line of fire! Do not shoot at anything or anyone!" When he got back to civilization, he intended to file a full report against this stupid woman. Capper, standing next to Central, started to go after Ivy. Central saw him start to move and grabbed him by the arm. "You go out there, and I swear to Christ I'll shoot your legs off!" he shouted. Capper could see Ivy outlined in the bright light of the flaming van; he knew the gas tank had already exploded, and there were no more shots coming from the vehicle, so he reasoned she probably was safe. He saw the iron will in the young officer's eyes and decided to stay put. For the moment.

Ivy moved cautiously around the front of the van. In the bright beam of the searchlight she had taken from the soldier she could see she was approaching a steep incline. She aimed the light down over the edge and saw only bushes.

Under the bushes Mooshu and Kathleen lay, not moving, looking up at the person holding the searchlight.

Standing in the brightness of the flaming van, her gun in her hand, Ivy was fully lighted.

Kathleen said to herself, *Ivy! What are you doing here?*

Satisfied there was no one down there, Ivy returned to the safe side of the burning wreck as Capper came up behind her and placed a hand on her elbow. "You okay?" he asked.

Ivy looked for a long moment into Capper's eyes. "Yeah, I'm fine. There's a dead woman in the van. She's African, I think. I doubt that the fire will leave enough of her to identify. She may have been the ILF buyer." She sighed and continued. "Let's call this off, and let Hardale know."

She leaned her head against Capper's shoulder and added, "Let's go home."

From where Kathleen and Mooshu lay concealed in the bushes, they could hear the sound of trucks leaving the area. The van fire burned itself out and soon all was quiet.

"I say we get away from here," Kathleen said, "It sounds like everyone's gone, but they could have left a lookout up there."

"Right," Mooshu agreed. "And a search of this area is likely. I think if we go farther down the hill we'll come to the Tokwe River."

"Good. I need to get to the airport. Sooner the better."

"Not so fast, Miss O'Toole," Mooshu said. "Between here and the airport there are many ways to die."

"What are you talking about?"

"Soldiers like Katumbo, for one thing. Wild animals for another. No, unescorted and unaided, I doubt you could get to the airport alive."

"And wouldn't you help, then?"

"Yes. I want to help you get home. But not by trying to escort you through the jungle. I don't even have a gun. No, I think I can help you by getting us to our destination."

"Our destination?" Kathleen asked.

"The intersection of two dry river beds, the Baba and the Amai. Unless you have a better idea."

"We're going to Mombe?"

"If I can remember the way. I read something about those two rivers some years ago. I know the general area. I think I can help the people of Mombe make those rivers flow again and get their cattle back. My hunch is they will be so grateful they'll help you get home."

"Good idea, Mooshu," Kathleen exclaimed. "And you? What about your home?"

"My home is long gone, Miss O'Toole."

"Under the circumstances, don't you think it would be alright if you call me Kathleen?"

He smiled and said, "Thank you, Kathleen."

The two new friends started off together through the forest. Mooshu's mind was on the challenge ahead of him. Kathleen's was on being home, as soon as possible.

They had reached the river and had been walking along its bank for more than an hour when Kathleen asked, "Mooshu, how long do you think it's going to take to make the Baba and the Amai flow again?"

Mooshu continued pushing through the undergrowth. It appeared to Kathleen that he didn't want to answer her.

"Mooshu," Kathleen insisted. "How long is it going to take?"

"A day. A month. A hundred years. I don't know."

"Mbuya Nehanda sent us!" Mooshu screamed in Shona. The arrow had missed his head by inches and lodged deep in a tree. Kathleen dropped flat to the ground an instant before another arrow came whistling out of the bushes and passed where she had been standing.

Mooshu dropped to the ground alongside Kathleen and screamed again, "Mbuya Nehanda sent us!"

"Where is she?" a voice called out in Shona from the bushes.

"If you are a man, let me see you," Mooshu replied in a loud voice. "If you are the ngozi, then go away, for I have done nothing wrong!"

The bushes parted noisily and two men stepped out. They were dressed in animal skins, their faces were painted with white streaks, they wore a quiver of arrows on their backs, and in their hands they each held a bow with an arrow nocked to shoot.

"Who are you?" the larger of the two men asked in Shona.

"My name is Mooshu. The white woman is a friend."

"Where is Mbuya Nehanda?" the large one asked.

"Mulungu has called her home to Him," Mooshu replied.

The large one aimed to shoot Mooshu. "She said you would receive us as her friends!" Mooshu shouted. "We were her friends!"

"Swear by almighty Mulungu that you did not kill her, that you did not harm her!" the warrior demanded.

"I swear it! I swear it!" Mooshu affirmed. "Let me prove it to you. Mbuya told me your people need water. I can bring you water. That is why I am here."

"I see no water!" the warrior said. "You lie!"

"No, no! I can bring you water out of the mountain! I can make the Baba and the Amai flow again."

The one who had aimed at Mooshu lowered his bow, and his companion did likewise. They walked forward and sat in the grass facing Mooshu & Kathleen. "Talk," said the large one.

"We may have a chance," Mooshu said to Kathleen.

"What is that talk you make to the woman? I don't know what you are saying."

"It is white people's talk. She comes from far away, and wants only to go home. We escaped from the bad man who caused Mbuya Nehanda to be killed, and he almost killed us."

Mooshu then outlined what had happened, from when he and Kathleen were first placed under Mbuya Nehanda's guard.

"Are you a spirit who makes dry rivers run again?" Mooshu was asked.

"No, I am a man like you. I have seen many rivers. I know rivers, and how water comes to be in them."

This seemed to impress the two warriors. When asked how he was going to make the Baba and the Amai flow again, Mooshu said he would know that only after he had seen what had happened.

"Then let us go now to the Baba and the Amai," the large man said, his manner showing he had decided to trust the strange man and his white woman, and the four started the trek to Mombe.

As they walked together, in a gesture toward friendship they exchanged names and told a little of their lives. The large man introduced himself as Fungai, which he said means "to think." The other said his name was Tichaona, which means "we will see," and that he was called Tichi, which he explained has no meaning at all, but is pleasing to the ear.

The two warriors could not pronounce Kathleen's name, so they decided her Shona name would be Chipo, or "gift."

"Yours is a funny name," Fungai told Mooshu. "It makes us laugh."

"Well, Chipo," Mooshu said to Kathleen. "What do you think of your new name? It means gift."

Kathleen grinned and said, "Chipo, eh? I wouldn't mind being thought of as a gift, but a cheap-o gift? Just between us, let's stick to Kathleen, shall we?" Mooshu laughed, and the two walked together side by side.

"That's the first time I've heard you laugh, Mooshu," Kathleen said.

"I have not found much cause for laughter in recent years. Not since I lost my family."

"I know, my friend," Kathleen said and placed her hand on his shoulder as they walked. "I know." She paused a moment, and then added in a soft voice, "I wish for you a life filled with good reasons to laugh." She felt a hitch come to her throat with the thought, *And may I soon get back to my life.*

"Thank you, my dear Kathleen," Mooshu said with deep feeling as he looked into the grey eyes of this unusual woman who came from Ireland.

MOOSHU WAS BROUGHT TO where the two rivers of Mombe had been one before they split. Here, the head of the river, its place of origin, seemed to be the foot of a mountain. And here there was a little water. This was all that was keeping the villagers alive. It seemed to come from inside the mountain. But the water seeped back into the ground shortly after it made its appearance, and the rest of the river head was dry, as was the entire area. There was not a sign of moisture anywhere except for the trickle that came from behind the rocks that filled the river head.

Mooshu saw that there were huge slabs of rock imbedded in the side of the mountain, just above the old river bed, and these slabs were at odd angles.

Then he saw it. Holes. There were perfectly shaped round holes in the rock. The holes had been drilled.

"What happened here?" he asked Fungai.

"White men came. Long ago. They made great thunder, and part of the mountain fell. Then the men became angry and went away. They said this was a bad place, an empty place. Soon after, our rivers dried up. Then our cattle died of thirst."

"Well," Mooshu said. "I believe I know what happened to your water. Pretty simple, actually. It's called dynamiting for diamonds. You can be glad those men didn't find what they were looking for, or they surely would have destroyed this place and killed all of you. But what I don't understand is, when you lost your rivers why didn't you simply move? Move your cattle, move your village."

"Some of us wanted to. A few did go. Most of those came back. We believe we must stay here and wait. We believe the water will return. We believe our cattle will return. The great Mbuya Nehanda said this, and we believe her. This has been our home for many generations. We don't want to go. We don't like the world of soldiers and fighting. Some of our people who left Mombe were forced to fight in armies when the revolution began. They were treated like slaves. And that is why it is better for us to stay here, where the armies can't find us."

Late that afternoon, Kathleen had a chance to be alone with Mooshu. "Can you bring water back to the rivers?" she asked him.

He shrugged his shoulders. "Sure. With enough dynamite, and with a few people skilled in how to use it. It could be done in a day. But all dynamite on the African continent is controlled by the diamond industry. It's very hard for anyone else to get their hands on dynamite. Some people have tried to smuggle it in from offshore, but that has never succeeded. And we know the diamond hunters have already been here, and they found no diamonds. They're not likely to come back, and blow up the face of this mountain just because we ask them to." He sighed and continued, "I know nothing of death from thirst but my guess is these people are close to the end."

That evening the village gathered around a fire. Fungai stood and made an announcement, which Mooshu translated for Kathleen.

"Mooshu has learned why our rivers went dry," Fungai said in a loud voice. "It is because of the white men who came here long ago and made thunder. Their thunder caused the side of the mountain to stop the water. Now the mountain can not fill our Baba and Amai with water any more."

The people of the village became agitated and talked together in loud and angry voices. Again, Mooshu translated for Kathleen. "They say all outsiders, white or black, are evil and should be killed. I'm afraid they are talking about us."

"Translate for me, Mooshu," Kathleen said, and jumped to her feet.

"Good people of Mombe! Listen to me!" she shouted, with Mooshu quickly translating. He thought she sounded like she was running for office. "Mbuya Nehanda sent us here to be your friends. She gave us powers to help you. Do not be angry with me and Mooshu. We are not the people who made the mountain fall."

While she paused to let Mooshu catch up with the translation, Kathleen looked around. The mention of their village's spirit-medium seemed to have calmed the people somewhat but there was still a look of anger in the crowd.

"I know you are angry," Kathleen said, making calming gestures with her hands. "You have good reason to be angry. Your lives have been hurt. Your cattle are gone, and now Mombe is a dying place. Soon, like your cattle before you, you will all die as well."

Kathleen added in a low voice, "Here in Mombe, my name is Chipo. You have said my name means gift. Now Chipo will make you a gift. I will help Mooshu bring water to the Baba and the Amai. And I will bring you new cattle. You will have your lives back again."

Mooshu's voice showed his bewilderment as he finished translating. He stared at Kathleen. *What was she doing?*

The silence was heavy. An old woman got to her feet and walked slowly to Kathleen. In one hand she carried a long knife. There was a look of anger on her face. She placed the tip of the knife at Kathleen's breast and held it there while she stared into Kathleen's eyes. For a long time she searched, moving her own face slowly from side to side as if to see what lay behind the white woman's eyes. Then she turned to the crowd.

"I believe her," was all the old woman said, and she put her knife away as she returned to her seat. There was a murmur. Another woman, also old, got to her feet and walked to Kathleen. She placed her hands in Kathleen's singed hair and studied it. She spoke to Mooshu, and he answered her.

"She asked what happened to your hair," Mooshu said. "I told her the fire that killed Mbuya Nehanda tried to kill you, but it could not kill you because Mbuya Nehanda wanted you to come here."

The old woman told the crowd, "I believe her," and also returned to her seat.

A small child, a boy who seemed to Kathleen about Michael's size when he was six years old, got to his feet. The boy began to walk across the open ring toward the two outsiders and the crowd grew silent once more. Mooshu choked up when he saw that the child had the same severe limp he had, and for the same reason: one leg was much shorter than the other.

The boy walked swiftly up to where Mooshu was seated on the ground, the child's face level with Mooshu's. He stood looking into Mooshu's face in silence for a brief moment, then he smiled and placed his hand on Mooshu's head. There was a gasp from the people, for this gesture meant commitment, an intent to bond. Then the boy turned and faced the crowd. There was total silence.

The boy said loudly, "My name is Tatenda."

A woman screamed. Many in the crowd began talking excitedly and pointing to the boy in amazement.

Fungai quickly whispered to Mooshu, who translated for Kathleen: "The boy has never spoken. The woman who screamed is his mother. The father is dead. The shame of being born with a short leg meant he would never speak. It seems he has found great courage today."

Mooshu stood. The boy smiled up at him, and placed his small hand in the man's large one.

Turning once more to the crowd, Tatenda called out loudly, "I want to be like Mooshu." The crowd fell silent again, astonished at the miraculous transformation in the child.

Two large tears ran down Mooshu's face as he picked the boy up and held him in his arms. The woman who had screamed in amazement came to stand beside her son, and she looked with wonder in the face of this powerful man.

LATER THAT EVENING, Tatenda's mother asked Fungai to invite Kathleen and Mooshu to sit with her and her son in front of their hut. Fungai explained that this, like placing one's hand on a person's head, was also an invitation to bond.

"Looks like you're getting a family," Kathleen said to Mooshu.

"I am honored. Tatenda is precious. His name means thank you. And it is I who give thanks at finding him. The mother is young and strong, and not hard to look at. Her name is Tapiwa, which means the given." Tapiwa, though she could not understand English, knew she was being talked about and she lowered her head in embarrassment. Mooshu placed his hand lightly on her head. Tapiwa raised her eyes to look at Mooshu, and in them Kathleen saw what looked like adoration.

"The three of you together like this, like a family, makes me feel glad and sad," Kathleen said.

"Oh?" Mooshu asked.

"I'm glad for you. Sad for me. I miss my family. I need to be with them."

"Yes, of course you do," Mooshu said. "But tell me, how will you keep the promises you made to these people? You know, to reopen the mountain spring I would need dynamite and an expert to use it. And I don't know how you intend to get cattle in here. With starvation throughout the land, your cattle would be stolen from you long before you could herd them here. You would need an army to protect them from any point of entry."

"There is a flat field just outside the village," Kathleen said. "It is very long and runs parallel to the mountain."

"Yes," Mooshu said. "Fungai told me it was cultivated as pasture when they had cattle."

"I thought as much. I walked it earlier today and noticed there are no rocks. The ground is flat, free of holes."

Mooshu's eyes lit up. "Of course! You're going to bring the cattle in by cargo plane! Brilliant!"

Kathleen smiled. "The plane will land here twice. First with dynamite and a crew that knows how to use it. With Baba and Amai flowing again, the plane will return with the cattle. Do you think thirty head would give the village a good start?"

"I'm sure of it," Mooshu said. Then he got a worried look on his face.

"This will cost a great deal of money. Will the IRA pay for it? I mean, why should they?"

Kathleen laughed. "No, the IRA will not pay for it. They would have no reason to, as you suggest. But I can pay, and I will." She added, "It will make me very happy."

"You have so much money?" Mooshu asked in astonishment.

"More than enough. It was from another Chipo maker, and he was my father. I was going to use part of my money to buy death and destruction. Instead, I will use it to buy life. That feels much better to me."

The words were out of Kathleen's mouth before she thought about what she was saying. The idea was strange, yet it seemed to come from a part of her that was firm, reliable. She knew at once that she could trust what she had said; that she could make it her life. A new life.

The airlift plan was relayed to Fungai and he reported it to the people. The villagers had often seen large silver birds fly overhead, and the thought that one would come visit them—*twice*—set them off like children who have been promised a holiday, and they danced madly.

Kathleen and Mooshu spent the next three days surveying the mountainside and how it seemed related to the Baba and the Amai. With a stick, Mooshu made drawings in the riverbank and did calculations. Kathleen learned exactly what he would need to restore the rivers. She wanted to be certain to include everything for opening up the mountain in the first shipment so that the airplane would need to make only two trips; two were dangerous enough, sneaking in beneath the radar in total violation of Zimbabwe air space.

Finally, though, the plan was complete and Kathleen was ready to go home. She was assigned six guards to lead her back to civilization. But before she left, she said goodbye to her best friend in Africa.

"Mooshu," she said softly as the two sat side by side holding hands, Tatenda sitting nearby and studying these two persons intently. "You saved my life back there in that fire. There is no way to thank you for that."

"Glad to do it, Kathleen," Mooshu said with a smile. "You saved my life, too. By helping me help these people, you have opened my life to a new purpose. There is no way I can thank you for that."

"You're a dear. Forgive me for the way I treated you when we met," she said with a shake of her head and a roll of her eyes. "The way I spoke to you."

Mooshu laughed. "I earned it. I was trying to look the fool. I guess I succeeded."

"A fool you are not, Mooshu. Anything but. And you bring these people your great skills. You are a genius."

"No, I am no genius; merely a man with some education. The only genius here is in the fate that brought us together. If we hadn't met, we might both be dead today."

Genius, Kathleen thought, *seems to have caring and intelligence—no matter whether man's Holy Books and prayers may know this Power as Allah, Yahweh, or God, or by any other name.* She felt a clear place open in her heart, where there had been only darkness since she was sixteen years old.

Kathleen looked deep into Mooshu's eyes. "And now we must say goodbye, probably never to meet again."

"I've heard it said of true friends: If you go live by the seashore and I go live at the top of the mountain, we shall still be together, always, and never be apart."

"That's lovely," Kathleen said softly and took the little man in her arms for a hug.

"Goodbye, my friend. I'll never forget you," she said with tears in her eyes. "Will you remember me?"

Dr. Mooshu's eyes, too, were full as he said with a tremble in his voice, "Ah yes!"

FUNGAI WAS WORRIED. The six-day walk through the jungle from Mombe to Harare would be dangerous for Kathleen. It would be dangerous for any white woman. Her guards would be armed only with bows and arrows, and spears. Fungai decided that Kathleen should not be a white woman. She should be disguised as a tribal matriarch. The women of the tribe laughed like children as they blackened Kathleen's face and hands with soot, tied bundles of cloth to her body to disguise her shape, and put her in a dress that had belonged to Mbuya Nehanda. Her head and face they covered with a shawl. All that was left to identify her as a white woman were her blue-gray eyes. She was counseled to never let anyone see them. With her own things wrapped as a small bundle carried over her shoulder, Kathleen was ready for the trek.

There were no incidents on the journey and the six men from Mombe escorted Kathleen directly to a thicket of tall bushes at the edge of the runway at the airport. An incoming jumbo jet looked like it was aiming for them. The site and roar of the huge airplane frightened the six men and they took off running, back to Mombe.

As an old black woman, Kathleen shuffled, stoop-shouldered, into the ladies room at the terminal; and she came out a vigorous young white woman. She reflected that she had been gone from home about three weeks. Her note to Omar had said she would be gone two days.

He must be frantic by now. And no one knew where I was going. I made sure of that, she said to herself. Being secretive was cruel, she thought, and her family did not deserve cruelty. She wondered why this had never occurred to her before. It seemed her visit to Mombe had taught her something of herself, and she was glad.

She decided to phone Omar in London. Even if he was off somewhere on business, she would go to the house. She would be with the boys.

She called direct. The familiar ring of the London exchange was comforting, but it also sent a chill up her spine.

Please, oh please, be there! A lot of time had gone by. Anything could have happened.

"Hello?" came the familiar voice.

A wave of relief washed over her. *I hear my life!* she thought.

But Kathleen buttoned up her emotions and sounded strong as ever when she said, breezily, "Hello, Omar. How are you?"

"Oh, my God, woman! Oh, dear God!" Omar said. His voice cracked and all Kathleen could hear was a muffled sound in the background. Omar was crying. Hard.

Kathleen felt her own tears rush from her heart. She hadn't expected Omar to react like this, and she was deeply touched.

With a weak and fractured voice she said, "Omar?" It was barely more than a whisper.

There was no answer but the line was open. She heard him clear his throat to break off the crying. He tried again. It wasn't working; he would have to try to talk through his tears.

"You're alive!" he said with a sob. "You're alive!"

"I couldn't get to a phone the whole time, Omar. It was like being stranded on a desert island. But it was a jungle. I'll explain," she said. "I'm so sorry!" Now she was crying too. She couldn't hold it back. "My Omar! How I've missed you, my darling! And our boys! Are they all right?"

"Yes, fine," Omar said through the gravel in his throat. "They're both fine. They've missed you; asked a lot of questions. I didn't want to let them know how frightened I was. They might have figured it out, I don't know. Where were you? I've sent people looking everywhere. Called Tom. He knew nothing. Called other IRA people. That got me nowhere."

He would have, easily could have, run on forever with chatter but he found himself crying again. She heard it, and cried too.

"Where are you?" he finally said through tears.

"Africa."

"Africa! I'll come and get you! I'll—"

"No, wait!" she said. "'I'm at Harare International right now, in Zimbabwe. It's faster if I take the next jet home. I've got quite a story to tell you."

"Yes, yes, of course," Omar said. "I'll call Tom and Peg right away. They are sick with worry. They call me almost every day." He paused before adding, "I love you so much."

After a pause, Kathleen said softly, "'I'll be at Heathrow in eleven hours. Can you meet me?"

"Can I meet you? I'll race the airplane down the runway!" he said.

Kathleen laughed, and Omar drank the sound of her laughter like a man craving water.

The End—Book One

. . . the story continues in Book Two and Book Three of

The Vengeance Trilogy

What's going to happen next? Get a sneak preview at
www.ophirpublishing.com

Printed in the United States
75549LV00002B/113

9 780978 765811